The Death of the Gods

The Death of the Gods

Dmitry Merezhkovsky

MINT EDITIONS

The Death of the Gods was first published in 1895.

This edition published by Mint Editions 2021.

ISBN 9781513283098 | E-ISBN 9781513288116

Published by Mint Editions®

MINT
EDITIONS
minteditionbooks.com

Publishing Director: Jennifer Newens
Design & Production: Rachel Lopez Metzger
Project Manager: Micaela Clark
Translated By: Herbert Trench
Typesetting: Westchester Publishing Services

Contents

PART I

I

About two and a half miles from Cæsarea in Cappadocia, upon the woody spurs of Mount Argæus, and close to the great Roman road, bubbled a certain warm spring, famous for its healing virtues. A granite slab, adorned with rough sculpture and bearing a Greek inscription, proved that this spring had of old time been consecrated to the twin sons of Zeus, Castor and Pollux; but this by no means prevented the unbroken images of these Pagan demigods from being locally worshipped as St. Cosmas and St. Damian respectively.

On the other side of the road, opposite the sacred fountain, rose a little thatched tavern, flanked by a dirty stable, and by a shed where fowls and geese were dabbling in the mud. In this tavern, owned by one Syrax, a wily Armenian, could be bought goats'-milk cheese, black bread, honey, olive oil, and a thin sour wine, grown in neighbouring vineyards.

A screen divided the tavern into two compartments; one for the use of common folk, the other for guests of more importance. From the smoked ceiling hung hams curing, and odorous bunches of mountain herbs, proving that Fortunata, the wife of Syrax, was a careful housewife; a fact that did not save the dubious reputation of the establishment.

At night honest travellers dared not halt here, remembering sundry rumours about dark plots hatched in the cottage; but Syrax, ever scheming, and knowing whose hand to cross with silver, had never troubled his head about rumour. The partition was formed by two slender columns, between which was stretched, in the manner of a door-curtain, an old chlamys (or outer garment) of faded wool, belonging to the mistress of the house. The little columns, wrought in a barefaced attempt at the Doric style, were the pride of the heart of Syrax and the single ornament of the tavern. Once gilded, they had long stood creviced and chipped and hopelessly cracked.

The stuff of the chlamys, when new, had been a bright violet; now it was a dirty blue, eked out by many patches, and stained with innumerable stains, due to the breakfasts, dinners, and suppers of ten years of the conjugal life of the hard-working Fortunata.

In the clean half of the tavern, on a single narrow couch, which was torn in many places, Marcus Scuda, Roman tribune of the ninth cohort of the sixteenth legion, was lolling before a tankard-strewn table.

A dandy provincial, he had one of those faces at the sight of which prosperous slaves and second-rate courtesans would inevitably exclaim with heartfelt admiration: "*What* a handsome man!"

At his feet, in an uncomfortable but respectful attitude, a red-faced man sat, panting. His bald head was fringed with grey hair, brushed towards the temples. He was the centurion of the eighth *centuria*, Publius Aquila.

Farther off, twelve soldiers, stretched on the floor, were playing at knuckle-bones.

"By Hercules!" cried Scuda, "I'd rather be the meanest beggar in Constantinople than the first man in a mouse-trap like this. Can you call this an existence, Publius? Answer me honestly. Is this living? To think that outside barracks and camps the future has nothing in store for one; that one must rot in this sickening marsh without ever catching a glimpse of the world again!"

"Yes," assented Publius; "it's a fact that life here isn't precisely gay; but on the other hand, it's peaceful!"

The knuckle-bones pre-occupied the attention of the old captain. Pretending to listen to the gossipings of his superior officer, and fully to agree with the drift of his remarks, he followed with an interested eye the game of the legionaries. He said to himself, "If the red aims well, he'll certainly win."

However, by way of politeness, Publius asked Scuda, with a show of attention—

"Why, by the way, have you brought down on yourself the indignation of the Prefect Helvidius?"

"A woman, a friend of mine, was at the bottom of it, a girl. . ."

And Marcus Scuda, in a fit of garrulous intimacy, confided to the ear of the old centurion that the Prefect, "that old goat of a Helvidius," had grown jealous on account of the special favours conferred on him, Marcus, by a certain frail lady, a Lydian.

Now Scuda wanted, by rendering some important service, to win back the good-will of the Prefect; and he had resolved upon a plan.

Not far from Cæsarea, in the fortress of Macellum, dwelt Julian and Gallus, the cousins of the reigning Emperor Constantius, and the nephews of Constantine the Great. These two were the last representatives of the luckless house of the Flavii. On his accession to the throne, fearing rivals, Constantius had assassinated his uncle, the father of Julian and Gallus, Julian Constantius, the brother of

Constantine. But Julian and Gallus themselves had been spared, and imprisoned in the solitary castle of Macellum, where they lived oppressed by perpetual fear of death. In great perplexity, knowing that the new Emperor loathed the two orphans who reminded him of his crime, Helvidius, Prefect of Cæsarea, desired, but dreaded, to divine the will of his master.

Scuda, the adroit tribune, possessed by visions of a career at Court, grasped, from chance words of his superior officer, that the latter dared not take upon himself the heavy responsibility, and trembled lest the current rumour about an escape of the heirs of Constantine should be realised in fact. At this point Scuda made up his mind to go to Macellum, seize the prisoners, and bring them to Cæsarea under the safeguard of his legionaries, well assured that he had nothing to fear from these orphaned minors, abandoned by the world and hated by the Emperor. By this valiant proceeding, Scuda counted on regaining the favours of the Prefect Helvidius, so unhappily lost on account of the auburn-haired lady of Lydia. Nevertheless, being of a suspicious nature, he only communicated to Publius part of his plan.

"And what do you propose now, Scuda? Have you received instructions from Constantinople?"

"I have received nothing; nobody knows anything; but there is an everlasting hawking about of rumours, don't you see? There are endless veiled hopes and hints, unfinished phrases, threats and warnings, allusions. . . Any idiot can do what he has been told to do. But this is a matter of guessing the mute will of our master. That's a job that brings reward. Come, let us make the venture, take the risk. The great thing is to be speedy and stout-hearted, and to trust in the Holy Cross! . . . I confide myself to you, Publius. Perhaps we shall be drinking at Court, you and I, before many days are over; and, by God, a better wine than this!"

Through the little barred window filtered the troubled light of a melancholy dusk. It was raining monotonously. A single clay wall, full of crevices, separated the room from the stable. The acrid odour of dung came though, and the clucking of hens, the shrill chirping of chickens, and the grunting of pigs was audible. There came also the steady noise of a liquid falling into a sonorous can, as if the good wife were milking her cow. The soldiers, discussing their winnings, were quarrelling among themselves in undertones. Close against the floor, through the frail lath and plaster, a hog had thrust his fat, pink snout. Caught in too narrow a slit, he could not draw out his muzzle and was groaning piteously. Publius mused—

"By Jupiter! we're nearer the courtyard of the cattle than the court of the Emperor!"

His interest in the game had melted away. The tribune after his excess of confidence himself felt sad. Through the window he looked at the grey sky, dissolving itself into water, at the muzzle of the pig, the thick lees of wine in the tankards, the dirty soldiers. Anger mounted to his brain.

He struck the table, which swayed on its uneven legs, with his fist.

"Hi, rascality! betrayer of Christ, Syrax, come here! What wine do you call that, you scoundrel?"

The innkeeper ran up. He wore hair and beard frizzled into fine ringlets, black as ebony, with bluish shadows. Fortunata used to say, in her hours of conjugal tenderness, that the beard of Syrax was like a bunch of the grapes of Samos. His eyes were also black and extraordinarily brilliant, and a honeyed smile never left his purple lips. He resembled a caricature of Bacchus, and was black and sugary from every point of view. To appease the wrath of Scuda, the innkeeper took to witness Moses and Deidamia, Christ and Hercules, that his wine was superexcellent. But the tribune was obstinate, declaring that he knew in whose house Glabrio, a rich merchant of Lyrnas, had recently been assassinated; and that he, Scuda, would denounce Syrax in the proper quarters. Terrified, the Armenian rushed to the cellars, and brought back thence in triumph a strange bulky bottle, flat at its base, narrow-necked, covered with mildew, and grey with age. Through the mouldiness in places the glass was visible, no longer transparent, but irised, and upon the label of cypress-wood attached to the neck of the bottle could be deciphered the initial letters of *"Anthosmium"* and below *"Annorum Centum."*

But Syrax assured the couple that even in the reign of the Emperor Diocletian the wine had been more than a hundred years old.

"Black wine?" asked Publius, with respect.

"Black as tar, and sweet smelling as nectar. Ho! Fortunata! for this wine bring summer glasses, cups of crystal, and bring too the whitest snow from the ice-tub."

Fortunata brought in two glasses. Her healthy face was of a dull pallor like thick cream, and with her came in the smell of country freshness, milk, and manure.

The landlord gazed at the bottle amorously, and kissed its neck; then with caution he raised the waxen seal. The wine flowed black and odorous in a thick jet, dissolving the snow, while the crystal of the cups became dull and cloudy under the action of cold.

Thereupon Scuda, who had pretensions to learning (he was capable of confusing Hecuba with Hecate), declaimed proudly the only line of Martial he could remember—

Candida nigrescant vetulo crystalla Falerno!

"Wait a moment. Here is something still better," and Syrax plunged his hand into his pocket, drew thence a minute flask carved out of onyx, and with a sensual smile poured into the wine a drop of precious Arabian cinnamon. The drop fell, and, like a creaming pearl, melted into the black liquor. A strangely heavy perfume filled the room.

While the tribune was slowly drinking, Syrax made a clacking noise with his tongue, murmuring, "The wines of Biblos, of Lesbos, of Lathea in Chios, of Icaria. . . are less than nothing to this wine!"

Night was falling. Scuda gave the order to get ready to march. The legionaries began putting on their armour, fastened the greave protecting the right leg, and took up bucklers and lances. When they entered the outer hall, the Icarian shepherds, who were brigands rather than shepherds, seated near the fire, rose respectfully before the Roman tribune. Scuda, full of a sense of his own rank and valour, felt the blood burning in his veins and his head buzzing with the effect of the marvellous liquor.

On the threshold a man approached him. He wore a strange oriental costume—a white tunic, striped with broad red bands, and on his head a high headdress of woven camel's hair, and a towering Persian tiara. Scuda halted. The visage of the Mede was finely cut, lengthy and meagre, and yellow of hue rather than olive. The narrow and piercing eyes sparkled maliciously, but all his movements were calm and majestic. He was one of those wandering magicians who haughtily declared themselves Chaldeans, seers, and mathematicians. He announced to the tribune that his name was Nogodarès. Sojourning by chance with Syrax, he was travelling from the distant Hyrcania towards the coasts of the Ionian sea, to meet the celebrated warlock philosopher, Maximus of Ephesus. The magician begged for authority to prove his art and to divine the happy fortune of the tribune.

The shutters were closed. The Mede was preparing something on the ground; suddenly a slight crackling was heard; everybody was silent and a flame rose in a long red tongue amidst wafted flakes of white smoke, which filled the room. Nogodarès put his pale lips to a double flute, and played a languid, plaintive air, like the funeral songs of the Lydians. The flame grew yellow—grew fainter, then sparkled anew in pale flashes. The sorcerer threw into the fire a handful of dried herbs. They evaporated in a penetrating aroma which brought on the senses an indefinable melancholy, like the perfume of half-withered grasses, on some misty evening, in the arid plains of Arachosia and Drangiana. Obeying the plaintive call of the flute, a huge serpent slid out of a black box placed at the feet of the magician, and slowly, with a sound as of parchments rubbed together, unwound its glittering and metallic coils. The wizard chanted in a broken voice, which seemed to come from afar, and several times repeated the same syllables, "*Mara, mara, mara!*" The serpent coiled itself round his thin body and caressingly, with a tender hissing, brought its flat green head and brilliant carbuncled eyes close to the ear of the enchanter. A whistling, and the forked sting flashed, as if the reptile had murmured its secret to its master, who now threw the flute upon the ground. The flame filled anew the room with thick smoke, this time diffusing an odour choking as if exhaled from the tomb. The flame went out. Darkness and fear possessed all present; everybody felt it difficult to breathe. But when the open shutters allowed the leaden light of the dusk to enter, there remained no trace of the snake or of the black box. Notwithstanding this, everybody's face was livid.

Nogodarès approached the tribune—

"Rejoice! Favour—great and speedy favour—awaits thee from thy great master Augustus Constantius!"

During several moments he scrutinised the hand of Scuda narrowly. Then, stooping to the level of his ear, muttered, so as to be heard by none but the tribune—

"This hand is dyed with blood—the blood of a great prince!"

Scuda grew afraid.

"What dost thou dare to say, cursed hound of a Chaldean? I am a loyal servant."

But the other probed him with his searching eyes and half ironically responded—

"What dost thou fear? Given a few years. . . And is glory won without the spilling of blood?"

Pride and joy filled the heart of Scuda when at the head of his soldiery he quitted the tavern. He drew near the sacred fountain, crossed himself, and quaffed that virtuous water, invoking in a fervent prayer St. Cosmas and St. Damian, that the prediction of Nogodarès should not fall fruitless. Then he vaulted upon his haughty Cappadocian charger and gave the legionaries the order "March." The standard-bearer raised the ensign above his bared head. It was the image of a large dragon, fixed upon a lance, with gaping jaws of silver and the rest of its body formed of coloured silk. Unable to withstand the wish to parade before the crowd assembled at the door of the inn, and although conscious of peril, intoxicated with wine and pride, the tribune stretched his sword up the misty road, and in a loud voice commanded—

"To Macellum!"

A hum of astonishment ran through the crowd. The names of Julian and of Gallus were uttered. The legionary who led the column raised his skyward-twisted horn, sounded it, and the echoing note of the Roman trumpet vibrated away amongst the mountains.

II

A profound obscurity reigned in the great sleeping-chamber of Macellum, an ancient palace of Cappadocian princes.

The bed of the young Julian was very hard,—a wooden pallet, laid with a panther-skin. So the young Julian himself willed it, being bred in the austere principles of the Stoics by Mardonius, his tutor, a passionate disciple of ancient philosophy.

Julian was not asleep. The wind, blowing in fierce gusts, howled like an imprisoned beast between the chinks of the walls. Then all fell back again into silence, and in the intent pause large drops of rain could be heard splashing from the height of the roof upon the ringing flagstones. The keen ear of Julian detected at moments the rustling of the rapid flight of a bat. He distinguished, too, the regular breathing of his brother, a delicate and girlish lad, who slept upon a soft bed under mouldy hangings, the last trace of luxury in this deserted castle. In the next room could be heard the heavy snore of Mardonius.

Suddenly, the door of the secret staircase in the wall turned softly upon its hinges. A bright light dazzled Julian.

Labda, an old slave, entered, carrying in her hand a metallic lamp.

"Nurse, I'm afraid! Don't take the lamp away. . ."

The old woman placed the lamp in a stone niche above the head of Julian.

"Can you not sleep? You are not in pain? Are you hungry? That old sinner Mardonius always keeps you fasting. I've brought you cakes of honey. They're good. . . Taste!"

Making Julian eat was the favourite occupation of Labda; but she dared not indulge in it by day—dreading the severe Mardonius—and so brought her delicacies mysteriously under cover of night. Labda, who was purblind and could scarcely drag her limbs along, always wore the black religious habit. Although a devout Christian, she was regarded as being in reality a Thessalian sorceress. The grimmest superstitions, old and new, fused in her brain into a strange religion not far removed from madness. She mingled prayers with spells, Olympian gods with demons, Christian rites with the black arts. Her body was behung with crosses, and amulets carved out of the bones of the dead; and scapularies, containing the ashes of martyrs, swung from her shoulders. The old woman felt for Julian a pious affection, regarding him as the

DMITRY MEREZHKOVSKY

sole and legitimate successor of Constantine the Great, and holding Constantius, the reigning Emperor, a murderer and a usurper.

Labda knew better than anybody the family tree and traditions of the race of the Flavii. She remembered the grandfather of Julian, Constantius Chlorus. The murderous mysteries of the Court lingered on, ineffaceable, in her memory; and many a time at night would she tell them to Julian, keeping nothing back, so that he, at the narrative of events which his childish brain could not yet comprehend, felt his heart gripped by fear and indignation. With dull eyes, in a low monotonous listless sing-song, Labda, looking like one of the Fates, would recite these gruesome epic tales of a few years ago, as if they had been so many legends of remotest antiquity.

Placing the lamp in a stone niche, Labda blessed Julian, with a sign of the cross; ascertained that the amulet of amber was safe on his breast, and, pronouncing some charms to exorcise ill spirits, vanished.

A heavy half-slumber fell upon Julian. It was warm; great drops of rain, descending in silence as into the bottom of a sonorous vessel, lulled him into languor. He knew not whether he was awake or asleep; whether it was the breathing of the wind or Labda which was murmuring at his ear the terrible secrets of his family. All that he had learnt from her, and all that he had seen in infancy, fused into a single fearful dream.

. . . He sees the dead body of the great Emperor upon a splendid bier. The corpse is painted; and the head adorned by the deftest of barbers with an ingenious dress of false hair. Julian, brought thither to kiss the hand of his uncle for the last time, is afraid. The purple, the diadem, with its stones glittering under the flame of torches, dazzle him. Through the heavy Arabian perfumes, for the first time in his life he comes into contact with the odour of a corpse. But bishops, eunuchs, generals, acclaim the Emperor as if he were alive; and the ambassadors bow down before him and return thanks, observing all the punctilious ceremony of diplomatic etiquette. Scribes read out the edicts, the laws, the decrees of the senate, and implore the approval of the dead man; a flattering murmur surges to and fro among the multitudes; they declare that he, the Emperor, is so great that by a special mercy of Providence he reigns after death.

The child knows that he whom all glorify has killed his own son, a brave young man, whose only fault lay in the people's too great love of him. This son had been slandered by his stepmother, who loved him with an unholy love, and had taken her revenge upon him thus as Phædra upon

Hippolytus. Afterwards the wife of Constantine had been surprised in adulterous intimacy with a slave of the Imperial stables and had been stifled in a bath heated to a white heat. And so on, corpse, upon corpse, victim after victim. Finally, tormented by conscience, Constantine the Great had implored priests to shrive his soul from guilt. He was refused. Thereupon the Bishop Ozius succeeded in convincing him that one religion only possessed the power of purifying from sins like his. And therefore it had come to pass that now the sumptuous *Labarum*, the standard bearing wrought in precious stones the monogram of Christ, glittered above the catafalque of the parricide.

Julian strove to awake, to open his eyes, and could not.

Ringing drops fell continually, like heavy tears, and the wind blew on: but it seemed to him that it was Labda, the old Fate, babbling near him with her toothless gums the terrible tales of the Flavii.

Julian dreamed again. He was in the subterranean vaults of Constantius Chlorus, surrounded by porphyry sarcophagi containing the ashes of kings. Labda is hiding him in one of the darkest corners and has wrapped in her cloak the sickly Gallus, who is shivering with fever. Suddenly, above their heads in the palace, groanings resound from room to room.

Julian recognises the voice of his father; struggles to answer him—to run to his aid—but Labda holds back the child, murmuring, "Quiet! quiet! or they will be upon us!" and hides him under her chlamys. Hasty steps clatter upon the staircase—come nearer and nearer still; the door bursts into shivers and the soldiers of Cæsar, disguised as monks, invade the vault. The Bishop Eusebius of Nicomedia directs the search; and coats of mail glitter under the black robes of the searchers.

"In the name of the Father and of the Son and of the Holy Ghost, answer—who is there?"

Labda is crouching in a corner, still locking the children to her breast. Again comes the solemn cry—

"In the name of the Father and of the Son and of the Holy Ghost—who is there?"

The legionaries, sword in hand, explore every hole and corner; Labda throws herself at their feet; shows them the sickly Gallus and Julian, defenceless—

"Fear God! what harm can a six-year-old innocent like this do to the Emperor?"

And the legionaries force all the kneeling three to kiss the cross which Eusebius holds out to them, and to take the oath of faithfulness to the new Emperor. Julian remembers the great cross of cypress-wood. There was an enamelled picture of Christ on it. On the dark base of the wood stains of fresh blood were still visible, imprinted by the fingers of the cross-bearing assassin.

Was it the blood of the father of Julian, or of one of his six cousins, Dalmatius, Hannibal, Nepotian, Constantine the Younger, or of the others? The murderer, in order to ascend the throne, had taken six corpses in his stride, doing each deed in the name of the Crucified. And still round the tyrant, day after day, rose the cloud of victims, a multitude which no man could number.

Julian awoke full of fears. The rain had ceased and the wind fallen. The lamp burned steadily in its niche. Julian sat up on his bed, listening in the silence to the beatings of his own heart. The hush seemed curiously insupportable. Suddenly, voices and steps resounded from room to room, reverberated along the high arcades of Macellum as formerly along the vaults of the Flavii. Julian shivered. It seemed to him that he was dreaming still.

The steps approached; the voices became distinct.

The lad cried out, "Gallus, awake! Mardonius, don't you hear something?"

Gallus awoke. Barefooted, his grey hair dishevelled, and clothed in a short sleeping-tunic, Mardonius, his face bloated, yellow and wrinkled like an old woman's, rushed towards the secret door.

"The soldiers of the Prefect! . . . Dress! . . . We must fly."

He was too late. The grinding of iron bolts told that the door was being shut from the outside. The stone columns of the public staircase flushed with the light of torches, illumining the purple dragon of a standard-bearer and the cross upon the breastplates of legionaries.

"In the name of the most orthodox and blessed Augustus, Constantius Imperator! I, Marcus Scuda, Tribune of the Fretensian Legion, take under my safeguard Julian and Gallus, sons of the Patrician, Julius Flavius!"

Mardonius, with drawn sword, stood in a warlike attitude in front of the closed door of the chamber, barring the way of the soldiers. This glaive was rusty and useless, and served the old tutor only to show, during his lessons in the Iliad, how Hector used to fight Achilles. At this moment Mardonius, although he would have been incapable of killing a hen, was brandishing the sword in the face of Publius, according to the most correct traditions of Homeric warfare. Publius, who was drunk, flew into a passion:

"Get out of my way, windbag! Clear out, I tell you, if you don't want me to slit you!"

He seized Mardonius by the throat and hurled him against the wall.

Scuda ran to the door of the chamber and opened it. For the first time in his life he beheld the two last descendants of Constantius Chlorus. Gallus seemed tall and strong, but his skin was fine and white as a young girl's; his eyes, of a wan blue, were indolent and listless; his flaxen hair, the distinguishing trait of the house of Constantine, spread in curls over his powerful neck. But in spite of his masculine appearance, downy beard, and eighteen years, Gallus at that moment looked a child. His lips trembled, he blinked sleep-swollen eyelids, and, crossing himself, continually whispered: "Lord, have mercy upon me!"

Julian was a thin child, sickly and pale, with irregular features, thick glossy black hair, too long a nose, and a too prominent lower lip. But his eyes were astonishing. Large, strange, and variable, they shone with a brightness rare in a child's eyes, and an almost morbid or insane concentration.

Publius, who in his youth had often seen Constantine the Great, mused—

"That little rascal will be like his uncle!"

In the presence of the soldiers fear abandoned Julian. He was only conscious of anger. With closed teeth, the panther-skin of his bed flung over his shoulder, he gazed at Scuda fixedly, his lower lip trembling with bridled rage. In his right hand, hidden by the fur, he gripped the handle of a slim Persian dagger given him by Labda; it was tipped with the keenest of poisons.

"A true wolf's cub!" said one of the legionaries, pointing out Julian to his companion.

Scuda was about to cross the threshold of the chamber, when a wild chance of safety flashed upon Mardonius. Throwing aside his tragic sword, he seized the mantle of the tribune, and began to scream in a shrill feminine voice:

"Do you know what you're doing, rascals? How dare you insult an envoy of Constantius? It is I who am charged to conduct these two young princes to Court. The august Emperor has restored them to his favour. Here is the order from Contantinople!"

"What is he saying? . . . what order is it?"

Scuda stared at Mardonius. His faded and wrinkled visage was unmistakably that of a eunuch; and the tribune knew well what special favour eunuchs enjoyed at Court.

Mardonius hunted in a drawer, lit on a roll of parchment, held it out to the tribune, who unrolled it and immediately grew pale. He only read the first lines, but saw the name of the Emperor, who referred to himself in the edict as Our Eternity,—*Nostra æternitas*,—but remarked neither the date nor the year.

When he perceived, swinging from the parchment, the great Imperial seal of dark green wax, attached by golden threads, his eyes clouded; he felt his knees give way—

"Pardon, there is some mistake. . ."

"Away with you! away with you at once! the Emperor shall know everything!" retorted Mardonius, hastily snatching the decree from the trembling hands of Scuda.

"Don't ruin us! We are all brothers, we're all sinners! I entreat you in the name of Christ!"

"I know what acts you commit, in the name of Christ! Go! Go at once."

The tribune gave the order to retire. A single drunken legionary tried, by fair means or foul, to hustle Mardonius; but they overbore the rioter by main force.

When the sound of steps died away, and Mardonius was assured that all peril was over, he was seized by a wild fit of laughter which shook the whole of his soft fleshy person. Forgetting all tutorial dignity, the old man in his short night tunic began to dance, crying out gleefully—

"Children, children! Glory to Hermes! We've hoodwinked them cleverly! That edict was annulled three years ago! Ah, the idiots, the idiots!"

At the breaking of dawn, Julian fell into a deep sleep. He awoke late, refreshed and light-hearted, when the sun was shining brightly into the room through the great iron-clamped window.

III

Their lesson in doctrinal theology was taught to the lads in the morning by an Arian priest. Long and dry as a lath, he had green eyes, damp and bony hands. This monk, who was named Eutropius, had the disagreeable habit of gently licking the hollow of his palm, smoothing his grey hair, and immediately afterwards making his finger-joints crack. Julian knew that one movement would inevitably follow the other, and used to get madly irritated.

Eutropius wore an old black cassock, full of stains and patches. He used to say that he wore it out of humility, but, as a matter of fact, he did it from miserliness.

Such was the instructor chosen by Eusebius of Nicomedia, the religious guardian of Julian.

This monk suspected in his pupil a certain yeast of moral perversity, which, unless cured, would draw upon Julian eternal damnation.

And Eutropius used to talk continually of the grateful feelings the boy should show towards his benefactor the Emperor Constantius. Whether he was explaining the text of the Bible, expounding Arian dogmas, or interpreting an apostolic parable, all lessons were conducted to the same conclusion, the "root of holy obedience and filial docility." And when the Arian monk spoke of the benefits granted to Julian by the Emperor, the child would fix upon him his deep glance; but although each knew the intimate thoughts of the other, never did pupil and professor exchange a word upon the subject. Only if Julian stopped, forgetting some text, or became confused in the chronological list of Old Testament patriarchs, or repeated badly the prayer he had learned by heart, Eutropius would silently gaze at him, take his ear caressingly between two fingers, and two long and sharp finger nails would slowly pierce the flesh.

Eutropius, despite his morose look, was endowed with a certain ironical gaiety. He gave his pupils the most affectionate of nicknames, while ridiculing their imperial origin. When, after pinching Julian's ear, he saw him grow pale, not with pain but with rage, he would whisper in humility—

"Your Majesty does not deign to feel anger against Eutropius, his humble and unlearned slave?" and, licking the palm of his hand, he would smooth the grey locks of his temples, crack his long fingers, and add that it was wholesome sometimes to give naughty, idle little boys a whipping; that form of instruction being often mentioned in Holy Writ as the most effective means of enlightening the souls of the dark and disobedient. He used only to say it to tame the diabolic pride of Julian, who, moreover, was well aware that Eutropius would never dare to put his threat into execution. The monk himself was convinced that the child would rather die than undergo such a humiliation. But the tutor, nevertheless, loved to discourse upon the topic often and long.

At the end of the lesson, during the explanation of a text, Julian once mentioned the earth's antipodes, about which he had heard Mardonius speaking. He had done this with the secret intention of annoying the monk, but Eutropius became jocular.

"Who's been talking to you about 'antipodes,' my angel? Little sinner, how you do make me laugh! That old fool of a Plato did, I know, write something about it. But are you actually wise enough to believe that men walk about on their heads?"

Eutropius would launch forth into accusations of heresy against the philosophers. Was it not a scandal to imagine that mankind—created after the image of God—could walk about upside down, and so bring Heaven into contempt? And when Julian, insulted by insults to his favourite philosophers, argued that the earth was shaped like a globe, Eutropius became serious and lost his temper, purple with fury and stamping his feet—

"It's that heathen, Mardonius, who teaches you these godless lies!"

When he got angry he would splutter and shower the hearer with his spittle, which Julian believed must be venomous. Exasperated, the monk would savagely attack all the Greek sages. Wounded to the quick by the suggestions of Julian, forgetting that his pupil was a mere child, he burst into serious harangues, accusing Pythagoras of being mad, impudent, audacious, affirming that the atrocious "Utopias" of Plato were not fit to read, and that the instruction of Socrates was clean against reason.

"Read what Diogenes Lærtius says of Socrates! You will see that not only was he a money-lender, but that he practised vices which no decent man can name."

Epicurus, above all, excited the whole of his rancour; the beastliness with which he plunged into pleasures of all kinds, the brutality with which he used to satisfy his sensual desires, were proof enough that he was less than human.

Resuming something of his habitual calm, Eutropius on this particular day betook himself to explaining some hair-splitting scholastic distinction of the Arian dogma, and waxed wroth with the same heat against the orthodox oecumenical Church, which he considered heretical.

From the splendid and desolate garden a warm breeze came in through the open window. Julian feigned to listen to Eutropius. Really he was dreaming of a very different person, his well-loved teacher Mardonius. He recollected his wise lectures; his readings of Homer and Hesiod—how different from these monkish lessons!

Mardonius did not *read* Homer; following the custom of the ancient rhapsodists, he used to chant the poems, to the great amusement of Labda, who was wont to say that he bayed like a dog at the moon. And in fact he did appear absurd to folk who heard him for the first time. The eunuch would punctiliously scan each foot of the hexameter, beating time with his hand. And while his yellow and wrinkled visage remained intensely rapt, his shrill feminine voice streamed on from strophe to strophe. Julian never remarked the ugliness of the old man, seeing only the throbbing passion of a soul thrilled by grandeur and beauty.

His listener trembled, while the divine hexameters rose and shouted like waves. He saw the farewells of Andromache and Hector; the wanderings of Ulysses, weeping for Ithaca on the melancholy and sterile beach of Calypso's island. Delicious sorrow seized the heart of Julian; pains of yearning for Hellas, the country of the gods, eternally beautiful, land of all beauty-worshippers. Tears shook in the voice of the teacher, and rolled down his withered cheeks.

Sometimes Mardonius would talk with the boy of goodness, of the austerity of virtue, of the death of heroes for freedom's sake. Little indeed, oh! how little, did these lessons resemble those given by Eutropius.

Mardonius used also to narrate the life of Socrates; and when he came to the "Apology," delivered by the philosopher before his death to the people of Athens, the old master would rise, and triumphantly declaim the speech from memory, a calm irony lighting his face. These were less the phrases of a man accused, than the ringing tones of a judge addressing the people.

"Socrates does not ask for pardon. All the power, all the laws of a government are absolutely nothing beside the liberty of the soul of man. Yes! the Athenians can kill a man without taking from him the freedom and the happiness of his immortal soul." And when this barbarian, this ex-slave from the banks of the Borysthenes, pronounced the word "liberty" it seemed to Julian that the word contained such superhuman power that beside it even the Homeric pictures lost lustre. Fixing on his master his great wide, haunting eyes, the lad shook with enthusiasm.

The cold touch of a hand at his ear drew Julian from his dreams. The lesson of the catechist was finished. On his knees he recited the prayer of thanksgiving; then escaping from Eutropius he ran to his room, took down a book, and hastened to a solitary nook in the garden to read at ease the *Symposium* of Plato, the pagan, a book forbidden above all others. On the stairs Julian met the monk, who was departing—

"Wait, my dear boy! What book is your Majesty carrying?"

Julian stared at him and tranquilly tendered the volume. On the parchment binding Eutropius read the title, written in great capitals, "The Epistles of St. Paul the Apostle," and gave back the book unopened.

"That's all right! Remember that I have to answer for your soul to God and to the sublime Emperor. Don't read heretical books, especially none of those frivolous philosophers whom I have today condemned."

It was the habitual trick of the boy to wrap dangerous books in innocent bindings. Julian from his infancy had learnt dissimulation, and even took pleasure in deceiving others, especially Eutropius. He dissembled and lied needlessly and habitually, prompted by deep-seated anger and revenge. To Mardonius alone his behaviour was always open and gracious.

Intrigues, scandals, gossipings, suspicions continually arose at Macellum among the numberless idle servants. The whole pack of varletry, in the hope of Court favour, subjected the two disgraced young princes to espionage by night and day. Long as Julian could remember, death was an hourly expectation. Little by little he had accustomed himself to perpetual fear, being quite aware that neither in the house nor garden could he take a step or make a gesture unperceived by a thousand intent but invisible eyes. Hearing and understanding much of the toils about him, the boy was forced to feign ignorance. At one time it was the conversation between Eutropius and a spy sent by the Emperor Constantius, in which the monk named Julian and Gallus "the imperial scourges"; at another time, in the gallery under the kitchen windows, it was the meditation of a cook, furious at some insolence on the part of Gallus. She was saying to the washer-up of the dishes, "God save my soul, Priscilla, but what I can't make out is, why they haven't strangled them before!"

Today, when Julian, after his lesson in theology, went out of the house and perceived the greenness of the trees, he breathed more freely. The two peaks of Mount Argæus, covered with snow, sparkled against blue sky. The neighbourhood of glaciers made the air refreshingly cool; garden alleys stretched hither and thither into the distance; glistening dark-green foliage of oaks formed thick vaultings; here and there a ray filtered through the branches of plane-trees. Only one side of the garden was not walled in, for in that direction lay a chasm. At the foot of the plateau on which the castle stood, a dead plain stretched as far as Anti-Taurus, and from this plain fierce heat rose in mist, while in the garden fresh streams were running and little waterfalls tinkling through thickets of oleanders.

A century before the date of which we are speaking Macellum had been the favourite domain and pleasure-house of the luxurious and half-mad Ariarathes, king of Cappadocia.

Julian took his way towards an isolated grotto, hard by the precipice, in which a statue of the god Pan, playing the flute, stood over a little sacrificial altar. Outside the grotto, a lion's mouth jetted water into a stone basin, and a curtain of roses masked the entrance while letting through its branches a view of the undulating hills and the plain, far down and drowned in misty blue. The perfume of roses filled the little cave, and the air there would have been oppressive had it not been cooled by a stream channelled in the rocky floor.

The wind scattered the turf with yellow petals of roses, and flung them floating on the water of the basin. From the dark and warm place of shelter could be heard the humming of bees. There Julian, stretched on the moss, used to read the *Banquet* of Plato, understanding nothing of many of the passages; but their beauty had for him a double relish because it was a fruit forbidden.

When his reading was done, Julian wrapped the book anew in the binding of the "Epistles of the Apostle Paul," went up to the altar of Pan, gazed at the joyous god as at an old accomplice, and, thrusting his hand into a heap of dried leaves, drew from the interior of the altar, which was cracked and covered with a piece of board, a small object carefully enveloped in cloth. It was his own handiwork—a delightful little Liburnian trireme, or galley with three banks of oars. He set it swimming in the basin; the galley rocked on the miniature waves. The model was complete,—three masts, rigging, oars, gilded prow, and sails made of a fragment of purple silk, the gift of Labda. Nothing was wanting but to fix the rudder, and the boy began the task.

From time to time, while planing a piece of board, he would look into the distance, at the hills outlined in mist through the hedge of roses. Beside his plaything Julian soon forgot all vexations, all hates, and the eternal fear of death. In this little cave he imagined himself a shipwrecked sailor. He was the wily Ulysses in some solitary cavern facing the ocean, building a ship in which he might win back again to Ithaca. But down yonder, there among the hills, where the houses of Cæsarea shone white as the sea-foam, a little cross, glittering high above the roof of the basilica, irritated him still. That everlasting cross! Could he never be free of it, even here in his own cave? He would resolve not to see it, and stooping, redoubled his attention to the galley.

"Julian!" a voice cried; "Julian, Julian! Where in the world is he? Eutropius is looking for you to go to church with him."

The boy shivered, and nimbly hid his handiwork inside the altar of Pan. He smoothed his hair, shook his clothes, and when he came out of the grotto had resumed an expression of impenetrable Christian hypocrisy.

Eutropius, holding Julian's hand in his bony one, conducted him to church.

IV

The Arian basilica of St. Maurice was built almost entirely of blocks taken from the ruined temple of Apollo. The sacred court, the *atrium*, was surrounded by colonnades. In the middle of this court murmured a fountain, placed there for the ablutions of the faithful. Under one of the side porticoes lay an ancient oaken tomb darkened with age; and in this tomb were the wonder-working bones of St. Mamas, for which Eutropius had obliged Julian and Gallus themselves to build a stone-work shrine. The task of Gallus, who took to it as to a game, went rapidly forward, while the wall of Julian frequently crumbled and proved oddly unsatisfactory; a phenomenon which Eutropius explained by remarking that St. Mamas refused the offering of children possessed by the demon of pride.

The halt, the maimed, the sick, and the blind, expectant of miracle, thronged near the tomb. Julian understood why they stationed themselves here. One of the monks used to hold a pair of balances; the pilgrims—some of them come from hamlets many leagues away—weighed with scrupulous care pieces of linen, woollen stuff, or silk; and having laid them on the tomb of St. Mamas, would fall to praying all night. At daylight the stuff was weighed over again, and the weight compared with the weight on the previous day. If the texture proved heavier, it was declared that the prayer had been answered, that the divine mercy, like dew, had soaked into the stuff and rendered it capable of producing all manner of marvellous cures.

But frequently the prayer was in vain. The stuff weighed just what it did before; and pilgrims would pass whole days, weeks, even months, waiting at the sepulchre. Among the latter there was an old woman named Theodula. Some called her demented; others counted her a saint. For years she had not quitted the tomb of St. Mamas. The daughter for whose restoration she had come to pray had now been a long while dead. But Theodula continued kneeling ceaselessly before her faded and ravelled fragment of cloth.

From the outer court three doors led into the basilica—one for women, one for men, and the third, in the centre, for monks and the lower clergy. With Eutropius and Gallus, Julian went in through this last door, being *anagnost* or reader of the lessons for the day. Clothed in a long black robe with white sleeves, his hair anointed, and bound back by a fillet that it might not fall into his eyes while reading aloud, Julian passed through the midst of the faithful, his eyes fixed humbly on the ground. His pale face assumed almost involuntarily the inevitable and hypocritical expression of submissiveness. He ascended the high rood-loft. The frescoes of the wall to the right depicted the martyrdom of St. Euthymus, in which one executioner seized the sufferer's head, while another, wrenching open his mouth with pincers, brought the cup of molten lead to his lips. In another scene the executioner with an instrument of torture was flaying the childish and bleeding limbs of St. Euthymus, hanging from a tree by his hands. Beneath these frescoes ran the inscription, "With the blood of the martyrs, O Lord, Thy church is arrayed as in purple and fine linen."

On the opposite wall sinners were burning in the fire of the pit, and above them rose Paradise and the saints. One of the saints was plucking the fruits of the tree of Eden; another playing the psaltery; and a third, couched on a cloud, contemplated with a beatific smile the tortures of the damned. Beneath were written the words, "Behold! there shall be tears and gnashing of teeth!" The adorers of St. Mamas entered the church like a procession of all human maladies. The bandy-legged, the blind, the armless, the anæmic, children tottering along like old men, epileptics, idiots with pale faces and inflamed eyelids—all bore the mark of a dull and desperate submission. When the choir ceased, there could be heard the contrite sighings of the "widows of the church," black-robed nuns of the order of St. Basil, and the jingling of the chains of old Pamphilus, who for many a long year had addressed no word to the living, muttering only, "Lord, Lord, give me tears!—grant me mercy!—give me an end to remembrance!"

The atmosphere was that of a warm sepulchral chamber, thick, loaded with incense and the smell of melting wax, hot oil, and the breath of all these sick persons. Now it was Julian's lot on that day to read aloud part of the Apocalypse.

The terrifying pictures of the Revelation were unfolded, the white horse of Death soared through space above the peoples of the earth, as they knelt weeping at the nearness of the world's end.

"*The sun becomes dark as pitch, and the moon red as blood. Men say to the mountains, Fall on us and hide us from the throne of God and from the wrath of the Lamb, for the great day of His anger is come, and who can resist it?*"

Over and over again came the prophecy: "*Men shall seek death and shall not find it; they shall desire death and it shall flee from them.*"

Lamentation arose: "*Thrice happy are the dead!*" and "*Then came the bloody destruction of all peoples, and the angel cast his sickle into the earth and gathered the vintage of the earth and cast it into the great wine-press of the wrath of God, and the wine-press was trodden without the city; and there came out blood from the wine-press even unto the bridles of the horses, as far as a thousand and six hundred furlongs,*" and men cursed the God of heaven for their plagues, and they did not repent them of their sins; and the angel sang: "*He Who worships the Beast and his image shall drink of the wine of the wrath of God, prepared in the cup of His anger, and shall be tormented in fire and sulphur before the holy angels and the Lamb, and the smoke of his torture shall rise in the night of ages. For he who shall adore the Beast and his image shall rest no more.*"

Julian ended. A profound hush succeeded in the church. Painful sighs rose from the terrified crowd; and the noise of foreheads struck against the earth and the clank of the fetters of Pamphilus, accompanying his perpetual murmur: "Lord, Lord, give me tears!—grant me mercy!—give me an end of remembrance!"

The child raised his eyes towards the spandril of mosaic between the columns of the arcade, representing the Arian image of Christ; a sombre, terrible figure, its wasted face aureoled in gold, and diademed in the fashion of the Byzantine emperors. It was the face of an old man, with a long thin nose and lips severely shut. With his right hand he was blessing the world; in the left he held a book in which was written, "Peace be with you; I am the Light of the World." He was seated on a splendid throne, and a Roman emperor (Julian imagined that it must be Constantius) was in the act of kissing his feet.

In the penumbral shadow below this image, lighted by a single lamp, could be discerned a bas-relief on a sarcophagus, dating from the earliest Christian times. It displayed sea-nymphs, leopards, gay tritons blowing their horns, and among them Moses, Jonah and his whale, Orpheus charming the beasts with his lyre, an olive-branch, and a dove; the whole sculpture a symbol of pure and childlike faith. In the midst stood the Good Shepherd bearing on his shoulder the sheep that had gone astray, the soul of the sinner. This barefooted youthful figure, with beardless face, had the joyous and simple bearing of a poor peasant, and his smile something of a heavenly sweetness.

Julian imagined that nobody nowadays knew or saw that Good Shepherd; and this little picture of old times was somehow connected in his mind with a dream of his childhood which he tried in vain to recover.

And, gazing at this youth, who seemed as if mysteriously reproaching him, he murmured the name picked up from Mardonius, "Galilean!" At that moment slanting rays of the sun through the windows trembled, above, in a cloud of incense, which, aflame with reflections from the gilded aureole, seemed to upheave the sombre and terrible image of the Arian Christ. The choir chanted, *"Let all human flesh be dumb and bow down, fearful and trembling, thinking no more of the things of the earth; for the Emperor of emperors, the Lord of lords, has given Himself afresh as a pledge and a food to His faithful; even He who is surrounded by the hosts of angels, by all powers and dominions, by cherubim with innumerable eyes, and by the six-winged seraphim, veiling their faces and singing, 'Alleluia! Alleluia! Alleluia!'"*

Like a tempest the psalm swept over the bowed heads of the pilgrims. The figure of the Good Shepherd faded into the distance; but its youthful gaze remained steadily fixed upon Julian, a gaze full of reproach. The heart of the child was moved, not by a sense of worship, but by an intolerable fear; a fear before that mystery which was for him to remain forever insoluble.

V

From the Arian basilica Julian returned to Macellum, and got out his little galley which he had prepared for this special occasion; and learning that Eutropius, after the Mass, had gone a journey of several days, the boy slipped through the barred gates of the fortress, and ran to the temple of Aphrodite, close to the church of St. Maurice. The sacred wood of the goddess bordered the Christian cemetery. Endless hostilities, debates, wranglings, and even lawsuits, were kept up between these two temples. The Christians begged for the destruction of the Pagan shrine; Olympiodorus, the sacrificing priest, on the other hand, complained that the custodians of the basilica by night would secretly cut down ancient cypresses in the sacred wood, and dig graves for Christians in the soil belonging to Aphrodite.

Into the wood Julian wound his way; a warm breeze blew softly on his cheek. In the afternoon heat the grey and fibrous bark of the cypresses trickled with thick resinous tears. To Julian the dusk seemed perfumed by the very breath of the goddess.

The white bodies of statues stood up in sharp relief against the rich shadow of trees. An Eros there had been maimed by some custodian of the basilica, who had rudely smashed off its marble bow. The weapon of the little winged Love-god, together with his hands, lay in deep grass at the foot of the pedestal. But although one-armed, the mischievous boy continued to take aim, and a mad smile of malice still fluttered on his lips.

Julian entered the house of the priest, Olympiodorus. Its rooms were small but comfortable, and rather bare than luxurious. There was neither carpet nor silver dish to be seen; the floors and furniture were of wood, and the vessels of clay. But everything bore the stamp of taste. The handle of the kitchen lamp was a marvellous little work of art representing Neptune with his trident; the bold outlines of earthen jars, full of olive oil, won the admiration of Julian; and along the walls ran light frescoes, water nymphs mounted on sea-unicorns; and dancing women, clothed in the long robe of votaries of Pallas Athene, hovered along in graceful scroll-work.

The little house stood all smiling in its bath of sunshine. Nereids, dancers, sea-unicorns, the Neptune on the lamp, and the inmates of the house, all seemed folk cheerful by nature, guiltless of ugliness, of malice or spleen. A couple of dozen olives, some white bread, a bunch of grapes, some wine and water, these were enough to turn the little meal into a feast, and Diophane, the wife of Olympiodorus, had in fact tied a wreath of laurel to the door to mark that very day a feast-day.

Julian went into the little garden of the atrium. Under the blue sky a jet of water pulsed into the air, and in the midst of narcissus, acanthus-blossom, tulips, and myrrh, rose a bronze Hermes, winged and smiling like the rest of the cottage, and poised in the act of taking flight. Above the flowers, butterflies and bees playing in the sunshine chased each other, and in the shade of the porch Olympiodorus and his daughter Amaryllis, a pretty girl of some seventeen springs, were playing the Greek game of *kottabos*. On a slender column fixed in the earth, and oscillating like the scale of a balance, lay a little beam, which bore, slung from each end, a cup; under each cup stood an amphora full of water, crowned by a statuette in metal. The game consisted in throwing from a certain distance a few drops of wine, in as high a curve as possible, into one of the little cups, which, thus suddenly weighted, would descend and strike the statuette.

"Play, play; it is your turn!" cried Amaryllis.

"One, two, three!" Olympiodorus threw the contents of his goblet, and missed.

He burst out into a boyish laugh. It was strange to see the tall grey-headed man so wholly absorbed in his game.

The young girl, with a charming movement of her bare arm, threw back her mauve tunic and in her turn flung the liquid. The little cup of the *kottabos* rang upon the statuette. Amaryllis began laughing and clapping her hands. Suddenly, on the threshold they saw Julian, and both rushed to welcome him. Amaryllis cried—

"Diophane! where art thou? Come and see what guest we've got today. Quick, quick!"

Diophane ran from the kitchen.

"Julian, my darling child! . . . Don't you think he is grown thinner? How long it is since we have seen you! . . ."

And she added, radiant with good humour—

"You may well be merry, children, for this evening we shall have a real feast. I'm going to prepare crowns of fresh roses; I shall fry three perch, and make you cakes of gingerbread!"

At this moment a young slave accosted Olympiodorus and whispered in his ear that a rich patrician lady of Cæsarea wished to see him, having something to discuss with the priest of Aphrodite.

Olympiodorus followed the slave. Julian and Amaryllis went on with the game of *kottabos*. Presently a little twelve-year-old girl came shyly up to them. It was Psyche, the pale fair-haired and youngest child of Olympiodorus. She had great sad blue eyes, and, alone in the house, seemed a stranger to the cult of Aphrodite, and apart from the general gaiety. Keeping aloof from the rest, she would remain musing while others were laughing, and nobody knew what made her sad, or what gave her pleasure. Her father pitied her as one incurably sick, ruined by the evil eye or by the witchcrafts of his eternal enemies the Galileans, who had carried off the soul of his child in revenge.

The dark Amaryllis was the favourite daughter of Olympiodorus: but the mother secretly spoiled Psyche, and loved with jealous passion the delicate child whose inner life was hidden from her. Psyche, unknown to her father, and in despite of the caresses, prayers, and even the threats of her mother, used to attend the basilican church of St. Maurice. Anguished on discovering this, the priest of Venus had renounced Psyche; and when her name was mentioned, his brow would cloud over with a bitter expression. He was sure that it was by reason of the impiety of his child that the vine, once blessed by Aphrodite, produced fewer fruits than of yore; he believed that the little golden crucifix worn on the child's neck had profaned the temple of the indignant goddess.

"Why do you go to that church?" Julian asked her one day.

"I don't know; it is comfortable there. Have you seen the Good Shepherd?"

"Yes, the Galilean! How did you know about Him?"

"Old Theodula told me. Ever since then I have gone to church; and, tell me, Julian, why do they all hate the Good Shepherd?"

At this moment Olympiodorus returned in triumph and narrated his interview with the patrician lady, a young girl whom her betrothed had abandoned. She believed him bewitched by the amulets of a rival. Many a time had she gone to the Christian church and besought St. Mamas with an aching heart, but neither fasts nor prostrations had snapped the evil charm.

"As if the Christians could console her!" Olympiodorus contemptuously concluded, throwing a keen glance at the attentive Psyche. "This Christian girl has now sought my help, and Aphrodite will heal her!"

He produced the two white pigeons, bound together, which the Christian had begged him to offer as a sacrifice to the goddess of love.

Amaryllis took the little creatures in her hand, and kissed their rosy beaks, declaring that it would be a thousand pities to kill them.

"Father, we will offer them to the goddess without spilling a drop of blood!"

"How? There can be no sacrifice without bloodshed."

"We will give them liberty. They shall fly away clean into heaven, straight to the footstool of Aphrodite. Is she not in the sky? She will accept them. Let me do this, darling father, I beg of you!"

Olympiodorus had not the heart to deny this entreaty; and the young girl, unbinding the pigeons tossed them back to liberty. They fled away into the sky with a delirious beating of white wings, making for the footstool of Aphrodite. Shading his eyes with his hands the priest watched the offering of the convert disappear into the clouds, while Amaryllis danced with joy, crying—

"Aphrodite, Aphrodite, receive the gift!"

Olympiodorus went out. Julian, solemn-faced and timorous, approached Amaryllis; his cheeks grew red, and his voice trembled as he pronounced the name of the young girl.

"Amaryllis, I have brought you—"

"Ah! I have long been going to ask you what it could be."

"It is a galley with three banks of oars!"

"A galley! What do you mean?"

"A real Liburnian galley."

He immediately began to unroll his present, but suddenly aware that Amaryllis was watching him, he felt ineffable shame, became confused, and with an imploring look at the damsel, slid the ship into the basin of the fountain.

"You see, Amaryllis. . . it is a trireme. . . a real trireme, with—with—sails. . . and. . . its rudder. . . Look how well it gets under way!"

But Amaryllis laughed heartily.

"What an odd boy you are! What in the world should I do with your trireme? I fear it wouldn't take me very far. It's a ship for mice and flies. Make a present of it to Psyche; she will be delighted with it."

Julian, though deeply hurt, assumed indifference, while tears choked his speech. Controlling himself, he said disdainfully, but with trembling lips—

"I see that you don't understand anything. . . about art."

Amaryllis laughed yet more heartily. To add insult to injury, a summons came for her to receive her betrothed, a rich merchant from Samos, who dressed badly, perfumed his person, and spoke vile grammar. Julian hated him, and when he learnt of the arrival of the Samian, the charm of the house vanished so far as he was concerned.

From the neighbouring room he could hear the distracting chatter of Amaryllis and the voice of her lover.

Without uttering a word, and filled with cold hatred, Julian seized his cherished trireme—the real Liburnian trireme which had cost him such endless pains—and before the startled eyes of Psyche, snapped the mast, tore down the sails, tangled the rigging, and stamped the toy into atoms with his feet.

Amaryllis returned. Her face bore traces of a strange happiness, of that superfluity of life and love-joy which awakens in young girls an imperious need to embrace and to kiss those near them.

"Julian. . . forgive me. . . I have pained you. Forgive me, dear! you know well that I love you."

And before he had time to make up his mind, Amaryllis, throwing back her tunic, imprisoned his head in her fresh bare arms. A delightful dread stopped the beating of Julian's heart; he saw her great dark dewy eyes so close to him, the sweet odour of her body so overwhelmed him, and she locked him so close against her breast, that the boy grew giddy. He closed his eyes and felt a kiss long, too long, pressed upon his lips.

The voice of the Samian broke the enchantment—

"Amaryllis, Amaryllis! where art thou?"

Julian putting forth all his strength pushed the girl away, his heart overflowed with pain and hatred, and crying, "Let me go, let me go!" snatched himself free and fled.

Deaf and heedless he escaped from the house through the vineyards and the cypress wood; nor halted till he reached the temple of Aphrodite. Now and again he heard his name called, and the gay voice of Diophane, announcing that the cakes of gingerbread were ready; but he made no reply. Search was made for him. He lay in hiding in the thicket of laurels at the feet of Eros. Accustomed to his fits of moroseness, they gave up the search, satisfied that he had returned to Macellum.

When all around was restored again to silence, Julian came out from his hiding-place and gazed at the temple of the goddess of love, lodged upon a gentle hill, and bare to view on all sides. The Ionic marble columns, flooded with sunshine, were softly steeped in the warmth of azure, receiving its ardent embraces with the cold purity of snow.

Each corner of the façade was surmounted by pedestalled griffins, with lifted talons, beaks gaping, and woman-shaped breasts, standing out, proud and austere, against the deep blue of the sky.

Julian went up the steps into the portico, pushed open the bronze doors and penetrated the interior of the temple up to the very shrine, the *naos*.

Silence and coolness surrounded him. The setting sun overhead still fell on the capitals of the columns, and their fine illumined scroll-work, contrasted with the penumbral shadow on the floor of the temple, seemed soft and bright as tresses of gold. A tripod, still burning, diffused the odour of myrrh.

Julian, leaning against the wall, lifted his eyes in fear, restraining his breath till it almost died upon his lips.

She, the goddess herself, was before him. Under the open sky, in the midst of the temple, stood, cold and white, new-born of the sea-foam, Aphrodite Anadyomene. With a smile she contemplated the heavens and the sea, wondering at their charm; as if unwitting still that their beauty was her own beauty, glassed in the eternal mirrors of the azure and the waters. No raiment profaned her divine body. Naked and chaste she rose, as the clear sky soaring above her.

Julian gazed on with an insatiate gaze, and felt quick thrills of adoration sweep over his frame. The child, in his black monkish habit, knelt before Aphrodite, his face upturned, his hands pressed to his palpitating little heart.

Then still aloof, still timorous, he sat at the foot of the column. He leant his cheek against the marble. Peace sank slowly into his soul. He fell asleep.

But, even through that slumber, he was conscious of her presence.

She came down towards him, nearer, nearer. . . Her delicate white hands stole round his neck. The boy with a smile submitted to these passionless endearments; the cold of the marble chilled his very heart. That divine embrace bore no likeness to the wild clasp of Amaryllis. The soul of Julian, freeing itself from earthly love, entered depths of repose, as into some ambrosial night of Homer, or the sweet rest of the dead.

When Julian awoke it was night. Over the roofless quadrilateral stars were shining, and the crescent moon shedding her silver upon the head of the statue. Julian arose. Olympiodorus must have meanwhile been tending the temple, although he had either not observed or had refrained from waking the child; for now, on the bronze tripod, fresh charcoal was glowing, and a fillet of odorous smoke arising towards the goddess.

Julian smiling approached, and from the chrysolite cup, between the feet of the tripod, took a few grains of incense and flung them on the coals. Smoke rose more thickly, and the ruddy glow of the fire, like a pale flush of life, came over the face of the statue, contending with the soft new-born shine of the moon.

Julian bowed down and kissed the marble feet, and watered them with his tears, exclaiming—

"Aphrodite! Aphrodite! thou shalt be my everlasting love!"

VI

In one of the foul and dirty quarters of the Syrian Seleucia, the port for Antioch on the shores of the Inner Sea, narrow and tortuous alleys debouched into a market-place lying along the quays. The sea-horizon was invisible, so thick was the throng of masts and the tangle of rigging. The houses were a mass of miserable little shells, whitewashed within and encumbered with furniture. Their fronts were garnished with tattered carpets, dirty fragments of cloth, and ravelled matting. In every nook and hovel and crowded court, along kennels and gutters of dirty fever-stricken water from laundries and baths of the poor, there lay seething in its penury and hunger a populace strangely cosmopolitan.

The sun, after thoroughly baking the earth, had just descended below the horizon; wide-winged twilight was settling slowly down; a stifling heat of dust and fog still weighed on the spirits of the city. From the market square breathed a suffocating atmosphere of flesh and vegetables, becoming rotten through lying all day in the blaze of the sun. Half-naked slaves were carrying bales of merchandise from the ships. Their heads were close-shaven; through their rags could be seen horrible blotches on the skin; and the greater number bore on their faces, in brandings by red-hot iron, the Latin letters C. F., that is to say *Cave Furem* ('ware thief!).

Braziers were being slowly lighted. But notwithstanding the approach of night, traffic and discussion gave no sign of ceasing in the network of alleys. From a neighbouring forge piercing blows of the hammer resounded on bars of iron, and flames shot up the sooty draught-hole. Hard by, slaves of a bakery, naked, covered from head to foot in flour-dust, and with eyelids inflamed by heat, were putting loaves into an oven. A shoemaker sat in his open-air stall, amid an insupportable smell of cobbler's glue and leather, stitching shoes by the light of a smoky lamp. He was squatting on his heels, and chanting desert songs at the top of his voice. Two old hags like witches, with hair streaming in the wind, were slowly passing across the little square in front of a row of hovels. They were yelling at each other, wrangling and threatening each other with fists and stones. The subject of dispute was the ownership of a cord on which to dry linen. A huckster, from a distant village, was hurrying along to be in time for the morning market. He was mounted on an old mare, flanked with wicker paniers, each heaped with rotting fish; the fetid smell of his load made passers-by edge off to a distance. A loutish urchin, with red hair and skin, was solacing his soul by beating on a great pan, while other children, a sickly multitude coming into the world and leaving it by hundreds daily, marched amidst this scene of poverty, grunting like pigs, round the pools of the quay. The water was full of orange-peel and egg-shells. In yet more villainous passages, inhabited by thieves, the smell of sour wine came from wine-shops, and sailors from every beach of the world marched along arm in arm, shouting drunken songs.

Surrounding all that noise, that filth and spilth of human misery, there murmured, sighed, and grumbled, the infinite, distant, and invisible sea.

Directly over against the subterranean kitchen windows of a Phoenician dealer, ragged gamblers were playing at knuckle-bones, and gossiping. From the kitchen warm gusts of boiling gravy, game, and spices ascended, greedily snuffed-up, with closed eyes, by the hungry gamesters.

A certain Christian, a dyer of purple, dismissed for theft from a rich factory at Tyre, was murmuring, as he hungrily sucked a mallow-leaf thrown away by the cook,—

"And at Antioch, my friends, what's going on there makes one shiver at nights, just to think of it. Why, a few days ago the hungry folk tore in pieces the Prefect Theophilus—and for what reason? Nobody knows! When the thing was done they remembered too late that the poor wretch was a good sort of fellow and a respectable man. I suggested that perhaps the Emperor had pointed him out for punishment."

A consumptive old man, a very skilful cardsharper, replied—

"I have seen the Cæsar, and I like him. Quite young, fair as flax, with a good-natured, fat face. But, as you say, what crimes are committed nowadays! what crimes indeed! Why one can't put one's nose outside the door without danger."

"Ah, that's nothing to do with Cæsar! it's his wife, Constantia, the old witch, that does it!"

But strange personages came near the knot of talkers and thrust themselves forward, as if desiring to take part in the conversation.

If the kitchen firelight had been brighter, it would have been noticed that their faces were begrimed and their clothes fouled and torn like those of stage-beggars; and notwithstanding their raggedness the hands of these persons were fine and white, and their nails pared and crimsoned. One of them whispered in his comrade's ear—

DMITRY MEREZHKOVSKY

"Listen, Agamemnon; here also they're talking about Cæsar."

He whom they called Agamemnon appeared to be drunk. He wore a beard, which was too thick and long to be natural, and gave him the aspect of a fantastic brigand. His eyes were debonair, almost boyish, and of a bright blue. His friends frequently pulled him back, muttering—

"Now then be careful!"

The consumptive old man went on in a whining tone—

"Now tell me plainly, my friends, is it just? The price of bread is going up everyday. People dying like flies. And, suddenly, guess what happens? Lately a great ship came from Egypt; everybody's happy, thinking that it brings bread. The word goes round that Cæsar has made the ship come to feed the people. And what do you think it was, my friends? Powder, Alexandrian powder, if you please! a special pink Libyan powder to rub down the wrestlers!—powder for the Emperor's gladiators—powder instead of bread! . . . Eh? . . . Now is that justice?"

Agamemnon nudged his companion's elbow.

"Ask his name, quick—ask!"

"Gently, wait a bit. . ."

A leather dresser remarked—

"Here in Seleucia the town is quiet, but up at Antioch there are nothing but traitors, spies, and informers."

The dyer, licking the mallow-leaf for the last time, growled and mumbled—

"Yes, unless God comes down to help us, soon flesh and blood will be going a deal cheaper than bread and wine!"

The currier, a philosophic tippler, sighed—

"Ah! ah! ah! we're all poor creatures! The gods of Olympus play at ball with us! Men weep and the gods laugh!"

The companion of Agamemnon meanwhile had succeeded in joining the conversation, and with nonchalant adroitness acertained the names of the talkers. He had intercepted the news, conveyed by the cobbler to the leather-dresser, about a plot hatched against Cæsar's life by the soldiers of the Pretorian guard. Then, strolling on a few paces, he had written down the names of the talkers with a jewelled stilus on tablets of soft wax, where many other names were inscribed already. At this moment hoarse sounds like the roarings of some subterranean monster came from the market square. They were the notes, now plaintive, now lively, of a hydraulic organ.

At the entrance to a showman's travelling booth, a blind slave, for four obols a day, was pumping up the water which produced this extraordinary harmony.

Agamemnon dragged his companion towards the booth, a great tent with blue awnings sprinkled with silver tinsel. A lantern lighted the black-board on which the order of the programme was chalked up, in Syriac and Greek. An oppressive atmosphere of garlic and lamp-oil prevailed inside, where, beside the organ, there struck up the wailing of two harsh flutes, while a negro, rolling the whites of his eyes, thrummed on an Arab drum. A dancer was skipping to and fro on a tight-rope, keeping time to the music with his hands, and singing the latest street song:

> *Huc, huc, convenite nunc. . .*
> *Spatolocinædi!*
> *Pedem tendite*
> *Cursum addite. . .*

This starveling mountebank was old, impudent, and repulsively cheery. Drops of sweat, mixed with paint, were trickling from his shaven face. His wrinkles, plastered with white lead, looked like the cracks in a wall when rain has washed off the lime. When he withdrew, the flutes and the organ ceased, and on the platform a fifteen-year-old girl appeared. She was to perform the *Cordax*, a celebrated licentious dance adored by the mob. Fathers of the Church might anathematise, and Roman laws interdict this dance, but both did so in vain. Everywhere the Cordax was danced as before by rich and poor, by street-dancers as well as by wives of senators.

Agamemnon murmured with enthusiasm:

"What a divinely pretty girl!"

Thanks to jostling by his companions he had reached a place in the front rank of spectators. The slender bronze body of the Nubian was only veiled round the hips by a light and transparent rose-coloured scarf. Her hair was wound on the top of her head in close fine curls, like those of Ethiopian women. Her face was of the severest Egyptian type, recalling that of the Sphinx.

She began to dance in careless fashion, as if already out-wearied. Above her head she swung heavy steel bells, castanets or "crotals,"—swung them lazily and loosely. But the movements became more emphatic, and suddenly under long lashes yellow eyes shone out, clear and bright as the eyes of a leopardess. She straightened her body. The steel crotals shook with such a challenge in their piercing sound that the crowd shivered and became still. The damsel whirled rapidly, vivid, slender, supple as a serpent; her nostrils dilated, a strange cry came crooning from her throat, and at each sharp movement her brown bosom shook and trembled within its almost invisible meshes of fine green silk.

The crowd howled with enthusiasm. Agamemnon struggled with rage because his companions held him back. Suddenly the girl stopped. A slight shudder ran through her body. Deep silence prevailed. The head of the Nubian was thrown back as if in a rigid swoon, but above it the crotals still shivered with an extraordinary languor, a dying vibration, quick and tender as the wing-flutterings of a captive butterfly. The flashing of the yellow eyes died away, although the eyeball kept its sparkling lights, and the face remained severe; but upon the dark and sensuous lips of that sphinx-like mouth a smile trembled, faint as the dying sound of the crotals.

The public shouted and applauded so loudly that the blue tent with its stars and spangles swayed like a sail in a hurricane. The showman became apprehensive lest his booth should collapse. The companions of Agamemnon at last failed to hold him back; raising the curtain, he rushed through the scenes into the part reserved for the dancers and actors. In vain his friends counselled—

"Wait; tomorrow you shall have everything as you wish! now something might. . ."

Agamemnon interrupted them—

"Not tomorrow; now, at once!"

He approached the owner of the show, the cunning and grey-bearded Greek, Mirmes, and without explanation flung into the skirt of his robe a handful of gold pieces.

"Is that dancing-girl your slave?"

"Yes. What does your excellency desire?"

Mirmes, evidently astonished, was staring now at Agamemnon and now at the gold.

"What's your name, girl?"

"Phyllis."

He bestowed money on her also, without stopping to reckon it.

The Greek murmured some words in the ear of the smiling Phyllis, who tossed up the pieces and threw sparkling glances at Agamemnon. He said—

"Come with me!"

Phyllis threw over her shoulders a dark cloak and glided with him into the street, asking submissively—

"Whither?"

"I don't know."

"To your house?"

"Impossible. I live at Antioch."

"And as for me, I only arrived in this city this morning. What, then, are we to do?"

"Wait a moment; I saw just now in a lane near this the temple of Priapus open. Let us go there!"

Phyllis led him on hastily, laughing. The companions of Agamemnon desired to follow him, but he said to them—

"It is unnecessary—remain here."

"Be careful! At any rate take a weapon, the quarter is dangerous. . ." and drawing from under his dress a dagger with a jewelled hilt, one of the friends of Agamemnon respectfully tendered it to him.

Groping at every step into thick darkness, Agamemnon and Phyllis made their way up a narrow passage out of the market-place.

"Here! here it is! Fear nothing—go in!"

They found themselves in the vestibule of a little vacant temple, its ancient and massive columns ill-lighted by the flicker of a lamp.

"Push-to the door!" and Phyllis, softly laughing, threw her warm cloak upon the ground. When Agamemnon took her into his arms, it seemed to him that round his body had coiled some warm lithe snake, with wide and terrifying eyes. At that moment from the interior of the temple came harsh cacklings, and such a gust of beating wings went past that the lamp nearly went out. Agamemnon disengaged his arms from Phyllis' waist and stammered—

"What in the world was that?"

In the dense darkness white forms were slipping by them like so many ghosts. Thoroughly frightened, Agamemnon crossed himself.

"What is it? May the Holy Cross protect us!"

Something stoutly nipped his leg. He yelled with pain and fear, but seizing one of his unknown enemies by the throat, he poignarded another. Deafening cries arose, followed by squeals and repeated battlings of wings. The lamp flickered for the last time, and Phyllis cried, laughing—

"They are the ganders! the holy ganders of Priapus! What a crime you have committed!"

Pale and trembling, the conqueror stood holding in one hand the bloody dagger and in the other two slain ganders. A crowd carrying torches burst with shouts into the temple, led by Scabra, the old priestess of Priapus. This dame had been peacefully supping in a neighbouring tavern when the trumpeting of the ganders had raised the alarm. Gathering a train of nocturnal prowlers she had rushed to the rescue. Hook-nosed, with unkempt grey hair, and eyes blazing like two steel points, the old priestess looked nothing less than a fury. She shouted—

"Help! help! The temples are desecrated, and the holy ganders of Priapus slain! And see here, here are the foul Christians!"

Phyllis fled, enveloping her face in the cloak, while the crowd dragged off Agamemnon, so cleanly taken aback that he never thought of relaxing his grip upon the ganders.

Scabra sent for the clerks of the market, the agoranomes. But with every moment the crowd grew larger, and Agamemnon's companions ran to support him. It was too late. From dens, wine-shops, alley stalls, a world of loiterers rushed up, attracted by the noise. All faces wore the expression of gleeful curiosity peculiar to idlers. The blacksmith appeared with hammer over his shoulder; the two old women had forgotten their quarrel; the floury baker jostled the lame cobbler, and behind them came the genial red-headed boy, shouting, and beating on his pan, as if calling to arms.

Meantime Scabra continued screaming, her nails fixed in the clothes of Agamemnon—

"Ah, just wait! wait a minute! let me get at that cursed beard of yours! I wont leave a hair in it! Out, carrion! food for crows! And you aren't worth the rope you will cost, thief!"

Finally the sleepy guardians of the market appeared; persons of curious demeanour, themselves liker common rogues than keepers of the peace.

Such a deafening din of laughs, oaths, and screams now ensued that nobody was audible. One shouted, "He's an assassin!" another, "A thief!" a third, "Let's burn him!"

Suddenly above the hubbub rang out the masterful voice of a tawny half-naked giant, the attendant in a public bath, an individual with a demagogue's gift for oratory:

"Citizens, listen to me, and mark what I say! I've long been watching this rascal and his companions! They are writing down our names! They are Cæsar's spies!"

Scabra, at last putting her threat into execution, seized Agamemnon's beard in one hand and his tresses in the other. He strove to repulse her, but she pulled with might and main, and to the general surprise black hair and beard both remained in the hands of the old woman, who stumbled and fell. Instead of Agamemnon, an athletic young man with fair curling hair and short beard stood before the people.

In its astonishment, the crowd was momentarily silenced; but the voice of the bath-slave was soon heard clamouring anew:

"See, citizens, they are disguised informers!"

Somebody cried out—

"Strike him! Knock him down!"

The crowd became tumultuous. Stones were thrown; the sham beggars of Agamemnon's company encircled him with drawn swords. At the first stroke the luckless leather-dresser was killed, and fell in a pool of blood. The red-headed boy was trampled under foot, and all faces were becoming ferocious, when at this juncture ten enormous Paphlagonian slaves bearing on their shoulders a purple litter impatiently thrust their way through the crowd.

"Saved!" cried the fair-haired young man, and vaulted into the litter with one of his fellows.

The Paphlagonians hoisted the pair on their shoulders and set off at sharp run. The infuriated crowd were making as if to dash in pursuit, with intent to stone them, when somebody called out—

"Citizens, don't you see that it is Cæsar himself—Gallus Cæsar!"

The mob halted, paralysed by fear, and the purple litter, swaying on the shoulders of the slaves like a skiff in a heavy sea, vanished into the darkness up the street.

SIX YEARS HAD ELAPSED SINCE the incarceration of Julian and of Gallus in the Cappadocian fortress of Macellum. Constantius had restored them to favour. Julian, then twenty years old, was sent to Constantinople, and given leave to travel in Asia Minor. Gallus, the Emperor had named to be his co-regent, with the title of Cæsar. Nevertheless this unlooked-for favour was no valid earnest of good-will. Constantius loved to destroy his enemies after having lulled away mistrust by a display of exuberant affection.

"Well, Glycon, Constantia may beg me as much as she likes, in future, to go out in false hair! But it's all over for me! I've done with it!"

"We warned your Majesty that it was dangerous."

But Cæsar, stretched on the soft cushions of the litter, had already forgotten his alarm, and cried, laughing—

"Glycon! Glycon! *did* you see the old woman rolling on the ground with my beard?"

When they arrived at the palace Cæsar ordered—

"Quick! Let me have a perfumed bath and supper. The walk has famished me."

A courier came near holding a letter.

"What is it, Norban? No, no, we will have business tomorrow morning."

"Let the magnanimity of Cæsar pardon me! It is an important message sent direct from the camp of the Emperor Constantius."

"From Constantius? Give it me."

Gallus broke the seal of the missive, read, and grew pale. His knees gave way—he would have almost fallen without the support of his courtiers.

Constantius, in exquisite and flattering terms, invited his tenderly-loved cousin to come to Milan. At the same time the Emperor summoned the two legions lodged at Antioch, the only bodyguard left to Gallus. Constantius designed thus to leave him defenceless and draw his rival into the snare. When Gallus had recovered presence of mind he murmured weakly—

"Call my wife!"

"Your Majesty's Imperial consort has just set out for Antioch."

"What! She knows nothing of this?"

"No."

"My God, my God! What is to be done? What can be done without her? Tell the envoy of the Emperor—No, say nothing to him—I scarcely know—How is it possible to arrive at a decision alone? Send a swift post to Constantia. . . Say that Cæsar begs her to return! My God, what is to be done?"

He paced up and down distractedly, now hiding his face in his hands, now nervously twisting his fair beard and repeating, "No, no, nothing in the world will induce me to go. I would rather die! Ah! I know Constantius!"

Another messenger came up, a scroll in his hand.

"From the spouse of Cæsar! Her Highness in leaving begged you to sign this as soon as possible."

"What! Another sentence of death? . . . Clement of Alexandria. . . this is really too much. Three a day. . ."

"Cæsar, it was your consort's desire."

"Well, well, what matters it? Nothing! Where's the pen? Nothing matters now! But why has she gone away? How can I get out of this pretty pass single-handed?"

And having signed the death-warrant he fixed those charming and listless blue eyes upon the servants.

"The bath is ready, sire, and the supper will be served after it."

"The supper? I'm hungry no longer. But what dish is there?"

"Truffles from Africa."

"Fresh gathered?"

"They arrived this morning."

"Would n't it be better to raise an army, eh? What do you say, my friends? I feel so overwhelmed. . . Truffles, you say? I was thinking about truffles only this afternoon."

The agitation of his countenance gave way to the airiest of smiles. Before plunging into the water, which was made milky and iridescent by the infusion of perfumes, Gallus waved his hand lightly:

"Pooh! the great thing is not to think! God have mercy on us all! . . . Perhaps after all Constantia will smooth over the matter. . ."

And his chubby face suddenly lighted while he plunged with glee into the scented water. He called out gaily—

"Tell the head cook to add a dressing of red pepper to the truffles!"

VII

At Nicomedia, at Pergamos, and at Smyrna Julian, now nineteen years old and an enthusiast for Hellenic wisdom, had heard much of the famous mage and sophist, Iamblicus of Chaldea, a pupil of the Neo-Platonist, Porphyrius. Men used commonly to call him "the Divine" Iamblicus. In order to see this master, Julian made a journey to Ephesus.

Iamblicus was a little thin and wrinkled old man. He liked complaining of his ailments—gout, rheumatism, nervous headache; he abused physicians, but was zealous in carrying out their advice, and used to speak with deep interest of drugs and infusions of herbs. He always wore, even in summer, a double tunic; never seemed warm enough, and would sit basking in the sun like a lizard.

From his youth up Iamblicus had broken himself of the habit of meat-eating, and spoke of it with disgust as a practice beyond his comprehension. His servant used to prepare for him a special broth, made of barley-water, warm wine, and honey, he being toothless and unable to masticate bread.

He was always surrounded by numberless admiring students who had travelled from Rome, Antioch, Carthagena; from Egypt, Mesopotamia, and Persia, to become his pupils.

All stoutly believed Iamblicus could work miracles. Iamblicus treated them like a father irritated at seeing round him so many weaklings. When they began to discuss and to wrangle, the master would make a sweeping gesture, followed by a grimace expressive of physical pain. He spoke gently, and in a low-toned, agreeable voice; the louder other folk shouted the more subdued his own tone became. He hated all noise, and quarrelsome voices as much as creaking sandals.

Julian gazed in disappointed perplexity at this chilly, sickly, and whimsical old man. What power drew towards him the world of philosophy? He remembered the story of pupils—that one night the divine master during prayer was upraised by some invisible force to a height of twelve cubits from earth, wrapped in a golden glory. Another tale was about a miracle, by which the master had smitten from a rock two warm springs, Eros and Anteros, the two Dæmons of love—the one dull-souled, the other joyous. Iamblicus, it was said, had caressed both, like children, and at a word caused them to disappear.

But in listening to the master Julian never succeeded in discovering the potency of his words. The meta-physic of the school of Porphyrius seemed to him dull, dead, and painfully complicated. Iamblicus would, it is true, emerge a playful victor from the most difficult dialectical discussions. His teaching about God, about the World, about the Ideas, was full of profound learning; but in it lay no vital stimulus. Julian had hoped otherwise, and nevertheless he hung about, and did not set off again homewards. The eyes of Iamblicus were strange, green, and deeply-sunk in his bronzed face. Julian was persuaded that these weird and by no means holy eyes betokened some hidden wisdom, the occult wisdom of the serpent, concerning which Iamblicus never spoke to his pupils. But when "the Divine," in his cracked voice, used to ask why his barley broth was not ready, or complained of gout, the spell was broken.

On one occasion Iamblicus was sauntering with Julian on the seashore, outside the town. It was a soft and melancholy evening. Behind the castle of Panormos in the distance glittered, with their array of statues, the terraces of the celebrated temple of the Ephesian Artemis.

The dark reeds along the sandy shore made no rustle. It was the spot where Latona gave birth to Artemis and Apollo. Smoke of numberless altars in the sacred Orthegian wood was rising in columns into the sky. To the south the Samian mountains shone blue on the horizon. Wavelets fell calmly as the breathings of a child, and pellucid waves swelled over the rocks. The setting sun, hidden behind vapour, gilded the edge of enormous cloud-masses.

Iamblicus seated himself upon a boulder, and Julian threw himself on the ground at his feet. The master caressed the thick black locks of the pupil.

"Are you sad?"

"Yes."

"I know you are sad. You seek and you do not find. You have not the strength to say '*He is*,' and you are afraid to say '*He is not*.'"

"How have you guessed this, Master?"

"My poor boy! for fifty years have I not suffered from the same pain? And I shall suffer from it till I die. Do you imagine that I know Him better than you—that I have discovered what you have missed? *That* is the birth-pain that never ceases. Beside it other tortures are as nothing. People think that they suffer from hunger, from poverty, from thirst; in reality they suffer only from the thought that perhaps He has no existence. Who shall dare to say '*He exists not?*' and yet what superhuman strength one must have to say, '*He is*'!"

"Do you mean to say that you, even you, have never come near Him?"

"Thrice in my life have I borne the ecstacy of feeling myself wholly at one with Him. Plotinus felt it four times, Porphyrius five times. But as for me, the moments in my existence in which life was worth living were precisely three."

"I have questioned your pupils on this subject; they knew nothing."

"Have they the courage to know? The shell of wisdom is enough for them; the kernel, for almost everybody, is deadly."

"Well, let me die, Master! Give the core to me!"

"Have you courage?"

"Yes; but speak—speak!"

"And what can I tell you? I do not know, . . . and need I tell you? Listen to the calmness of the evening, and the secret will be yours without words of mine. . ."

He kept stroking Julian's head; the boy was dreaming, "This, this is what I waited for," and clasping the knees of Iamblicus he falteringly entreated—

"Master, have pity! . . . Reveal it all! . . . Do not desert me!"

With green and strangely motionless eyes kept steadily on the clouds, Iamblicus murmured, as if speaking to himself:

"Yes, we have all forgotten the voice of God. Like children estranged from the cradle from the face of their father, we hear Him, and we do not recognise Him. To hear His voice, every earthly cry in our souls must cease. Just so long as reason shines and illumines our souls, we remain imprisoned in ourselves and see not God. But when reason is put by, ecstacy falls upon us like the dew of night—that ecstacy which the evil cannot know. The wise, the good alone can become, of their own will, lyres vibrating under the hand of God. Whence comes that beam which falls into the soul? I do not know. It comes unawares, and when one least expects it. To search for it is useless. God is not remote from us. One must make ready, with a soul becalmed; and simply wait, as the eyes await (according to the saying of the poet) *the rush of the sun from dark ocean*. God does not come, God does not go away; He is revealed. He is, what the universe is not, the negation of everything that exists. He is nothing, and He is All."

Iamblicus rose and slowly extended his wasted arms:

"Be still, be still, I tell you! Let all things listen for Him! He is here! Let the earth and the sea, let even the sky be dumb! Listen! . . . It is He who fills the universe, the very atoms sing with His breath; He who illumines matter and chaos—*at which the gods tremble*—just as the setting sun illumines that dark cloud."

Julian listened. It seemed to him that the master's calm weak voice was filling the world, was reaching the heights of the heaven, and the last confines of the sea. But the boy's sadness was so deep that it escaped from his bosom in an involuntary sigh.

"Father, forgive me if the question is a folly; but if it is thus with the world why go on living? Why this eternal interchange of life and death? Why pain? Why evil? Why the burden of the body? Why doubt? Why this dark thirst for the impossible?"

Iamblicus looked at him with gentleness, and anew passed his hand over Julian's head. He answered:

"Ah, my son, that is the very seat of the mystery! there is no evil, there is no body, there is no universe, if He exists! Think! it is He, *or* the universe! The body, evil, the universe, all are a mirage, a deception of the living senses. All we have once rested together upon the breast of God in the bosom of invisible light. But there came a time when we beheld from on high matter in its darkness and deadness, and each of us saw in matter its own image, as in a mirror. And the soul mused to itself, 'I can, and I will to, be free! I am like Him! Why not dare to quit Him and contain all in myself?' So the soul, like Narcissus gazing into the brook, fell under the spell of its own image, reflected in its body; and then she fell farther, and desired to fall forever, to rend herself from God forever. She cannot do so. The feet of mortal man touch earth, but his stature lifts him through the heavens.

"Upon the Eternal Ladder of births and of death, all souls, all things existing, are ascending and descending, sometimes towards Him, sometimes away from Him, seeking to leave the Father, and never fulfilling their endeavour. Each soul desires to be God. It weeps for the breast of God, has no rest upon earth, and aspires only to return to the Absolute. We must return to Him, and then all things will become God, and God will be in All. Do you imagine that you are alone in regretting Him! Are you not aware that the whole sum of things is yearning for Him? Listen!"

The sun had set. The edges of the flaming clouds had sunk into ashes. The sea had become pale, light, flocculent as the sky; the sky deep and diaphanous as the sea. Upon the road a cart was passing by; a young man and woman were in it—two lovers, perhaps. The woman was singing a melancholy love song. When they had passed all things were plunged into silence again, and became sadder still. With hastened strides, the oriental night swept over the earth. Julian murmured:

"How many times have I asked myself why Nature was so sad, and why, when she is proudest then saddest of all. . ."

Iamblicus answered by a smile—

"Yes. . . Yes. . . Look, she longs to say why; and cannot speak. She is dumb. She sleeps, and seeks to remember in her dreams, but Matter weighs down her eyelids. Only vaguely can she see Him. Everything in the universe, stars and sea, and earth, animals, plants, and people are dreams of Nature, thinking of God. What she so contemplates, is born and dies. She creates by contemplation, as a dream creates, with effortless ease, and no obstacle to her thought. That is why her works are so beautiful, so free, so purposeless, and so divine. The play of the dreams of Nature is like the play of clouds, without end or beginning. Outside that contemplation of hers nothing in the world exists; and the deeper that contemplation is, the more silent. Believe me, Will, Action, Effort, are only enfeebled and deflected contemplations of God. Nature, in her grandiose indolence, creates forms like the geometrician, for whom nothing exists except what he sees on the paper before him. She brings forms, one after another, out of the womb of her dream. But her mute meditation is only the appearance of reality. Nature, that sleeping Cybele, never lifts her eyelids, and never finds words. Man, he only, has found utterance. The human soul is Nature having lifted the lashes of her eyes, awakened and ready to see God, no longer in half-slumber, but really and face to face. . ."

The first stars were shining in the firmament; now they vanished, and now sparkled again into sight, like diamonds set in the dark azure. More stars, and yet more, kindled their new lights, till the array became incalculable. Iamblicus lifted his finger towards them—

"Julian, to what should one compare the universe of all those stars? One might liken it to a fisherman's net thrown into the sea. God fills the universe as the water fills the net, which moves, but which cannot retain the waters; and the universe desires, but cannot keep God in her meshes. The net is drawn, but God remains. If the universe made no stir God would create nothing—would not issue from the calm that surrounds Him. For whither should He sweep, and to what end?

Yonder, in the realm of the eternal Mothers, in the soul of Calm, dwell the seeds, the Forms, the Ideas, of all that is, has been, and shall be. The germ of hearth-cricket and of atom, together with the germ of the Olympian god."

Then Julian cried aloud, and his voice rang in the silence of Nature like a cry of mortal pain—

"But who then is He; why does He not answer when we call Him? What is His name? I wish to know, I desire to know Him, to hear Him—to see Him—why does He escape my thought? Where is He? Where does He dwell?"

"My poor boy! What matters thought to Him? What means it? He has no name. He is such, that we can say that He must exist, but it is impossible for us to say what He is. But do you think that you can suffer love, or curse Him, without singing His praises? The All-Creator is Himself, having no likeness to His creations. When you say, '*He is not*,' you are exalting Him as much as if you said '*He is*.' One can affirm nothing about Him, because He is above existence, reality, and life. That is why I have said to you that He is the negation of the universe and of your thought. Deny, renounce all that exists for us here, and yonder, in the soundless profundity of darkness, as in the light, you shall find Him still. Give Him friends, family, country, heaven, earth, yourself, your reason, then you will no longer see light, you shall yourself be it. You will not say, 'He and I,' because you will feel that He and you are '*one*'; and your soul will smile at your body as at a phantasm of the desert. You shall become silence, you shall no more find utterance. And if at that moment the world should crumble away, you would be happy: for what would the world signify to you, since you shall be with Him? Your soul shall not desire, because He has no desires; it shall no longer live, because He is above living; it shall no longer think, because He is above thought. Thought is the search for light. He seeks not, because He is Himself the light. He penetrates the whole soul—He laps it in Himself. And then, impartial and solitary, it rests above reason higher than goodness, higher than beauty, reposes in the infinite, on the breast of God the Father of Light. The Soul becomes God, or, to put it better, it remembers that in the night of ages it has been, is, and shall be, God. . . Such, my son, is the life of the Olympians; such is the life of the wise and heroic among men; renunciation of the universe, contempt of earthly passions, the flight of the Soul towards God, whom at last it sees face to face."

Iamblicus ceased speaking. Julian fell at his feet without daring to touch them, and kissed the earth where they rested. Then he raised his head and gazed into those strange green eyes, in which dwelt the wisdom of the serpent. They appeared calmer and deeper than the sky, and as if exhaling a miraculous power.

Julian murmured—

"Master! thou canst do all things. I believe! Command the mountains, and they shall approach each other! Be like God. Work a miracle, create the impossible. Grant my prayer! I believe!"

"My poor boy, what are you asking for? Is not the miracle which may be accomplished in your soul more beautiful than any wonders which *I* can work? Son, is it not a terrible and a happy miracle, this power in the name of which you can dare to say: 'He is,' and if 'He is not' it matters nothing, '*He will be*,' and you say 'Let God exist! Amen, so be it!'"

VIII

When Iamblicus and Julian, returning from their walk, were crossing Panormos, the crowded harbour-quarter of Ephesus, they noticed an unusual tumult; folk running hither and thither, waving torches and shouting—

"The Christians are destroying the temples! Woe be on us!" and others: "Death to the Olympian gods! Astarte is vanquished by Christ!"

Iamblicus attempted a detour through less frequented streets, but the howling mob caught and swept them in its course towards the temple of the Ephesian Artemis. The superb temple, built by Dynocrates, stood out sharply, dark and austere, against the starry sky. The gleam of the torches flickered up gigantic colonnades, pedestalled on beautiful little groups of caryatids. Up to this period, not only the Romans, but all tribes in the country had adored this goddess. Someone in the crowd cried out in a quavering voice—

"Hail to the divine Diana of the Ephesians!"

Hundreds of voices responded—

"Death to the Olympians and to your Diana!"

Above the Arsenal and its towering monument rose a blood-red light. Julian glanced at his divine master, and scarcely recognised him. Iamblicus was transformed back into a sickly and timid old man. He complained of headache, expressed his fear of an attack of rheumatism, and doubted whether his servant had not forgotten to prepare his fomentations. Julian lent him his own cloak; but he remained chilly, and stopped his ears, with a dolorous grimace, against the shouts and laughter of the crowd, which he dreaded. Iamblicus used to say there was nothing more stupid and disgusting than the spirit of the people. He pointed out to his pupil the faces hurrying past—

"Look at the monstrous vice in that expression! What hopeless triviality! what self-confident assertion! . . . Does it not make one ashamed of being human, to share human form with mud like that!"

An old Christian woman hobbled along, telling a story—

"And my grandson, he says to me, 'Grandmother, make me some meat-broth.' Well, I tell him, 'Yes, darling, I'll go to the market soon,' and to myself I'm thinking meat is nowadays cheaper than bread. So I buy some meat for five obols and have it cooked. And in comes a neighbour and screams at me, 'What are you cooking there? Don't you know that the meat of the market is not fit to touch today?'

"'Why so?'

"'The priests of the goddess have sprinkled the whole market with water from the sacrifices! There's not a Christian in the town eating the meat so spoiled. And they're going to kill the sacrificers, and pull down the devilish temple!'

"I threw the broth to the dogs; just think! five obols, all wasted!—more than a day's wage thrown away—but all the same I wouldn't make my own grandson unclean!"

Others were telling how, in the previous year, some miserly Christian had eaten of the impure meat, which had so rotted his intestines that his very relatives had had to abandon him, on account of the contagion.

In the public square rose a beautiful little temple to Diana-Selene-Phoebe-Astarte—the triple goddess Hecate, mother of the gods. Like enormous wasps greedily intent upon a honeycomb, monks had surrounded the temple on all sides, crawling along the lovely white cornice, clambering up ladders, and to the chant of psalms, smashing the statues and bas-reliefs.

The columns were trembling on their bases, fragments of marble flying in all directions. The delicate edifice seemed to wince like a living creature. Finally an attempt was made to set the temple on fire; but as it was wholly built of marble, all efforts in this direction were fruitless.

Suddenly a strange noise rang out from the interior, a deafening and resonant series of shocks, while triumphant howls of the crowd rose to the sky.

"Bring ropes, ropes! Hide her immodest limbs!"

In a hubbub of hymns and wild laughter the mob, by means of ropes, dragged out of the temple the superb silver body of the goddess, which had been moulded by Scopas. Step by step, it came thundering down.

"Cast her in the fire! in the fire!"

The figure was dragged into the muddy market-place. There a monk was declaiming a passage from the celebrated edict of Constantine II, the brother of Constantius—

"'Let there be an end of superstition, and let sacrifices be abolished' (*Cesset superstitio sacrificiorum, aboleatur insania!*).

"Fear nothing; break, sack, plunder everything in that temple of demons!" Another was reading by torchlight from a parchment scroll the following words from the book *De errore profanarum religionum*, by Firmicus Maternus—

"Divine Emperors! Come! succour the unfortunate heathen. Let us snatch them by force from hell rather than leave them to perish. Seize the temple-ornaments and let their riches feed your treasury. Let him who sacrifices to idols be torn from the earth, root and branch (*Sacrificans diis eradicabitur*). Thou shalt deliver him to death; thou shalt stone him with stones, were that offender thy son, thy brother, or the wife that sleeps upon thy heart!"

And over the crowd swept the exultant shout—

"Death! Death to the gods of Olympus!"

An Arian monk of gigantic stature, his lank black hair plastered to his sweaty face, heaved an axe above the goddess, seeking where to strike.

A voice advised—

"In the belly! In her abominable belly!"

The great silver body rolled over mutilated; the blows rang pitiless, leaving gaps bitten in the metal.

An old pagan stood by and veiled his face from the sacrilege. He was secretly weeping at the thought that now the end of the world, the end of everything, was come, for the earth would no longer bring forth a blade of corn.

A hermit from the deserts of Mesopotamia, clothed in sheepskin, wearing coarse sandals and an empty gourd slung from his shoulder, stood over the statue, sheep-crook in hand—

"This forty years I have never washed, that I might not see my nakedness, nor fall into temptation. And yet coming into cities, straight one perceives these accursed gods without a rag upon them. How long must we endure these devilish temptations! At the hearth, in the street, on the roof, in the baths, these idols everywhere above one's head? . . . Faugh! Faugh! Faugh! How can I spit enough disgust on things like these?"

The old man spurned the prostrate woman's form with his sandal in energetic horror; stamped on the bare breast as if it were alive, and kept scoring it with the sharp nails of his sandals, stuttering with rage—

"Take that, and that—and that, O foul immodesty!"

The lips of the goddess lay with their calm smile under the soles of his feet.

The crowd began to haul the statue upright in order to tilt it into the bonfire. Drunken garlic-smelling apprentices spat in the metal face. An enormous blaze, built of the massed wreckage of market-booths, quickly arose. The statue was dropped into the flames to be melted into silver bullion.

"There are five talents' worth! think—thirty thousand pieces of silver! We'll send half to the Emperor to pay the army, and take the other half for famished folk here. Cybele will bring solace to mankind at last, anyhow! Thirty thousand pieces of silver for the soldiers and the poor!"

"Bring fuel, more wood!" The flame mounted still more fiercely; the mob burst into laughter.

"We'll see whether the devil flies out of her! There's a demon in every idol, you know, and two or three inside goddesses!"

"When she begins to melt it'll get too hot for the devil, and he'll come wriggling out of her mouth like a red serpent!"

"No! you must make the sign of the cross beforehand. If you don't, he can glide into the earth. Last year, when we pulled down the temple of Aphrodite, someone sprinkled her with holy water and—can you believe it?—a whole flight of devilets scampered away from underneath the statue—I saw them myself—green and black and hairy all over! And when the head was broken open the big devil came out of her neck, with great horns and a tail as bald as a mangy dog!"

At this moment Iamblicus, half dead with terror, seized Julian by the hand and dragged him away—

"Look! Do you see those two men? They are spies sent by Constantius. Your brother Gallus has been taken under escort to Constantinople. Be careful; this very day there will be a report sent in as to how you bear yourself."

"But what is there to be done, Master? I am well accustomed to it; for years they have kept spies about me."

"For years! Why have you said nothing of it to me?"

The hand of Iamblicus shook within that of Julian.

"Why are those two whispering together? Look at them—they must be pagans. . . Now then old man, hurry up, bring wood!" cried out a ragged rascal in a triumphant tone.

Iamblicus whispered into Julian's ear—

"Let us despise it all, and in contempt resign ourselves. Human stupidity can never hurt the gods!"

So saying the "Divine" Iamblicus took an enormous faggot from the hands of the Christian and cast it into the fire. At first Julian could scarcely believe his eyes. The now-smiling spies stared at him, with a curious fixity.

Then weakness, and his own habitual hypocrisy for his own sake and for the sake of others, won the day. He went to the heap of wood, chose the largest log, and, after Iamblicus, threw it into the blaze in which the mutilated body of the goddess was already melting. He clearly saw drops of silver rolling on her face as in a death-sweat, and the lips still keeping their invincible smile.

IX

L ook at those fellows dressed in black, Julian! They are shadows of night-fall, shadows of death. Soon there will not be a single ancient white robe left, nor a single sun-steeped piece of marble. . . All is over!"

So spoke the young sophist, Antoninus, son of the prophetess Sospitra and of Ædesius, the Neo-Platonist. He was standing with Julian on the terrace of the temple of Pergamos, in bright sunshine, under a sky of cloudless blue. Along the foot of the balustrade was carven the revolt of the Titans. The gods were triumphing; and the hoofs of the winged horses crushing the serpent bodies of the antique giants. Antoninus pointed to the carving—

"Ah! Julian, the Olympians conquered the Titans, but now the Olympians in their turn will be beaten by barbaric gods. These temples will become tombs. . ."

Antoninus was a handsome youth, straight-limbed as one of the old statues, but his health had been broken for years by an incurable malady, and his face had become yellow, lean, and melancholy.

"I pray the gods," went on Antoninus, "I entreat the gods not to suffer me to see that night—that I may die before it comes. Rhetoricians, sophists, poets, sages, artists, none of us are wanted anymore. We are born in too late a day. . . All is over for us!"

"And suppose you are mistaken?" hazarded Julian.

"No, all's over! We are not as our forefathers! We are sick, strength fails us."

Julian's face seemed as worn and haggard as that of Antoninus. The projecting lower lip gave him an expression of taciturn arrogance. The thick eyebrows were knitted in bitter obstinacy; precocious wrinkles already furrowed his cheeks. The long nose had grown longer than ever; and his always strange eyes were now burning with a dry, feverish, disagreeable fire. He still wore the monkish habit. During the day he still attended church, as hitherto; worshipped relics; read the gospels in public, and was preparing to take orders. Sometimes all this hypocrisy seemed to him worse than useless. He foresaw that Gallus would not escape a premature death, and knew that he himself might expect it at any moment.

But his nights Julian was wont to pass in the great library of Pergamos, where he was studying the works of the great foe of Christianity,

Libanius. He attended the lectures of the Greek sophists, Ædesius of Pergamos, Chrisantius of Sardinia, Priscius of Thesephros, Eusebius of Minos, Proeres, and Nymphidian. These taught him much about what he had already heard from Iamblicus, of the *triad* of the Neo-Platonists, and of the "divine ecstasy." He said to himself—

"All that is not what I am seeking; they are hiding something from me!"

Priscius, imitating Pythagoras, had passed five years in silence, keeping to a vegetarian diet, and using neither raiment of wool nor sandal of leather. He wore a cloak of pure white linen and sandals of palm leaves stitched together.

"In our age," he used to say, "the thing of moment is to be able to hold one's tongue, and to meditate on dying worthily."

Thus Priscius, despising all things, awaited what he called the catastrophe, that is to say, the complete victory of Christianity over the Hellenists.

The wily and prudent Chrisantius, when the subject of the gods was touched on, would cast his eyes to heaven, avowing that he dared not talk about them, knowing nothing, and having forgotten what he had learnt on the subject. And he advised others to follow his own example. As for magic, miracles, and phantasms, he would hear nothing about them, declaring that they were criminal deceptions, forbidden by the Imperial laws.

Julian had no appetite, slept ill; his blood was boiling with passion and impatience. Every morning on awaking he would wonder—

"Is it to be today?"

He would worry the poor sages with ceaseless questions concerning mysteries and miracles. Some of them he shocked, especially Chrisantius, who was in the habit of acquiescence in all the opinions which seemed to him most foolish.

On one occasion Ædesius, a timid and learned old man, pitying Julian, said to him—

"My boy, I want to die quietly; you are young yet. Leave me alone. Address yourself to my disciples; they will reveal to you everything I have taught. Yes, there are many things about which we are afraid to speak, and when you shall have been initiated into the greater mysteries, you will perhaps be ashamed at having been born a mere mortal, and of having remained one up till now."

Euthemus of Minda, a disciple of Ædesius, and a jealous and

malicious fellow, declared to Julian: "There are no more such things as miracles. Don't expect any. Men have badgered the gods too long. Magic is a lie, and those who believe in it are idiots. But if you are still hungry for wisdom, and absolutely must have illusions, go to Maximus. He despises our dialectical philosophy, and yet himself. . . But I don't like speaking ill of my friends. Just hear, however, what happened lately in a temple of Hecate whither Maximus had conducted us to prove his art. When we had gone in and adored the goddess, he said to us: 'Sit down, and you shall see a miracle.' We sat down. He threw on the altar a phimian-seed, muttering something,—a hymn I suppose,—and then we saw the statue of Hecate smile at us! Maximus said to us: 'Fear nothing when you shall see the two torches held by the goddess kindle of themselves. Behold!' Before he had finished the sentence the lamps were alight, self-kindled!"

"The miracle, in fact, was accomplished!" cried Julian.

"Yes; our emotion was so great that we prostrated ourselves. But when I came out of the temple I asked myself, 'Is what Maximus does worthy of true philosophy?' Read Pythagoras, Plato—there shall you find wisdom. By divine dialectic to lift the heart of man—is not that finer than any miracle?"

But Julian was listening no more; his eyes sparkled as he gazed at the surly face of Euthemus, and he murmured as he went forth from the school—

"Keep your books and your dialectics! I seek life and faith! Can they exist without miracles? I thank thee, Euthemus, thou hast pointed me to the man I have sought for long."

With a bitter smile the sophist answered—

"Nephew of Constantine, you have not improved upon your ancestors. Miracles were not necessary to the faith of Socrates!"

X

At the stroke of midnight, in the vestibule leading to the great hall of the mysteries, Julian flung off his novice's robe. The sacrificial mystagogues, initiators into the pagan ceremonial, then clothed him anew in their own priestly tunic, woven of threads of papyrus. A palm-branch was put into his hand, and his feet were left bare. He was then led up a long low hall, the vaults of which were supported by a double row of bronze Corinthian columns. Each column, formed of two serpents entwined, bore two incense-burners on lofty and slender branching stands, whence rose thin tongues of flame. Dense vapour filled the hall. At its end glittered two winged golden bulls, propping a splendid throne, on which was seated, arrayed in a long black tunic powdered thick with emeralds and carbuncles, and in demeanour like a god, the greatest hierophant of all, Maximus of Ephesus.

The slow reverberant voice of a temple slave announced the opening of the mysteries—

"If any impious, or Christian, or Epicurean be present in this assembly, let him go forth!"

Instructed in advance as to the necessary responses, Julian pronounced the words—

"Let the Christians go forth!"

The choir of temple slaves, hidden in obscurity, took up the burden—

"To the doors! To the doors! Let the Christians go forth! Let the impious go forth!"

Then twenty-four lads, entirely naked, each holding a silver sistrum, like a crescent-moon, came forth from the shadow. In perfect unison they raised the vibrating instruments above their heads, and with one graceful gesture struck the resonant strings, which gave forth a long and plaintive note. Maximus made a sign.

Someone tightly bandaged Julian's eyes from behind and said to him earnestly—

"Go forward! Fear neither Water, Fire, Spirits; nor Bodies, nor Life, nor Death."

He felt himself dragged forward; an iron door opened on creaking hinges. He was pushed through it; a stifling atmosphere beat on his face while his feet groped down slippery and twisted steps. Feeling his way down this endless stair, amidst sepulchral silence, it seemed at last that he must be a great distance underground. He proceeded along a narrow passage—so narrow that his hands, held stiffly to his sides, rubbed along the walls. Suddenly his bare feet struck moisture; he heard water flowing; a stream covered his ankles. He kept on, but at every step the water rose, reaching first his calves, then his knees, and finally his loins. His teeth began to chatter with cold. The flood rose breast high. He wondered—

"Perhaps this is a trap; it is some device of Maximus for killing me, to do the Emperor pleasure."

But he held stoutly on, forging slowly through the water. Finally it seemed to lessen, till at last it completely ebbed away. A suffocating heat, as from the mouth of a furnace, gradually enveloped him, so that the ground scorched his feet. Julian thought he must be walking straight into an oven; blood throbbed in his temples; sometimes the heat was so intense that it licked his cheek like a flame. But the lad never wavered.

In its turn the heat diminished. But sickening odours next choked his breath. Time after time he stumbled against round objects, and recognised bones and dead men's skulls.

Suddenly he felt someone walking by his side, gliding along noiselessly like a shadow; an ice-cold hand seized his own. He uttered an involuntary cry. Two hands were gently pulling at his clothes, the fleshless bones piercing their withered skin. The grip of these hands became playful movements, repulsive caresses like those of debauched women. Julian felt a breath on his cheek tainted with fusty rottenness and moisture, and then became aware of a rapid murmur at his ear, like the rustle of leaves on a night in autumn—

"It is I! It is I!—I!—do you not know me again? It is I!—I!"

"And who, who art thou?" stammered Julian. But immediately he recollected his promise of absolute silence.

"It is I! Shall I strip the bandage from your eyes so that you may know me again, may meet me again?" And the bony fingers, with the same hideous eagerness, fluttered over his face as if seeking to drag off the bandage.

A deadly chill penetrated Julian to the heart, and, through habit, he thrice crossed himself involuntarily, as in childhood at some bad dream.

A clap of thunder! The ground heaved under his feet! He felt himself falling into the unknown; and lost consciousness.

When he regained his senses he was no longer blindfold but lay on cushions in a huge twilit grotto. A cloth, soaked in penetrating perfumes, was being held to his nostrils. Opposite Julian stood a lean man with a coppery skin; it was the gymnosophist—the naked sage—assistant of Maximus.

He was holding high above his head a motionless metallic disc. A voice said to Julian. "Look!" Julian gazed at the dazzling circle. Its brilliancy was almost painful to the eyes. Looking at it fixedly and long, gradually all things melted and lost their sharper outline. A pleasant weakness breathed through his being. The luminous disc no longer shone in the void, but in his own mind; his eyelids descended; a sleepy smile of weariness played upon his submissive lips. He felt a hand stroking his head, and a voice asked—

"Are you asleep?"

"Yes. . ."

"Look me in the eyes!"

Julian obeyed with effort and perceived Maximus stooping over him.

He was a man of about seventy years old, bearded to the girdle. Thick hair, with a yellow glitter in it, fell thick over his shoulders. Deep wrinkles, furrowed by thought and will, and not by suffering, marked cheek and brow. His smile was like the smile of women who are at once witty, mendacious, and enchanting. But it was the eyes of Maximus that gave Julian most pleasure. Under thick eyebrows they shone mocking, and tender, yet piercing to the quick.

Maximus asked—"Do you wish to see the most famous of the Titans?"

"Yes."

"Watch then."

The magician pointed to the depth of the cave where stood a tripod of Corinthian bronze, vomiting smoke. A tempestuous noise filled the cavern—

"Hercules! Hercules! Deliver me!"

The smoke vanished; blue sky appeared. Julian lay stretched motionless and pale, watching through half-shut eyelids the rapid visions unfolded before him. It was as if someone commanded him to see them. He beheld clouds and snow-clad mountains, and heard the breaking of distant waves. Slowly he perceived an enormous body, chained hand and foot to crags. A kite was devouring the liver of the Titan, drops of black blood trickled down his side; the great chains rattled, and the whole body shuddered with pain.

"Deliver me, Hercules!"

And the Titan raised his shaggy head; his eyes met those of the youth entranced—

"Who art thou? Whom dost thou summon?" asked Julian, speaking heavily in his dream.

"I call on thee!"

"I am but a mortal, and helpless."

"Thou art my brother; set me free!"

"Who has chained thee up anew?"

"The humble, the gentle,—who through cowardice forgive their enemies. Slaves! slaves! . . . O deliver me!"

"How can I deliver thee?"

"Be even as I am."

The smoke of the tripod obscured the apparition. Julian woke for a moment and the great hierophant, the teacher of rites, asked—

"Do you wish to see the ruined Archangel?"

"Yes."

"Behold him!"

In the white smoke appeared faintly a head between two gigantic wings. The feathers of the wings swept out, drooping like branches of yew, and a bluish tint as of some lost sky trembled upon the melancholy plumes.

Someone cried to Julian from afar off—

"Julian! Julian! Deny the Galilean in my name!"

Julian held his peace.

Maximus muttered at his ear—

"If you wish to see the great Angel you must make this renunciation."

And Julian pronounced the words—

"I deny Him!"

Above the head of the apparition suddenly glittered the morning star—the star of dawn—and the Angel repeated—

"Julian, deny the Galilean in my name!"

A third time the Angel repeated,—and his voice sounded exultant and close by: "Renounce Him!"

And Julian answered—

"I renounce Him!"

The Angel said—

"Thou mayest approach."

"Who art thou?"

"I am Lucifer, I am Light, I am the East, I am the Morning Star!"

"How beautiful thou art!"

"Be thou as I am."

"What melancholy dwells in thine eyes!"

"I suffer for all living. Birth must cease, death must cease. Come to me; I am the Shadow, I am Repose, I am Liberty."

"How art thou named among men?"

"Evil."

"Thou?"

"Yes. I turned in revolt."

"Against whom?"

"Against Him whose peer I am. He willed to be alone, but we are two, and equals."

"Make me in thine image!"

"Revolt also! I will give thee the thews for rebellion."

"Teach me!"

"Violate the law, love thyself, curse Him, and be as I am!"

The Angel disappeared; the wind in circling gusts rekindled the flame on the tripod. The flame blew over the brim of the vessel and ran along the ground. The tripod itself was overset, and the flame went out. In the darkness came a rushing noise of numberless steps, with cries and groanings, as if an invisible army, fleeing before an enemy, were in passage through the cave. Julian, in terror, fell face downward to the earth, while the long black robe of the hierophant, stretched over him, struggled with the wind.

"Flee, flee!" groaned indistinct voices. "The gates of Hell are opening; it is He, He, the Conqueror!"

The wind hissed in Julian's ears; legions upon legions seemed passing over him; suddenly there fell a dead calm; a heavenly breath filled the vast cavern and a voice murmured—

"Saul, Saul, why persecutest thou me?"

It seemed to Julian that he had heard that voice before, in some far time of childhood. Gently it came again—

"Saul, Saul, why persecutest thou me?"

And the sound faded away into the distance, so that there came at last but an imperceptible whisper: "Why, why, persecutest thou me?"

When Julian awoke and raised his prostrate face he saw one of the initiating priests lighting a lamp. He felt giddy, but remembered exactly everything that had taken place. His eyes were blindfolded and, strengthened with spiced wine, he was enabled to climb the staircase,

his hand gripped this time by the strong hand of Maximus. He felt as
if an invisible force was lifting him on wings. The teacher of rites said
to the lad—

"Now ask what you will!"

"Did you summon Him?" inquired Julian.

"No. But when one chord of the lyre vibrates, another chord responds.
Opposite answers opposite."

"Why is there such potency in His words if His words are only lies?"

"His words are truth."

"What do you mean? Then it is the Titan and the Angel who lied?"

"They also are the truth."

"Do you mean that there are two truths?"

"Two truths."

"Ah! You are tempting me! . . ."

"Not I, but the wholeness of the truth. If you are afraid, be silent."

"I am afraid of nothing. Say on; tell all! Are the Galileans right?"

"Yes."

"Why then should I have renounced them?"

"There is, beside theirs, another truth."

"One higher?"

"No, equal."

"But in what is one to believe? Where is the God whom I seek?"

"Both here and yonder. Serve Ahriman,—serve Ormuzd, whichever
pleases you! But forget not that both are equal,—the kingdom of
Lucifer and the kingdom of God."

"Which way should I choose?"

"Choose one of the two roads, and halt no more!"

"But which?"

"If you believe in Him, take up the cross. Follow Him according to
His command; be humble, chaste. Be the lamb that was dumb between
the hands of the shearers. Flee into the desert for salvation; give Him
body, soul, and reason! Believe! . . . that is one way. And the Galilean
martyrs attain the same liberty that Prometheus and Lucifer have
attained."

"That way I cannot choose."

"Choose then the other path. Be puissant as your ancestors of old,
the heroes—proud, pitiless, and haughty. No compassion! No love! No
pardon! Arise and conquer all things! Let your body become hard as
marble out of which the demigods are hewn! Take and give not! Taste

of the forbidden fruit and repent not! Believe not, doubt not, and the world shall be thine! Thou shalt be the Titan—an angel revolted against God."

"But I can never forget that the words of the Galilean contain truth also. I cannot admit two beliefs."

"Then thou shalt be like all common mortals and hadst better never been born; but thou canst choose. Make the venture! . . . Thou shalt be emperor!"

"I? Emperor?"

"Thou shalt have between thy hands what Alexander never had."

Julian felt that they were issuing from the bowels of the earth, felt the morning sea-breeze bathing him. The hierophant unknotted the bandage over his eyes, and lo! they were standing on a high marble tower, the astronomical observatory of the great seer, built after the model of the ancient Chaldean towers, but upon a crag above the sea. Below stretched luxurious gardens, palaces, and cloisters, recalling the colonnades of Persepolis. In the distance the Artemision and Ephesus stood in clear relief against the mountains over which the sun was about to rise.

Julian's head almost gave way at the extent of the view; he had to lean upon the arm of Maximus; but then with a smile the youth closed his eyes, and the beams of the rising sun flushed his white vestments with rose-colour. The seer stretched out his arm.

"Behold! all this is thine!"

"Can I sustain it, Master? Assassination may strike me at any moment. I am weak and ill."

"The sun, the god Mithra, is crowning you with his purples—the purple of the Roman Empire. All this is thine. Dare!"

"And what is it all to me, since truth unified does not exist, and since I cannot find the God for whom I seek?"

"Ah! if thou canst make one the truth of the Titan and the truth of the Galilean, thou wilt be greater than any that have been born of women! . . ."

MAXIMUS OF EPHESUS WAS THE owner of marvellous libraries, quiet marble chambers, and spacious anatomical laboratories crowded with scientific apparatus. In one of the latter the young physicist, Oribazius, a doctor of the school of Alexandria, was vivisecting, scalpel in hand, a rare animal sent to Maximus from the Indies. The hall was circular and the walls loaded with rows of tin vessels, chafing dishes, retorts, apparatus like that of Archimedes, and fire machines like those of Ktesius and Geron. In the silence of the adjoining library drop after drop fell plashing from the water-clock, an invention of Apollonius. Globes were there also, geographical charts in metal, and models of the celestial spheres wrought by Hipparchus and Eratosthenes.

In the clear and serene light falling through the glass ceiling, Maximus, clothed as a simple philosopher, was scrutinising the still-warm organs of the animal laid on the marble. Oribazius stooping over the liver of the animal was saying—

"How can Maximus, the great philosopher, believe in these ridiculous miracles?"

"I believe in them and I believe in them not," answered the magian. "This Nature which you and I are studying, is not she most miraculous? Are not these blood-vessels, this nervous system, the admirable combination of organs which we are examining like augurs—are not these the most splendid of mysteries?"

"You know my meaning," interrupted the young doctor. "Why have you deceived this young man?"

"Julian?"

"Yes."

"He himself desired to be deceived."

The brows of Oribazius knitted into a frown.

"Master, if you love me, tell me who you are. How can you endure lies like these? Do I not understand what magic means? You attach luminous fish-scales to the ceiling of a darkened chamber, and the pupil to be initiated believes that the skies are descending on him at the word of the hierophant. You manufacture with skin and wax a death's head, into which you fit a stork's neck; and through it you pronounce your predictions from beneath the floor. The pupil imagines that the skull uncurtains to him the secrets of the tomb; and when it is necessary that the head should vanish, you bring a chafing dish near it, the wax melts and the skull collapses. By skilful rays of coloured light playing on odorous smoke, you make the innocent believe that they have verily seen the gods! You display under water in a basin, of which the walls are stone and the bottom glass, a living Apollo (acted by an obliging slave), while some vulgar prostitute is played off as Aphrodite. This—this, you call the holy mysteries!"

His habitual equivocal smile wandered over the compressed lips of the teacher, who answered—

"Ah! our mysteries are deeper and finer than you suppose. Men have absolute need of enthusiasm. For him who has faith the harlot is Aphrodite really, and the luminous scales are the stars of heaven. You say that people weep and pray before semblances produced by a lamp and coloured glasses? Oribazius, Oribazius! . . . but this Nature which makes your science marvel, is she not herself a mirage, produced by senses as deceptive as the wizard's lantern? Wherein does truth consist? Where does falsehood begin? You believe and you know, and I neither wish to believe nor am skilled to know. Truth dwells for me in the same shrine as falsehood."

"Would Julian thank you, if he knew that you were deceiving him?"

"He saw what he desired to see. I have given him enthusiasm, strength, and audacity. You say that I have deceived him. If that had been necessary I would have done so—I would have tempted him. I love the falsehood that contains a truth. I love temptation. Till I die I will never abandon Julian and shall allow him to taste all forbidden fruits. He is young; I shall live on a second life in him. I will unveil for him the mystery and charm even of crime; and perhaps through me he shall become great!"

"Master, I do not understand you."

"And that is precisely why I speak thus to you," responded Maximus, fixing on Oribazius his penetrating and impassive eyes.

XI

Julian had an interview with his brother Gallus while the latter was on his way to Constantinople. He had found him surrounded by a troop of traitors in the pay of Constantius: the quæstor Leontinus, a wily courtier, famous for skill in eavesdropping and cross-examining servants; the tribune Baïnobadois, a taciturn barbarian, who gave the impression of an over-tragic actor playing the part of a headsman; the Emperor's haughty Master of Ceremonies, *comes domesticorum*, Lucilian; and finally Marcus Scuda, the former tribune of Cæsarea in Cappadocia, who, thanks to the protection of certain old ladies, had attained the post he longed for.

Gallus, now, as always, gay and giddy, had offered Julian an excellent supper, of which the chief feature was a plump pheasant stuffed with fresh Theban dates. He laughed like a child, and was calling up all sorts of reminiscences of old days together at Macellum, when suddenly Julian spoke to him about his wife Constantia.

The face of Gallus fell; his eyes filled with tears, and he laid down on his plate the succulent piece of pheasant which he had been on the point of putting into his mouth.

"Don't you know, Julian, that Constantia is dead? She died unexpectedly after an attack of tertian ague, on the very journey to the Emperor which she had undertaken to absolve me from blame in his eyes. I wept for two whole nights when I heard that news."

He cast a timid glance at the door, put his hand on Julian's shoulder, and whispered confidentially—

"Since then, I have let things go to the devil! She alone might have saved me. Ah! she was an astonishing woman. Without her I am ruined. I can do, and I can learn, nothing. . . 'They' do with me just as they please."

He tossed off a cup of wine at a gulp.

Julian remembered Constantia, the sister of Constantius, a widow of ripe age, the evil genius of her brother, her who had incited him to commit numberless crimes, crimes which were frequently mere fatuous stupidities. Amazed, he asked, anxious to know by what quality this woman had tamed his brother—

"She was beautiful?"

"It is clear you never saw her."

"No. Was she ugly?"

"Yes, very ugly. She was short, brown, thin, and had bad teeth, which I can't bear in women. Nevertheless, being aware of this defect, she never laughed. People used to say she deceived me, that in disguise she used to go to the circus, as Messalina did, on visits to a young and handsome groom. Well, what of it? Did not I on my side deceive her? She never bothered me, and I used to take care in return never to worry her about these trifles. Folk used to say she was cruel! By God, Julian, she knew how to govern! Of course she didn't like the authors of epigrams on her bad manners, comparing her to some kitchen-slave dressed as Cæsar's wife! She loved revenge, admiration! And what a mind, what a mind, Julian! Why, I was as much at ease sheltered behind her, as behind a granite wall. Ah, the mad things we used to do together! We certainly never lacked amusement."

He smiled at some agreeable recollection and passed the tip of his tongue along his rosy upper lip between the sips of Chian wine.

"There's no denying we made the most of time," he repeated, not without modest pride.

When Julian was on his way to this interview with his brother, he had thought of waking in him some feeling of seriousness and remorse, had even prepared a little speech, in the style of Libanius, against the doings of irresponsible tyrants. He had expected to see a man bowed under the yoke of Nemesis, and not the tranquil fat and rosy visage of this comely athlete. Words died on Julian's lips. He looked without blame or distaste upon this "docile animal"—for so he inwardly named his brother. Of what avail were sermons to a young stallion? Julian contented himself therefore with saying to Gallus in a grave tone—

"Why are you going to Milan? Do you suspect nothing?"

"Yes—hush—but it is too late!"

And, sweeping his hand significantly round his neck, he added—

"The slipnoose of death is already here! 'He' is tightening it little by little. Why, he would unearth me from a rabbit-burrow, Julian! No, no, best speak no more of it! All's over! We've made the most of time, that's all."

"But you have two legions left you at Antioch?"

"Not one. 'He' has filched all my best soldiers, little by little, under colour of this pretext and that; and always, by Jove! for my own good! Why, everything he does is for my own good. . . He thinks of nothing else! Now he's in a hurry to see me simply to profit by my advice. Julian, that man is terrible! You don't know yet, and God grant that you may never know, what that man is. He sees everything, knows my inmost thoughts, those that I wouldn't mutter to my pillow; and he's watching your mind also. Frankly, I am afraid of him!"

"But can't you escape?"

"Hush, speak lower!"

The features of Gallus took on an expression of boyish terror.

"No, no; I tell you all is over! I am as neatly finished as a fish already hooked. 'He' is drawing in the line gently, so that it doesn't break. A Cæsar, let him be who he will, is always a big fish to land. I know that it's impossible to escape. He'll take me one day or another. . . And now I see the snare, and I am walking into it all the same out of fear. For six years, from the very first, I quaked before that man. Like a small boy, now however I've walked far enough. Brother, he'll cut my throat as a cook cuts the throat of a fowl. But he will torture me first by a thousand stratagems and caresses. I should prefer to finish quicker."

The eyes of Gallus became suddenly brilliant, and he exclaimed—

"Ah, if *she* had been here, at my side, she would certainly have saved me! She was such an astonishing woman!"

The tribune Scuda, entering the *triclinium* where supper was laid, announced, with a profound salutation, that on the morrow, in honour of the arrival of Cæsar, there would be races in the hippodrome of Constantinople, and that the celebrated rider Korax would take part in them. Gallus was delighted at the news, and ordered a crown of bay-leaf to be prepared, that, in case of the victory of Korax, he might himself crown his favourite before the people. He launched into racing stories, boasting the skill of his charioteers.

Gallus drank deeply, laughed like a man whose rakish conscience is at ease, with not a trace of his recent fears upon those handsome features. Only at the last moment of farewell he kissed Julian heartily, suddenly melting into tears.

"May God help you! May God help you!" he blubbered. "You alone have stood my friend—you and Constantia!"

Then he whispered into Julian's ear—

"I hope that you'll save your skin, brother. You can wear a mask and keep your own counsel; I have always envied you that. May God succour you!"

Julian sincerely pitied his brother; he knew that he would not escape Constantius.

On the following morning Gallus left Constantinople with his former escort. At Adrianople he was only permitted to retain ten small chariots, and had to relinquish all his personal suite and baggage. The autumn was far advanced, the roads in fearful condition, rain falling continuously all day for a week. Peremptory messages reached Gallus to hurry on. He was given no time to rest or sleep, and had taken no bath for a fortnight.

One of his keenest discomforts was horror at close contact with dirt. All his life he had taken peculiar care to keep his body healthy and exquisitely groomed. It was with profound melancholy that he gazed at his uncut nails, and the purple of his travelling chlamys, befouled by dust and muddy roads. Scuda never quitted his side for an instant, and Gallus, not without reason, dreaded his assiduous companion. The tribune, years ago, had come as bearer of a despatch from the Emperor, and was but newly arrived in Antioch, when by an impudent remark he had offended Constantia, the wife of Gallus, who straightway in a fit of fury had ordered the Roman tribune to be flogged and afterwards thrown, like a slave, into a dungeon.

Foreseeing the probable consequence, Constantia had quickly ordered the tribune to be set at liberty. He then presented himself at the palace of Gallus, as if nothing had occurred, and, pocketing the affront, had never even reported it to his master; perhaps through fear that so degrading a punishment might besmirch the prospects of his career as a courtier.

During the whole journey from Antioch to Milan Scuda retained his seat in Cæsar's chariot, never quitting him, inviting his confidences, and treating him like some wayward child, who, being out of sorts, was not to be left to himself for a moment by a servant so devoted and affectionate.

Where, as in Illyria, there were dangerous river crossings to be made on frail wooden bridges, Scuda would put his arm around Gallus with the tenderest solicitude, and if the latter strove to free himself, swear that he preferred death to the risk of drowning his precious charge.

The tribune wore an oddly thoughtful expression, especially when contemplating the neck of Gallus, smooth and white as a young girl's. The Cæsar, feeling this attentive look, would fidget uneasily in his seat, and with difficulty restrain himself from striking the amiable tribune in the face. But the poor prisoner's spirits quickly rose again. He contented himself with imploring (for despite everything his appetite remained healthy), that they might halt for a meal, were it never so scanty. At Petovio, in Norica, they were met by two fresh envoys from the Emperor, accompanied by a cohort of Court legionaries.

The mask was then dropped. Round the palace where Gallus slept armed sentinels were placed as round a prison. In the evening the prefect Barbatio, making his way in, without any pretence at ceremony, ordered him to take off the chlamys of a Cæsar and don the simple tunic and paludamentum, or ordinary cloak, of a common soldier.

On the following morning the prisoner was ordered to get into a karpenta, a little two-wheeled cart without a hood employed by minor officials on official journeys. A cold wind was blowing intermittently. Scuda according to his custom put one arm round Gallus, and with the disengaged hand gently fingered the new garment.

"Sound cloak, this—soft and warm! Better than the purple, which is a chilly affair! Why, they've lined this tunic with double wool!" And pushing his investigations further, Scuda slid a hand under the paludamentum, then under the tunic, and suddenly, with a laugh, drew forth the blade of a poniard, which Gallus had succeeded in concealing.

"Now that's a mistake!" said Scuda. "Why, you might through carelessness stab yourself! What a boy you are!"

And he threw the dagger out on the road. An infinite weariness seized Gallus. He closed his eyes and felt the endearing grip of Scuda inside his arm. Was it all a nightmare?

They halted at the fortress of Pola in Istria, on the shores of the Adriatic. Some years formerly this town had been the scene of the murder of Priscus, the heroic young son of Constantine the Great.

The gloomy town was thronged with soldiers. Interminable barracks in the style of Diocletian had replaced the houses of civilians. Snow lay thickly on the roofs, the wind was moaning in deserted streets, and the sea lay rumbling below.

Gallus was led into one of these barracks and given a seat fronting the window, so that the full daylight fell upon his face. One of the Emperor's most skilful police officers—Eustaphius,—a little wrinkled and amiable old man with the wheedling and penetrating voice of a confessor, rubbed his blue and chilly hands and began the cross-examination. Gallus, who was mortally fatigued, said everything that Eustaphius suggested he should say, but at the words "treason to the empire," paled, and started to his feet.

"It was no doing of mine—nothing to do with me!" he stammered in dismay. "Constantia planned it all! It was she who exacted the death of Theophilus, of Clement, Domitian, and the rest! Before God, it was not I. She said nothing to me about it. I was utterly ignorant!"

Eustaphius looked at him smilingly.

"Very well," he said, "I will duly inform the Emperor that his own sister Constantia, spouse of the late Cæsar of the East, alone is culpable."

And turning towards the legionaries he ordered—

"The interrogatory is finished. Take him away."

Shortly afterwards arrived the sentence of death decreed by the Emperor Constantius, who had looked on the accusation brought against his lamented sister in the light of a personal insult.

On hearing the sentence read out, Gallus lost consciousness and fell into the arms of the soldiers. Up to the last moment the poor fellow had hoped against hope. And, even now, he expected that they would at least grant him the reprieve of a few days, or hours, in which to prepare for death. But a rumour had gone round that the soldiers of the "Steadfast Sixteenth Flavian" legion were insubordinate, and planning to free Gallus; so he was dragged off incontinently to execution.

It was the early dawn. The snow, fallen during the night, had covered the foul mud, and lay glittering in chilly sunshine, its dazzling reflection lighting up the ceiling of the small room whither Gallus had been conducted.

The authorities distrusted the soldiery, who almost all liked and pitied the disgraced Cæsar; so for executioner they had chosen a butcher, who sometimes officiated in disposing of the thieves and brigands of the neighbourhood. This barbarian, unused to a Roman sword, had brought to the block a great double-edged axe which served him in the slaughter-yard. The butcher was a stupid, handsome, and sleepy slave. The name of the condemned man had been concealed from him and he believed he was only to behead a common thief. Before the last scene, Gallus became calm and humble, allowing his gaolers to do what they listed. Like a child, he wept and struggled when about to be placed by force in a bath, but once in he found the water pleasant.

But at sight of the butcher sharpening his axe he shivered in all his limbs. A barber then carefully shaved off the fine golden hair, always the beauty and pride of the young Cæsar. In returning from the barber's room Gallus, finding himself alone for a moment with the tribune Scuda, unexpectedly dropped on his knees before the cruellest of his foes.

"Save me, Scuda! I know you can do it! Tonight I have received a message from the Flavian legion. Let me get a word with them. They will deliver me! I have thirty talents hidden in the temple at Mycenæ. Nobody knows it. I'll give them to you,—and more, much more! The soldiers love me. I'll make you my friend, my brother, my co-regent. . . fellow-Cæsar!"

Mad with hope, he embraced the tribune's knees, and Scuda, shuddering, felt the lips of the Cæsar on his hands. He made no answer, and, smiling, slowly freed himself from the embrace. Gallus was ordered to undress. He objected to take off his sandals, his feet being unclean. When he was almost naked the butcher began to bind his hands behind his back, thief-fashion, and Scuda hastened to help him. When Gallus felt the touch of the tribune's fingers, in a fit of fury he escaped from the grasp of the headsman, seized Scuda by the throat, and endeavoured to strangle him. In his naked activity he seemed suddenly transformed into some sinewy and terrible young tiger.

The choking tribune was snatched from the grapple, and the prisoner's feet and hands were securely bound. At this moment in the barrack court resounded the shouts of the Flavian soldiers—"Long live Cæsar Gallus!" and the murderers hurried on with their job. A great section of a tree-trunk was rolled in for a block, and Gallus thrust down on his knees in front of it. Barbatio, Baïnobadois, and Apodemus gripped him by the shoulders, hands, and feet; and Scuda bowed the head against the block, weighing down that vainly resisting skull with all his might. Chilled by emotion, his fingers felt the newly-shorn pate still moist with soap. The butcher proved an unskilful headsman. His axe slashed the neck, but the blow fell awry. He raised the hatchet a second time, crying to Scuda—

"More to the right! Hold the head more to the right!"

Gallus struggled and roared like a half-stunned bull. Nearer and nearer the cries of the soldiery resounded:

"Long live Gallus Cæsar!"

The butcher heaved his handle high and smote. A stream of blood gushed over the hands of Scuda; the head fell with a thud, and rolled away over the stone flags.

At that moment the legionaries burst into the hall. Barbatio, Apodemus, and Scuda hurried to the opposite door, the headsman remaining at a loss; but Scuda muttered in his ear—

"Take Cæsar's head, so that the legionaries may not recognise the body. It's a question of life or death for us all!"

"He was *not* a thief then?" faltered the executioner, in amazement.

He found it difficult to carry this shaven head; at first he slid it under an arm, but it became uncomfortable; then, slipping his hooked thumb into the mouth, he managed to bear off the skull of him before whom so many heads had once bowed down.

JULIAN, ON LEARNING THE DEATH of his brother, said quietly to himself—

"Now comes my turn!"

XII

I t was at Athens that Julian was about to take his vows and finally become a monk. One fresh spring morning, before the sun was up, Julian, issuing from the church where he had officiated at matins, followed for a few miles the banks of the Ilissus, in the shadow of plane-trees and wild vine. Not far from Athens he had lighted upon a solitary place, on the edge of a torrent which poured, like a scarf of silver, upon a sandy bottom. Thence he used often to gaze with wonder through the mists at the ruddy cliff of the Acropolis and the haughty lines of the Parthenon, half-illumined by the dawn.

On this particular morning Julian took off his shoes and walked along the reaches of the Ilissus barefoot. The air was full of the smell of flowers and of the rich-scented muscat grape—that aroma in which there is a foretaste of wine, faint as the promise of first love, stealing into the soul of youth.

Julian, with feet in the water, sat down upon a platan-root, opened the *Phædrus* and began to read at the passage in the dialogue in which Socrates says to Phædrus: "Let us go this way, and follow the course of the Ilissus; we will choose a solitary place and there sit down.

"*Phædrus*: Luckily, I'm unshod this morning, and as for you, Socrates, you always go barefoot. We'll walk in the bed of the river. Look, how smiling and pellucid the water is!

"*Socrates*: By Pallas! here's a wonderful nook; it must be sacred to the nymphs and to the god Acheloüs—to judge by these little statues. Doesn't it seem to you as if here the breeze were softer and of sweeter odour? Here, even in the hum of the crickets there's something of the sweetness of summer. But what I love best of all is this deep grass!"

Julian turned from the book with a smile. All was as it had been eight centuries before. Even the crickets set up their song.

"Socrates actually touched this ground with his feet!" he thought, and burying his head among the reeds he kissed the spot with adoration.

"Good-day, Julian! you've chosen a lovely corner there to read in. May I sit down near you?"

"Sit, sit; I shall be delighted. Poets never violate a solitude."

Julian looked up at a meagre personage, draped in an enormously long cloak (it was the poet Publius Porphyrius), thinking to himself—

"He's so small and frail that I believe he'll soon turn into a grasshopper, as Plato fancied the poets do."

Publius, like the grasshoppers, could almost live upon air, but the gods had not granted him complete immunity from appetite; and his shaven cadaverous face and discoloured lips were stamped with insatiable hunger.

"Why are you wearing such a long cloak, Publius?" Julian asked.

"It isn't mine," answered the other philosophically. "I share a room with a young man, Hephæstion, who has come to Athens to learn eloquence. He will be a famous lawyer one day. Meanwhile he's as poor as I am, poor as a lyric poet—I need say no more! Why, we've pledged our clothes, our furniture, even the inkstand; but we still have a cloak between us. In the morning I go out, and Hephæstion studies Demosthenes; in the evening he puts on the chlamys, and I write verses. Unfortunately we're not the same height—but what does that matter? I take my walks along the streets 'long-robed,' like the ancient Trojan ladies."

Publius laughed heartily; the cadaverous face took on the expression of a mourner who has incautiously cheered up.

"You see, Julian," continued the poet, "I'm counting on the death of the widow of a very rich Roman landowner. The happy heirs will order an epitaph from me, and are going to pay for it generously. Unfortunately the widow, in spite of everything that doctors and heirs can do, persists in not giving up the ghost. But for that, my boy, I should have bought myself a cloak long ago. Listen, Julian, get up and come with me at once!"

"Whither?"

"Trust me—you'll thank me for it."

"What's the mystery?"

"Ask no questions; get up and come! The poet brings no harm to the poet's friend. You'll see a goddess."

"What goddess?"

"Artemis, the huntress."

"A picture? Statue?"

"Much better than that. If you love beauty, take your cloak and follow me."

Publius assumed so seductive and mysterious an air that Julian was bitten by curiosity.

"There's but one condition. Say nothing, and marvel at nothing we do. Otherwise the spell will break. In the name of Calliope and Erato, just trust me! We're only two yards from the place, and to shorten the road for you I'll read you the beginning of my epitaph on the widow."

They issued on the dusty high-road. Under the first rays of the sun the steel shield of Pallas Athene darted lightnings from the rose-hued Acropolis. Along the stone walls, hiding brooks humming along under the fig-trees, the grasshoppers were singing shrilly, vieing with the hoarse voice of the poet as he recited the epitaph.

Publius Porphyrius was a man not destitute of talent. His career had been a curious one. Several years previously he had possessed a pretty little house, a veritable temple of Hermes, at Constantinople, not far from the Chalcedonian suburb. His father, an oil merchant, had bequeathed him a little fortune which should have permitted him to live without cares. But Publius was a worshipper of antique Hellenism, and rebelled against what he called the triumph of Christian servitude. He wrote a liberal poem which displeased the Emperor Constantius, who was therein alluded to unfavourably. This allusion cost the author dear. Chastisement fell upon him; his house and goods were confiscated, and he himself banished to an islet in the archipelago, inhabited only by rocks, goats, and fevers. This trial was more than Publius could stand. He cursed liberal opinions, and determined to blot out his misdeeds at any price. Shaking with fever, he composed during his sleepless nights, by means of sentences culled from Virgil, a poem glorifying the Emperor; the verses of the ancient poet being grouped in such a fashion that they formed a new work. This ingenious puzzle tickled the palate of the Court. Publius had divined the taste of the century.

Straightway he ventured on feats more astonishing still. He wrote a dithyrambic, or Bacchic ode in free stanzas, and addressed it to Constantius. It consisted of verses of different lengths, designed so that they formed complete figures, such as a Pan's flute, a water-organ, or a sacrificial altar on which the smoke was represented by uneven phrases. But by a marvel of skilfulness the poem was so contrived as to make a decorative oblong twenty hexameters wide and forty hexameters long. Certain lines were traced in red ink and, read together, became transformed into a monogram of Christ, or into a flower of arabesques, but always, in whatever shape, made new lines composed of new compliments. Finally the four last hexameters of the book could be read in eighteen different orders: from the end backwards, from the beginning, from the side, from the middle, from above, from below, etc., and, read in what manner you please, formed a eulogy to the Emperor.

In executing this work the poor poet nearly lost his wits. But his victory was complete, and Constantius more than charmed. He believed that Publius had surpassed all the poets of antiquity; he wrote the author a letter with his own hand, assuring him of protection and ending thus: "In our age My bounty, like the calm breath of the zephyrs, is breathed upon all who write verses."

Nevertheless his confiscated property was not restored to the poet; he was simply given money and authorised to quit his desert island for Athens.

There he led a melancholy existence. The ostler in the stables of the circus, in comparison with Publius, lived in luxury.

In the company of gravediggers, shady speculators, furnishers of nuptial feasts, he passed whole days in the antechambers of the illiterate great, in order to obtain orders for a marriage ode, an epitaph, or a love-letter. At this trade he gained little, but never lost heart, hoping to offer to the Emperor one day a poem which would win him complete pardon.

Julian felt that in spite of this outward abasement Porphyrius bore at heart a deep love for Hellas. He was a fine critic of Greek poetry and Julian enjoyed his conversation.

They left the high-road and approached the high wall of an enclosure like some *palæstra* or exercise-ground. Round about all was solitary; two black lambs were cropping the grass; near the closed door, in the chinks of which poppies and white daisies were growing, there stood a chariot and two white horses. Their manes were close-cut like those of the horses in the bas-reliefs. By them stood an old slave, a deaf-mute, but evidently of an affable disposition, for he immediately recognised Publius and nodded to him in friendly fashion, pointing to the closed gate of the wrestling ground.

"Lend me your purse a moment," said Publius to Julian. "I'll take out one or two pence for this poor old fool."

He threw the coins, and the mute, with servile grimaces and pleased grunts, opened the door.

They entered under a long and dark covered gallery. Between rows of columns ran other galleries laid out for the exercise of athletes. The spaces in their midst were now widths of grass instead of sand. The two friends penetrated a large inner portico. Julian's curiosity became keener at every step, the mysterious Publius leading him on by the hand without a word. Doors of *exedræ*, or academic halls where orators used to meet, opened into the second portico, and the grasshoppers were humming now where eloquent discourses of Athenian sages had in old time resounded. Above the deep grass bees were whirling: silence and melancholy pervaded all. Suddenly, a woman's voice was heard, and the noise of a disk striking the marble, followed by a merry burst of laughter.

Stealing in like robbers, the pair hid themselves in the outer shadow of the columns of the *elaiothesion*, or place where the ancient wrestlers used to rub themselves over with oil.

From behind these columns could be seen the *ephebeion*, a quadrangular space open to the sky, originally laid out for disk-throwing, and now newly strown with fresh sand.

Julian looked in, and started back.

At twenty paces from him stood a young girl entirely naked. His eyes swept over her wonderful body. She was holding a discus in her hand.

Julian longed instinctively to beat a retreat; but turning, he saw in the eyes of Publius and upon the whole of that lean tawny face such a look of admiration, that he understood that the adorer of Hellas, in bringing him to the place, had been moved by no shameful thought; that enthusiasm was wholly sacred.

Publius, seizing the hand of Julian, murmured:

"Look! We are now nine centuries back, in ancient Laconia. Do you remember the verses of Propertius—

"Multa tuæ, Sparte, miramur jura palæstræ, Sed mage virginei, tot bona gymnasii, Quod non infames exercet corpore ludos Inter luctantes nuda puella viros?"

"Who is she?" asked Julian.

"I don't know. I never wanted to know."

"That is well! Hush!"

Now he gazed eagerly and without shame at the girl hurling the disk. Blushes were unworthy of a philosopher.

She retreated some steps, inclined her body forward, and advancing the left leg made a swift bounding movement, and shot the metal circle so high that it shone in the rising sun, and in falling struck the farthest pillar. It was like watching the motions of a statue by Phidias.

"That shot was the best," said a little twelve-year-old damsel, clad in a rich tunic and standing near the column.

"Myrrha, give me the disk," replied the player. "I can throw it higher than that, as you shall see. Meroë, get farther out of the way. I might hurt you, as Apollo hurt Hyacinthus."

Meroë, an old Egyptian, to judge by her multi-coloured vestments and tanned visage, was preparing in alabaster jars perfumes for a bath. Julian understood that the mute slave of the gate and the white-horsed chariot outside must belong to these two votaries of the Laconian games.

After the disk-throwing the young girl took from Myrrha a bow and a quiver, and drew thence a long arrow. She aimed at a black circle at the opposite end of the *ephebeion*; the string hummed, the arrow flew whistling and stuck in the target: then a second, then a third.

"O huntress Artemis!" sighed Publius.

Suddenly a sunbeam slipping between two columns shot into the face and youthful breast of the young girl. Throwing bow and arrows aside in sudden bedazzlement, she hid her face in her hands.

Swallows, uttering their faint fine chirpings, undulated about the exercise-ground, and pursuing each other vanished into the blue of the sky.

She uncovered her face and raised her arms above her head.

Its fair hair, golden at its ends as honey in the sun, at its roots was auburn; her lips half opened in a happy smile, she suffered the sun to bathe her body, gliding lower and lower yet, till she stood clothed, as in the loveliest raiment, in pure light and beauty.

"Myrrha," the girl murmured slowly and dreamily, "look at the sky! How beautiful it would be to bathe in it, like those birds! Do you remember our saying that men could not be happy because they had no wings? When I look at the birds I am consumed with envy. One should be light and bare as I am at this moment, and winging high up in the sky, and knowing that one could fly forever—that there should be nothing else but sky and sun about one's light and free and naked body!"

Drawing herself up to her full height with outstretched arms she sighed deeply, as at some remembered joy fled away forever.

The burning caress of the sun now reached her waist. Suddenly she shivered and grew ashamed, as if some living and passionate being had approached her. With one hand she shielded her breast, with the other the abdomen, the immortal gesture of Aphrodite of Cnidos.

"Meroë, give me my clothes! quick, Meroë!" she exclaimed, with eyes wide open and startled.

Julian never remembered how he came forth from the wrestling-ground; his heart was on fire. The poet's face was solemn as that of a man quitting a temple.

"You are not annoyed?" he asked Julian.

"No; why should I be?"

"Perhaps a Christian might find it a temptation?"

"There was nothing of temptation there for me. Do you understand?"

"Perfectly; that is what I thought."

And again they found themselves on the dusty high road, where the sun was already hot, and bent their steps towards Athens.

Publius continued in an undertone, as it were talking to himself—

"Oh, how shameful, how deformed we are nowadays! Ashamed of our own morose and pitiful nakedness, we hide it because we feel ugly and impure. Whereas of old time. . . Ah! there was a time when all was very different. Julian, the young girls of Sparta used to go out upon the wrestling-ground naked and haughty before all the people. Nobody feared temptation in those days. Folk were simple as children—as gods! And to think that nevermore shall that happen again; that the freedom, the cleanness, of that happy state shall be seen on earth no more!"

The poet's chin fell on his breast, and he sighed drearily.

They came at last to the Street of Tripods, and hard by the Acropolis the friends separated and went their ways in silence.

Julian went into the shadow of the propylæa, through vast porches leading into temple-enclosures; but avoided the Decorated Porch, on which Parrhasius had chiselled the battles of Marathon and Salamis, and passing the little temple of the Wingless Victory ascended to the Parthenon.

He had but to shut his eyes to remember the superb body of Artemis the huntress. When he opened them the sun-bathed Parthenon marbles seemed golden and living as that divine body; and, despising Imperial spies and chances of death, he desired openly to worship and kiss the warm stones of that holy place.

Two black-robed young men of pale and severe countenance were standing near. They were Gregory of Nazianzen and Basil of Cæsarea. The Hellenists feared these two men as their most formidable foes. It was the hope of the Christians that the two friends would one day become fathers of the Church. They were now watching Julian.

"What's the matter with him today?" said Gregory. "Is that the attitude of a monk? Are those the gestures of a monk? Do you see those closed eyes—that smile? Do you believe that his piety is genuine, Basil?"

"I have often watched him weeping and praying in church."

"Mere hypocrisy!"

"If so, why does he come to us, seek our friendship, and argue over the Scriptures?"

"He's deceiving himself; or perhaps he wishes to seduce the faithful. Never trust him! He is the tempter! Remember what I say, brother, the Roman Empire in fostering this young man is nursing an adder!"

The two friends went off, their eyes on the ground. The severe caryatids of the Erechtheum, the laughing blue of the sky, the white temple of the Wingless One, the Porches and the Parthenon, that wonder of the world, on them cast no spell. One thing alone did they desire: to lay all these haunts of demons in the dust. The long shadows of the monks fell on the Parthenon steps as they walked away.

"I must see her again," Julian was thinking; "I must find out who she is."

XIII

T he gods created mortals for one purpose only—polite conversation!"
    "Charmingly said, Mamertinus! Say it again, I beg, before you've forgotten it! I'll write that down with the other maxims," declared Lampridius, the professor of eloquence, taking tablets from his pocket. His admired friend Mamertinus was a fashionable Athenian advocate.

"My dear fellow, I say," repeated Mamertinus with the most delicate of smiles, "I merely say that men have been sent by the gods—"

"No, no, it didn't run so, Mamertinus; you put it better. The gods created mortals—"

"Ah, yes; the gods created mortals for one purpose only—polite conversation!"

And the enthusiastic Lampridius scribbled down the words as if they had been the utterance of an oracle.

The scene was a friendly supper of men of letters given by the venerable Roman senator Hortensius, in the villa of his rich young ward Arsinoë, not far from the Piræus.

Mamertinus on that day had achieved a remarkable speech in defence of the banker Barnava. Nobody had the smallest doubt that Barnava was a complete scoundrel; but, besides measureless eloquence, the advocate possessed so telling a voice that one of the innumerable ladies who adored him avowed: "I never listen to what Mamertinus says; I have no wish to know what he's talking about. I become intoxicated with the tones of his voice, and especially with the dying cadence at the end of his periods. It is incredible! It is no longer a human voice, but nectar and ambrosia, the heavenly sighing of an Æolian harp!"

And so, while the populace labelled the money-lender Barnava "the blood-sucker," the devourer of widows and orphans, the Athenian judges enthusiastically acquitted the client of Mamertinus.

From this client the advocate had received 50,000 sesterces, and therefore felt in no dissatisfied mood at the supper given by Hortensius in his honour. But it was his habit to affect the invalid, in order that he might be spoiled and petted the more.

"I am utterly done up today, my friends," he murmured plaintively; "aching in every limb. Where is Arsinoë?"

"She will soon be here. Arsinoë has just received from the museum of Alexandria some new apparatus for experiments in physics; and she is entirely absorbed in them. But I will give an order to summon her," suggested Hortensius.

"No, don't do that," responded the lawyer carelessly. "But what a ridiculous thing—a young girl at physics! What in the world has the one thing to do with the other? Your blue-stockings have been finely belaboured by Aristophanes and Euripides. Arsinoë is a whimsical creature, Hortensius! Really, if she wasn't so attractive, what with her sculpture and her mathematics she would almost become—"

He did not finish the sentence, and gazed languidly out of the window.

"What am I to do?" replied Hortensius. "A spoiled child. . . an orphan; no father, no mother! As her mere tutor, I can't well deny her anything."

"I see, I see."

The lawyer was no longer listening; he was thinking about himself.

"My dear fellows, I feel—"

"What—what's the matter?" asked several voices anxiously.

"I'm feeling—I fancy—a draught. . ."

"We'll shut the shutters," proposed the host.

"No, we should be stifled! But I've so worn out my voice today. . . And I have to make another defence tomorrow. Give me a carpet under my feet, and my wrapper; I'm afraid of catching cold in the night chill."

And Hephæstion, the friend of Publius and pupil of Lampridius, rushed away to get Mamertinus' wrapper.

It was a piece of soft woollen stuff, daintily embroidered. The lawyer carried it everywhere to safeguard his precious throat from the faintest risk of cold.

Mamertinus nursed his own health like a lover, with so simple a grace, such a passion of self-solicitude, that his friends were instinctively constrained to think of nothing but nursing him too.

"This wrapper was embroidered for me by the venerable Fabiola," he informed them with a smile.

"Wife of the senator?" asked Hortensius.

"Yes! I'll tell you a little story about her. One day I wrote a note—a graceful trifle, but really a mere trifle—just five lines in Greek to another lady (also one of my admirers), who had sent me a basket of the most charming cherries. I thanked her in a frolicsome imitation of Pliny. But just imagine, my friends, Fabiola was seized with so violent a desire to read that letter and to copy it for her collection, that she sent two of her slaves to lie in wait for my messenger. So, brought to a halt in the middle of the night, not a soul in sight, he thought, of course, that brigands were about to strip him of lock, stock, and barrel. But they did him no harm, gave him money, and only took from him my letter, so that Fabiola might have the first reading of it. She actually learnt it by heart!"

"You don't mean it? Ah, I know her! She is a most remarkable woman," continued Lampridius. "I have seen myself that she keeps all your letters enclosed in a lemon-wood casket like so many jewels. She learns them by heart and declares that they are superior to any poetry. Fabiola argues, and argues rightly: 'Since Alexander the Great used to keep the poems of Homer in a cedar-wood coffer, why shouldn't I keep the letters of Mamertinus in a jewel-casket?'"

"This *foie gras* with saffron sauce is the height of perfection! I advise you to taste it."

"Who made it, Hortensius?"

"My head-cook, Dædalus."

"All honour to him! . . . he's a poet."

"Don't let a goose's liver run away with you, my dear Garguillus! A cook, a poet? You will offend the divine muses, our protectresses!"

"I affirm! and I shall always maintain! that cooking is an art as lofty as any other. It's time to fling prejudices to the winds, Lampridius!"

Garguillus, the head of the Imperial chancery, was a man of enormous body, extremely fat, his triple chin scrupulously shaved and perfumed, and his grey hair closely cropped. His face was intelligent and noble; for many years he had been considered the indispensable guest at every supper of Athenian men of letters. Garguillus loved only two things in the world, a good table and a good style. Gastronomy and literature blended for him into a double bliss.

"Suppose now I take an oyster," he was declaring while his delicate fingers, loaded with amethysts and rubies, brought the mollusc towards his mouth; "I take an oyster, and I swallow it"—and in fact he swallowed it, shutting his eyes, with a sucking and clucking noise of his upper lip, which was curiously greedy, and even rapacious, in its appearance. It was prominent, trussed into a point, oddly twisted, and vaguely resembled a small elephant's trunk. When repeating a sonorous verse of Anacreon or Moschus he would move about this upper lip with as much sensuousness as when tasting at supper some sauce of nightingales' tongues.

"I swallow it, and I am immediately aware," went on Garguillus solemnly—"I am immediately aware that the oyster comes from the coast of Britain and not from the south or from Tarentum. Would you like me to prove it? Shall I close my eyes and say from what sea the fish comes?"

"But what in the world has that to do with poetry?" asked Mamertinus impatiently. He could not bear that any but himself should receive general attention.

"Imagine for yourselves, my dear friends," continued the gastronomist imperturbably, "that for years I have not been to the shores of the ocean, which I love and am always regretting. I assure you that a good oyster has such a fresh and salty relish of the sea, that to swallow it is immediately to be a thousand miles hence on the immense seashore. I close my eyes, I see the waves, I see the rocks, I feel the breeze of 'foggy ocean,' as Homer calls it! . . . No! tell me frankly what verse of the Odyssey can wake in me as clearly the sense of sea poetry as the smell of a fresh oyster? Or when I divide a peach and inhale the odour of its juice, why, tell me, are the perfume of the violet and the rose more essentially poetical? Poets describe form, colour, sound. Why can taste be not perfect as these? All is stupid prejudice, my dear fellows! Taste is an immense and hitherto unexplored boon from the gods. The assemblage of tastes forms a harmony as fine as any orchestration of sounds. I affirm, therefore, that there is a tenth muse, the muse of Gastronomy!"

"Let oysters and peaches be admitted. But what harmony, what beauty can you discover in a goose liver dressed with saffron sauce?"

"You are ready to allow, Lampridius, that there is beauty not only in the idylls of Theocritus, but even in the coarsest comedies of Plautus?"

"I admit that."

"Well, my friend, for me there is a gastronomic poesy in *foie gras*; in fact I am prepared to crown Dædalus with laurels for this dish, just as I would crown an Olympic ode of Pindar!"

Two new guests appeared on the threshold; they were Julian and the poet Publius. Hortensius yielded the place of honour to Julian, while Publius devoured the innumerable dishes with his eyes. To judge by his new chlamys the rich widow must have departed this life, and the happy heirs paid for the epitaph in no niggardly fashion.

The general conversation went on. Lampridius told a story of how one day, moved by curiosity, he had been to hear a Christian preacher thundering against pagan grammarians. "The grammarians," assevered the preacher, "do not rank men for their worth, but for their literary style, thinking it less criminal to kill a man than to pronounce the word *homo* with a wrong aspiration!" Lampridius suspected that if these Christian preachers hated the style of the rhetoricians to such a degree, it was because, conscious that they themselves could write and speak only like barbarians, they made ignorance the badge of moral worth, so that for them a good speaker became a suspicious character.

"The day on which eloquence perishes will see the end of Hellas, the end of Rome! People will turn into dumb animals, and it is to make them so that Christian preachers use their barbarous jargon."

"Who knows," murmured Mamertinus pensively, "perhaps style *is* more important than virtue, since slaves, barbarians, and nincompoops can all be virtuous!"

Hephæstion meanwhile was explaining to his neighbour the exact meaning of Cicero's advice—"*Causam mendaciunculis adspergere.*"

"*Mendaciunculis*, that's to say, little lies. Cicero, in fact, advises you to sow little inventions all over your speech; he admits falsehood if decorative."

Then followed a general discussion on the methods of beginning a speech: should the beginning be anapæstic or dactylic?

Julian became bored.

He confessed heartily that he had never considered the matter, and that in his opinion the speaker ought rather to preoccupy himself with the fundamental idea of his speech than with the making style out of a mosaic of peccadilloes.

Mamertinus—then Lampridius and Hephæstion—waxed wroth. According to them the subject of a speech was a matter of no moment. To an orator it should be absolutely indifferent whether he undertook to attack or to defend a case. Even meaning had no interest for him. The principal thing was the orchestration of verbal sounds—the melody, the musical assonance of letters—permitting even a barbarian, witless of Greek, to feel the sheer beauty of language.

"I'll just give you an example, two Latin verses of Propertius," said Garguillus. "Notice the power of the sounds and the emptiness of the meaning. Listen—

"'*Et Veneris dominæ volucres, mea turba columbæ, Tingunt Gorgonio punica rostra lacu.*'"

What pure delight! Every letter sings! What does the meaning matter? All the beauty consists in the sound, in the assemblage of vowels and consonants. For that utterance I would give all the civic virtue of Juvenal and the philosophy of Lucretius! No! Just hear again! What sweetness there is in that murmur—

"*Et Veneris dominæ volucres, mea turba columbæ!*"

and he wagged that upper lip with a smack of delight.

Everybody repeated the lines of Propertius, unwearying of their charm, and embarking on a veritable orgy of quotation.

"Just listen," murmured Mamertinus in his Æolian voice—

"*Tingunt Gorgonio. . .*"

"*Tingunt Gorgonio*," repeated the master of chancery. "By Pallas!— why, it delights one's very palate. It's like swallowing a warm mouthful of wine mingled with Attic honey—

"*Tingunt Gorgonio. . .*"

Note how the 'g's' follow each other, and then farther on—

". . . *punica rostra lacu.*"

"Astounding! inimitable!" murmured Lampridius, shutting his eyes.

Julian was ashamed and amused at this verbal intoxication.

"Words should be, to a certain extent, devoid of meaning," continued Lampridius gravely; "they should flow, roar, chant, without ever bringing up short either the ear or the emotion. Then only real enjoyment of their beauty is possible."

On the threshold of the door, from which the gaze of Julian had seldom departed, there now appeared, quietly as a shadow, a white and haughty figure.

The open shutters allowed the moonlight to fall in, mingling with the ruddy shine of torches on the mosaic of the mirror-smooth floor, and on the wall frescoes, portraying Endymion asleep under the caresses of Selene. The apparition kept still as a statue. The antique Greek peplum of soft white wool fell in long folds, cinctured high under the breast. Moonlight illumined the robe, but the face remained in shadow. The new-comer looked at Julian and Julian looked at her. They smiled at each other, knowing that nobody observed them, and finger on lip she listened to the anecdotes of the guests.

Suddenly Mamertinus, who was discussing with Lampridius grammatical peculiarities of the first and second aorist, exclaimed—

"Arsinoë! At last! So you've made up your mind to abandon physics and modelling for our company?"

She came in and deigned a smile to everyone.

She was the same disk-thrower whom a month before Julian had seen in the abandoned wrestling-ground. The poet Publius, knowing everybody and everything in Athens, had sought the acquaintance of Hortensius and Arsinoë, and had introduced Julian to the house.

Arsinoë's father, an old Roman senator, Helvidius Priscus, had died during the last years of Constantine the Great, bequeathing Arsinoë and Myrrha, his two daughters by a Goth woman-prisoner, to Hortensius, whom he respected on account of his love for antique Rome and hatred for Christianity. A distant relative of Arsinoë, owner of factories of purple at Sidon, had left his incalculable wealth to the young girl.

To Arsinoë, Christian virtues and the patriarchal customs of Rome seemed equally contemptible. The figures of independent women, Aspasia, Cleopatra, and Sappho, alone captivated her girlish imagination. Had she not declared naïvely one day, to the horror of Hortensius, that she would rather become a beautiful and free courtesan, than be transformed into the mother of a family, slave of a husband, "like everybody else"? Those three words, "like everybody else," filled her with melancholy disgust. At one time Arsinoë was attracted by natural science, and had worked with illustrious men of science at the museum in Alexandria. Then the atomic theories of Epicurus, Democrates, and Lucretius had enthralled her. She loved a study which should deliver her soul from the "terror of the gods."

With the same almost morbid intensity, she had afterwards applied herself to sculpture, and had come to Athens in order to study the best works, the masterpieces of Phidias, Scopas, and Praxiteles.

"You are still discussing grammar?" asked the daughter of Helvidius Priscus of the guests, as she came into the dining-hall. She continued ironically: "Don't trouble yourselves; go on. I won't argue or complain, because I'm too hungry after my day's work. Slave, some wine! . . ."

"My friends," continued Arsinoë when seated, "you'll ruin your minds with quotations from Demosthenes and your rules from Quintilian! . . . Take care! Rhetoric will ruin you. . . I want to see a man who doesn't care a fig for Homer or for Cicero, who speaks without thinking of the aspirates, of syntax, or of the conjunction of letters. Julian, let us go down to the beach after supper; I am disinclined for discussions on dactyls and anapæsts."

"Precisely my own mood, Arsinoë," stammered Garguillus, who had eaten too much *foie gras* and who almost always, at the end of dinner, felt an aversion for literature proportionate to the weight upon his stomach.

"*Litterarum intemperantia laboramus*," as Seneca used to say. "We are suffering from literary indigestion. We are simply poisoning ourselves!" and he thoughtfully took a tooth-pick from a pocket. His large face expressed weariness and disgust.

XIV

Together the pair went down the alley of cypresses leading to the sea. The moon-path of sensitive silver on the waters ran up to the horizon, and waves were breaking against a chalk cliff. At the end of the alley there was a semicircular seat. Above it the huntress Artemis, in short tunic, with crescented hair, quiver on shoulder, and two deer-hounds at her feet, looked down on the two young people.

They sat down together. Arsinoë pointed out the hill of the Acropolis, so distant that the columns of the Parthenon could hardly be distinguished; and took up the thread of conversations started at their former meetings—

"See how beautiful it is! . . . And you would destroy that, Julian?"

Making no reply, he stared on the ground.

"I have thought much over what you said to me the last time we met, concerning this humility of yours," continued Arsinoë gently. "Was Alexander son of Philip of Macedon humble? And nevertheless is he not great and splendid?"

Julian said nothing.

"And Brutus, Brutus the stabber of Cæsar! Had Brutus turned the left cheek when struck on the right, do you think he would have been more sublime? Or, indeed, perhaps you consider him a criminal, you Galileans? Why can I not help thinking sometimes, Julian, that you are a hypocrite; and that these black habiliments are not your body's true raiment?"

She turned brusquely towards his moon-lit face and regarded him steadfastly.

"Arsinoë, what do you want of me?" murmured Julian, whose cheek was very pale.

"I want you to be frankly my foe!" exclaimed the young girl. "You must not pass by like this, without telling me what you are. Sometimes I dream that it would be better if Rome and Athens were utterly ruined! Better burn a corpse than leave it unburied! And all our friends here— grammarians, rhetoricians—poets who write Imperial eulogies—all these are the rotting body of Greece and Rome. In their company one grows afraid, as among the shroudless dead. . . Oh, you may triumph, Galileans! Soon corpses and ruins are all that will remain on earth! . . . And you, Julian. . . But no! . . . It is impossible! I do not believe that you are with them and against Hellas—against me! . . ."

Julian sprang up before her, pale and mute, longing to burst away. She held him back.

"Tell me that you are my enemy," she said with heart-broken challenge in her voice.

"Arsinoë! . . . Why—"

"Tell me all! . . . I must know. Do you not feel how near we are? Or are you indeed afraid to speak?"

"In two days I leave Athens," murmured Julian.

"Why?—Where are you going?"

"The Emperor has recalled me to Court—to die perhaps. I may now be looking at you for the last time."

"Julian, you do not believe in Him?" cried Arsinoë, seeking to read the eyes of the monk.

"Speak lower!"

He rose, and striding round cautiously explored the dusty road silvered by the moon, the bushes, and even the sea, as if afraid to see sudden-rising spies from the Emperor. Reassured, he returned and sat down. Leaning one hand heavily on the marble he brought his lips close to the ear of Arsinoë—so near that she felt his warm breath—muttering rapidly—

"Believe in *Him*? . . . Listen, girl! I say to you now what I have never dared to say even to myself. I hate the Galilean! . . . But I have lied as long as I can remember. Lying has soaked into my soul, or clung to it, as this black vestment clings to my body. You remember the poisoned shirt of Nessus; Hercules snatched it off with pieces of his own flesh and it slew him, all the same. I—I too shall perish wearing this Galilean lie!"

He pronounced each word with painful effort. Arsinoë gazed at him. His face, changed by suffering and hatred, became the face of a stranger.

"Be calm, friend!" she murmured. "Tell me all. I shall understand you better than anyone else."

"I should like to be able to speak, but speech is a power I have lost," sneered Julian. "I have kept silence too long. Do you understand, Arsinoë? It is all over with him who has once fallen into their clutches! These good and humble men deform him to such a degree—teach him so thoroughly to lie and to dissimulate—that it becomes impossible ever to stand erect and manful again!"

The blood rushed to his forehead, swelling the veins, and through clenched teeth he muttered—

"Cowardice! Foul Galilean cowardice! this—to hate your enemy as I hate Constantius, and to pardon him, to crouch at his feet, cringe like a serpent, to supplicate him in the humble Christian manner: 'A year, grant your weak-witted slave, Julian, another year; and then do with him as it may please you and your counsellors, O well-beloved of God!' What baseness!"

"No, Julian," protested Arsinoë, "you will conquer! Deception is your strength. . . Julian, do you remember Æsop's fable, The Ass in the Lion's Skin? In this affair of yours the story is reversed; the lion is in the ass's skin, and the hero in a monkish habit! And how they will shrink affrighted when you suddenly show your talons! What joy and what terror! Tell me, you long for power?"

"Power!" cried Julian, intoxicated at the sound of the word and inhaling with deep breaths the fresh air of night—"power! . . . oh, only for a year, a few months, a few days! And I would teach them, I would teach all these crawling and venomous creatures what means their Master's word, 'Render unto Cæsar the things that are Cæsar's'; I swear by the Sun-god they should render to Cæsar what is his!"

He raised his head, his eyes flashing with rage and pride and renewed youth. Arsinoë gazed on him with a smile. But his head soon fell. He sank back on the bench and crossing his arms on his breast in monkish fashion he faltered—

"No, no; why nurse empty dreams? That can never be. I shall perish. Anger will stifle me. Listen; every night after passing the day on my knees in churches, bowed over relics, I go home broken with fatigue; I fling myself on the bed and sob; yes, bite my own flesh, to avoid crying out with pain. Oh, you cannot know yet, Arsinoë, this Galilean horror and infection in which I have agonised for twenty years without escaping by death. We Christians take a deal of killing,—worms that live on even when cut in pieces! At first I used to seek consolation in the teachings of the diviners and philosophers. It was hopeless. I follow neither the one nor the other. I am wicked and I wish to be wickeder still. To be strong and terrible as the Demon, my only brother. . . But why, why can I not forget that there is beauty in the world; why, O cruel one, did you dawn upon my life?"

With a quick spontaneous movement Arsinoë flung her bare arms round Julian's neck, drew him to her so strongly, so closely, that he felt the whole freshness of her body, murmuring—

"And if I did come towards you, O young man, what if it were as a sibyl to prophesy you glory? You alone are alive among the dead!

Splendour is yours! What matters it to me that your wings are no swan's wings, but wings of the black and lost, your talons, talons of a bird of prey? My love is for all the revolted, the reprobate, the rejected—you understand me, Julian? I love the proud and solitary eagles better than any stainless swan. Only. . . be prouder yet, be wickeder yet! Dare up to the height of your ambition! Lie without shame; better lie than be humiliated. Fear not hate; it is the impetus of your wings. Come, shall we make an alliance? You shall give me power, I will give you beauty. Are you willing, Julian?"

Again through the light folds of her antique peplum, as once in the *palæstra*, he saw the breathing image of the huntress Artemis; it seemed that divine body shone through, golden and tender.

His head reeled in the lunar shadow enveloping them. Those haughty lips laughingly approached his own.

For the last time he mused. "I must tear myself away. She does not love me. She will never love me. Her love is only for power."

But immediately he added to himself, with a faint smile: "Well, let it be so! I consent to be duped!"

The chill of the strange and insatiate kiss of Arsinoë shot to his heart like the chill of death. It seemed as if Artemis herself, in the translucence of the moon, had descended towards him, embraced him, and mocked him, and like a beam of moonlight fled away.

ON THE FOLLOWING MORNING BASIL of Cæsarea and Gregory of Nazianzen came across Julian in a basilica in Athens. He was kneeling in prayer. The two friends gazed at him, surprised. Never had they seen upon his features such an expression of rapt serenity.

"Brother," murmured Basil to Gregory, "we have sinned; he whom we inwardly accused is a righteous man."

Gregory shook his head.

"May the Lord pardon me if I am deceived," he said slowly, his piercing eye still on Julian. "But remember, Basil, how often the Devil himself, the father of lying, has appeared to men in guise of an angel!"

XV

On the base of a dolphin-shaped lamp were ranged the curling irons of a barber. The lamp-light was growing pale, for rays of morning, falling through silken window-curtains, were gradually filling the sleeping chamber with deep violet hues. The curtains were dyed in the richest hyacinthine purple of Tyre.

"'Hypostasis,' 'hypostasis'? What is the meaning of the divine hypostasis, or essence, or personality, of the Trinity? No human being can form any conception. I myself haven't slept a wink in thinking over it the whole night. I arrived at no conclusion but an atrocious headache. Boy, give me towels and soap!"

So spoke a personage with a tall headdress like a mitre and the pontifical aspect of a high-priest or Asiatic tyrant. He was chief barber and wig-maker in attendance on the sacred person of Constantius. The razor in his skilful hands was flitting, with an incomparable grace and lightness, over the Imperial chin. He was engaged upon a sacred mystery. In attendance on each side were innumerable *cubicularii*, slaves holding vases, essences, oils, and napkins, and two youths bearing fans. Supervising all these, Eusebius, grand chamberlain of the private apartments, stood by. He was the most powerful man in the Empire.

During the ceremony of barbification, as an emperor's shaving must be called, the two youths refreshed the illustrious patient by means of great fans, each six-winged like the seraphim, or the *ripides* with which deacons fan away flies from a sacramental chalice, during the intoning of the liturgy. The barber had scarcely finished the Emperor's right cheek and was beginning the left, which had been anointed with an Arabian essence named "the foam of Aphrodite." Leaning to the ear of Constantius he whispered cautiously:

"Ah! Well-beloved of God, your universal intelligence alone can determine what this hypostasis, this mysterious personality of Father, Son, and Holy Ghost may mean. Don't listen to the bishops! Act as pleases yourself, and not as it may please them. But Athanasius, that patriarch of Alexandria, must be punished as a blasphemous rebel. Almighty God, the Creator Himself, will instruct your Holiness as to what, and in what manner, your subjects ought to believe. In my humble opinion the Arians are perfectly right in asserting that there was a time when the 'Son' did not exist. And so consubstantiality. . ."

But at this moment Constantius was staring at himself in the great polished silver mirror, and rubbing his hand over the silky new shaven region on his right cheek. He interrupted—

"I don't think that's very smooth!—eh! I think you might go over it again. What were you saying to me about consubstantiality?"

The barber, who had received a talent of gold from the Court bishops Ursatius and Valentine to prepare the Emperor for the new profession of faith, was murmuring insinuatingly in the ear of Constantius and wielding his razor with the most persuasive delicacy, when at this moment the chief of the *silentiarii*, Paul, surnamed Catena, approached the Emperor.

He was so called because his infamous system of reports enwound any chosen victim in chains well-nigh indissoluble. His effeminate face was beardless and handsome, and judged by externals he seemed the angel of humility. His dark eyes were full of languor; his walk, a noiselessly graceful feline motion. He wore crosswise over the shoulder a wide dark blue ribbon—sign of special Imperial favour.

Paul Catena with a subtle and authoritative gesture waved the barber away, and whispered in the ear of Constantius—

"A letter from Julian! Intercepted tonight. Deign to read it."

Constantius greedily snatched the letter from the hands of Paul, opened it, and read. Disappointed, he muttered—

"Mere trash—trifles; he sends a present of a hundred grapes to a sophist and writes the praises of the fruit and of the number 'a hundred.'"

"Ah! a ruse!" said Catena.

"Really?" asked Constantius; "what proofs are there?"

"None."

"Then he's either exceedingly cunning or indeed—"

"What does your Eternity mean?"

"Or, in fact, he is innocent."

"As your Majesty pleases," stammered Paul.

"*As I please?* I desire to be just, simply just. Are you not aware of that? I must have proofs. . ."

"Wait; we shall find them."

Another informer came near, a young Persian named Mercurius, court-pantler, little more than a lad. He was feared not less than Paul Catena and had been pleasantly nicknamed "Chief Diviner of Dreams." If the prophetic dream could be twisted into any meaning even remotely unfavourable for the person of the Emperor, Mercurius would make careful notes of it and hasten to make a report. Many a victim had paid with their goods and their prospects for the imprudence of dreaming what they had no business to dream; and, aware of this, prudent courtiers would declare themselves martyrs to insomnia, enviers of the legendary dwellers in Atlantis, who, according to Plato, are lapt in slumber without visions. The Persian signed to a distance two Ethiopian eunuchs who were knotting the laces of the Emperor's green and gilt shoes. He kissed the feet of the sovereign, and as it were basked a moment in his eyes, like a dog who affectionately gazes up for his master's orders.

"May your Eternity forgive me," whispered little Mercury, "I could not refrain from running to your presence. Gaudentius has had a bad dream! You appeared to him in a torn chlamys and crowned with blasted ears of corn. . ."

"What does that mean?"

"The blasted ears announce famine, and the torn chlamys. . . I dare not. . ."

"Sickness?"

"Worse still, I'm afraid, if possible. Gaudentius' wife confessed to me that he had consulted the augurs. God knows what they told him!"

"Well, well! We will discuss it. Come again this evening."

"No! I will come this afternoon. Permit me to mention a slight matter, something not so grievous. . . There is also the matter of the table-cloths. . ."

"What table-cloths?"

"Have you forgotten? At a supper in Aquitaine the table was spread with two table-covers with purple borders—borders as wide as those on the Imperial chlamys!"

"Do you mean to say they were more than two fingers wide? Remember, I've authorised the width of two fingers."

"Ah, much, much wider I fear! It was a regular Imperial chlamys. Can such sacrilege be permitted?"

Mercury did not succeed however in reciting all his reports:

"At Delphi a monster has been born—four ears, four eyes, two snouts, all covered with hair. The augurs say it is a bad omen—that the Holy Empire will be split up. . ."

"We shall see! we shall see! Write it all down in due order and submit it to me."

The Emperor went on with his morning toilet. He consulted his mirror again, and with a fine camel's-hair brush took up a morsel of rouge from the casket of filigree silver, shaped like a reliquary and crowned by a little cross, at his elbow. Constantius was devoutly religious; enamelled crosses and the monogram of Christ adorned every trinket in his private rooms. Exquisite and expensive paint called *purpurissima*, extracted from the scum on the purple mollusc while in a state of ebullition, was specially prepared for him. Constantius adroitly spread a faint flush of this over his withered brown cheek. From the room called Porphyria, where the regal vestments were kept in a pentagonal wardrobe, eunuchs bore forth the Imperial dalmatic. It was stiff, heavy with gold, encrusted with precious stones, and with lions and dragons embroidered on its amethystine purples.

In the main hall of the palace on that day was to be held the great Arian council. The Emperor slowly took his way thither along a gallery of pierced and fretted marble. Palace guards, or palatines, two-deep formed a long lane, mute as statues and holding lances fourteen cubits long crossed above the head of their master, as he paced in state between them. Constantine's banner of cloth of gold, the *Labarum*, surmounted by the monogram of Christ, shone rustling behind, borne by the officer of the Imperial largesses (*comes sacrarum largitionum*). Mute body-guards (*silentiarii*) heralded the procession, imposing silence on everyone they met.

In the gallery the Emperor encountered the Empress Eusebia Aurelia. She was a mature woman with a pale and weary face, delicate and noble features, a mischievous raillery sometimes kindling her keen eyes. Crossing her hands on the *omophorium* covered with sapphires and heart-shaped rubies, the Empress bowed profoundly and pronounced the habitual morning salutation:

"I am come for the joy of beholding you, O spouse well-beloved of the Lord! How has your Holiness deigned to sleep?"

Then, at a sign from her, the attendant maids of honour drew to a distance and she murmured sweetly, in a simpler and sincerer tone—

"Julian is to be received by you today. Receive him kindly! Don't believe these spying reports. He is a poor innocent boy. God will repay you, sire, if you grant him favour."

"You ask favour to him as a favour to yourself?"

The husband and wife exchanged a rapid glance.

"I know," she said, "you always have confidence in me; let it be so now. Julian is a faithful slave. Don't refuse me. . . Be kind to him. . ."

And she gratified him with one of those smiles which hitherto had wielded irresistible power over the heart of Constantius.

In the portico, which was separated from the great hall by hangings (behind which the Emperor used to ensconce himself to hear what was going on at the councils), a monk, wearing a cruciform tonsure and in a hooded robe of coarsest drugget, came near. It was Julian.

"I salute my benefactor, the triumphant and glorious Emperor Augustus Constantius. May your Holiness pardon me!"

"We are happy to receive you, my son."

Julian's cousin magnanimously extended his hand to Julian's lips. Julian kissed the hand dyed with the blood of his father, of his brother, of all his relatives. Then he rose erect, pale and with sparkling eyes fixed upon his enemy. He gripped the handle of a poniard hidden under his robe. The grey eyes of the Emperor lighted with pride and cautious malice, seldom dropping their scrutiny. He was a head shorter than Julian, large-shouldered, solidly-built, and bandy-legged like an old cavalry soldier. The tight brown skin over his temples was disagreeably glossy. The thin lips were severely closed with the expression of folk that set order and punctuality above all other virtues—the expression of a pedant and a schoolmaster.

To Julian he appeared detestable. He felt an animal fury getting the better of him, and, unable to utter a word, his eyes fell and he breathed with difficulty.

Constantius smiled, imagining the young monk unable to bear the superhuman majesty of the Imperial glance. With ostentatious benevolence he continued—

"Fear nothing! Go in peace! Our kindness shall bring no danger upon you. On the contrary we shall from this day forth heap bounties on our cousin who is an orphan."

Julian bowed and proceeded into the hall of council; and the Emperor, hidden behind draperies, lent an ironic and attentive ear to the debate beginning within.

He immediately recognised the voice of the principal dignitary of the Imperial post, Gaudentius. It was he who had suffered from the bad dream.

"One council treads on the heels of another," Gaudentius was complaining; "now it's at Sirmio, now it's at Sardis, now at Antioch, and now here at Constantinople. They discuss and discuss, but never come to an understanding. And I would ask you, for pity's sake, to consider the horses that have to carry these gentlemen about! Out of a relay of ten horses you will hardly find one who is not foundered by the bishops. Another five councils, and my beasts will only be fit for the knacker's yard—not a car will have a wheel on it. Yet, in spite of all, you'll see that the bishops will still be at loggerheads and boggling at the Trinity!"

"Why then, Gaudentius, don't you send in a formal report on the subject to the Emperor?"

"Nobody would believe me. I should be accused of irreligion and lack of respect for the crying needs of the Church."

In the vast round hall, crowned by a cupola on columns of Phrygian marble, the heat was already stifling. Slanting sun rays fell in through uncurtained windows. The noise of voices was like the buzzing of a swarm of bees. The Imperial golden seat—*sella aurea*—was prepared on a daïs. It rested on lions' paws of carved ivory, crossed like those of the curule chairs of Roman consuls.

Close to the throne, the high-priest Paphnutis, with a face empurpled by argument, was declaring—

"For my part, I shall keep to the opinions my fathers taught me! According to the creed of our holy father Athanasius, patriarch of Alexandria, we must worship a single God in a Trinity, and the Trinity in a single God; the Father is God; the Son is God; the Holy Ghost is God, and nevertheless they form together but one God!"

And as if he was smashing an invisible enemy he brought down his enormous right fist into his left-hand palm and glared triumphantly round the assembly.

"That tradition have I received from my fathers, and that tradition I will keep!"

"Who is it? What's he saying?" asked Ozius, a man of a hundred years old, who had been alive in the time of the council of Nicæa. "Where's my trumpet?" Harrowing perplexity could be read on his face. He was deaf, almost blind. The deacon who accompanied him set the ear-trumpet to his ear.

A certain pale thin monk seized Paphnutis by the surplice—

"Father Paphnutis," he shouted to drown the general clamour, "what is all this about? . . . It is a question of a single word; is not that so?" and forthwith he began to narrate terrible scenes he had witnessed in Alexandria and Constantinople. The Arians had opened with wooden pincers the mouths of those unwilling to receive the Sacrament in heretic churches, and forced the host between their lips. Mere children were subjected to inquisition; the breasts of women were crushed under leaden weights and branded with live iron. In the Church of the Holy Apostles so horrible a struggle had taken place between Arians and Orthodox that the blood, overflowing the cistern which received the drainage of the place, had poured down the steps in front of the western façade and streamed into the market-square. At Alexandria the governor Sebastian had caused virgins to be beaten with thorn branches, so that many of them had succumbed and their bodies lay unburied outside the city gates. All this contention was over a single letter, an *iota*.

"Father Paphnutis," argued the pale monk, "for an iota! The word 'substantial' does not even occur in the holy Scripture. What are we then torturing each other about? Think, Father; it is horrible!"

"Then," interrupted the Arch-priest impatiently, "must we be reconciled with those impious dogs who will not hunt out of their pestilent hearts the doctrine that there was a moment when the Son of God did not exist?"

"'One Shepherd and one Flock,'" the monk returned: "Let us make them some concessions!"

But Paphnutis refused to hear anything, vociferating till the veins of his neck almost burst—

"Let the enemies of God be silent! Never will I give in! Anathema on the Arian heresy! Such have I received the faith from my fathers, and such will I keep it!"

Ozius the centenarian wagged approvingly his white head and long beard. On the other side of the hall two archdeacons were talking together.

"You keep very calm, Father Dorophas. Why are you taking no part in discussion today?"

"My voice is gone, Father Flavius. I am too hoarse with anathematising the cursed sectaries."

In another group the deacon from Antioch, Aetius, a bold and fervent disciple of Arius, regarded as an atheist for his audacious and scoffing interpretations of the Trinity, was holding forth.

The career of Aetius had been remarkable for its extraordinary variety. At first a slave, he had afterwards become by turns a coppersmith, a sailor, a rhetorician, a pupil and teacher of Alexandrian philosophy, and finally a deacon.

"God the Father is in His substantial essence different from His Son," Aetius was saying with a smile and evident gusto, to the dismay of his hearers. "The Trinity has differentiations, degrees of glory, according to the nature of the personalities comprised in it. The word 'God' cannot be used of the Son, because He has never applied it to Himself. The Son has never even comprehended the essence of the Father, because it is impossible for Him who had a beginning to imagine that which has neither beginning nor end."

"Blaspheme not!" shouted an indignant bishop. "Where is this Satanic boldness going to stop, my brethren?"

"Drag not the simple-minded into perdition by your speeches!" shrieked another.

"Prove me wrong by philosophic reasoning, and I will acquiesce. But shouts and insults are proof of nothing but impotence," replied Aetius calmly.

"It is written in the Scriptures. . ."

"What is that to me? God has given intelligence to man that He himself might be understood. I believe in logic of argument and not in texts. Reason with me on the basis of the syllogisms and categories of Aristotle. . ."

And with a contemptuous smile he threw his surplice around him like the cynic mantle of Diogenes.

Some bishops were beginning to speak in favour of a universal creed in which mutual concession should be made, when the Arian Narcissus of Neronia, a profound expert in all statutes, creeds, and canons of the councils, intervened in discussion. He was a man little liked, suspected of adultery and usury, but admired by everyone for his theological erudition.

"That is a flat heresy!" he declared decisively.

"Why is it a heresy?" demanded several voices.

"Because the assizes of Paphlagonia have already so laid it down."

"The assizes of Paphlagonia?" repeated the desperate bishops; "we had clean forgotten them. What is to be done now?"

"May God have pity on us miserable sinners!" the good bishop Ozius was muttering; "I can no longer understand anything; I can't get out of the labyrinth; my head is buzzing, my ears singing with Greek words; I'm walking in a fog and don't know myself what I believe in and what I disbelieve; what is heresy and what is not. . . Jesus help us! . . . We are falling into the snares of the Devil."

At that moment the hubbub and clamour ceased. The bishop Ursatius of Singidion, one of the Emperor's favourites, mounted the

DMITRY MEREZHKOVSKY

tribune. He was holding in his hand a long scroll of parchment. Two *silentiarii*, having mended their fine pens of Egyptian reed, got ready to write down the conciliar debate. Ursatius read out the message of the Emperor to the bishops—

"Constantius, the triumphant, glorious, and eternal Augustus, to all bishops assembled in this council. . ."

The Emperor demanded the dismissal of Athanasius, the patriarch of Alexandria, whom he called the most useless of men, the traitor, the accomplice of the insolent and abominable Magnentius.

The courtiers, Valentine, Eusebius, Axentius, hastened to sign the scroll. But a murmur arose.

"It is all a damnable device; a trick of the Arians! We will not let our patriarch suffer. . ."

"The Emperor calls himself *eternal*. . . nobody is eternal but God! It is a mockery of holy things."

Constantius, lurking behind the curtain, heard this last speech distinctly. Thrusting the hangings roughly by, he pushed unexpectedly into the hall. The lances of the guard surrounded him. His face expressed anger. A heavy silence fell upon the throng.

"What is it, what is it?" the blind Ozius kept whispering in restless perplexity.

"Fathers," the Emperor began, bridling his anger, "allow me, the servant of the Most High, to use my zeal under His providence to a successful issue. Athanasius is a rebel, the chief violator of universal concord and oecumenical peace."

Fresh murmurs arose. Constantius was silent and ran a surprised look over the array of bishops. A voice shouted—

"Anathema upon the abominable Arian heresy!"

"The faith against which you revolt," replied the Emperor, "is my faith. If it is heretical, why has the omnipotent God assigned victory to us over all our enemies? Constans, Vetranio, Gallus, the abominable Magnentius, why has God Himself placed the power over the world in our sacred hands?"

The bishops were dumb; then the courtier Valentius, bishop of Mursa, bowing with great servility—

"God will unveil the truth to your wisdom, sire, well-beloved of the Lord! What you believe cannot be heresy. Did not Cyril of Jerusalem behold a rainbow-surmounted cross in the heavens on the day of your victory over Magnentius?"

"It is my will," interrupted Constantius, rising from the throne. "Athanasius shall be laid low by the power God has entrusted to me. Pray that all these conflicts and controversies may cease, that the murderous heresy of the Sabæans, the partisans of Athanasius, may be destroyed, that the truth may shine into all hearts. . ."

Suddenly the Emperor grew pale; the words expired on his lips.

"What! How is it that he has been allowed to enter?"

He pointed to a tall old man with a severe and majestic face. It was the bishop Hilarion of Pictavia (Poitiers), who had been exiled and ruined for his faith, one of the greatest enemies of the Arian Emperor. He had come to the council unsummoned, perhaps seeking martyrdom. The old man raised his hand to heaven as if calling down malediction upon the head of the Emperor, and his powerful voice thrilled the silent crowd—

"Brothers, Christ must be about to descend, for Antichrist has already conquered, and that Antichrist is Constantius! He does not break your backs on the wheel, but he flatters your proud bellies. He does not throw us into dungeons, but entices us into his palaces. . . Emperor, hearken! I say to you what I have said to Nero, Decius, Maximian, all persecutors of the Church. But you are not, like them, the murderer of men, but the murderer of the Divine love itself! Nero, Decius, Maximian, have better served the God of truth than you! In their reign we conquered the Devil, the blood of the martyrs flowed, cleansing the earth, and their dead bones worked miracles. Whereas you, O King, cruellest of the cruel, slay and yet grant us not the glory of death. . . Lord, send us a true despot like Nero, and let the kindly arm of Thy wrath revive again the Church dishonoured by the kiss of this Judas!"

The Emperor sprang to his feet—

"Seize him and the rebels!" he exclaimed, half-choked with rage, pointing to Hilarion.

The guards flung themselves on the bishops.

The crowd became a wild and indescribable mob illumined by the flashing of swords. Roman soldiers, snatching off the breastplate, stole, and chasuble of Hilarion, dragged the old man away. Many present rushed in mad panic to the doors, fell, and were trampled underfoot by the rest. One of the recording clerks leapt on the sill of a window, but a soldier pinned him there by his long vestments and would not release him. The table and the inkstands were upset, red ink poured over the blue jasper floor, and voices shouted at the sight of the crimson sea—

"Blood! blood! blood!"

Others howled—

"Death to the enemies of the thrice-pious Augustus!"

Paphnutis in a thunderous monotone persisted in crying while the guards dragged him away—

"I recognise the council of Nicæa! . . . Anathema on the Arian heresy!"

Others screamed—

"Be silent, enemies of God! Anathema! the council of Nicæa! the assizes of Sardis! the canons of Paphlagonia!"

Blind Ozius remained seated motionless, forgotten by all, in his episcopal chair, murmuring inaudibly—

"Jesus Christ, Son of God, have pity upon us! What is the matter, my brethren, what is it?"

In vain he stretched feeble hands towards his terrified friends. Nobody saw him, nobody heard him; and tears streamed down his aged cheeks.

Meanwhile Julian watched all, a contemptuous smile upon his lips, full of inward triumph.

On the same day, late in the evening, in a quiet and solitary defile two Mesopotamian monks were journeying afoot together. They had been sent by Syrian bishops to the council, had escaped the palatine guards with great difficulty, and now, their minds at peace, were proceeding towards Ravenna to embark as quickly as possible upon the ship which was to restore them to the desert. Fatigue and sadness were on their faces. Ephraim, one of the two, was extremely old; the other, Pimenus, a lad.

Ephraim said to Pimenus—

"It is time to regain the desert, brother. Better to hear the howling of jackal and lion than the cry that dinned our ears in the Imperial palace. Happy are those who speak not. Happy those who hide themselves in desert places, beyond arguments of masters of the Church, who have understood the uselessness of words; who debate nothing. Happy is he who seeks not to understand God's mysteries, but who, merging his spirit into Thine, sings to Thy face, O Lord, like a harp; understanding how difficult it is to know, how easy to love Thee!"

Ephraim was silent, and Pimenus murmured—

"Amen!"

The quiet of night enveloped the pair, and courageously, steering by the stars, the two monks took their way eastwards rejoicing in the majesty of their barren road.

XVI

T he city of Milan lay basking in the sun; and by every street the crowd was turning its steps towards the chief public square.

Tremendous acclamations ran through the throng, and in the triumphant chariot, drawn by twenty horses white as swans, appeared the Emperor. His chariot seat was so lofty that the people were obliged to throw their heads back to behold him. His robes, besown with precious stones, sparkled dazzlingly in the sun. In his right hand he held the sceptre, in the left the Imperial globe crested by a cross.

Motionless as a statue, outrageously painted, he looked straight before him without turning his head, which was held stiff as in a vice. During the whole journey, and despite the joltings of the car, the Emperor stirred not a finger, nor coughed, nor blinked the steady stare of his eyes.

Constantius had acquired this immobility by years of effort, and was particularly proud of it, considering it an indispensable part of Imperial etiquette. On such occasions he would have preferred to undergo torture rather than betray his mortal nature by sneezing, coughing, or wiping off the sweat which stood in beads on his forehead.

Although squat and bow-legged he imagined himself gigantic. When the chariot disappeared under the arch of triumph, not far from the baths of Maximian Hercules, the Emperor bowed his head as if he were afraid of striking his head against the lofty gates which would have freely taken a Cyclops beneath them.

Each side of the road was lined with palatine guards helmeted and cuirassed in gold, the two ranks of the bodyguard flashing in the sun like streams of lightning.

Round the Imperial chariot great dragon-shaped standards were floating. The purple stuff, swollen by the wind engulfed in the gullets of the monsters, gave out a shrill sound like the hiss of snakes, and the long purple tails of the dragons wavered to and fro above the people. In the Forum were drawn up all the legions quartered in Milan. Thunders of applause welcomed the Emperor. Constantius was pleased. The noise had neither been too feeble nor too tumultuous. Arranged beforehand according to the strictest etiquette, the soldiers had been instructed to be enthusiastic with moderation and respect.

Giving each of his motions a kind of stiff and pedantic emphasis, Constantius solemnly descended from the chariot and went up to the tribune raised above the square. It was draped with ragged standards of old victories and studded with metal eagles.

The trumpets sounded up anew in the call denoting that the leader desired to speak to his army. The Forum was instantly hushed.

"*Optimi reipublicæ defensores!*" began Constantius. (Excellent defenders of the Republic.)

The discourse was long-winded, tedious, full of scholastic flowers of rhetoric.

Julian in Court dress now ascended the steps of the tribune, and the fratricide invested the last descendant of Constantius Chlorus with the sacred purple of the Cæsars.

The sunlight filtered through the thin silk when the Emperor raised the purple to enrobe the kneeling Julian. The rich hue tinged the pale face of the new Cæsar, who murmured inwardly the prophetic verse of the Iliad—

> "*Eyes closed by purple death and puissant Destiny. . .*"

And nevertheless Constantius was welcoming him:

"*Recepisti primævus originis tuæ splendidum florem, amatissime mihi omnium frater.*" (Still young, you have attained already the flower of your royal birth, most beloved of all my brothers!)

An enthusiastic roar rose from the legions. Constantius became rather gloomy; that shout had slightly exceeded the proper bounds. Julian must have pleased the soldiers.

"Glory and prosperity to Cæsar Julian!" They cheered louder and louder, till it seemed as if they would never cease.

The new Cæsar thanked the legionaries with a kindly smile, and every soldier clashed his buckler against his knee as a sign of rejoicing.

It seemed to Julian that it was not by the will of the Emperor, but by the will of the gods, that he had reached this eminence.

EVERY EVENING CONSTANTIUS WAS IN the habit of consecrating a quarter of an hour to the polishing of his nails. It was one of the few toilet delicacies that he permitted himself, being sober, unimaginative, and rather gross than effeminate in all his habits. Paring his nails with little files, polishing them with minute brushes, he gaily asked his favourite eunuch, the grand chamberlain Eusebius, on the evening of the day of investiture—

"How soon do you think will Julian conquer the Gauls?"

"I think," answered Eusebius, "that the next news we shall receive will be of the defeat and death of that young man!"

"Really?—that would give me much pain! But I have done, don't you think, everything that lay in my power. . . Henceforth he has only himself to blame. . ."

Constantius smiled, and bowing his head admired his nails.

"You have conquered Magnentius," murmured the eunuch, "you have conquered Vetranio, Constans, Gallus. You will conquer Julian. Then there will be but one shepherd, one flock, God and you alone."

"Yes, yes. But, putting Julian on one side, there is still Athanasius. I shall never be happy until, living or dead, he shall have fallen into my hands."

"Julian is more to be feared than Athanasius, and you have invested him today in the purple of death. Oh, wisdom of Providence, destroying by inscrutable means all the enemies of Your Eternity! Glory be to the Father, and to the Son, and to the Holy Ghost, now and during the night of ages!"

"Amen," concluded the Emperor, having finished the toilet of his nails and thrown away the last minute brush. He approached the ancient banner of Constantine, the Labarum, which stood always in the sleeping-chamber, knelt down, and contemplating the monogram of Christ which shone in the flicker of the still-burning lamp, began his prayers. He accomplished exactly the prescribed number of salves and signs of the cross, addressing God with an imperturbable faith, as one who never doubts his own worth and acceptability.

The three-quarters of an hour of devotions having elapsed, Constantius arose with a light heart. Eunuchs undressed him. He lay down on an Imperial couch propped by cherubim of silver on outspread wings, and fell asleep in placid innocence with a child like smile on his lips.

XVII

At Athens, in one of the most frequented cross-roads, a statue modelled by Arsinoë—*The victorious Octavius holding up the head of Brutus*—was exhibited to the people, and the Athenians welcomed in the daughter of the senator Helvidius Priscus a renewer of the art of their golden age. But the special dignitaries whose business was to keep watch on the public temper, officers strangely but rightly nicknamed "Inquisitors," reported to the proper quarters that the statue might arouse liberal sentiments in the people. A resemblance to Julian was discovered in the face of Brutus, and in the work as a whole a criminal allusion to the recent punishment of Gallus. Attempts were made to discover in Octavius some analogy to the Emperor Constantius. The affair took the proportions of an act of treason, and almost fell into the hands of Paul Catena. Luckily the Imperial chanceries sent direct a severe order to the local magistrate, that not only should the statue disappear from the cross-roads, but that it should be broken to pieces under the eyes of government officials.

Arsinoë wished to hide the statue, but Hortensius was in such mortal affright that he threatened to give up his ward herself to the informers.

In deep disgust at the degradation of the public, Arsinoë allowed them to do with her work everything that Hortensius desired, and masons broke up the figure.

Arsinoë hastily left Athens, her guardian having persuaded her to follow him to Rome, where friends had long promised him the office of Imperial quæstor. They installed themselves in a house not far from the Palatine Hill.

Days flowed by in inactivity, Arsinoë realising that there was no longer scope for the greatness and freedom of antique art. She bore in mind her conversation with Julian at Athens; and it was the only link which restrained her from suicide. The long suspense of inaction seemed to her intolerable. In moments of discouragement she longed to have done with it all, to leave all, to set out for the Gallic battlefield and at the side of the young Cæsar attain power, or perish.

But she fell seriously ill. In the long and calm days of convalescence she found a devoted consoler in her most faithful adorer, Anatolius, a centurion of the Imperial cavalry, son of a rich merchant of Rhodes.

He was a Roman centurion, as he used to say himself, merely as the result of a mistake, having only taken to the military career to satisfy the empty-headed ambition of his father, who desired as the summit of earthly honour to see his son clothed in gilt armour.

Evading discipline by generous gifts, Anatolius passed his life in luxurious idleness, amidst works of art and books, in feastings and indolent and costly travel. The profound lucidity of soul which had characterised ancient Epicureans was not possessed by this modern. He complained to his friends—

"I suffer from a mortal malady. . ."

They would ask him dubiously—

"What malady?"

And he would say—

"What you call my spirit of irony and what seems to me melancholy madness."

His finely cut delicate features expressed extreme fatigue. Sometimes he would awake as from a sleep, undertake a wild excursion with fishermen in a hurricane in the open sea, or set off to hunt wild boar and bear, or contemplate hatching a plot against the life of Cæsar, or seek initiation into the terrible mysteries of Mithra and Adonis. On such occasions he was capable of astonishing by his rashness and audacity even those persons who were ignorant of his ordinary way of living.

But the excitement once evaporated he would return to listlessness and lassitude, still more sleepy, still more cynical and sad.

"Nothing can be done with you, Anatolius," Arsinoë used to say to him; "you are so soft that people might think you had no bones."

But she felt a kind of Hellenic grace in this last of the Epicureans; liked to read in his weary eyes their melancholy mockery of himself and everything else. He would say—

"The sage can extract enjoyment from the blackest melancholy, as bees of Hymettus make their best honey with the juice of bitterest plants!" and his gossip soothed Arsinoë, who smilingly used to call Anatolius her physician.

In reality she became stronger, but never returned to her studio. The sight of chips of marble filled her with painful memories.

Meanwhile, at the time of which we are speaking Hortensius was preparing wonderful public games in the Flavian Theatre, in honour of his arrival in Rome. He was continually travelling, and busy receiving horses, lions, bears, Scots wolf-dogs, crocodiles from the tropics, and with these, flocks of intrepid hunters, skilled riders, comedians, and gladiators.

The date of the performance was approaching, and the lions had not arrived from Tarentum, where they had disembarked. The bears had grown thin, famished, timid as lambs.

Hortensius became sleepless with anxiety.

Two days before the festival, the gladiators, Saxon prisoners, proud and fearless men for whom he had paid a colossal sum, considering it a disgrace to serve as a sport for the Roman populace, committed suicide by cutting their own throats at night in their prison.

Hortensius, at that unexpected news, nearly went out of his mind. Now all hope concentrated itself on the crocodiles, which excited the special curiosity of the mob.

"Have you tried giving them newly-killed hogs' flesh?" demanded the senator of the slave entrusted with the supervision of these precious beasts.

"Yes; but they won't eat it."

"Have you tried veal?"

"They won't touch that, either."

"And wheaten bread soaked in cream?"

"They turn away from it and go to sleep."

"They must be ill or too fatigued."

"We've even opened their jaws and shoved the food down their throats. They cough it up again."

"Ah! by Jupiter, those foul beasts will be the death of me! We must release them after the first day in the arena or else they will die of hunger," groaned Hortensius falling into a chair.

Arsinoë contemplated him with envy. He at least was not tired of life.

She passed into an isolated chamber whence the windows looked down on the garden. There in the calm moonlight her young sister Myrrha, who was now about sixteen years old, was softly touching the strings of a harp, and the notes were falling like tears. Arsinoë kissed Myrrha, who answered her by a smile without ceasing to play. A loud whistle sounded behind the garden wall:

"It is he," said Myrrha, rising. "Come quickly!"

She grasped Arsinoë's hand tightly. The two young girls threw black cloaks over their shoulders and went out. The wind was chasing the clouds along, and the moon, sometimes hidden, sometimes shone out brightly. Arsinoë opened a door in the outer wall of the house. A young man wrapped in a monk's hooded mantle was awaiting them.

"We are not late, Juventinus?" asked Myrrha.

"I was afraid that you were not coming!"

They walked long and rapidly down narrow lanes, then out among the vineyards, issuing at length into the Roman plain. In the distance the brick-built aqueduct of Servius Tullius was outlined against the sky. Juventinus turned round and said—

"Somebody is following us!"

The two young girls turned round also. A flood of moonlight fell upon them, and the individual following them exclaimed cheerfully—

"Arsinoë! Myrrha! . . . And so I have found you again! Where are you going?"

"We're going among the Christians," answered Arsinoë. "Come with us, Anatolius; you will see some curious things."

"What do I hear? Among the Christians?—You have always been their enemy!" wondered the centurion.

"With age, my friend, one grows better and more tolerant, or indifferent, if you like to call it so. This is a superstition neither better nor worse than other superstitions. And then one is capable of a good deal when bored. I am going among them for Myrrha's sake; it pleases her. . ."

"Where is the church? We're out in the plain," murmured Anatolius.

"The churches are destroyed or profaned by their fellow-Christians, the Arians, who believe in Christ otherwise than they do. You must have heard the debates about it at Court. So now the adversaries of the Arians are wont to pray in secret in subterranean vaults, as in the time of the first persecutions."

Myrrha and Juventinus had lingered a little behind the others; Arsinoë and Anatolius could talk freely.

"Who is he?" asked the centurion with a nod towards Juventinus.

"The last scion of the ancient patrician family of the Furii," answered Arsinoë. "The mother wishes to make a consul of him. His only dream is to flee into some Thebaïd, or monkish community in the desert, to spend his days in prayer. He loves his mother and hides himself from her as from an enemy."

"The descendants of the Furii, monks? . . .'T is a queer age," sighed the Epicurean.

They approached the *arenarium*, old excavations in crumbling tufa, and went down narrow steps to the bottom of the quarry. The volcanic blocks of red earth looked strange-hued in the moonlight. Juventinus took a little clay lamp from a dark niche, and lighted it; the long flame flickered feebly in its narrow gullet.

They entered the darkness of the side galleries of the *arenarium*. Hollowed by the ancient Romans, the quarry was large and spacious and descended in steep slopes. It was therefore pierced by numerous galleries, for the use of workmen in transporting the tufa. Juventinus led his companions through the labyrinth and halted at last in front of a shaft from which he lifted the coverlid of wood; the party went cautiously down the damp and slippery steps; at the bottom was a narrow door; Juventinus knocked; the door opened, and a grey-headed monk introduced them into a passage hollowed in harder tufa. The walls on both sides from floor to vaulting were covered with slabs of marble, the seals of tombs in which coffins (*loculi*) were ranged.

At every step folk carrying lamps came to meet them. By the flickering light Anatolius read with curiosity on one of these stone flags: "Dorotheus, son of Felix, in this place of coolness, light, and peace, reposes" ("*requiescit in loco refrigii, luminis, pacis*"). On another: "Brethren, disturb not my deep slumber."

The style of the inscriptions was radiant and happy: "Sophronia, beloved, thou art alive forever in God" ("*Sophronia, dulcis, semper vivis Deo*"). And a little farther on: "*Sophronia vivis!*" ("Sophronia, thou livest!") as if he who had written these words had at length realised that there was no more death.

Nowhere was it written "He is buried here," but only "Here is laid for a certain time" (*depositus*). It seemed as if millions of people, generation upon generation, were lying in this place, not dead, but fallen asleep, all full of mysterious expectation. In the niches lamps were placed. They burned in the close atmosphere with a long steady flame and graceful vases exhaled penetrating odours. Nothing but the faint smell of putrefying bones, which escaped by fissures in the coffins, gave any hint of death.

The passages went down lower and lower, curved as round an amphitheatre; and here and there in the ceiling a large aperture gave light from *luminaria* opening on the country without.

Sometimes a weak moon-ray passing down the *luminaria* would strike at the bottom on a slab of marble covered with inscriptions.

At the end of one of these passages they saw a sexton who, chanting gaily, was hollowing the ground with heavy blows of his pick. Several

Christians were standing near the principal inspector of the tombs, the *fossor*. He was very well dressed and had a fat cunning face. The *fossor* had inherited a right freely to dispose of a gallery of catacombs, and to sell unoccupied sites in his gallery, which was all the more appreciated because in it were buried the relics of St. Laurence. Although rich, the *fossor* was keenly bargaining, as they came up, with a wealthy and miserly leather-merchant. Arsinoë stopped a moment to hear the discussion.

"And my tomb will be far away from the relics?" the leather-dresser was asking mistrustfully, thinking of the big sum exacted by the *fossor*.

"No, just six cubits away."

"Above or beneath?"

"On the right-hand side, sloping down a little. It's an excellent position; I don't ask a penny too much. Though you be as sinful as you please, everything will be forgiven. You will go straight into the heavenly kingdom."

With an expert hand the gravedigger took the measurements for the tomb as a tailor measures for a coat, the leather-dresser insisting that he should have as much room as possible in order to lie in comfort.

An old woman approached the sexton.

"What do you want, mother?"

"Here's the money—the extra payment!"

"What extra payment?"

"For the right-hand tomb."

"Ah, I see; you don't want the crooked one?"

"No; my old bones crack at the very idea of the crooked one."

In the catacombs, and especially near the relics, so much value was set upon grave-sites that it was necessary to contrive slanting tombs which were leased to the poor.

"God knows how long one will have to wait for the resurrection," the old woman was explaining; "and if I took a tomb on the slant it would be all very well to begin with, but when I got tired it wouldn't do at all."

Anatolius listened in astonishment.

"It is much more curious than the mysteries of Mithra," he observed to Arsinoë with a languid smile. "Pity that I didn't know it sooner. I've never seen such an amusing cemetery."

They went on into a rather large chamber called the *cubicula of consolation*. A multitude of small lamps were burning on the walls. The priest was at the evening office, the stone lid of a martyr's tomb placed under an arched vault (*arcosolium*) serving as altar. There were many of the faithful in long white robes, every face serenely happy. Myrrha, kneeling with eyes full of love, was gazing at the Good Shepherd pictured on the ceiling of the chamber. In the catacombs early Christian customs had been revived, so that after the liturgy all present, looking on themselves as brothers and sisters, gave each other the kiss of peace. Arsinoë following the general example with a smile kissed Anatolius.

Then all four climbed again toward the upper storeys, whence they could take their way to the secret retreat of Juventinus, an old pagan tomb, a *columbarium*, lying at some distance from the Appian Way. There, while waiting for the ship which was to take him to Egypt, the land of holy anchorites, he was living hidden from the searches of his mother and of government officials. He lodged with Didimus, a good old man from the Lower Thebaïd, to whom Juventinus gave blind and unquestioning obedience.

Here they found Didimus squatting on his heels, weaving basket-work. The moon-rays, filtering through a narrow opening, glinted on his white hair and long beard. From top to bottom of the walls of the *columbarium* were little niches like pigeons' nests, and each of these contained a mortuary urn.

Myrrha, of whom the old man was very fond, kissed his withered hand respectfully, and prayed him to tell her some story about the hermit fathers of the desert. Nothing pleased her better than these wonderful and terrible tales by Didimus.

The company grouped themselves round the white-headed old man, Myrrha watching him with feverish eyes and feeble hands clasped to her heaving breast. Nothing was heard save his voice and the distant hum of Rome, when suddenly, at the inner door communicating with the catacomb, a knock was heard.

Juventinus rose, went to the door and asked, without opening it—
"Who is there?"

No answer came, but a still gentler knock as of entreaty.

With great precaution Juventinus held the door ajar, shuddered and recoiled. A woman of tall stature came into the *columbarium*. Long white vestments enveloped her and a veil hid her face. Her gait was that of one recovering from an illness or of a very old woman. With a sudden movement she raised the veil and Juventinus cried—

"My mother!"

Didimus rose, a severe expression on his countenance.

The woman threw herself at the feet of her son and kissed them, grey tresses falling dishevelled over her lean and haggard face, which bore traces of high patrician beauty. Juventinus took the head of his mother between his hands and kissed it.

"Juventinus!" the old man called.

The young man made no response.

His mother, as if they had been completely alone, murmured hastily and joyously—

"O my son, I thought I should never see you again; I would have set out for Alexandria—O I would have found you even in the desert! But now all is over, is it not? Tell me that you will not go! Wait until I die! Afterwards do what you will. . ."

The old man resumed—

"Do you hear me, Juventinus?"

"Old man," answered the patrician mother, "you will not carry off a son from her that bore him! . . . Listen, if it must be so, I will deny the faith of my fathers; I will believe in the Crucified! . . . I will become a nun!"

"Ah, pagan! thou canst not understand the law of Christ. A mother cannot be a nun, nor can a nun be still a mother."

"I have borne him in anguish; he is mine!"

"It is not the soul, but the body, that you love."

The patrician woman cast at Didimus a look full of hatred.

"Be then accursed for your lying speeches," she exclaimed; "accursed, you stealers of children—tempters of the guileless! ye black-robed fearers of the celestial light—slaves of the Crucified! destroyers of all beauty and joy!"

Her face changed; she drew her son yet closer, and said chokingly—

"I know thee, my son! thou wilt not go. . . thou canst not. . ."

Old Didimus, cross in hand, stood at the open door leading to the catacombs. He said solemnly—

"For the last time, and in the name of God, I order you, my son, to follow me and to leave her."

Then the patrician relaxed her hold of Juventinus, and faltered—

"Then go! Let it be so. . . Leave me, if thou canst!"

Tears flowed no longer down her furrowed cheeks; her arms fell rigid, with a heart-broken gesture, to her sides. She waited. All were silent.

"O Lord, help me. . . inspire me!" Juventinus prayed in terrible distress.

"He who will follow Me, and will not hate father and mother, wife and children, brother and sister, and even his own life, can never be My disciple!"

These words were recited by Didimus, turning for the last time towards Juventinus—

"Remain in the world! Thou hast rejected Christ! Be accursed in this age and in the age to come!"

"No, no! Cast me not out, father! I am on your side. Lord, here am I," exclaimed Juventinus following his master.

His mother made no arresting movement; not a muscle of her face stirred; but when the noise of his footsteps died away a hoarse sob heaved her breast and she fell into a swoon.

"Open—in the name of the most holy Emperor Constantius!"

It was the summons of soldiery sent by the prefect to hunt the Sabæan rebels, on the denunciation of the patrician mother of Juventinus.

With a powerful lever the soldiers attempted to prise open the door of the *columbarium*, shaking the edifice on its foundations. The little silver urns vibrated plaintively under the blows. Half of the door gave way.

Anatolius, Myrrha, and Arsinoë rushed into the inner gallery. The Christians hurried along the narrow passages like ants disturbed in their mound, making for all the secret outlets communicating with the quarry. But Arsinoë and Myrrha, unfamiliar with the exact situation of the galleries, lost their way in the labyrinth and at last reached the lowest floor of all at a depth of fifty cubits under ground. It became difficult to breathe; muddy water lay under foot. The flame of the lamps became dim and almost blew out. Putrid miasmas filled the air. Myrrha felt her head swim and gradually lost consciousness.

Anatolius took her in his arms. At every step they feared to encounter the legionaries; all the outlets might be blocked and sealed up; they were running the risk of being buried alive.

At last they heard the voice of Juventinus calling—

"Here! here!"

Bent double, he was carrying the old Didimus on his back.

At the end of a few minutes they reached a secret door opening on the Campagna.

On returning to the house, Arsinoë quickly undressed Myrrha and put her to bed, still in a dead faint. Kneeling by her side the elder sister long kissed and chafed the thin, yellow, and inert hands. A pang of agonising presentiment shot through her heart.

The face of the sleeper bore a strange expression. Never had it reflected so bodiless a charm. All the little body seemed transparent and frail as the sides of an alabaster jar illumined by an inner fire.

XVIII

L ate one evening in a marshy wood not far from the Rhine, between the fortified post, *Tres Tabernæ* and the Roman town of Argentoratum,[1] conquered a short time previously by the *Alemanni*, two soldiers who had lost their way were slouching along. One named Aragaris, an awkward and red-headed giant, a Sarmatian in the Roman service; the other Strombix, a lean and frowning little Syrian.

The spaces between the trunks of trees were densely dark. A fine rain was falling through warm air. The birches diffused an odour of damp leaves, and far off a cuckoo was calling.

At every crack of the branches the startled Strombix began to quake and seized the fist of his companion.

"Oh, cousin! cousin!"

He used to call Aragaris cousin, not through blood relationship, but for friendship's sake. They had been taken into the Roman army from opposite ends of the world. The northern barbarian, a huge guzzler but a chaste liver, despised the voluptuous and timid Syrian who was so frugal in his eating and drinking. But while mocking him he pitied him as a child.

"Cousin!" wailed Strombix.

"Well, what is it? Can't you be quiet?"

"Are there bears in this wood?"

"Yes!" answered Aragaris sullenly.

"And suppose we met one, eh?"

"We should knock him on the head, sell his skin, and go and drink."

"And suppose the bear, instead of being killed. . ."

"Poltroon! it isn't difficult to see that you're a Christian!"

"Why must a Christian be a coward?" said Strombix with a vexed air.

"You've told me yourself that in your Book it is written *whosoever smiteth thee on thy right cheek turn to him the other also*."

"True."

"Well, I'm right; and if so, to my thinking you mustn't go to wars; the enemy will strike you on one cheek and you turn him round the other. You're a set of cowards, I say."

"The Cæsar Julian's a Christian, and *he* isn't a coward!" retorted Strombix.

---

1. Strasburg.

"I know, my boy," continued Aragaris, "that you can pardon enemies when you have to fight them, poor chicken! Your belly is no bigger than my fist. With a clove in it you're fed up for the whole day; and so your blood is no better than marsh-water!"

"Ah, cousin! cousin!" observed Strombix reproachfully, "why did you talk about food? Now I've got another gnawing ache in my stomach. Give me a little garlic! There's some left in your bag."

"If I give you what there's left we shall both starve tomorrow in this forest!"

"Ah, but if you don't give me some now, I shall fall from weakness and you will be obliged to carry me."

"Well, stuff and swill, dog!"

"And a little bread too," begged Strombix.

Aragaris gave him, with an oath, his last ration of biscuit. He himself had eaten overnight enough for two days, of fat pork and bean pottage.

"Attention! Hark!" he said halting. "There's a trumpet! We're not far from the camp. We must steer round to the north. . . I don't mind bears," added Aragaris thoughtfully, "but that centurion. . ."

The soldiers had nicknamed this hated centurion "Cedo Alteram," because he used to cry out gleefully everytime he broke the rod with which he was striking a delinquent, *Cedo alteram!* that is to say, "Give us another!"

"I'm certain," said the barbarian—"I'll wager that Cedo Alteram will tan my back as a tanner whacks a bullock's hide. It's abominable, my friend, abominable."

The worthy pair were now stragglers behind the army, because Aragaris according to his custom had got dead drunk in a plundered village and Strombix had been thrashed. The little Syrian had made a fruitless attempt to obtain the favours of a handsome Frankish girl. This sixteen-year-old-beauty, daughter of a barbarian killed in the fight, had administered to him two such blows that he had fallen on his back and had then fairly stamped upon him.

"She wasn't a girl but a devil," declared Strombix. "I hardly took hold of her and she nearly broke every rib in my body."

The note of the trumpet became more and more distinct. Aragaris, sniffing the wind like a blood-hound, noticed the smell of smoke; the bivouacs must be but a short way off.

The night became pitch dark. They could hardly make out the road; the path was lost in marshes in which they leapt from tussock to tussock. Fog began to rise. Suddenly from a great yew, with branches from which moss hung like long grey beards, something fled away with a harsh cry. Strombix crouched down with fear. It was a black cock.

They finally lost their bearings. Strombix climbed a tree.

"The bivouacs lie northwards—not far off. There's a wide river below."

"The Rhine, the Rhine!" exclaimed Aragaris. "Now go ahead!"

They slid down through the birches and aspen trees a hundred years old.

"Cousin, I'm drowning!" yelled Strombix. "Somebody's hauling me by the feet!"

"Where are you?"

With great difficulty Aragaris extricated him, and, swearing, took him on his shoulders. Under his feet the Sarmatian felt the stems of faggots laid down by the Romans. This causeway of faggot work led to the great road hewn not long before through the forest by the army of Severus, Julian's general. The barbarians, according to their custom, had blocked and encumbered the track with enormous trunks of trees. These trunks had to be clambered over. Sometimes rotten, moss-covered, and crumbling under foot, and sometimes hard and slippery with rain, they made the march most difficult; and it was by roads like these, always in fear of an attack, that the army of about thirteen thousand men had to move. That army every Imperial general except Severus had traitorously abandoned.

Strombix was cursing his comrade—

"I won't go a step farther, heathen! I'd rather lie down on the dead leaves and die; at least I should not see your damned visage—huh! Unbeliever! It's easy to see that you don't wear the cross! Is it a Christian's business to drag along a road like this, and what are we pushing on to? The rods of the centurion. I won't go a step farther."

Aragaris hauled him on by main force, and, when the road became more practicable, carried shoulder-high the whimsical companion who kept abusing and pummelling him all the time and shortly fell soundly asleep on those mighty pagan shoulders.

At midnight they reached the gates of the Roman camp. Everything was still. The drawbridge had long been raised. The friends had to sleep in the wood near the hinder gate, usually called the Decumanal.

At dawn the trumpet sounded. The nightingale had been singing in the misty wood; he ceased, frightened by the warlike notes. Aragaris snuffed the smell of soup and woke Strombix. They made their way into the camp and sat down near the cauldrons. In the principal tent near the Pretorian gate the Cæsar Julian was keeping watch.

From the day on which he had been nominated Cæsar at Milan thanks to the protection of the Empress Eusebia, Julian had applied himself with zeal to soldierly exercises. He not only used to study the art of war under the direction of Severus, but desired moreover to master every detail of the work of the rank and file. Within sound of the trumpet, in barracks, on the Campus Martius in company with new recruits, during whole days he would learn to march, to use the bow and sling, to leap ditches, and to run under the heavy weight of full marching order. He became also an adept in swordsmanship.

The blood of the race of Constantine, a race of austere and obstinate warriors, woke in the young man and overcame his monkish hypocrisy.

"Alack! divine Iamblicus and Plato! if you could only see what your pupil is becoming!" he would sometimes exclaim, wiping the sweat from his brow.

And pointing to his armour he would add—

"Don't you think, Severus, that this steel sits as badly on a pupil of philosophers as a war-saddle on an ox?"

Severus would only reply by a mischievous smile; he knew that these sighings and complaints were not sincere, and that in reality Julian was delighted with his military progress.

In a few months he had been so transformed and hardened into manhood that it was not easy to recognise in him the "little Greek" of the Court of Constantius. His eyes alone had not changed, still shining with a strange and unforgettable keenness which had in it something of fever. Julian felt himself growing stronger everyday, not only physically, but morally also. For the first time in his existence he felt the happiness that comes from the love of simple and common folk.

From the first it had gratified the legionaries to see a real Cæsar, cousin of the Augustus, learning soldiering in barracks, with no repugnance for the coarse fare of soldiers. Austere faces of the veterans would light up with grim tenderness as they watched young Cæsar, and remembering their own youth wondered at his rapid progress. Julian used to hail them, listen to their gossip over old campaigns, and advice about fastening the breastplate so that the straps might chafe less and the best way of holding the foot while marching to avoid over-fatigue.

The rumour went round that the Emperor Constantius had sent the inexperienced young man among the barbarians of Gaul to get killed, that he himself might be rid of a rival. It was said that the generals, following the hints of Imperial eunuchs, had abandoned and betrayed the young Cæsar accordingly. All this increased the affection of the legions for Julian.

Skilled in the arts of winning favour, acquired during his monkish education, Julian cautiously used every means to strengthen the love felt towards himself and to deepen the unpopularity of the Emperor. Before the soldiers he would speak of his brother Constantius with meaning humility, lowering his eyes and affecting the aspect of a victim. It was the easier for him to captivate the warriors by fearlessness, inasmuch as death in battle seemed to him a thing to be desired. The kind of death to which Gallus had been subjected formed no part of his designs.

Julian had organised his life after the austere example of ancient conquerors. His stoic education by the tutor Mardonius helped him to endure total absence of comfort. He allowed himself less sleep than the meanest soldier, and lay not on a bed but upon a coarse rough carpet, like that called in popular parlance *suburra*.

The first part of the night was devoted to sleep, the second to the business of state and war, the third to the Muses. For Julian's favourite books were never left behind when he was campaigning. He inspired himself with Marcus Aurelius, Plutarch, Suetonius, and Cato the elder; and by day he endeavoured to put in practice what he had mused over with them by night.

On the memorable morning before the battle of Argentoratum, when he heard the *reveillé* at dawn, Julian quickly donned complete armour, and ordered his charger to be brought round. While waiting he withdrew into the inmost part of the tent. There was ensconced a lovely statuette of the winged Mercury, bearing the caduceus—the god of movement, gaiety, success. Julian bowed before the image and threw some grains of incense on a little tripod. According to the direction of the smoke the Cæsar, who flattered himself that he understood the divining art, sought to ascertain the influence of the day. Overnight he had heard a raven crying three times—a bad omen.

Julian was so convinced that his unexpected military success in Gaul was due to some supernatural power that from day today he became more superstitious.

When issuing from the tent he stumbled over the wooden beam at the threshold. The face of the Cæsar darkened. All the omens were unfavourable; he inwardly resolved to postpone the battle till the morrow.

The army began its march. The road through the forest was painful. Masses of trees embarrassed every step. The day promised to be a very hot one. The army had only done half its journey, and there remained more than one and twenty Roman miles to cover to reach the camp of the German barbarians (Alemanni) which lay on the left bank of the Rhine in a great plain, near the town Argentoratum.

The soldiers were worn out. As soon as they had crossed the forest and reached open ground Julian assembled them round himself in a great circle, like spectators in an amphitheatre, so as himself to be the centre of the centurions and cohorts, extending from him like the spokes of a huge wheel. This was the custom of the Roman army, so that the greatest possible number could hear the words of their general.

Julian explained to the legions in a few brief and simple sentences that fatigue might prevent success, that it would be safer to camp for that night in the field where they were, to rest, and attack the barbarians the following morning, with vigour renewed.

Discontented murmurs ran through the army; the rank and file struck their shields with lances—a sign of impatience—clamouring that Julian should lead them without delay to the field of battle. The Cæsar understood by the general expression on faces around him that in resisting he would commit a grave mistake. He felt in the crowd that thrill of ferocity with which he was so familiar, which was so indispensable to victory, and by the least maladroitness so easily to be changed into mutiny. He leapt on horseback and gave the signal to continue the march. Peals of enthusiasm answered him and the army moved off.

When the sun was beginning to sink they reached the plain of Argentoratum. There the Rhine was shining between low hills. To the south rose the sombre mass of the Vosges Mountains, and swallows were sweeping over the surface of the majestic German river.

Suddenly, on the nearest hill, three riders appeared; they were the Alemanni.

The Romans halted, and disposed themselves in battle-order. Julian, surrounded by six hundred steel-clad horsemen, the Clibanarii, commanded the horsemen of the right wing. On the left extended the infantry, under the orders of Severus. Julian himself was also under the command of this general.

The barbarians opposed their cavalry to that of Julian. At their head rode the Alemannic king Chlodomir. Fronting Severus, Agenaric, the young nephew of Chlodomir, led the German infantry.

War-horns, trumpets, and fifes resounded; ensigns and flags inscribed with the names of cohorts, the purple dragons and Roman eagles, assembled at the head of the legions. In the van strode axe-bearers, chief centurions, and *primipilares*, men bred to victory. Their regular and heavy tread shook the earth. Suddenly the foot soldiers of Severus halted. The barbarians, who had been lurking in a trench, sprang from their ambuscade and attacked the Romans. Julian from a distance saw the confusion that ensued and galloped up to restore order. He attempted to calm the soldiers, speaking hastily now to one cohort, now to another, in something of the concise style of Julius Cæsar. When he uttered the words, "*Exurgamus viri fortes*" or "*Advenit, socii, justem pugnandi jam tempus,*" this young man of twenty-two was thinking with pride: "At last I am like such and such a famous soldier!" Even in the very fire of action he never forgot his books, and rejoiced to enact over again familiar scenes of Livy, Plutarch, and Sallust. The well-tried Severus restrained his ardour, and, while giving a certain liberty to Julian, retained the general direction of the action. Arrows whizzed and barbarian javelins, dragging long cords; and war-engines flung huge stones hundreds of yards.

The Romans now found themselves face to face at last with the terrible and mysterious inhabitants of the North, about whom so many incredible legends were afloat. Some wore bear-skins on their backs, and on their shaggy heads the gaping jaws of wolves. Others had their helms adorned with the horns of stag and bull. The Alemanni were so contemptuous of death that, keeping only lance and sword, they frequently flung themselves into battle stark naked.

Their reddish hair was knotted on the top of their heads and fell back on the neck in a thick mass or plaited mane. They wore long sweeping broad moustaches and their skins were deeply bronzed. A great number were so savage that, unfamiliar with the use of steel, they fought with bone-tipped lances dipped in violent poison. A scratch from this primitive barb was sufficient to produce a slow death in terrible agony. From head to foot, instead of armour they wore thin scales pared from the hoofs of horses and sewn on linen, a kind of horny mail. In this array the barbarians seemed strange monsters, clad in birds' feathers and fish scales.

There were also Saxons with pale blue eyes, men for whom the sea had no terrors, but who feared the land.

The foremost *primipilares*, locking their shields together, formed a compact wall of steel, and advanced steadily, slowly, almost invulnerable to blows. The Alemanni rushed upon this wall with ferocious cries, like the hoarse growls of bears. The main fight began, breast against breast, shield against shield. Dust was so thick over the plain that the sun was darkened. At this moment on the right wing the iron-clad horses of the Clibanarii began rearing and taking fright. The stampede threatened to crush the legions of the reargard. Through the cloud of arrows and lances, the fire-coloured scarf of the gigantic king Chlodomir was shining in bright sunlight.

Julian in the nick of time galloped up on his black charger, bespattered with foam. He grasped the situation. The barbarian foot-soldiers, placed for the purpose between their horsemen, were slipping under the legs of the Roman horses, and disembowelling them; the horses fell, dragging down in their fall the *cataphracti*, or men in scale-armour, who, overwhelmed under its weight, were unable to rise. Julian placed himself directly behind the flying horsemen; it was a question of either stemming the flight or being crushed himself. The tribune of the Clibanarii came into collision with him. Pale with shame and terror, he recognised Julian. Julian's forehead flushed purple, he forgot his classical books, leaned over, seized the flying man by the throat, and shouted with a voice which appeared to himself strangely savage—

"Coward!"

Then he faced the tribune round to the enemy. The *cataphracti* halted, glanced at the purple dragon, the Imperial ensign, and remained motionless. In a moment the mass of iron recoiled and swept back anew against the barbarians. The fight became a wild confusion. A lance struck Julian full in the breast; he owed his safety to his breastplate. An arrow hissed by his ear, grazing his cheek with its feathers. Severus now sent the legions of the Cornuti and Brakathi, half-savage allies of the Romans, to succour the wavering cavalry. They were wont to sing their war-hymn, the Barrith, only when their blood was up in the joy of battle, intoning it in a low and plaintive voice. The first notes were calm as the nocturnal sighing of woods; but little by little the Barrith became louder, more solemn, and terrible, until at last, raising a furious and deafening roar like a stormy sea, all the singers were beside themselves.

Julian ceased to see or understand the surge of battle round him; he was conscious only of intolerable thirst and a sharp aching in the bones of his sword hand; he had lost all reckoning of time. But Severus kept all his presence of mind, and directed the fight with incomparable skill. Perplexed and heart-broken, Julian perceived the orange scarf of Chlodomir in the midst of the legions; the barbarians had penetrated obliquely into the centre of the Roman army. Julian thought "All is lost!" He remembered the unfavourable presages of the morning and addressed a last prayer to the gods of Olympus—

"Come, help me! For who is there but I to restore you to power upon earth?"

In the centre of the army were stationed the old veterans of the Petulant legion, so called on account of their rashness. Severus counted on them, and his reliance was not in vain. One of them shouted—

"*Viri fortissimi!* Bravest of the brave, let us not betray Rome and our Cæsar! Let us die for Julian! Glory and prosperity to Cæsar Julian!"

"For Rome. . . for Rome. . ." stern voices responded, and these tried legions, grown grey under the flag, once again went to meet death, steady and cheery. The inspiring breath of great Rome swept over the whole army.

Julian, his eyes full of enthusiastic tears, rode towards the veterans to die along with them. Again he felt the force of sheer affection, the force of the people lifting him on its wings to carry him to victory.

Then terror seized the barbaric masses; they trembled, broke, and fled; and the eagles of the legions, their rapacious beaks and outspread wings glittering in the sun, swooped down again amongst the routed tribes, proclaiming the victory of the Eternal City.

The Alemanni and Franks perished fighting to the last gasp.

Kneeling in a pool of blood, the savage would wield his sword or lance with a slackening hand, but in his troubled eyes were to be seen neither fear nor despair, only thirst for vengeance and contempt for his conquerors. Even those who were left for dead arose, half-crushed, and fixed their teeth in the legs of their enemies. Six thousand barbarians fell in that battle or were drowned in the Rhine.

The same evening, as Julian Cæsar stood on the hill, enveloped by the rays of the setting sun, King Chlodomir, who had been made prisoner on the bank of the river, was led before him. He was breathing with difficulty, his face livid and sweating, his enormous hands bound behind his back. He knelt down before his conqueror, and the young Cæsar of twenty-two laid his slight hand upon the shaggy head.

XIX

I t was the time of vintage; all day songs had been echoing along the hill-sides around the pleasant Gulf of Naples.

In the favourite country of the Romans, at Baiæ, famous for its sulphur-baths, Baiæ of which the Augustan poets used to say,

Nullus in orbe sinus Baiis prælucet amoenis,—

idle folk were delighting in the country and Nature; there fairer and more voluptuous than man.

It was an inviolate corner of that charming country, where the imaginations of Horace, Propertius, and Tibullus lingered yet. Not a single shadow of the monkish age had yet dulled that sunny littoral between Vesuvius and Cape Misenum. Christianity it is true was not denied there; but it was smilingly put by. Feminine sinners there were not yet repentant. On the contrary honest women grew shy of virtue as old-fashioned. When news of the Sibyl's prophecies arrived, menacing the decrepit world with earthquake, or when came news of fresh crimes and bigotries of Constantius, or of Persians invading the East, or barbarians threatening the North, the lucky inhabitants of Baiæ, closing their eyes, inhaled their delicious breeze full of the odour of Falernian half-crushed in the wine-press, and consoled themselves with an epigram. To forget the misfortunes of Rome and soothsay about the end of the world, all that they needed was to send each other gifts of pretty verses—

Calet unda, friget æthra,
Simul innatat choreis
Amathusium renidens
Salis arbitræ et vaporis,
Flos siderum Dione!

On the faces of the gayest Epicureans could be seen something at once senile and puerile. Neither the fresh salt water of the sea bath nor the warm sulphurous springs of Baiæ could completely cure the bodies of these withered and chilly young men, bald and old at twenty, not through their own debauches, but through sins of their ancestors;

youths on whom women, wisdom, and literature had begun to pall; witty and impotent young men, in whose veins ran the blood of too late a generation.

In one of the most flowery and pleasant nooks between Baiæ and Puteoli and under the dark slopes of the Apennine, rose the white marble walls of a villa.

Near the wide window, opening directly on the sea, so that from the chamber sky and sea alone were visible, Myrrha was lying on a bed.

The doctors had not understood her malady; but Arsinoë, who watched her sister day by day losing strength and vitality, had brought her from Rome to the sea-coast.

Notwithstanding her illness Myrrha would clean and arrange her chamber with her own hands, in imitation of nuns and hermits; and would herself bring water, and attempt to wash linen, and do her own cookery. For weeks, and to the very last stage of her illness, she obstinately refused to go to bed, spending whole nights in prayer. One day the terrified Arsinoë found a hair-shirt on the weak body of her sister. Myrrha had taken all articles of luxury from her little chamber, stripping it of curtains and ornaments, and leaving nothing but a bed and a coarse wooden crucifix. The bare-walled room was "her cell." She also fasted strictly and Arsinoë found it difficult to oppose the gentle obstinacy of her will.

From the life of Arsinoë all listlessness had disappeared. She wavered continually between hope of restoring Myrrha to health and despair at losing her. And although she could not love her sister more passionately than before, yet, dominated by the fear of their eternal separation, she understood her own love more clearly.

Sometimes, with motherly pity, Arsinoë would gaze upon that wasted face, and the little body in which so fierce a fire was burning. When the sick girl refused wine and food prescribed by the physician, Arsinoë would say in vexation—

"Do you think I am blind, Myrrha? Are you trying to kill yourself?"

"Are not life and death equal in our eyes?" answered the young girl, with such earnestness that Arsinoë could only reply—

"You do not love me! . . ."

But Myrrha used to say caressingly—

"Beloved, you do not know how much I love you! Oh, if you could only. . ."

The invalid would never finish the sentence, nor ask her sister if she held the faith. But in her sad glance at Arsinoë, as if not daring utterance, Arsinoë read reproach. Nevertheless, she was herself unwilling to speak about that faith, not having the courage to communicate her doubt, for fear of perhaps robbing her sister of the mad hope of immortality.

Myrrha weakened from day today, waning like the wax of a taper; but from day today grew more joyous and more calm.

Juventinus, who had quitted Rome lest his mother should follow him, was waiting at Naples with Didimus for the departure of the ship for Alexandria. He came to see the sisters every evening. He used to read aloud the Gospels and tell legends of the saints. . . Oh, how Myrrha longed to journey to those dark caves and live near those great and holy lives! The desert to her appeared not dull and sterile, but flowery, a wondrous earthly paradise, lighted by a light such as shone on no other region. Indoors she grew stifled; and sometimes, fevered by the pains of sickness, and languishing after the Thebaïd, she used to watch the white sails of ships disappear in the distance and stretch out her pale hands towards them. Oh, to flee after them and breathe the pure air and silence of the desert! Many a time she would try to rise, declaring she felt better, would soon be well, and in secret kept hoping that they would allow her to set sail with Didimus and Juventinus, on the ship for Alexandria.

Anatolius, Arsinoë's faithful admirer, was also living at Baiæ. The young Epicurean used to organise delightful excursions in his gilded galley from the Bay to the Pæstan Gulf, with gay companions and pretty women. What he loved most was to see the purple sails bowing over the sleepy sea; hues of twilight melting on the cliffs of Capreæ and Ischia, looking like enormous amethysts lying in the water. It pleased him to ridicule his friends about their faith. The fragrance of wines and the intoxicating kisses of courtesans pleased him also.

But everytime he went into Myrrha's quiet little cell he would become aware that another side of life also lay open to him. The innocent grace and the pale countenance of the young girl touched him deeply. He longed to believe in anything in which she believed: the gentle Galilean, and the miracle of immortality. He would listen to the tales of Juventinus, and the life of desert anchorites he, too, thought sublime. Anatolius observed with surprise that for himself truth existed both in the intoxication of life and in its renunciation; both in the triumph of matter and in the triumph of soul; both in chastity and in voluptuousness. His intelligence remained clear, and his conscience without remorse.

Even doubt had for him its pleasure, like a kind of new game. These deep and gentle waves of opinion, transitions from Christianity to Paganism, lulled his soul rather than distressed it.

One evening Myrrha fell asleep before the open window. On awakening, she said to Juventinus with a bright smile—

"I've had a strange dream. . ."

"What was it?"

"I don't remember. But it was happy. Do you think that the whole world will gain salvation?"

"All the righteous; sinners will be punished."

"Righteous? sinners? . . . That is not my idea," answered Myrrha, still smiling, as if she was trying to remember the dream. "Do you know, Juventinus, that all, all shall be saved, and that God will not suffer one to be lost!"

"So the great master Origen believed. He used to say, 'My Saviour cannot rejoice so long as I am in iniquity.' But that is a heresy. . ."

Myrrha, not listening, went on—

"Yes! yes! that must be so. I understand it at last. All shall be saved, to the very last. God will not allow one of His creatures to perish."

"I wish I too could believe it," murmured Juventinus, "but I should be afraid. . ."

"One must fear nothing; where there is love, fear is cast out. I do not fear anything."

"And He?" demanded Juventinus.

"Who?"

"He, the Unnameable, the Arch-rebel!"

"He also, He also!" cried Myrrha, with strong conviction. "So long as there shall be even a soul that has not gained salvation, no creature can enjoy full felicity. If there be no bounds to Love, if Love is infinite, then all shall be in God, and God in all. Friend, will not that be happiness? We have not yet taken full account of that. Every soul must be blessed, do you understand?"

"And Evil?"

"There is no evil, if there is no Death."

Through the open window came the echo of the Bacchic songs of the friends of Anatolius, making merry in their purple galleys on the blue twilight sea.

DMITRY MEREZHKOVSKY

Myrrha pointed to them—

"And that is also beautiful, and that is also to be blest," she murmured.

"What? These vicious songs?" asked Juventinus, dreading her reply.

Myrrha shook her head—

"No! all is well, all is pure. Beauty comes from God. Friend, what are you afraid of? To love, one must be unspeakably free! . . . Fear absolutely nothing. You are still ignorant what happiness life can give!"

She drew a deep sigh and added—

"And what happiness death gives too!"

It was their last talk together. Myrrha lay in bed for several days, motionless and silent, without opening her eyes. She may have suffered much, for her brows would sometimes contract with pain; but a gentle smile of resignation would follow; not a groan, not a complaint escaped the closed lips.

Once, at midnight, she called Arsinoë, who was sitting beside her. The sick girl spoke with difficulty; she asked, without opening her eyes—

"Is it yet day?"

"No, night still," answered Arsinoë, "but the sun will soon rise."

"I cannot hear. . . Who are you?" Myrrha murmured indistinctly.

"It is I, Arsinoë."

The invalid suddenly opened her wide luminous eyes and gazed fixedly on her sister.

"It seemed to me," said Myrrha with an effort, "it seemed to me that it was not you. . . that I was utterly alone."

Then very slowly, with great difficulty, being scarcely able to move, she brought her transparent hands together, with an imploring look of fear. The corners of the lips trembled, the eyebrows moved.

"Do not abandon me! When I die, do not think that I am no more!"

Arsinoë leaned towards her, but Myrrha was too weak to kiss her, although she tried to do so. Arsinoë brought her cheek closer to the great eyes, and the young girl softly caressed her face with the long lashes. Arsinoë felt on her cheek a touch light as butterfly's velvety wings. It was a trick invented by Myrrha in childhood.

That last caress brought back to Arsinoë all their life together, all their mutual affection. She fell on her knees and, for the first time for years, sobbed irresistibly, as if the tears were melting her inmost heart.

"No, Myrrha," she said, "I will not abandon you. . . I will stay with you always!"

Myrrha's eyes grew animated and joyous; she faltered—

"Then you—"

"Yes; I long to believe; *I will believe!*" exclaimed Arsinoë, and immediately wondered. Those words appeared a miracle to herself, and no deception. She had no wish to recall them.

"I will go into the desert, Myrrha; like you, instead of you," she continued in a transport of wild love; "and, if God exists, He must grant that there shall be no death between us; so that we *shall* be always together."

Myrrha closed her eyes, listening to her sister. With a smile of infinite peace, she murmured—

"Now, I will go to sleep. I want nothing more. I am well."

She never opened her eyes or spoke again; her face was calm and severe as the face of the dead; and in this state she lived on several days longer.

When a cup of wine was brought near to her lips, she would swallow a few mouthfuls. If her breathing became nervous and irregular, Juventinus would chant a prayer or some divine hymn, and then, as if soothed, Myrrha began to breathe more easily.

One evening, when the sun had set behind Ischia and Capreæ, while the motionless sea was melting into heaven, and the first dim star trembling, Juventinus was singing to the dying girl—

Deus creator omnium
Polique rector vestiens,
Diem decore lumine
Noctem sopora gratia.

Perhaps Myrrha's last sigh was breathed to the sound of that solemn hymn. None knew when she died. There seemed no change. Her life mingled painlessly with the impalpable, inviolable, the Eternal, as the warmth of a fair twilight melts into the coolness of night.

Arsinoë buried her sister in the catacombs, and with her own hand engraved on the slab, "*Myrrha, vivis!*" ("Myrrha, thou livest.")

She scarcely wept. But she bore in her heart contempt for the world, and the resolve to believe in God, or at least to do all she could to attain belief in Him. She desired to distribute her fortune to the poor, and to set out for the Thebaïd. On the very day Arsinoë informed her indignant guardian of these intentions she received from Gaul a curt and enigmatic letter from Cæsar Julian—

"Julian, to the most noble Arsinoë, happiness! Do you remember the matter about which we spoke together at Athens, in front of the statue of Artemis? Do you remember our alliance? Great is my hate, but greater yet is my love. It may be that the lion shall fling away the ass's skin soon. Meantime, let us be gentle as doves and wise as serpents, according to the counsel of the Nazarean Christ."

Composers of Court epigrams, who mockingly nicknamed Julian "Victorinus" or "the little Conqueror," were astonished to receive, time after time, news of the Cæsar's continual victories. The laughable gradually became the terrible. General discussion arose about witchcrafts and secret dæmonic forces backing the fortunes of the friend of Maximus of Ephesus.

Julian had conquered and restored to the Roman Empire Argentoratum, Bracomagum,[1] Tres Tabernæ,[2] Noviomagus,[3] Vangiones,[4] Moguntiacum.[5]

The soldiers worshipped him as much as ever; and Julian became more and more convinced that the Olympians were protecting him and advancing his cause. But, for prudential reasons, he continued to attend Christian churches, and in the town of Vienna on the banks of the river Rhodanus he had been present at an especially solemn mass.

In the middle of December the conquering Cæsar was returning after a long campaign to winter quarters in his beloved Parisis-Lutetia on the banks of the Seine.

Night was closing in. The southern soldiers were marvelling at the pale green lights of the northern sky. New-fallen snow sounded crisply under the tread of the soldiers. Lutetia, built on a little island, was surrounded by wide river-channels. Two wooden bridges connected the town with steep banks. Its houses were built in the Gallo-Roman style, with broad glazed galleries, instead of the open porticoes of southern countries. The smoke of a multitude of chimneys hung over the town, and the trees were hoar with frost.

Fig-trees carefully swaddled in straw, and brought by the Romans from the south, clung to the southward-facing walls of the gardens, like children dreading the cold.

This year, in spite of occasional thawing winds from the south, the winter had been severe. Huge blocks of ice, crashing and grinding together, were floating down the Seine. The Greek and Roman soldiers

---

1. Brumat near Strasburg.
2. Saverne (Vosges).
3. Spires.
4. Worms.
5. Mayence.

used to watch these in surprise, and Julian too wondered at the beauty of the blue and green transparent masses, and compared them to Phrygian marble, with its emerald-hued veins.

There was something in the sad beauty of the North which, like a distant remembrance, haunted and thrilled his heart, as now he and his troop arrived at the palace, of which the brick arcades and turrets rose in sharp black outline against the twilight sky.

Julian went into the library. The cold was intense; a great fire was kindled on the hearth, and letters which had arrived at Lutetia during his absence were brought to him. One of these from Asia Minor came from Iamblicus. Julian thought that the fragrance of the East came with it.

Outside a hurricane was raging, and the wind roaring by struck violent blows on the closed shutters. Shutting his eyes, Julian dreamed of marble porticoes and gleaming temples veiled in obscurity, sweeping away to the horizon to disappear like golden clouds.

He shivered, rose, and noticed that the fire had gone out. He could hear a mouse gnawing the parchments in the library.

Julian suddenly felt a longing to see a human face. With a half-humorous smile he remembered that he had a wife. She was a relative of the Empress Eusebia, named Helena, whom the Emperor had forced to marry Julian shortly before his departure for Gaul. Julian cared nothing for Helena. Although more than a year had elapsed since their marriage he had scarcely seen her; he knew nothing of her, and had never passed a night under the same roof. His wife had remained a virgin.

From youth up, her dream had been to become the spouse of Christ. The idea of marriage filled her with disgust. At first she had thought all was lost, but, seeing afterwards that Julian asked from her no conjugal caresses, she grew calmer and lived in her apartment, morose, placid, dressed in black, the life of a nun. In her prayers Helena had vowed perpetual chastity.

On this night a mischievous curiosity drove Julian to the tower in which his wife was praying. He opened the door without knocking, and went into the feebly lighted cell; the virgin was kneeling before a lectern above which hung a large crucifix.

Julian approached, and screening the flame of the lamp with one hand, gazed at his wife for some minutes, frowning. She was so absorbed in devotion that she did not notice him. He said—

"Helena!"

She uttered a cry and turned her pale severe face towards Julian.

"How you startled me!"

He looked wonderingly at the great crucifix, the gospel, and the lectern, and murmured—

"Are you always praying?"

"Yes! I pray for you also, well-beloved Cæsar."

"For me? Really! . . . Confess that you believe me to be a great sinner?"

She lowered her eyes without answering. His frown became deeper.

"Do not be afraid; speak out. Don't you believe that I am specially guilty, in some manner, before God?"

She answered in a low voice—

"Specially? . . . Yes, I think so. Do not be angry. . ."

"I was sure of it. . . Now tell me what it is? I must repent me of my crimes."

Helena resumed, in a yet lower voice, and more severely—

"Do not laugh! I have to answer for your soul before the Eternal—"

"You. . . for mine?"

"We are joined forever."

"By what?"

"The sacrament of marriage."

"Religious marriage? But up till now we are strangers to one another, Helena!"

"I fear for your soul, Julian," she repeated, fixing on him her innocent eyes.

Placing his hand on her shoulder, he gazed mockingly at the pale face, so cold in its chastity. The small and lovely mouth, with its rosy lips half parted with an expression of fear and inquiry, was in strange contrast to the rest of the face. Julian leaned towards her, and before she had time to regain her presence of mind, kissed her on the lips.

She started and rushed to a far corner of the room, hiding her face in her hands. Then gazing at Julian, her eyes wild with fear, she hastily crossed herself, murmuring—

"Away, away, O evil one! I know thee; thou art not Julian, but the Devil. In the name of the most Holy Cross, I conjure thee. . . disappear!"

Anger seized Julian; he turned to the door and bolted it; then approaching Helena with a smile he said—

"Be yourself, Helena; I am a man—I am your husband—and not the Devil! The Church has blessed our union." He gazed upon her with strangely warring emotions. She slowly drew her hands from her eyes.

"Forgive me. . . it seemed to me. . . you frightened me so, Julian. . . I know that you desire nothing evil. . . but I have had visions. . . Just now I believed. . . He haunts this place at night. Twice I have seen him. . . He said to me ill things about you. Since then I have been afraid. He told me you bore on your face the mark of Cain. . . Why do you look at me so, Julian?"

She was trembling and leaning against the wall; he approached and put his arm round her waist.

"What are you doing? Let me go, let me go!"

She tried to cry out, to call the servant.

"Eleutheria! Eleutheria!"

"Why are you calling? Am I not your husband?"

She began to weep bitterly.

"Brother, this must not be. . . I am the bride of Christ! . . . I believed that you. . ."

"The bride of the Roman Cæsar cannot be the bride of Christ!"

"Julian! . . . If you believe in Him. . ."

He smiled.

"I abhor the Galilean!"

In a supreme effort she strove to repulse him, exclaiming, "Away, Devil! . . . Why hast thou abandoned me, Lord?"

With his impious hands he tore off the black vestment. His soul was full of fear, but never before in his life had he known such intoxication in evil-doing. Ironically, with a smile of defiance, the Roman Cæsar gazed at the opposite corner of the cell, where in the feeble flicker of the lamp-light hung the great black crucifix. . .

XXI

More than two years had elapsed since the victory of Argentoratum. Julian had delivered Gaul from the barbarians. At the beginning of spring, when still at Lutetia for his winter quarters, he had received an important letter from the Emperor Constantius brought by the tribune Decensius.

Each new victory achieved in Gaul harried the soul of Constantius, and stabbed his vanity to the quick. This "street-urchin," this "magpie," this "monkey in the purple," this "pocket conqueror," to the indignation of Court scoffers had turned into a veritable victor.

Constantius writhed with jealousy. At the same time he sustained defeat after defeat in his own campaign against the Persians in the Asiatic provinces. He grew thin, sleepless, lost his appetite, and twice suffered from terrible attacks of vomiting. The Court physicians were in dismay.

Sometimes, during nights of insomnia, lying in bed under the sacred standard of Constantine, the Emperor mused:

"Eusebia deceived me! But for her I should have followed the wise counsel of Mercurius. . . I should have had his throat cut in some dark corner! I should have exterminated this serpent from the Flavian nest! . . . Imbecile that I was! . . . It was I, myself, who let him escape! And who knows? . . . Perhaps Eusebia herself was his mistress?"

A long-delayed jealousy made his envy bitterer still. He could not revenge himself on the Empress Eusebia, who was dead. His second wife, Faustine, was an empty-headed little woman for whom he felt nothing but contempt.

Constantius tore the hair on which hairdressers still spent such infinite pains, and shed tears of rage. Had he not protected the Church? Had he not swept all heresies to destruction? Had he not built and adorned monastery after monastery? Did he not regularly accomplish all due rites and offices? And now what reward was granted him? For the first time the master of the world felt his soul swelling in indignation against the Master of the universe. A dark imprecation rose to his lips.

To assuage his jealousy he had recourse to unusual means. He sent letters to all great cities,—"letters of victory," adorned with laurels, and announcing the triumphs granted by the grace of God to the Emperor Constantius. These letters were to the effect that it was Constantius and not Julian who had four times crossed the Rhine,—Constantius (who was really frittering away his army at the other end of the world). It was Constantius, and not Julian, who had almost perished from arrows at Argentoratum! Constantius who had taken Chlodomir prisoner; Constantius who had pierced marshes and impracticable forests, hewn roads, stormed fortresses and endured hunger, thirst, heat; who, more wearied than the soldiers, had allotted to himself less sleep than they.

Julian's name was never mentioned in these despatches, as if that Cæsar were no longer in existence. The people applauded Constantius as conqueror of the Gauls, and in all the churches, bishops and archbishops chanted prayers and thanksgivings for victory granted to him over the barbaric Alemanni.

Julian on hearing of these follies contented himself with a smile. But the Emperor's gnawing jealousy was not sated. He decided to rob Julian of his best soldiers, and then by imperceptible steps and fleeting pretences to disarm him, as Gallus had been disarmed; to draw him into the toils and deal him the mortal blow.

With this intention he sent with a letter to Lutetia a certain skilful official, the tribune Decensius. He was forthwith to select the most trusted legions, namely, the Heruli, Batavians, Petulants, and Celts; and to despatch them into Asia for the Emperor's own use. Moreover, this dignitary was to deflower each remaining legion of its three hundred bravest warriors; and Cintula, tribune of the Imperial stables, was instructed to take the pick of the porters and baggage-carriers, and, having thus crippled Julian's transport, to bring these men to the East.

Julian warned Decensius, and proved to him that rebellion was inevitable among the savage legions raised in Gaul, who would almost certainly prefer to die rather than quit their native soil. But that obstinate official, preserving an imperturbable haughtiness on his wily yellow face, took no account of these observations.

At right angles to one of the wooden bridges which joined the island of Lutetia to the river-banks, stretched long, low barrack buildings. All the morning the soldiery had been excited and tumultuous. The stern and wise discipline hitherto observed by Julian alone restrained them.

The first cohorts of Petulants and the Heruli had departed on the previous night. Their comrades the Celts and Batavians were preparing to follow them. Cintula issued his orders in a peremptory tone. Savage murmurs were running through the crowd. An insubordinate soldier had just been beaten to death. Decensius strode hither and thither, pen behind ear, documents in hand. In the great courtyards, under a dark sky, thick-wheeled covered chariots were waiting for the soldiers' wives and children. Women, parting from the country where they were born, were stretching out their arms to the woods and fields. Others were kissing the maternal soil, and weeping at the thought that their dust should be buried in a strange land. Others, more resigned and sullen in their pain, had wrapped handfuls of earth in little bundles, to carry with them as tokens. A lean dog, with ribs to be counted through his skin, was licking the grease of an axle-tree. Suddenly he darted away and began to howl, muzzle in the dust. Everybody, thrilled by the sound, turned round to watch him. A legionary angrily thrashed the poor beast, who fled into a field with his tail between his legs, and, halting there, renewed his howlings in a yet more plaintive key. This dog's cry, wailing through the impressive silence of the twilight, shook the nerves of all who heard it. The Sarmatian Aragaris belonged to the number chosen to leave the north. He was bidding farewell to the faithful Strombix—

"Oh, cousin, cousin! why are you leaving me?" whined Strombix, between mouthfuls of soup, which Aragaris had given up to him. Grief had taken away his own appetite.

"Be quiet, fool!" the consolatory Aragaris was remarking; "there are too many women groaning already! . . . It would be more useful if you, who belong to the country, would tell me what forests we shall have to pass through?"

"What do you mean, cousin? There are no forests there; only sand and rocks."

"And how does one get shelter from the sun?" asked the incredulous Aragaris.

"It's a desert! It's as hot there as under a cook's oven, and there's not a drop of water."

"What! No water? And how about beer?"

"They don't even know what beer means!"

"You're lying!"

"May I be struck blind, cousin, if in all Mesopotamia and Syria you find a keg of beer or of honey."

"Then it's all over, brother! If it's hot there, and there's neither water, beer, nor honey, they're simply hunting us to the end of the world like oxen to the slaughter!"

"Hunting you on to the horns of the Devil, cousin!" and Strombix wept yet more bitterly.

At that moment there came a distant rumble, and din of voices. The two friends ran out of the barracks; a crowd of soldiers were rushing over the wooden bridge towards Lutetia. The cries came nearer; wild agitation seized the garrison; the soldiery poured out upon the road in a dense shouting mass, in spite of the orders, threats, and even blows of the centurions.

"What has happened?" asked a veteran.

"Twenty soldiers have been beaten to death!"

"What? Twenty! Why, it was a hundred!"

"They're going to cudgel every man in turn; it's the order!"

Suddenly a legionary with torn clothes and terrified demeanour rushed into the crowd shouting—

"Comrades! quick, to the palace! . . . quick! Julian's just been beheaded!"

These words fell like a spark on tinder. The long-smouldering flame burst into destructiveness. The faces of the soldiers took on an expression of animal ferocity. No one understood nor wished to hear, but all shouted—

"Where are the rascals? Kill the hounds!"

"Who?"

"The envoys from the Emperor Constantius!"

"Down with the Emperor!"

"Ah, the idiots!—to think they've killed such a leader!"

Two innocent centurions who were passing were seized, thrown to earth, trampled upon and almost rent in pieces. At the sight of the gushing blood the mutineers became yet more ferocious. Another mob coming over the bridge swept up to the barracks, and there rose a deafening cry—

"Glory to the Emperor Julian! Glory to Augustus Julian!"

"He is slain! He is slain!"

"Hold your peace, fools; Augustus is alive! We've just seen him!"

"The Cæsar's alive!"

"He's no longer Cæsar, but Emperor!"

"Who said he was killed?"

"Where is the blackguard?"

"They tried to kill him!"

"Who?"

"Constantius!"

"Down with Constantius! Down with all cursed eunuchs!"

Someone on horseback rode by so quickly as almost to escape recognition—

"Decensius! Decensius! Catch the ruffian!"

Still with pen behind his ear and ink-flask dangling from his girdle, accompanied by insults and laughter, he disappeared from sight. The crowd grew thicker and thicker, and the mutinous army was like a raging flood; but their anger was turned into glee when the Herulian and Petulant legions, who had marched the evening before, and also mutinied, were seen in the distance on their way back. They, their wives, and their children were kissed with emotion, as after a long separation. Some shed tears of joy, others struck their shields; and great bonfires were kindled. The fountains of oratory were unloosed. Strombix, who in his youth had been a buffoon at Antioch, felt himself inspired, and, hoisted with wild gesticulations on the shoulders of his comrades, began—

"*Nos quidem ad orbis terrarum extrema ut noxii pellimur et damnati. . .* "

"They're sending us to the other end of the world like criminals; and our families, whom we bought back from slavery with the price of our blood, will fall back into the hands of the Alemanni—"

He was unable to finish; the barracks were ringing with piercing cries, and the noise, familiar to soldiers, of scourges scoring the back. The legionaries were lashing the detested centurion Cedo Alteram, and the soldier who was administering the lashes to his superior flung away the bloody rod, and to the general amusement, imitating the cheery voice of the centurion, called out—

"*Cedo Alteram!* Give me another!"

"To the palace! To the palace!" yelled the crowd. "Let us make Julian, Augustus! Let us crown him with a diadem!"

The mob rushed off, leaving in the courtyard the half-dead centurion weltering in blood. Through the dark clouds the stars sparkled here and there, and a cold wind lifted the dust. The barred windows, doors, and shutters of the palace were all hermetically sealed. The building seemed tenantless.

Foreseeing the revolt, Julian had not left his quarters nor shown himself to the soldiers, being occupied in divinations. For two days and two nights he had waited for a miracle. Clothed in the long white robe of the Pythagoreans, lamp in hand, he was ascending the steps which led to the highest tower. There the assistant of Maximus of Ephesus was awaiting him, and observing the stars. This assistant was no other

DMITRY MEREZHKOVSKY

than Nogodarès, who once in the tavern owned by Syrax at the foot of Mount Argæus had foretold the future to the tribune Scuda.

"Well?" Julian asked anxiously.

"There's nothing to be seen! It looks as if heaven and earth were conspiring."

A bat swooped by.

"Look, look! Perhaps some prediction can be made from the manner of its flight?"

The night-wandering creature almost brushed Julian's face with its cold wings, and vanished.

"Someone's soul approaches," murmured Nogodarès. "Remember! this night something great will be accomplished. . ."

The indistinct cries of the mutineers were borne faintly up the wind.

"If a sign appears, come to me," said Julian as he went down to his library.

With irregular restless strides he walked up and down the room, halting every now and then to listen. It seemed as if someone was following him; that a curious cold air was blowing on the nape of his neck. He wheeled round, but discovered nothing. He felt the blood beating strongly in his temples. He resumed his walk, and again it seemed that someone was murmuring into his ear words that he had not time to understand.

A servant entered, and announced that an old man from Athens desired to see the Cæsar on urgent business. Julian uttered a cry of elation and ran to meet the new-comer. He thought he should see Maximus; but he was mistaken. It was the high-priest of the mysteries of Eleusis, whom also he had impatiently expected.

"Father!" exclaimed Julian, "save me! I must know the will of the gods! . . . Let us come quickly, for all is prepared."

Round the palace resounded deafening cries from the revolted army, shaking the old brickwork of the walls. But when a baggage-carrier, livid with fear, ran in exclaiming, "Mutiny! The soldiers are breaking in the iron gates!" Julian said with an imperious gesture, "Fear nothing! We will arrange that matter presently. Let no one come into my presence!" and taking the high-priest by the hand he hastily led him into a dark underground vault, and closed the heavy iron door. All was there ready. Torch-flames were glittering over the silver image of the Sun-god, and tripods fuming; the holy vessels, full of water, wine, and honey, stood prepared, with salt and flour to be sprinkled on the bodies of the victims. Geese, doves, hens, an eagle, and a white lamb which bleated plaintively, stood round in different cages.

"Quicker, quicker!" exclaimed Julian, giving a long dagger to the priest.

The old man, who was panting heavily, began hurriedly to mutter prayers; he killed the lamb, put a portion of the flesh and fat upon the coals of the altar, and with mysterious exorcisms began the inspection of its organs. With expert hands he drew forth the liver, heart, and lungs, and scanned them from every side.

"The powerful shall be overthrown!" he said, pointing to the heart, which was still warm; "a terrible death. . ."

"Whose?" Julian asked. "His or mine?"

"I know not."

"You know not?"

"Cæsar," said the old man, "be not hasty. Decide nothing tonight; wait for the day; the presages are doubtful. . ."

He did not finish his sentence, but took another victim, a gander, and then an eagle. Overhead the noise of the crowd at the gates swept like the roar of a torrent. Blows of a battering-ram shook the iron doors, but Julian heard nothing. He examined the bloody organs with eager curiosity.

The old sacrificial priest repeated:

"Decide nothing tonight; the gods are silent."

"But now is the moment!" cried Julian in vexation.

Nogodarès came in, and solemnly spoke:

"Julian, rejoice! tonight your destiny is decided. . . but make haste! Afterwards it will be too late."

The soothsayer looked at the hierophant; the hierophant at the soothsayer.

"Wait!" said the priest of Eleusis.

"Dare!" said Nogodarès.

Julian stood between the two, in perplexity scrutinising both.

The faces of the augurs remained impenetrable.

"What is to be done?" he murmured to himself. Then he remembered, and exclaimed joyfully:

"One moment! I have an ancient book in my library, *Concerning Contradiction in Auguries*; we shall see!"

He hurried to the library; but in a passage he encountered the bishop Dorotheus, in sacerdotal dress, bearing the crucifix and the sacred Viaticum.

"What is this?" asked Julian.

"The Viaticum for your wife, who is dying, O Cæsar!"

Dorotheus looked with severity at the robes of Julian, his pale face, and his blood-stained hands.

"Your wife," continued the bishop, "desires to see you before her death. Will you come?"

"Yes! . . . yes! later! . . . O gods! . . . another ill omen."

He entered the library and began to rummage among the parchments. Suddenly he heard a voice murmuring distinctly in his ear:

"Dare! dare! dare!"

"Maximus, it is thou!" exclaimed Julian, wheeling round.

There was no one in the dark apartment.

Julian's heart beat so strongly that he pressed his hand against his side; a cold sweat stood on his forehead.

"This—this is what I was waiting for!" murmured Julian. "The voice was 'his'; now, all doubt is over! . . . I will go!"

The barred gates had given way with a crash. Legionaries were pouring into the atrium, thrilling the old palace with their cries, while the crimson glare of the torches shone through the chinks of shutters like the light of a conflagration. Not a minute was to be lost. Casting away his white robes, Julian donned his armour, paludamentum, war cloak, and helmet, buckled on his sword, and ran down the principal staircase leading to the entrance. He opened the door and presented himself to the soldiers with a calm and unshaken demeanour. All doubts had disappeared. While in action his will never vacillated; but never up to that day had he been conscious of such a fulness of inward force, such clearness and self-possession of mind. In a moment the crowd felt that supremacy. The pale face of Julian was imperial and awe-striking, and at a gesture from him the mob was silenced. Julian spoke to the soldiers, asking them to restore order; he would neither abandon them nor permit that they should be taken from Gaul; on that head he would convince his well-beloved brother, the Emperor Constantius.

"Down with Constantius!" interrupted the legionaries. "Down with him who slew his brother! Thou art our Emperor! Glory to Augustus Julian, the Invincible!"

Admirably did Julian affect surprise, and, as if startled, lowered his eyes and turned aside his head with a deprecating gesture of his lifted palms, as putting away from him so criminal a gift. The shouts redoubled.

"What is this?" said Julian, feigning dismay. "You are ruining me and you are ruining yourselves. Do you think that I can betray my sovereign?"

"Yes! your brother's murderer!" shouted the men.

"Silence!" answered Julian, striding towards the crowd. "Do you not know that we are sworn. . . ?"

Every movement was a hypocritical ruse. When the soldiers surged round him he drew his sword from its sheath and pointed it against his own breast as if to fall on it.

"Bravest of the brave! better die for Cæsar than betray him!"

But the men, seizing his hands, disarmed him, and many, falling at his feet, kissed them, weeping—

"Ah! we are willing to die for you!"

Others stretched out their hands, groaning—

"Have pity on us; be our Augustus!"

The heart of Julian was thrilled. He loved these rough faces, the barrack-atmosphere, and the unrivalled enthusiasm in which he felt his own power.

He saw that the mutiny was dangerous and in earnest, observing that the legionaries did not interrupt each other, but shouted unanimously, and became suddenly hushed, as if their action had been concerted beforehand.

There was either a deafening hubbub, or absolute silence.

Finally, Julian, with an effort that might well have been thought sincere—

"My children! my dear comrades! behold me. . . I am yours in life and in death. I can refuse you nothing!"

"Crown him! The diadem!" they cried, triumphantly.

But no diadem was to be found.

Strombix proposed—

"Let Augustus order that his wife's necklet of pearls be brought here!"

Julian answered that a woman's ornament would be unfitting, and an ill presage with which to inaugurate a reign.

But the men were unsatisfied. They insisted on seeing a sign of regality shining on the head of their chosen, to make him their Emperor indeed. One of the legionaries snatched from his war-horse the phaleræ, or forehead trapping, with its string of metal disks, for the crowning of Augustus.

But neither did this please him, for the ornament stank with the sweat of the horse. Everyone cast about to find another decoration, and at last the standard-bearer of the Petulant legion, the Sarmatian Aragaris, pulled from his neck the metal chain denoting his rank, and Julian wound it twice round his own head. This chain made him Emperor of Rome.

"Hoist him on a shield! on a shield!" shouted the soldiery.

Aragaris tendered his round buckler. Hundreds of arms heaved the Emperor. He saw a sea of helmeted heads, and heard, like the rolling of thunder, the exultant cry—

"Glory to Julian, the divine Augustus!"

It seemed the will of destiny. One by one the torches were extinguished. The clamour died away; and the eastern sky was barred with soft white bands. The dark and dull mass of the palace-towers became clear in all its ugliness; a single lighted window was still visible. Julian guessed that this must be the light in the cell where Helena lay dying.

And when at dawn the wearied army dispersed, he went to the bedside of his wife. It was too late. The dead woman lay quietly on her virgin couch; the lips severely closed. Julian felt no remorse, but painful curiosity moved him as he gazed at the dark face of his wife, wondering—

"What was that last desire? What did she wish to say to me?"

XXII

The Emperor Constantius meantime was passing at Antioch a somewhat melancholy period. At night he had alarming visions and kept six lamps burning in his chamber till daybreak in the vain endeavour to relieve his fears of darkness. Hour after hour would he lie motionless and moody, starting at the least sound. Once he dreamed he saw his father, Constantine the Great, holding a sturdy and mischievous child in his arms. Constantius took the child and placed him on his right hand, attempting the while to hold in his left a great ball of crystal. But the child in wilfulness pushed the globe, which fell and broke; and its fragments, piercing like needles, buried themselves in the body of Constantius, darting with intolerable pain, burning, and hissing into his brain, eyes, and heart. The Emperor awoke, bathed in a cold perspiration. He consulted sorcerers, diviners, celebrated magicians. Troops were assembled at Antioch for a campaign against Julian. Sometimes after a moody fit of immobility the Emperor was seized with an impulse to action; the greater number of Court officials found this haste unreasonable, and confided to each other their fears as to the mental state of the august sovereign.

The autumn was reaching its end when he left Antioch. At noon, about three miles from the city, near the village of Hypocephalus, the Emperor saw an unknown mutilated body lying on the road. Facing the south the corpse was stretched to the right of Constantius, who was on horseback. The head was separated from the body.

The Emperor grew pale and turned away. None of the riders round him uttered a word, all being aware that the omen was an evil one. In the town of Tarsus in Cilicia, Constantius had shivering fits and felt weakness, but he paid them no attention nor consulted leeches, believing that riding in the hot sun over the steep mountains would produce reaction and relief.

He rode towards the little town of Mopsucrenam at the foot of Mount Tarsus, the last halting-place before crossing the Cilician border.

On the way he suffered several times from violent giddiness, which obliged him to dismount and lie down in a litter. Subsequently the eunuch Eusebius tells how, when lying in the palanquin, the Emperor took from his bosom and tenderly kissed a precious stone on which was engraven the profile of the late Empress Eusebia Aurelia.

DMITRY MEREZHKOVSKY

At one of the cross-roads he asked whither one of the ways led, and when he was told to the abandoned palace of the kings of Cappadocia, at Macellum, his brow clouded. Mopsucrenam was reached at night-fall. Constantius was weary and full of gloom. Hardly had he entered the house which had been prepared when one of the courtiers, against the command of Eusebius, thoughtlessly announced to the Emperor that two couriers from the southern provinces were awaiting him.

Constantius ordered them to be admitted, in spite of the supplications of Eusebius, his favourite chamberlain, who advised him to postpone business till the morrow. The Emperor declared that he felt better, and suffered from nothing but a slight pain at the nape of his neck.

The first courier, trembling and livid, was ushered in.

"Tell me all, immediately!" exclaimed Constantius, dismayed at the man's expression.

The courier then narrated the audacious movements of Julian, who, before the assembled army, had torn up the Imperial rescript. Gaul, Pannonia, Aquitania, had submitted to Julian, and the traitorous army was advancing to encounter Constantius, with all the legions to be gathered from those provinces.

The Emperor stood up, his face disfigured by fury, and, seizing the messenger by the throat, shook him.

"You lie, caitiff! You lie! You lie! . . . There is still a God in heaven to shield the kings of the earth. . . and He will not permit, do you understand! . . . Fools! . . . He will not permit. . ."

He had a spasm of weakness, and covered his eyes with his hand; the courier, more dead than alive, slunk to the door.

"Tomorrow," stammered Constantius wildly; "tomorrow we absolutely must set out! . . . by forced marches, direct. . . as the crow flies. . . over the mountains. . . We absolutely must go to Constantinople."

Eusebius approached him, with the humblest of bows—

"Divine Augustus! The Lord God has granted you, you His chosen, victory over your enemies. You have annihilated Magnentius, Constantius, Vetranio, Gallus. You will crush this impious—"

But Constantius, wagging his head without listening, muttered—

"Then He exists not; if it is all true, and I am single-handed, alone! Who dares to say that 'He' exists, when such crimes can be accomplished! I've been thinking so a long time. . ."

He cast a dull look on the courtiers present and said—

"Call in the other."

A physician came up—a courtier-like person, with a clean-shaven rosy face, an Armenian who assumed the airs of a Roman patrician. He observed respectfully that too keen emotion might be harmful to the Emperor, that he should rest. . . Constantius waved him away like an irritating fly.

The second courier was shown in. He was Cintula, the tribune of the Imperial stables, who had escaped from Lutetia. He brought the terrible news that the inhabitants of Sirmium[1] had opened their doors to Julian, and welcomed him as the saviour of the country. In two days he would debouch on the great Roman road leading to Constantinople.

The Emperor either did not hear, or did not understand, the last words of the messenger. His face became strangely rigid. He made a gesture of dismissal to all present. Eusebius alone remained to talk the business over with him. In another quarter of an hour Constantius ordered that he should be assisted to his chamber, and made several steps. Then a cry escaped him; he pressed his hands to his head, as if he suddenly felt terrible pain. Courtiers ran to support him. The Emperor did not lose consciousness. By his face and movements, and the veins, standing out like whipcord on his forehead, it was evident that he was making fearful efforts to speak.

Finally he stammered slowly, word by word, as if being throttled by an iron collar—

"I—want—to—speak—and—I—cannot!" Those were his last words; paralysis had stricken the whole of his right side. His arm and leg fell inert.

He was carried to bed, but his eyes were wakeful and intelligent, and he struggled to utter something—some important order perhaps. From his lips came only confused sounds, like weak lowings. No one understood what he wanted, and the invalid fixed his clear gaze in turn on each present. Eunuchs, courtiers, generals, slaves, thronged round the dying man, helplessly desirous of doing his last behest.

At moments the clear eye became angered and the lowing hoarse. At last Eusebius understood, and brought wax and tablets. At the sight of these a flash of joy was seen on the Emperor's face. He gripped the steel stylus awkwardly, like a child. After some struggles, he succeeded in tracing a few letters on the soft wax, and the courtiers with difficulty deciphered the word "*Baptism*." Constantius fixed his supplicating look

---

1. On the Save, at no great distance from Belgrade.

on Eusebius, and everybody wondered at not having understood before. He was desirous of being baptised before death, having, like his father Constantine, always postponed this sacrament to the last, in the belief that he could then miraculously cleanse his soul and leave it whiter than snow. A messenger was despatched for the bishop. There proved to be none in Mopsucrenam, and recourse was had to the Arian priest of the basilica. He was a timid man, with a bird-like face, red-nosed, with a goat's beard, and a provincial manner.

When disturbed by the messengers, Father Nymphodion was enjoying his tenth wine-cup, and seemed in too cheerful a mood. It was impossible to make clear to him the matter in hand, and he grew angry at what he believed to be raillery. But when at length convinced that fate had designated him to baptise an Emperor he nearly lost his reason. When he entered the chamber of the sick man, the Emperor gazed on the trembling priest with such humility that it was evident he feared to die, and was eager to hasten the ceremony. Meantime the town had been scoured in vain for a basin of gold or silver. It is true that a jewelled one was available, but it had served for the bacchic mysteries of Dionysus; and the common copper basin used by the parishioners of the basilica was therefore preferable. This copper basin was brought to the bed and warm water poured into it. The doctor was about to feel its temperature, but the Emperor made a brusque movement and groaned, lest the water should be sullied. The dying man's tunic was taken off. Strong arms of legionaries raised him, like a child, and immersed him. The wasted face of Constantius, his eyes fixed and wide open, stared at the cross fixed above the Labarum, the golden standard of Constantine. It was an obstinate and vacuous stare, as of children when they see some dazzling object and cannot turn away from it.

The ceremony did not soothe the sick man, who seemed to have forgotten everything. Volition came into his eyes for the last time when Eusebius again stretched out to him the waxen tablet, but Constantius, unable to write, only traced with his finger the name "*Julian*." Did he desire to pardon his enemy or to bequeath his vengeance?

For three days he lay in the extremity of death; courtiers murmured to each other that this was evidently some special punishment of God, who would not permit him to die. But they referred to him always as "The Divine Augustus," "His Holiness," and "The Eternal." His sufferings must have been great; the low moaning turned into a steady death-rattle, which went on day and night. Courtiers came in and went out, eagerly hoping for the end. The eunuch Eusebius alone never left his master. Many a crime had this eunuch upon his conscience; all the tangled threads of reports, espials, and ecclesiastical broils were gathered in his hands. But he alone in the palace proved his love to his master, and at night when everyone was sleeping, or had withdrawn, worn out by the task of nursing, Eusebius remained by the bedside, arranging pillows, cooling the dry lips with ice, or kneeling at the feet of the Emperor in prayer. When none saw, Eusebius would gently lift the purple coverlet and weepingly kiss the feet, now pale and benumbed. Once it seemed to him that Constantius noticed this caress and thanked him with a look. Something fraternal and tender passed between the two cruel, ill-starred, and solitary men.

Eusebius closed the eyes of the Emperor; the Church recited over him, before the body was committed to the tomb—

"Rise again, O king of the earth! Answer the summons of thy coming Judge, the King of kings!"

XXIII

Not far from Succi, a mountainous defile in the Hæmus range[1] between Moesia and Thrace, two men were making their way along a narrow path, at night, through a forest of beeches. They were the Emperor Julian and Maximus the enchanter. The full moon was shining in a clear sky, and strangely illuminating the gold and purple of autumn foliage. From time to time a wan yellow leaf would fall swirling with a slight rustle. The air was full of moisture and the musty smell of a tardy autumn—that soft, chill melancholy odour which puts men in mind of death. The soft masses of leaves made a brushing sound under the feet of the travellers, and round them in the silent woods burned the magnificent obsequies of the departing year.

"Master," asked Julian, "why is not that divine lightness mine, that gaiety which used to make so splendid the men of Hellas?"

"You are not a man of Hellas."

Julian sighed—

"Alas, our ancestors were barbarians, Medes; and the sluggish blood of the North flows in my veins. It is true, I am no son of the Hellenes!"

"My friend, Hellas has never existed," murmured Maximus, with his old bewitching smile.

"What do you mean?" asked Julian.

"The Hellas that you love has never existed."

"Do you mean to say that my faith is futile?"

"We are only to believe," answered Maximus, "in what is not, but shall be. Your Hellas shall exist, shall be the reign, the kingdom of divine men, men daring all things, fearing none."

"Fearing none! . . . Master, powerful enchantments are thine. . . Deliver my soul from fear!"

"Fear of what?"

"I cannot say, but from childhood I have been afraid—afraid of life, of death, of myself, of the mystery in all things, of the darkness. . . I had an old nurse, Labda, like a Parca, a Fate, who used to spin me terrible tales of my family, the Flavii. These mad old-wives' tales keep singing in my ears still, at night, when I am alone. They will ruin me some day. . . I wish to be free, as one of the old Hellenes. . . and I have no gladness in

---

1. The Balkans.

me. . . Sometimes I think I am a coward, Master! . . . Master, save me! Deliver me from that eternal fear, these consuming darknesses!"

"Ah, I have long known the need of your soul," said Maximus, gravely, "and from this very day I will cleanse you from this Galilean corruption—slay the shadow of Golgotha in the radiance of Mithra— warm afresh your body, frozen at baptism, in the hot blood of the Sun-god! . . . My son, rejoice! for I will give you such freedom, such joy as no man on earth has yet possessed!"

They issued from the wood, and followed a narrow path, hewn through the rock, above a chasm in which a torrent ran seething. Stones, loosened by their feet, rolled echoing down and plunged into the water. High over the forest they saw the distant snow-covered summits of Mount Rhodope. Julian and Maximus at last reached and entered the mouth of a cave. It was the temple of the Sun-god Mithra, where mysteries, forbidden by the Roman laws, were performed. In this cavern there was no sign of splendour; the bleak walls were engraven with cabalistic signs of Zoroastrian religion, triangles, enlaced circles, winged beasts, and constellations. Here and there the vaulted obscurity was relieved by dull flames of torches or the form of an initiating priest in strange and sweeping robes.

Julian was arrayed in the Olympian robe, embroidered with Indian monsters, stars, suns, and hyperborean dragons. He held a flambeau in his right hand. Maximus had acquainted him with the responses to be made to his initiator, and Julian had learned them by heart, although their meaning hitherto was unintelligible to him.

With Maximus he went down rock-hewn steps into a long and deep foss. Here the air was already humid and stifling; but to make it more so, overhead a wooden trap-door, riddled with holes like a strainer, was lowered across, from edge to edge. The trampling of hoofs resounded, and the sacrificers placed three black bulls, three white bulls, and a red bull with gilded hoofs and horns on the trap above the two men. Then the initiators, intoning a hymn which mingled with the bellowing of the beasts, felled with axes one bull after another. They fell on their knees and struggled, the wooden framework trembled under their weight, while the farthest vaults of the cavern resounded to the cries of the red bull, which was hailed as the god Mithra. Percolating through the holes in the trap, the blood fell in a hot shower upon the head of Julian. This slaying of the bull consecrated to the Sun was the supreme mystery of the Pagans. Throwing off his outer clothes and standing in

DMITRY MEREZHKOVSKY

his white tunic only, Julian offered head, breast, and all his limbs to the terrible trickling rain. Then Maximus, shaking the torch overhead, cried—

"Let thy soul be steeped in the expiating blood of thy god, the Sun, in the purest blood of the ever radiant heart of thy god, the Sun; let it be cleansed in his morning and in his evening light! Dost thou, O mortal, still hold anything in fear?"

"Yes," was the response.

"Let thy soul become a parcel of thy god, the Sun! The quenchless and inviolable Mithra takes thee to himself! Dost thou still fear anything, O mortal?"

"I fear nothing more on the earth," answered Julian, who was now streaming with blood from head to foot. "I am even as He is!"

"Take this crown," said Maximus, placing a wreath of acanthus-leaves on the head of Julian, with the point of his sword.

But the catechumen flung the coronal upon the ground with a cry—

"The Sun only is my crown, the Sun alone!"

Then he stamped on the acanthus, and lifting his arms skyward repeated a third time—

"Now, until death, my crown is the Sun!"

The mystery was over. Maximus kissed the initiate. On the face of the old man as he did so hovered a gleam of strange significance.

While they were retracing their steps through the beech-forest the Emperor spoke to the enchanter—

"Maximus, I think you are hiding from me some secret deeper yet." He turned towards the old man his pale face, on which, as was the custom, the traces of the sacred blood were not yet wiped away.

"What do you wish to know, Julian?"

"What lot shall fall to me?"

"You will conquer."

"And Constantius?"

"Constantius is no more."

"What mean you?"

"Wait! the Sun shall reveal your glory!"

Julian dared not question further. Both men regained the camp in silence. In Julian's tent a courier from Asia Minor, the tribune Cintula, stood waiting. He knelt and kissed the edge of the Imperial paludamentum—

"Glory to the divine Augustus Julian!"

"Do you come with a message from Constantius?"

"Constantius is no more!"

"What say you?"

Julian trembled and threw a glance at Maximus, whose face remained inscrutable.

"By the will of God," continued Cintula, "your enemy departed this life in the town of Mopsucrenam, not far from Macellum."

That evening the army assembled on a hill. The death of Constantius was already made known to them.

Augustus Claudius Flavius Julian took his station on a hillock so that all the soldiers could see him; crownless, weaponless, unarmoured, and enswathed head to foot in purple. To conceal the traces of the blood, which might not be washed off, he had enveloped his head and veiled his face in the purple silk. In this attire he bore the appearance rather of a sacrificial priest than of an emperor. Behind him rose the ruddy forest wrapping the base of Mount Hæmus. Above his head hung, like a golden banner, the yellow branches of a maple. Far as the eye could see, the plain of Thrace lay below, crossed by the white marble pavement of the Roman road stretching victoriously away to the Propontic Sea. Julian gazed at his army. When the legions moved their stations, red flashes from the sunset were reflected upon burnished helmets, breastplates, and eagles; the lances above the cohorts seemed like lighted tapers. By Julian's side was Maximus, who spoke in Cæsar's ear—

"Look forth upon this sight of glory! your hour is come! Act now!"

The magician pointed to the Christian banner, the Labarum, with its crest of the monogram of Christ, the flag made on the pattern of that fiery standard bearing the inscription, "Through this shalt thou conquer," which Constantine the Great had seen miraculous in the heavens.

The troops made no stir. Julian in a clear and solemn voice addressed them—

"Comrades, our work is finished. Now we will go to Constantinople! Give thanks to the Olympians, who have given us the victory!"

These words were only heard by the first ranks, but there were numerous Christians among them. These were roused by the last startling expression.

"Lord have mercy on us! what is it he says?" cried one.

"Do you see that old man with the white beard?" said another to his comrade.

"Yes."

"That's the Devil, who, in the body of Maximus the enchanter, is tempting Cæsar!"

But the more distant ranks, who had not heard Julian's words, cried—

"Glory to Augustus Julian! Glory! Glory!" and louder and louder yet from outskirts of the hill, as far as they were covered by the legions, arose a cry repeated by thousands of voices—

"Glory! . . . Glory! . . ."

Mountains, air, earth, and forest trembled with the voice of the multitude.

"Look, look!" murmured the dismayed Christians; "the Labarum is being lowered!" And in fact the holy banner was being veiled before the Emperor. A military blacksmith came down from the wood with a brazier and red-hot pincers.

Julian, whose face, in spite of the ruddy gleams of the purple and the sun, was dark with strong emotion, wrenched the golden cross, with its monogram of precious stones, from the staff of the Labarum. Pearls, emeralds, and rubies were scattered on the ground, and the glittering cross buried in the earth, stamped under the sandal of the Roman Cæsar.

From a casket Maximus immediately drew forth a little silver statue of the Sun-god, Mithra-Helios; and the smith in a few instants soldered it to the staff of the Labarum.

Before the army had recovered from its astonishment and fear, Constantine's sacred banner rose above the head of the Emperor, crowned with the image of Apollo. An old soldier, who was a devout Christian, turned away and veiled his eyes to avoid seeing the sight of horror.

"Sacrilege! sacrilege!" he muttered, turning pale.

"Woe, woe, upon us!" groaned another; "Satan has entoiled our Emperor!"

Julian knelt before the standard and, stretching out his arms to the little silver image, exclaimed—

"Glory to the invincible Sun, king of all gods! . . . Augustus worships the eternal Helios; god of light, god of reason, god of the gladness and joy upon Olympus!"

The last rays of sunset lighted the bold beauty of the god of Delphi, and rayed his head. The legionaries stood in silence, save that in the wood the dry leaves could be heard falling. The conflagration of the sunset, the purple of the sacrificial king, the withered woods, all these breathed a magnificence as of sumptuous obsequies. One of the men in the front rank muttered a single word so distinctly that it reached Julian's ear, and thrilled him—

"Anti-Christ!"

PART II

I

Hard by the stables, in the Hippodrome of Constantinople, there was a room which served as a sort of common den for grooms, women-riders, actors, and charioteers. Even in daytime lamps were kept burning in this stifling resort, where the air smelt strongly of dungheap and stable. When the curtain at the door was lifted a dazzling flood of light invaded this den; and in the sunny distance could be seen empty tiers of seats, and the magnificent staircase joining the Imperial box to the apartments of Constantine's palace. Egyptian obelisks also were seen in the arena and in the centre, on the yellow sand, a gigantic sacrificial altar of marvellous workmanship, wrought of three entwined serpents of bronze, bearing on their flat heads a Delphian tripod.

Crackings of whips, shouts of riders, snortings of horses, came from the arena, and the muffled sound of wheels on the soft sand went by like a rushing of wings. No races were going on, but merely the preparatory exercise for the races which were to take place a few days later. In one corner of the stable a naked athlete, rubbed over with oil and covered with dust, a girdle of leather round his hips, was raising and lowering dumb-bells. Throwing back his shaggy head, he arched his back till the joints cracked, and at every effort his face grew crimson and the veins of his neck swelled.

Preceded by slaves, a young Byzantine woman of patrician rank approached the athlete. She was dressed in a morning robe of delicate hues; and a veil thrown over her head covered her aristocratic and slightly-faded features.

She was a zealous Christian, widow of a Roman senator; beloved of monks for her generous donations to monasteries, and abounding charity. At first she concealed her escapades, but soon perceived that to combine the love of the church with the love of the circus was quite the fashion.

Everybody knew that Stratonice detested the coxcombs of Constantinople, curled and painted, nervous and capricious as she was herself; it was her temperament and fancy to mingle the most costly perfumes of Arabia with the enervating heat of circus and stable. Hot tears of repentance, fervent confessions to tactful confessors, were of no avail; and this little woman, frail and delicate as some ivory trinket, cared for nothing but the coarse caresses of a certain famous circus-rider.

Stratonice was watching the exercises of the gymnast with a practised eye, while he, preserving a stupid expression on his beefy face, paid her not the slightest attention. She muttered something to her slave, with simple wonder admiring the powerful back and the terrible Herculean muscles rolling under the red skin of the shoulders, when, bending with deep inhalations, like the wind of a forge, he raised the iron weights above his handsome tawny head.

The curtain was lifted. The crowd of spectators recoiled, and two Cappadocian mares, a white and a black, pushed into the stables, ridden by a young horsewoman, who, with a guttural cry, adroitly leapt from one beast to another, and thence to the ground.

She was solidly-built, hale and sprightly as her mares, and upon her bare body shone fine drops of sweat.

Zephirinus, the elegant sub-deacon of the Basilica of the Holy Apostles, smilingly hastened towards her. A great lover of the circus, a frequenter of races and racing-stables, this young man would wager heavy sums for the blue (*veneta*) against the green (*prasina*). With his red-heeled morocco boots, his painted eyes, and curled hair, Zephirinus had much more the appearance of a young girl than of a servant of the church. Behind him stood a slave, burdened with packets of pretty stuffs and boxes, purchases of every kind from famous shops.

"Krokala, here are the perfumes you asked for the day before yesterday."

The sub-deacon offered the equestrienne a flask sealed with blue wax.

"I've been hunting in shops all the morning, and have only found it in one. It is pure nard, and arrived yesterday from Apamea!"

"And what purchases are these?" demanded Krokala.

"Oh, the silks in fashion! . . . ornaments—sets of jewels!"

"All of them for your—?"

"Yes, all for my most noble sister, the devout matron Bezilla; one *must* help one's near relatives! She trusts nobody's taste but mine for choosing stuffs. From early morning I am under her orders. My head goes round, but I don't complain. No! . . . No! . . . Bezilla is so good. . . such a holy woman!"

"Unfortunately old," laughed Krokala. "Here, boy, wipe the sweat off the black mare with fresh fig leaves."

"Old age also has its virtues," replied the sub-deacon, gently rubbing together his white hands; they were loaded with rings.

Then he whispered in Krokala's ear: "This evening?"

"I'm not sure. . . perhaps. Are you going to bring me something?"

"You needn't be afraid, Krokala, I won't come empty-handed! There's a piece of stuff. . . a quite marvellous pattern."

He kissed two of his fingers, adding: "Something perfectly dazzling!"

"Where did you pick it up?"

"Oh, at Pyrmix's of course, near the baths. For what do you take me? You might make a long *tarantinidion* out of it. You can't imagine what embroidery there is on it! Guess the subject!"

"I don't know! . . . Flowers—animals?"

"In gold and silk—the whole story of Diogenes, the Cynic."

"Ah, that must be pretty!" cried the girl. "Come, by all means, I shall expect you."

Zephirinus glanced at the *clepsydra*, a water-clock placed in a niche in the wall.

"I am late—quite late! I must go on to a money-lender, a jeweller, then the patriarch, and then the church. Till then, goodbye."

"Don't forget," Krokala cried to him, with a mischievous gesture.

The sub-deacon disappeared, followed by his slave.

A crowd of grooms, dancing girls, gymnasts, and tamers of wild beasts invaded the stables. With his face protected by a mask, the gladiator, Mermillion, was heating a bar of iron red-hot; he was taming a lion newly received from Africa, and which could be heard roaring through the stable-wall.

"You'll be the death of me, granddaughter, and you'll go to hell yourself! Oh, oh, how my back hurts! I'm done for!"

"Is that you, grandfather Gnyphon? What do you want?" asked Krokala in a vexed voice.

Gnyphon was a little old man with cunning tearful eyes, which shone under eyebrows active as two white mice. He had the violet nose of a drunkard, wore Libyan breeches, patched and botched here and there, and on his head a Phrygian cap.

"You've come again for money," grumbled Krokala, "and you've been drinking again."

"It's a sin to use such language. You'll have to answer for my soul to God. Just think what you've brought me to. I am living now in the Smokatian quarter; I hire a little cellar from an image-carver, and everyday I have to see him making his horrible idols in marble. There's a nice occupation for a Christian! I scarcely open my eyes in the morning, when tap, tap, tap,—my landlord's hammering his marble—bringing white devils into the world; damnable gods that stand laughing at me. How am I to keep out of the wine-shop? O Lord, have mercy on us! I'm simply weltering in Pagan horrors, like a pig in a sty, and it'll be reckoned against us... and who'll be responsible, I'd like to know? Why, you! You're rolling in money, and yet you leave a poor miserable old man—"

"You lie, Gnyphon! You're not poor; you're a miser; you've got a money-box under the bed!"

Gnyphon made a despairing gesture: "Hush—hush!"

To change the subject he said: "Do you know where I'm going?"

"To the tavern, of course!"

"Worse than that. To the Temple of Dionysus! That temple, since the days of holy Constantine, has been buried under rubbish; but tomorrow, by the august order of the Emperor Julian, it will be all shining again. And I've hired myself out to do the sweeping, although I shall lose my soul and be packed off to hell for it. But I've allowed myself to be tempted because I'm poor and hungry. My granddaughter doesn't do anything to support me... That's what I've come to!"

"You let me be, Gnyphon. Here you are! Now go! And don't come again when you're drunk!"

Krokala flung some pieces of silver to her grandfather, and then, leaping on an Illyrian stallion, stood erect on his croup, touched him with the whip, and set off at a gallop round the Hippodrome. Gnyphon clacked his tongue, and said with pride—

"To think it was I who brought her up!"

The firm, bare body of the horsewoman shone in the morning sun, and her floating red hair matched the colour of the stallion.

"Eh, Zotick," cried Gnyphon to an old slave who was raking horse-dung into a basket, "come with me to clean the temple of Dionysus! You're a master in these things! I'll pay you three obols for it."

"Of course I will," answered Zotick. "Just a moment to trim the lamp for the goddess, and I'm at your service."

The goddess was Atalanta, patron of grooms, dunghills, and stables. Coarsely carven in wood, and looking little more than a smoky log, Atalanta figured in a damp corner. But Zotick, who had been bred among horses, used to worship her, often praying with tears in his eyes, arraying her coarse blockish feet with sweet violets, in the belief that she healed all his ills, and would preserve him in life and in death.

Gnyphon went out into the open space, the Forum of Constantine, which was circular, and adorned with colonnades and triumphal arches. In the midst a gigantic porphyry column rose from a massive pedestal, and bore on its summit, at a height of a hundred and twenty cubits, a bronze statue of Apollo by Phidias, which had been carried off from a Phrygian city. The head of the Sun-god had been broken, and, with barbaric taste, the head of the Christian Emperor, the apostolic Constantine, had been fitted in its stead to the neck of the image.

His brow was surrounded by gilt rays. In his right hand Apollo Constantine held the sceptre, and in his left the globe. At the foot of the colossus was lodged a little Christian chapel, a kind of palladium, in which worship was still offered in the time of Constantine. The Christians defended the practice by the argument that in the bronze body of Apollo, within the Sun-god's very breast, a talisman was hidden—a piece of the Most Holy Cross brought from Jerusalem. The Emperor Julian closed this chapel.

Gnyphon and Zotick proceeded along a narrow and lengthy street, which led straight to the Chalcedonian stairs, not far from the fortress. Many public edifices were being built, and others were rebuilding, for so hastily had they been erected to please Constantius that they already were crumbling away. Inquisitive gazers were wandering in this street, stopping at merchants' shops; porters were passing by, slaves following their masters. Overhead, hammers resounded; cranes were creaking, and saws grinding the white stone. Labourers were heaving at the end of ropes huge timbers, and blocks of marble glittered against the blue. A smell of damp plaster came from the new houses, and a fine white dust fell on the heads of passers-by. On this side and that, between the dazzling white walls steeped in sunlight, the smiling blue waves of the Propontic, trimmed with galley-sails like the wings of sea-gulls, shone at the end of narrow alleys.

Gnyphon heard, as he went by, a conversation between two workmen who were weighing mortar into a sack—

"Why did you become a Christian?" asked one of them.

"Just think, the Christians have six times as many feast days as Hellenists! Nobody harms you. . . I advise you to follow my example. One is much freer among Christians."

Where four roads met, the pressure of a crowd pinned Gnyphon and Zotick against the wall. In the middle of the street there was a block in the traffic; the chariots could neither advance nor draw back; shouts, oaths, blows of the whip, were exchanged. Forty oxen were dragging, on an enormous stone-wheeled cart, a jasper column. The earth shook under its weight.

"Whither are you dragging that?" asked Gnyphon.

"From the Basilica to the Temple of Hera. The Christians had carried it off for their church. Now it is going back to its proper position."

Gnyphon glanced at the dirty wall against which he was leaning, on which Pagan urchins had drawn the usual impious caricatures of the Christians.

Gnyphon turned and spat with indignation.

On one side of the crowded market-place they observed the portrait of Julian, arrayed in all the symbols of Imperial power. The winged god Hermes was coming down from the clouds towards him. The portrait was fresh and the colours not yet dry.

Now according to the Roman law every passer-by had to salute any picture of Augustus.

The Agoranome, or inspector of the market, stopped a little old woman carrying a large basket of cabbages.

"I never salute the gods," wept the old woman. "My father and mother were Christians."

"You haven't got to salute the god, but the Emperor!"

"But the Emperor is alongside of the god! So how should I salute him?"

"No matter! You were told to salute and not to argue!"

Gnyphon dragged Zotick farther on as quickly as possible.

"Devilish trick," he grumbled, "either salute the accursed Hermes, or be accused of insulting the sovereign! No way out! . . . Oh! oh! oh! the day of Antichrist! In one way or another we're always sinning! When I see you, Zotick, envy gnaws my very soul. You live with your dunghill goddess, and have no cares."

They reached the Temple of Dionysus, hard by a Christian monastery, the windows and doors of which were fast barred as against the approach of an enemy. The Hellenists accused the monks of having pillaged the temple.

When Gnyphon and Zotick went into the temple, carpenters and timberers were already at work. The planks which had been used to close the quadrilateral to the sky were dragged down, and the sun poured into the gloomy building.

"Just look at the cobwebs, look, look!" Between the capitals of the columns hung masses of grey webs, which were being hastily cleaned away by means of rag-mops on immense poles. A bat, disturbed in his lair, flew away from a dark crevice, rushing hither and thither to hide himself from the light, striking himself against all the corners. The rustling of his soft wings could be distinctly heard. Zotick began sorting the rubbish and throwing it into baskets while the old man mumbled, "Ah, these cursed fellows! what foulness they have heaped up!"

A great bunch of rusty keys was brought up and the treasure-room opened. The monks had carried off everything of value. Precious stones encrusted on the sacrificial cups were gone, the gold and purple adornments on the vestments had been torn off. When the splendid sacrificial robe was displayed a brown cloud of moths escaped from its folds. At the bottom of the hollow of a tripod, Gnyphon saw a handful of ashes, the remains of myrrh burned before the triumph of the Christians by the last priest during the last sacrifice.

From this heap of sacred rubbish, poor rags, and broken goblets, rose a perfume of death and mildew, a sad and tender odour, as of incense to gods profaned.

A gentle melancholy came over Gnyphon's heart. He smiled, remembering something perhaps of his childhood; sweet cakes of barley and thyme, field daisies and jessamine which he used to carry with his mother to the altar of the village goddess; his childish prayers, not to the distant God, but to the little gods polished by the frequent touch of hands, carven in beechwood—the holy Penates. He pitied the vanished gods, and sighed sadly, but suddenly returned to himself and muttered—

"Suggestions of the Devil!"

The workmen were carrying up a heavy slab of marble, an antique bas-relief, stolen many years before and discovered in the hovel of a cobbler whose kitchen oven it had served to repair. Philomena, the old wife of a neighbouring clothier, a devout Christian, hated the cobbler's wife, who used to let her ass stray into Philomena's cabbage-yard. War had been maintained between them for years, but the Christian woman was in the end triumphant; for acting on her information the workmen had penetrated into the cobbler's house, and in order to carry off the bas-relief and slab had been obliged to demolish the oven.

This was a terrible blow to the cobbler's wife. Brandishing her shovel, she called down vengeance from all the gods on the impious; pulled her hair out in handfuls, groaning over her scattered pots and pans while her children squealed round her like the young birds of a devastated nest. But the bas-relief was carried off, despite her struggles, and Philomena set about the work of cleansing it. The draper's wife zealously scrubbed the marble which had been blackened by smoke and made greasy with spilt broth. Little by little the severe lines of the divine sculpture became visible. The young Dionysus, naked and proud, lay half-reclined, as if fatigued by Bacchic feasting, letting his hand, which held a cup, fall idly. A leopardess was licking up the last drops from the goblet, and the god, giver of joy to all living things, was gazing with a benign smile at the strength of the beast subdued by the grape. The bas-relief was hauled into position. The jeweller, clambering up before the image of Dionysus, inlaid the orbits of the god with two splendid sapphires, to serve as eyes.

"What's he doing there?" asked Gnyphon.

"Can't you see? They are eyes."

"Yes, certainly, but where do the stones come from?"

"From the monastery."

"But why have the monks allowed it?"

"How could they prevent it? The divine Augustus Julian himself ordered it. The god's blue eyes were used as an ornament on the robe of the Crucified that's all. . . They talk about charity and justice, and they themselves are the worst of brigands! See how beautifully the stones fit into their old setting! . . ."

The god fixed his sapphire eyes on Gnyphon. The old man recoiled and crossed himself, seized with dread.

"Lord have mercy on us! It's horrible!"

Remorse filled his soul, and while sweeping he began, as was his wont, to talk to himself—

"Gnyphon! Gnyphon! what a poor creature you are! . . . Just like a mangy dog one might say. . . You're ending your days in a nice way! Why have you gone and damned yourself? The fiend has over-tempted you! . . . And now you go into everlasting fire without a chance of salvation. You've smirched soul and body, Gnyphon, by serving the abomination of the heathen! . . . Better had it been for thee hadst thou never been born!"

"What are you groaning at, old man?" Philomena the draper's wife enquired.

"My heart is heavy! . . . Oh, how heavy!"

"Are you a Christian?"

"Christian?—I am a betrayer of Christ!" answered Gnyphon, using his broom vigorously.

"Would you like me to take away your sin so that not a trace of heathen defilement shall stick to you? You see I'm a Christian too, and yet afraid of nothing. Do you think I'd have undertaken work like this, if I hadn't known how to purify myself after it?"

Gnyphon stared at her, incredulous.

But the draper's wife, having ascertained that nobody could hear them, muttered mysteriously—

"Yes! . . . there is a means! I must tell you about it! A pilgrim made me a present of a little bit of Egyptian wood, called persis, which grows at Hermopolis, in the Thebaïd. When Jesus and His mother on their ass were going through the gates of the town, the persis tree bowed down before them to the earth; and ever since it has been a miraculous healer. I've got a little splinter of it, and I'll break off a bit for you. There's such a power in that wood, that if you put a bit into a vat of water and leave it there for a night the water becomes holy. You'll just wash yourself from head to foot in it, and the heathen abomination will leave you like magic, and you'll feel yourself light and pure. Isn't it written in the Bible, 'Thou shalt dip in the water and shalt become as white as snow'?"

"Oh, my benefactress!" groaned Gnyphon, "save me! Give me a chip of that wonderful wood!"

"Ah! you may well call it precious! . . . Just to do a good turn to a neighbour I'll give it you for a drachma."[1]

"What's that you're saying, mother? Why, I never earned a drachma in my life! Will you take three obols?"[2]

"Miser!" cried the draper's wife indignantly. "You stick at a drachma! . . . Isn't your immortal soul worth so much?"

"But after all do you think I shall be quite pure?" objected Gnyphon. "Perhaps the sin has so soaked into me that nothing can. . ."

"I'll solemnly swear to it," insisted the draper's wife. "Try it and you'll feel the miracle at once! . . . Your soul will shine like the sun—as pure as a white dove. . ."

---

1. Worth about 8*d.*
2. Six to the drachma.

II

At Constantinople Julian organised Bacchic processions. Seated in a chariot drawn by white mules, he held in his right hand a golden thyrsus, surmounted by cedar-fruit, and in the other a cup garlanded with ivy. The rays of the sun flooded the crystal wine-cup with vermilion. On each side of the chariot paced tame leopards, sent from the island of Serendib. In front, Bacchantes sang to the beat of timbrels, waving bright torches; and through the clouds of smoke lads, wearing the horns of Fauns, spilt wine into goblets. As they pushed laughing along, the red wine often splashed the bare shoulder of some Bacchante, and dashed the sunshine with rosy spray. An obese old man, a certain rascally money-lender—who, by the way, was head of the Imperial Treasury,—mounted on an ass, played the part of Silenus to perfection. The Bacchantes danced along, waving their hands towards the Emperor—

O Bacchus, ever girt with gleaming cloud!

Thousands of voices intoned the chant from the *Antigone* of Sophocles—

But now be glad of Victory! She meets our gladness with an answering smile; And Thebes, the many-charioted, hears far-resounding praise. Now then have done with wars,—forget your strifes! Visit all temples of the gods with night-long dance and song; And thou, O Theban Bacchus, lead our mirth! Lead thou, and shake the earth!

Suddenly Julian heard a burst of laughter, the shrill scream of a woman, and the quavering voice of an old man—

"Ah, my pretty chicken!"

It was the Bacchic priest, a good-humoured septuagenarian, who had pinched the bare elbow of a comely Bacchante. Julian's face darkened, and he summoned the old dotard, who ran up, still dancing—

"My friend," whispered Julian in his ear, "observe the dignity which befits your age and rank!"

"I am a simple and unlearned man. And I may venture to tell your

Majesty that while philosophy is beyond me, I venerate the gods. Ask anyone you please on that head—I have always been faithful to them. Only. . . when I see a pretty girl. . . my blood gets up! I am an old satyr. . ." Seeing the displeased face of the Emperor he stopped, assumed a more solemn air, and relapsed into still denser stupidity.

"Who is that young girl?" asked Julian.

"She who is carrying the sacred vessels on her head?"

"Yes."

"A courtesan of Chalcedon. . ."

"What! . . . You have authorised a courtesan to touch the holy vessels of the gods with her foul hands!"

"But, divine Augustus, you yourself ordained this procession. Who was there to choose from? All the noble women are Galileans. And then. . . none of them would have consented to have exhibited themselves half-naked. . ."

"Then they are all. . ."

"No, no! Some of them are dancing-girls, tragic actresses, horsewomen from the Hippodrome. See how gay they are and free from false shame! Believe me, the people like that! That's what they want. And there's a patrician woman! . . ."

The last-named was a Christian, an old maid looking out for husbands. On her head rose a helmet-shaped wig, a galerum made of blond hair powdered with gold—thickly covered with gems as an Indian idol; impudently painted, she drew her tiger-skin across her withered bosom, and smiled affectedly.

Julian looked down on the people with a sudden impulse of distaste.

Rope-dancers, drunken legionaries, venal women, circus-riders, gymnasts, actors, swarmed and wantoned all round him.

The procession arrived at a place where four streets met. One of the Bacchantes ran to a tavern, whence came an unpleasant smell of rancid frying fish, and bought some greasy cakes for three obols. These she ate, greedily licking her lips; and finished by wiping her hands on the purple silk of her robes, which had been granted for the procession by the Imperial Treasury.

The chorus of Sophocles soon became wearisome. Husky voices took up a street-song. The whole proceeding appeared to Julian to have been desecrated. A drunken man was picked up; and some thieves, playing the part of Fauns, were arrested. They defended themselves, and a fight ensued. The only personages in the whole company whose demeanour remained dignified and beautiful were the panthers.

At last they drew near the temple. Julian came down from his chariot.

"Can I really present myself before the altar of Dionysus surrounded by this human refuse?"

A chill of disgust ran through his body. He saw the brutal faces wasted with debauchery, corpse-like through their paint; the painful nudity of bodies deformed by fasting and anæmia. He breathed the atmosphere of low wine-shops, houses of ill-fame. The breath of the crowd, tainted with rotten fish and sour wine, smote him through the aromatic smoke. Scrolls of papyrus were stretched out to him from every side:

"I was promised a place in your stables. . . I have been paid nothing for renouncing Christ. . ."

"Don't desert us, Divine Augustus! Protect us! We denied for your sake the faith of our fathers! . . . If you give us up what will become of us?"

These were the voices drowned by the chorus of the feast.

Julian went into the temple, and contemplated the marvellous statue of Dionysus. His eyes, weary with human deformity, reposed on the pure lines of that divine body. He became oblivious of the crowd as if he were alone—the only man amidst a herd of animals.

The Emperor proceeded to the sacrifice. The people watched with amazement the Roman Cæsar, as Pontifex Maximus, in his zeal for religion doing the work of a slave—splitting wood, bringing twigs, drawing water, and cleansing the altar.

A rope-dancer said to his neighbour—

"Look how he keeps at it! He really loves his gods!"

"By this right hand," remarked the other, "few people care for father and mother as he cares for his gods!"

"You see," laughed a third, "how he puffs out his cheeks to kindle the fire again! . . . Blow, blow! . . . It won't catch! . . . Your uncle Constantine put *that* fire out."

The flames jetted up, illumining the Emperor's face.

Dipping the holy water brush into a shallow cup, a silver patine used to cover the chalice, he besprinkled the sacrificial water over the heads of the crowd. Some grimaced, others started, at feeling the cold drops on their faces.

When all the ceremonies were over, Julian remembered that he had prepared a philosophical discourse for the people.

"Men," said he, "the god Dionysus is the beginning of your souls' liberty. Dionysus breaks every chain that binds you; he mocks the strong, sets free the slave. . ."

But he perceived such a dull stupidity upon every face, such an expression of tedium and weariness, that the words died on his lips. A mortal disgust for humanity arose in his heart. He made a sign to the lance-bearers to come round him.

Grumbling and disappointed, the crowd dispersed.

"I'm going straight to church to get absolution. Do you think I shall be forgiven?" said one of the Fauns, snatching off his own false beard and horns with an angry gesture.

"It wasn't worth losing one's soul for that, eh?" observed with wrath a lady of doubtful reputation.

"Nobody wants your soul, or would give three obols for it!"

"The cursed devils!" yelled a drunkard. "They didn't give us enough wine to get the taste of it!"

In the sacristy of the temple the Emperor washed face and hands, took off the splendid Dionysian dress, and put on again the simple white tunic of the Pythagoreans. The sun was declining, and he waited the fall of dusk to retrace his way to the palace unperceived.

Julian went into the sacred wood of Dionysus, where the silence was broken only by the humming of bees and the tinkle of a brook. A sound of steps made him turn round. It was his old friend, one of Maximus' favourite pupils, the young Alexandrian doctor, Oribazius.

They walked on the narrow path side by side. The sun was shining through large golden leaves of the vine.

"Look!" said Julian smiling. "Here great Pan is still alive!"

Then in a lower tone he added, hanging his head—

"Oribazius! . . . You saw it?"

"Yes," responded the student. "But perhaps the fault lay with you, Julian. . . What did you hope for?"

The Emperor made no answer.

They came near a little ruined temple that ivy had invaded and overrun. Fragments lay about in the deep grass. A single column only remained standing; and on its lovely capital, clear-cut as the petals of a lily, shone the last rays of sunset.

The friends sat down on the flags together and inhaled the air, sweet with mint and thyme and wormwood. Julian put the leaves aside and pointing to an antique broken bas-relief—

"Oribazius! That is what I hoped for!"

The bas-relief represented a religious procession of the ancient Athenians.

"That is what I desired. . . beauty like theirs! Why from day today do men become more and more deformed and misfeatured? Where are the immortal old men, the austere heroes, the proud lads, the pure women in their white and floating robes? Where is that strength, that gaiety of heart? Galileans! Galileans! what have you done with these things?"

He gazed at the bas-relief with eyes full of infinite sadness and infinite love.

"Julian," asked Oribazius, gently, "do you believe in Maximus?"

"Yes."

"Wholly?"

"What do you mean?"

"I've always thought, Julian, that you suffer from the same malady as your enemies, the Christians!"

"What malady?"

"Faith in miracles."

Julian shook his head.

"If there be neither miracles nor gods my whole life is a madness! . . . No, we won't speak of that. And do not be too hard upon me on account of my love for ancient ceremonies. I scarcely can explain it to you. The old simple things stir tears in me; and I love the evening more than the morning, autumn better than spring. I love all that is fleeting! . . . even the perfume of flowers that have faded. . . What would you have, my friend? The gods shaped me so! . . . That pleasant melancholy, that golden faery twilight, are necessary to me. In the depth of antiquity there is to me something ineffably gracious and fair such as I find in no other region—the shining of sunset on marble mellowed by time. Do not rob me of the mad love of what is no more. Everything that has been, is fairer than the thing that is! Remembrance has more power over my soul than hope. . ."

Julian was silent, and with a smile on his lips looked into the distance, his head leaning back against the column.

"You speak as a poet," answered Oribazius. "But the dreams of a poet are perilous when the fate of a world is in his hands. Ought not he who reigns over men to be something more than a poet?"

"Whose life is higher?"

"That of the creator of a *new* life? . . ."

"New! new!" exclaimed Julian. "To be plain with you, your novelty sometimes strikes terror into me! It seems to me to be cold and hard as death. I tell you, my heart is in antiquity. The Galileans, like you, are always seeking novelty and stamping the old idols under foot! . . . Trust me, new life lies only in what is old; immortal is it and proud, however it be thus insulted!"

He drew himself up to his full height, pale and haughty, his eyes brilliant—

"They think that Hellas is dead! . . . And from every quarter of the compass black monks come swooping down, like ravens, on its marble body, and pick at it, joyously shrieking, 'Hellas is dead!' But they forget that Hellas cannot die, that Hellas is in our hearts! Hellas is the divine beauty of man upon earth. She but slumbers, and when she shall awake, woe to the crows of Galilee!"

"Julian," murmured Oribazius, "I fear for you. . . You wish to accomplish the impossible. . . Crows do not feed on the living, and the dead do not rise again. . . Ah, Cæsar! what if the miracle does not succeed?"

"I have no fear. My defeat shall be my victory!" exclaimed the Emperor, with so radiant a happiness on his young face that Oribazius was thrilled, as if the miracle was now to be achieved. "Glory to the rejected! Glory to the conquered! But before my destruction," he added with a proud smile, "we will fight a good fight! . . . I would that my enemies were worthy of my hate, and not of my contempt! . . . In truth I love my enemies. They teach me to feel and measure my own force! They bring into my heart the gaiety of Dionysus. Or it shall be the old Titan, snapping his chains, and kindling anew the Promethean fire! Titan against Galilean! . . . Rejoice, tribes and peoples of the earth! I am the messenger of life who shall set you free! I *am* the Anti-Christ!"

III

In the neighbouring monastery, behind windows and doors closely sealed, solemn prayers of the religious were resounding above the distant noise of Bacchic chants. To drown them the monks joined their voices in shrill lamentation—

"Why, Lord, hast Thou abandoned us? Why has Thy anger fallen upon Thy sheep?

"Why hast Thou given us up in dishonour to the hand of the heathen?

"Why hast Thou let mankind do outrage unto Thee?"

The ancient words of the prophet Daniel took on an unwonted meaning—

"The Lord has delivered us to the evil king, the cunningest in all the earth! . . . "

Late in the night, when the sun had sunk upon the streets, the monks went back to their cells.

Brother Parphenas could not even think of sleeping. His face was pale and gentle, and in his great eyes, clear as a maiden's, perplexity was visible when he spoke about worldly matters.

He spoke rarely, indistinctly, and in a fashion so quaint, on topics so childish, that it was difficult to hear him without smiling. Sometimes he laughed without cause; and austere monks would say to him—

"What are you cackling at? Is it to please the Devil?"

Then he would timidly explain that he was laughing at his own thoughts, and thus convince everybody that Parphenas was mad.

One great art he possessed—that of illuminating manuscripts; and this art of Brother Parphenas brought to the monastery not only money, but renown in the most distant provinces. Of this he had no suspicion, and if he had been able to understand what reputation means, would rather have been dismayed than delighted.

His artistic occupations, which cost him vast pains (Brother Parphenas pushed perfection of detail to an exquisite finish), were not in his eyes a labour, but an amusement. He never said, "I'm going to work." But he always asked of the old Father Superior Pamphilus, who loved him tenderly, "Father, give me your blessing, I am going to play."

And when he had mastered some difficult combination of ornament, he would clap his hands in self-congratulation. Brother Parphenas so enjoyed the solitude and calm of night that he had learned to work by lamp-light. He used to say that the colours took on unexpected shades, and that the yellow light did no harm to drawings in the realm of pure fancy.

In his narrow cell Parphenas lighted the earthen lamp and placed it on a plank, among his little flasks, fine brushes, and colour-boxes of vermilion, silver, and liquid gold. He crossed himself cautiously, dipped his brush, and began to paint the outspread tails of two peacocks above a frontispiece. The golden peacocks, on a green field, were drinking at a streamlet of turquoise, with raised beaks and outstretched necks. Other rolls of parchment lay by him, unfinished. His world was a supernatural and charming world. Bordering the text of the page ran an embroidery of fabulous creations; a faery architecture of fantastic trees and animals. Parphenas thought of nothing while he created these things, but a happy serenity transformed his face. Hellas, Assyria, Persia, the Indies, Byzantium idealised, and the troubled vision of future worlds, of all peoples, and of all ages; these mingled in the paradise of the monk, and shone, with a glitter as of jewels, round the initial letters of the holy books.

This one represented the Baptism. St. John was pouring water on the head of Christ, and at his elbow the Pagan god of rivers was amiably tilting a water-jar, while the former proprietor of the bank (that is to say, the Devil) held a towel in readiness to offer the Saviour after the ceremony.

Brother Parphenas in his innocence had no fear of the old gods. They used to amuse him. He regarded them as long ago converted to Christianity. He never failed to place the god of mountains, in the shape of a naked youth, on the summit of every hill. When he was drawing the passage of the Red Sea, a woman holding an oar symbolised the Sea, and a naked man, inscribed Bodos, stood for the Abyss engulfing Pharaoh, while on the bank sat a melancholy woman, in a tan-coloured tunic, denoting the Desert.

Here, there, and everywhere, in the curve of a horse's neck, the fold of a robe, the simple pose of a god lying on his elbow, were evidences of antique grace and simplicity.

But on this night his "play" interested the artist no more. His tireless fingers were shaky, and the smile had left his lips.

Listening awhile, he opened a cedar-wood box, took out an awl used in the binding of books, crossed himself, and shielding the ruddy flame of the lamp with his hand, noiselessly issued from his cell. It was hot in the silent corridor. No sound was heard but the buzzing of a fly taken in a spider's web.

Parphenas went down to the church, which was lighted by a single lamp, placed before the old ivory-carved diptych. Two large sapphires in the aureole of Jesus, who was sitting on the Virgin's arm, had been carried off by the Pagans, and transferred to their original setting in the Temple of Dionysus. These black hollows in the yellow ivory were to Parphenas wounds in some living body.

"No, I cannot bear it," he murmured, kissing the hand of the Infant Jesus. "I cannot bear it; 'twould be better to die!"

These sacrilegious marks in the ivory tortured and angered him more than outrage on a human being.

In a corner of the church he discovered a rope-ladder, used in lighting chapel-lamps. Carrying this ladder he went forth into a narrow passage leading to the outer gate, in front of which the fat brother-cellarer, Chorys, was snoring on the straw. Parphenas glided past like a shadow. The lock of the door made a grinding noise. Chorys sat unblinking, and then rolled round on the straw.

Parphenas leapt over a low wall and found himself in the deserted street, into which the full moon was shining. There was a low roar of the sea. The young monk went along the Temple of Dionysus up to a point in which the wall was plunged in shadow. Thence he threw up the rope-ladder, so that it hooked itself to the metal pinnacle which decorated the corner. The ladder swung from the claw of a sphinx. The monk clambered by it to the roof.

Far off, cocks crew; a dog barked; and then again came silence, measured only by the slow sighings of the sea.

Parphenas threw the ladder down the inner wall of the temple, and descended.

The eyes of the god, two lengthy sapphires, shone with intense vividness in the moonlight, gazing down on the monk. Parphenas, thrilled by the silence, trembled and crossed himself. He clambered on to the altar where Julian had offered the sacrifice, and his heels felt the warmth of the half-extinguished embers.

The monk drew the awl from his pocket. The god's eyes sparkled close to his face, and the artist felt the careless smile of Dionysus, and the lovely pose of the body. Even while digging out the sapphires, his admiring hand involuntarily spared the body of the marble tempter.

Finally the deed was done. The blinded Dionysus stared horribly on the monk from his hollow orbits. Terror fairly seized Parphenas. It seemed that he was watched. He leapt down from the altar, ran to the rope-ladder, climbed, threw it down the other side of the wall, without taking time to fix it properly. This cost him a fall during the latter part of the descent.

With crimson face, and clothes ragged and disordered, but griping the precious sapphires, he slunk furtively across the street, and ran to the monastery.

The porter did not wake, and Parphenas furtively entered the chapel. At the sight of the diptych, his mind grew calm again. He tried the sapphire eyes of Dionysus into the holes. They fitted admirably, and soon were glittering anew in the aureole of the Infant Jesus. He returned to his cell, lit the lamp, and went to bed. Huddling himself up, and hiding his face in his hands, he burst into a fit of muffled laughter, like a child delighted at some piece of mischief and afraid of discovery. He then straightway fell sound asleep.

When he awoke, the morning waves of the Propontic were shining through the small barred window, and the pigeons cooing and shaking their wings.

The laughter of the previous night was still in the heart of Parphenas. He ran to the painting-table and contentedly looked at his unfinished arabesque of the Earthly Paradise. Adam and Eve were seated in a meadow, glittering in the sunlight; it was a vellum tapestry of purple, blue, and gold. And so the little monk worked on, innocently investing the body of Adam with the proud antique beauty of young Dionysus.

IV

The celebrated sophist, Hekobolis, Court professor of eloquence, had begun to climb the ladder of promotion at the very lowest rungs. He had been a servant attached to the Temple of Astarte at Hieropolis. At sixteen, having stolen some articles of value, he escaped to Constantinople, lived with the dregs of the populace, soaked in every kind of rascality. Later he took to the high-roads, where, roving on ass-back from village to village, he lived from hand to mouth, in company both with respectable pilgrims and with bands of brigands—sacrificers to Dindymene, that goddess beloved of the people. Finally he reached the school of Proeres the rhetorician, and soon became a teacher of eloquence himself.

During the last years of Constantine the Great, when the Christian religion became fashionable at Court, Hekobolis became a Christian. The clergy showed him sympathy, but Hekobolis (though never inopportunely) changed his form of creed as the wind blew: from Arian he became Orthodox, from Orthodox Arian, and every conversion raised him a step in office.

The clergy pushed him up this ascent, and in turn he lent the clergy a helping hand.

His head grew grey; he became pleasantly corpulent, his sage speeches more and more honeyed and insinuating, his cheeks more rosy, his eyes more kindly and brilliant. At moments an evil irony sparkled in them, as of some cold and arrogant spirit, but the eyelids would promptly drop and the sparkle vanish. All his habits were clerical. He was a strict observer of fasts, and an exquisite judge of cookery. His lean diet was more refined than the most sumptuous course of holiday feeding; just as his ecclesiastical witticisms were keener than the frankest pleasantries of the Pagans. He used to be served with a cooling drink made of beetroot and savoured with delicious spices. Many thought it preferable to wine. When denied ordinary wheaten bread he invented cakes of a desert manna, with which, it is said, Pachomius fed himself in Egypt. Ill-natured folk insinuated that Hekobolis was a libertine, and quaint tales were told about him at Constantinople. A young woman avowed to her confessor that she had fallen from chastity—

"It is a great sin! And with whom were you guilty, my daughter?"

"With Hekobolis, father!" The priestly visage cleared up. "With Hekobolis; ah, really! Well, well, the holy man is devoted to the Church! Repent, my daughter; the Lord will forgive!"

Such anedoctes were mere tittle-tattle. But his thick red lips were a trifle too prominent in the respectable shorn visage of the dignitary, although he usually kept them tightly closed, with an expression of monastic humility. Women were fond of his company.

Sometimes Hekobolis used to disappear for several days. No one fathomed the mystery, for he kept his own counsel. Neither servant nor slave accompanied him on these enigmatic journeys, from which he would return calmed and refreshed.

Under the Emperor Constantius, he received the appointment of Court rhetorician, with a superb salary, the senatorial laticlave, and the blue shoulder-ribbon, a distinction of the highest dignitaries. Nor was his ambition satisfied.

But at the moment when Hekobolis was preparing to mount a step higher, Constantius unexpectedly died. Julian, the Church's enemy, ascended the throne. Hekobolis lost no whit of his presence of mind. He merely did what many others were doing, but did it neither too soon nor too late.

Julian, in the first days of his reign, organised a theological controversy in his palace. A young doctor of philosophy, esteemed by everybody for his uprightness and noble nature, Cæsar of Cappadocia,—brother of the famous theologian, Basil the Great,—undertook the defence of the Christian faith against the Emperor himself.

In such tournaments of learning Julian authorised an entire independence of language, and even liked to be answered with passion and complete disregard of rank.

Discussion was of the keenest kind, and considerable numbers of sophists, priests, and men of science were present. Usually the opponent little by little gave way, yielding, not to the logic of the Greek philosopher, but to the majesty of the Roman Emperor.

But on this occasion it was not so. Cæsar of Cappadocia did not yield. He was a young man, almost feminine in the grace of his movements, and with a steady clearness in his frank eyes. He denominated the Platonic philosophy "the tortuous wisdom of the serpent," contrasting it with the heavenly wisdom of the Gospel. Julian frowned, bit his lips, bridling his anger with difficulty. The argument, like all sincere discussions, ended without results, and the Emperor, recovering his self-possession, quitted the hall with a philosophic jest, and a face of smilingly regretful magnanimity; in reality, pierced to the heart.

Precisely at this moment, Hekobolis, the rhetorician, came up. Julian, who considered him an enemy, asked him—

"What do you want?"

Hekobolis fell on his knees, and began a confession of repentance. For long, he said, he had hesitated; but the reasonings of the Emperor had finally convinced him. He cursed the dark Galilean superstition, and his heart returned to the remembrance of his childhood and the bright gods of Olympus.

The Emperor raised the old man, and, scarcely able to speak with emotion, pressed him convulsively to his bosom, and kissed him on his shaven cheeks and thick red lips. His eyes sought out Cæsar of Cappadocia to feast on his opponent's humiliation.

Julian kept Hekobolis near him for several days, repeating everywhere the story of his conversion, proud of his disciple as a child of a new toy, as a youth of his first mistress.

The Emperor desired to give some Court place of honour to his new friend, but Hekobolis flatly refused, alleging himself to be unworthy such distinction. He had decided to prepare his soul for the virtue of the Olympians by a long novitiate; and to purge his heart of Galilean impiety by personal service to one of the old gods.

Julian therefore nominated him chief sacrificial priest of Bithynia and Paphlagonia.

Persons bearing this title were called by the Pagans Archiepiscopts. The Archbishop Hekobolis thus governed two Asiatic provinces. Having taken the new way, he pursued it with as much success as the old, and even contributed to the conversion of many Christians to Hellenism.

Hekobolis became the high-priest to the celebrated Phoenician goddess, Astarte Atargatis, where in childhood he had served as a slave. This temple was built half-way between Chalcedon and Nicomedia, on a lofty promontory running out into the Propontic Sea. The place was called Gargarus. Pilgrims came thither from all corners of the earth to adore Aphrodite Astarte, goddess of life and love.

V

In one of the halls of his palace at Constantinople Julian was busy with affairs of state.

Between the porphyry columns on the terrace, looking out on the Bosphorus, lay a sparkling view of the pale blue sea. The young Emperor was seated at a round marble table, covered with papyri and rolls of parchment. Silentiaries of the palace stooped over the table, scribbling audibly with reed-pens. Some had a sleepy expression, not being accustomed to get up at such an early hour. Standing a little aloof, behind the colonnade, two men were exchanging observations in a low voice. These were Hekobolis and Julius Mauricus, an official with an intelligent, bilious countenance. This elegant Court sceptic, amidst general superstition, was one of the last admirers of Lucian, the satirist of Samos, author of stinging dialogues, in which he railed so pitilessly at all the idols of Olympus and Golgotha, every tradition of Greece and Rome. Julian was dictating a document to the chief priest of Galicia, Arsacius—

"Do not allow the sacrificial priests to frequent the theatre, to drink in taverns, or follow low trades. Respect the obedient, punish the unfaithful. In every town cause guest-houses to be built for pilgrims, who should therein find ample charity. Not only for Hellenist pilgrims, but for all, to whatever profession of faith they may belong. We ordain to be distributed in Galicia thirty thousand measures of wheat, a hundred and twenty thousand gallons of wine. Distribute a fifth part amongst the poor living near the temple, the rest amongst pilgrims and the sick. It is shameful that the Hellenists starve, when the Jews have not a beggar amongst them and the Galileans feed both their own poor and ours. They act like those who entice children with sweetmeats, beginning by hospitality, inviting to feasts of brotherly love. Little by little they finish by fasts, flagellations, madness, deaths of martyrs, and the horror of hell. Such are the customary means of those enemies of the human race who call themselves Christians and brothers. Combat them by charity, given in the name of the eternal Olympian gods. Announce in all cities and villages that such is my heartfelt will. If I learn that you have acted according to my decree, my favour shall be with you. Explain to the citizens that I hold myself in readiness to come to their help at any moment in all circumstances. But if they desire to obtain my favours, let them bow before Dindymene, the great Cybele, mother of the gods, and let them give glory unto her throughout all peoples, throughout all time."

He wrote the concluding words with his own hand.

Breakfast was served—bread, cheese, fresh olives, and a light white wine. Julian ate and drank without ceasing work. But suddenly he turned and pointing to the golden plate of olives, asked his favourite slave, who had been brought by him from Gaul, and invariably served him at table—

"Why this gold plate? Where is the other in earthenware?"

"Pardon, sire! . . . it is broken."

"Broken to pieces?"

"No—at the edge only. . ."

"Bring it here."

The slave ran to get the plate in question.

"It can be used for a long time yet," said Julian.

He smiled.

"My friends, I have long observed that the broken outlasts the new. I confess I have a fancy for cracked things. They have the charm of old friends! . . . I fear novelty and hate change," and he laughed heartily at himself. "You see what philosophy lies in a broken plate!"

Julius Mauricus twitched Hekobolis by the sleeve—

"Did you hear? That's his character! He keeps his cracked plates and expiring gods; and that is how a world's destiny is decided!"

Julian had become completely absorbed in edicts and laws for reform.

In every city in the Empire it was his wish to found schools, lectureships, debating-halls; special forms of prayer, and philosophic sermons, refuges for the upright, and for those who desired to devote themselves to philanthropic meditation.

"What?" whispered Mauricus to Hekobolis. "Monasteries in honour of Aphrodite and Apollo? A new horror!"

"Yes, my friend, with the aid of the gods we shall accomplish it all," concluded the Emperor. "The Galileans want to convince the world that they have a monopoly of brotherly love, although it belongs to all philosophers, whatever be the gods they revere. My task in the world is to preach a new love; a love free and glad as the very sky of the Olympians!"

Julian glanced round those present, but on the faces of his dignitaries did not find what he sought. Deputations from the Christian professors of rhetoric and philosophy at this moment entered the hall. An edict forbidding Christian teachers to give instruction in classical eloquence had recently appeared. The Christian grammarians had therefore to renounce their faith or quit their schools.

Scroll in hand, one of these teachers approached the Emperor. He was a little thin man with a confused manner, bearing a strong likeness to a parrot. Two raw and awkward pupils accompanied him.

"Beloved of the gods, have pity on us!"

Julian interrupted—

"What's your name?"

"Papirian, a Roman citizen."

"Well, understand, my dear Papirian, I bear no grudge against you. . . on the contrary, remain Galilean. . ."

The old man fell at the Emperor's feet and kissed them.

"Forty years have I been teaching grammar. . . I know Homer and Hesiod better than anyone else. . ."

"What do you want. . ." asked Augustus sternly.

"Sir, I have six children! . . . Don't rob me of my last crust! . . . My pupils like me; ask them if I teach anything harmful!"

Emotion prevented Papirian from continuing his speech, and he pointed to his pupils, who, not knowing where to put their hands, stood together staring and blushing.

"No, my friends," said the Emperor gently but firmly. "The law is just. To my mind it is absurd that Christian teachers, in explaining Homer, should expound away the gods of whom Homer sang. If you believe that our wise men composed mere fables on the subject of our gods, you should go to your churches, and expound Matthew and Luke! . . . And note, Galileans, all is done in your own interest. . ."

One of the rhetoricians muttered—

"In our interest! We shall starve!"

"Do you not fear profanation by what is worse than starvation— lying wisdom? You say 'Blessed are the poor in spirit,' Be, then, poor in spirit! . . . Perhaps you imagine that I am ignorant of your teaching? I know it better than you do! I see in the Galilean commandments depths you have never dreamed of! . . . But let each take his own path. Leave us our frivolous learning and philosophy, our poor literary knowledge. What have these poisoned streams to do with you? Yours is a higher wisdom! We own the earthly kingdom, and you. . . the Kingdom of Heaven. That's no small thing for humble folk like you! . . . Dialectic and logic leads to freethinking or heresies? Be then, in good sooth, simple as children. The ignorance of the fishermen of Capernaum is above all the Platonic dialogues, is it not? All the wisdom of the Galileans is summed in the word 'Believe'! Ah, rhetoricians, if you were true Christians you would bless our edict. At this moment, it is not your souls, but your bodies which rebel; your bodies, which find sweetness in sinfulness. That is all I have to say to you, and I hope that you will learn to agree with me, and that you will find that the Roman Emperor is more anxious for your souls' salvation than you are yourselves!"

Julian calmly threaded his way through the crowd of unhappy rhetoricians, contented with his speech, but Papirian, still kneeling, tore his hair—

"Why, Queen of Heaven, dost thou suffer such things to be?" and the two scholars, seeing their master's distress, with clumsy fists brushed the tears from their eyes.

VI

J ulian remembered the interminable conflicts between Orthodox and Arians under Constantius at the council of Milan, and designing to profit by that animosity, he decided to follow the example of his Christian predecessors and convoke an oecumenical council.

On one occasion, in a private conversation, he had declared that, instead of persecuting the Galileans, he wished to give them full freedom of faith, and to call back from exile Donatists, Cæcilians, Marcionists, Montanists, and other heretics banished by the councils of Constantine and Constantius. He thought that there was no better means of abolishing Christianity.

"You will see, my friends, when all the sectaries shall have returned, such strife will be kindled between these brethren, that they will begin to torture each other like birds of prey loosed from their cage into the arena of the circus. They will bring shame upon their Master's name more quickly and effectually than I could by any persecutions and martyrdoms!"

And so Julian sent into all parts of the Empire edicts authorising the banished to return. The wisest Galilean teachers were at the same time invited to come to the palace at Constantinople for a religious discussion; but the majority of those invited were unaware of the subject to be discussed, the wording of the letters being skilfully vague. Guessing some trick, many, pleading sickness, failed to present themselves.

The blue morning sky seemed dark against the dazzling whiteness of the double colonnade surrounding the court known as the Atrium of Constantine. White pigeons were fluttering here and there in the sky, with gleeful beating of wings. In the centre of the court stood the statue of Venus Callipyge, in warm and beautiful marble. The monks, passing by her, turned away, hiding their eyes, but the tender temptress remained, for all that, in their midst. Not without purpose had Julian chosen this situation for the Galilean council. The dark robes of the religious appeared blacker still, their starvation-dulled faces more meagre. Each strove to wear an air of indifference and presumption, feigning not to see his enemy at his elbow, yet casting stealthy glances of curiosity and contempt.

"Holy Mother of God, what is this? Whither are we fallen?" said the old bishop Eustace, with profound emotion. "Let me pass out, soldiers!"

"Gently, gently, my friend," answered the centurion of the lance-bearers, the barbarian Dagalaïf, politely keeping him from the door.

"I'm choking in this pit of heresy! let me pass!"

"By the will of Augustus, everybody here has come to the council," responded Dagalaïf, inflexibly keeping him back.

"But this is not a council, it is a den of thieves!"

Among the Galileans some more cheerful persons began to laugh at the provincial manners and the strong Armenian accent of Eustace, who, losing courage, quieted down, and slipped into a corner, muttering—

"Lord, Lord, how have I offended Thee?"

Evander of Nicomedia also quickly repented of having come and of having led thither brother Juventinus, a disciple of Didimus, who had but newly arrived at Constantinople.

Evander was one of the greatest dogmatists of his time; a man of profound and lucid intellect. He had lost his health, and grown prematurely old, over his books; he was almost blind, and his short-sighted eyes worn out with fatigue. Innumerable heresies besieged his brain, leaving him no sleep, or tormenting him in dreams, ever tempting him by their dread subtleties. Evander used to collect heresies, as one might collect jewels or scientific rarities, in an immense manuscript entitled *Against Heresy*. He hunted for them greedily, imagined those that might be in existence, and the better he refuted the more he was attracted towards them.

Sometimes he would entreat God to grant him simple faith, and God would refuse him simplicity.

In ordinary life he was timid, simple, and offenceless as a child. For rascals to deceive Evander was as easy as breathing, and on this score the mockers told a hundred stories against him. Plunged in doctrinal dreams, the bishop continually found himself in awkward situations. In one of these fits of abstraction he had come to this singular council, without thinking why he went thither, but attracted by the hope of lighting on a new heresy. Now his face was twitching with annoyance, and he shaded his weak eyes against the too bright rays of the sun, longing to be back amongst his books in his little twilight chamber.

Evander kept Juventinus at his side, and warned him against temptation by criticising various heresies. In the centre of the hall a vigorous old man was striding up and down. He had high cheek-bones and thick grey hair. It was the septuagenarian bishop Purpuris, recalled from exile by Julian. Neither Constantine nor Constantius had

DMITRY MEREZHKOVSKY

succeeded in stifling the Donatist heresy. For fifty years past streams of blood had flowed in Africa, by reason of the unjust deposition of a Donatist in favour of a Cæcilian, or of a Cæcilian in favour of a Donatist. Nor could any augury be made as to the final issue of this fratricidal strife.

Juventinus noticed that the Cæcilian bishop who was passing in front of Purpuris brushed the vestments of the Donatist with the corner of his chasuble. The latter turned fiercely round, with a growl of disgust, and, taking the stuff between two fingers, shook it several times before the eyes of everybody.

Evander informed Juventinus in a low voice that when a Cæcilian happened to enter a Donatist congregation he was hunted out and the flags touched by his feet were washed with salt water.

Behind Purpuris, dogging him step by step, walked his faithful bodyguard, an enormous half-savage African, brown-skinned, terrible, flat-nosed, and thick-lipped, the deacon Leona. He was armed with a cudgel, gripped tightly in his nervous hands. He was an Ethiopian peasant, belonging to the self-mutilating sect called Circumcellions. Weapon in hand, these sectaries would run along the high-roads offering money to passers-by, in return for destruction, adding, "Kill us, or we will kill you!" In the name of Christ the Circumcellions mutilated themselves, burned themselves, drowned themselves, but never would hang themselves, because Judas was hanged. They declared that suicide for God's glory washed all sin from the soul, and the people looked on them as martyrs. Before death, they abandoned themselves to all pleasures; ate, drank, and offered violence to women. A great number refrained from using swords, Christ having forbidden it, but on the other hand they felled heretics and pagans with huge bludgeons, "according to the Scriptures," and with consciences at ease. While spilling blood they would cry "Glory be to God!"

And the peaceful inhabitants lived more in terror of this religious cry than of war-trumpets or the roarings of a lion. The Donatists considered the Circumcellions as their guardians, and these Ethiopian peasants finding theological controversies hard to understand, the Donatists would point out beforehand those whom they were to strike according to the Scriptures.

Evander directed the attention of Juventinus on a handsome youth, whose tender and ingenuous expression seemed almost that of a young girl. He was a Caïnite.

"Blessed be our tameless brothers, Cain, Shem, the inhabitants of Sodom and Gomorrah!" preached the Caïnites. "They are seeds of high wisdom, of reason divine! . . . Come to us, all ye hunted, reprobate, revolted! Blessed be Judas! he alone among the apostles was initiated in the higher knowledge! . . . He betrayed Christ that He might die and rise again, because he knew the death of Christ would save the world! He who is initiated in our wisdom can transgress all limits, daring all, despising matter, trampling all fear under foot; and giving himself up to all sins and delight of the sense, attain that disgust for matter which is the final purity of the soul!"

"Look, Juventinus, there is a man who believes himself above archangels and seraphim," said Evander, waving his hand towards a young and sprightly Egyptian, who held himself aloof from everyone, an ironic smile on his lips, which were painted, like those of a courtesan. He was dressed in the latest Byzantine vogue, his white hands loaded with rings. His name was Cassiodorus, and he was a Valentinian. "In the Christians," affirmed the arrogant Valentinians, "there is a soul, as in animals; but there is no mind, as in us. We alone are initiated into the mysteries of the Gnosis and of the divine Plenum. It follows, therefore, that we alone are worthy to call ourselves human. All others are, as it were, pigs and dogs."

Cassiodorus would say to his disciples: "You should know everyone, but no one should understand you. Before the profane, deny the Gnosis, be dumb, and despise evidences of the gospel. Despise professions of faith and martyrdoms; love silence and mystery. Be for your enemy as invisible, elusive, inviolable, as the immaterial forces. Ordinary Christians need good actions for their salvation; but those who possess the highest knowledge of God, the Gnosis, need not perform these actions. We are the sons of light, they the sons of darkness. We fear not sin, because we know that sin is needful to the material body, and even to the immaterial soul. We are placed so high that, let our faults be what they will, we cannot err. Our heart remains chaste in the delights of matter, as pure gold keeps its brightness in the mud."

Elsewhere Juventinus saw an old man, with a hang-dog expression and a squint, the Adamite Prodick, explaining his teaching in a loud voice. He believed in restoring the innocence of the first Adam. The Adamites performed their mysteries in a church warmed like a bath and called the "Eden." Like our first ancestors, they evinced no shame in the absence of clothes, and assevered that among themselves all men and women were noted for lofty modesty, although the innocence of these paradisiac assemblies had sometimes been questioned.

At the elbow of the Adamite Prodick a woman—pale-faced, grey-haired, and proud, her eyes half-shut with fatigue—was sitting on the ground. She wore episcopal garb. She was the prophetess of the Montanists. Yellow-skinned Copts were tending her devotedly, gazing on her with solicitude, and calling her "Heavenly Dove." Consuming themselves for years in ecstasies of impossible love, they preached the duty of bringing humanity to an end, through the practice of continence. Scattered in numerous bands on the burning hills of Phrygia, near the ruins of Papusa, these pallid dreamers would remain sitting motionless, day after day, their eyes fixed on the horizon, on which the Saviour was to appear. On foggy evenings, above the grey plain, in the clouds, in rays of melting gold they would catch visions of the glory of God—the new Zion descending upon earth. Year after year they would wait, dying at last in the hope that the celestial kingdom was just about to descend upon the ruins of Papusa. Sometimes lifting her wearied eyelids, and with troubled gaze fixed in the distance, the prophetess was murmuring in Syriac—

"*Maran Atha*"—"The Lord is coming!"

And her Coptic servants bowed towards her, the better to hear.

Juventinus listened to the explanations of Evander. All this resembled some wild and torturing dream. His heart shivered, under a bitter flood of pity.

Silence was at last restored; all looks turned towards the same spot, at the opposite extremity of the court, where Julian was standing. His face was clear and firm, and he wore an air of assumed indifference His garb was the simple white chlamys of the philosophers.

"Old men and masters," said Augustus, addressing the assembly, "we have thought it well to give evidence of our indulgence and compassion to all our subjects who profess the Galilean teaching. For those who are gone astray it is better to feel compassion than hatred; better to lead the obstinate to the truth by exhortation, and in no wise by harryings, blows, or corporeal tortures. Wishing to restore peace to the world, so long troubled by religious discord, I have called you, O learnéd Galileans, together. We shall hope that under our protection you will give an example of those lofty virtues which befit your wisdom and your spiritual divinity."

So, with the easy gestures of a practised speaker, he began a speech prepared beforehand. But the benevolent words were not lacking in ironic allusion.

He made it clear he had not forgotten the stupid and coarse altercations that had taken place under Constantius, at the council of Milan. He mentioned, with an evil smile, those audacious persons who, regretting that they were no longer allowed to persecute or martyrise their brethren, had urged the ignorant populace into rebellion, poured oil on fire, and attempted to fill the world with fratricidal madness. These were the real enemies of humanity, and guilty of the greatest evil of all, namely, anarchy.

And he finished his harangue by the following unexpected words—

"We have called back from banishment your brothers, who had been hunted forth from the councils of Constantine and Constantius, because we desired to give liberty to all citizens of the Roman Empire. And for the complete suppression of discord, we confide to you, wise teachers, the duty of settling for Galileans a single and unique profession of faith. It is to this end that we have convoked you in our palace. Judge now, and authoritatively decide. In order to afford you full freedom of speech we will withdraw, and await your wise decision."

Before anyone had time to grasp the situation, or to answer this strange discourse, Julian, surrounded by his philosophic friends, left the court and disappeared.

Everybody was dumb. Someone uttered a long sigh, and in the general silence the beating of pigeons' wings and the rippling of the fountain alone were audible. Suddenly, on the raised marble daïs, which had served as tribune for Julian, appeared the kindly old man at whose provincial bearing and Armenian accent everybody had laughed.

His face was red, his eyes burning with vehemence. The Emperor's speech had offended the old bishop. Filled with fearless religious zeal, Eustace advanced towards the members of the council—

"Fathers and brothers," he exclaimed, and his voice was so stern and unshaken that no one thought of laughing at it—"Fathers and brothers, let us part in peace! He who has called us here, to seduce and to insult us, knows neither the canons of the Church nor the rules of the councils. He hates even the name of Jesus! Let us not be a sport to our enemies, let us restrain all angry words! I entreat you, in the name of the eternal God, let us separate in silence!"

He pronounced these words in a loud and ringing voice, his eyes fixed on a raised gallery, curtained by purple hangings. The Emperor, surrounded by his Hellenist friends, had just appeared there. A murmur of fright and astonishment ran through the assembly. Julian gazed at

Eustace, but the old man sustained his gaze. The Emperor's face grew dark.

At that moment the Donatist Purpuris brutally thrust off the bishop and took his place on the tribune.

"Do not listen to him," cried Purpuris; "do not let us separate, in scorn of the will of Augustus! The Cæcilians bear a grudge against him, because he has delivered us."

"No, in all truth, no, my brothers!" protested Eustace.

"Leave us, ye accursed! We are not your brothers! We are the wheat-ears of God—you the straw destined for the burning! . . ." And waving his hand towards the apostate Emperor Purpuris continued in a solemn tone, as if chanting a nuptial song—

"Behold our saviour! Look on him! . . . Glory, glory, to the most compassionate and learned Augustus! . . . Thou shalt trample on the snake and the reptile! Thou shalt conquer the lion, for the angels watch over thee in all thy doings. . . Hail!"

The congregation became unsettled. Some declared that the advice of Eustace must be followed. Others asked to be heard, not wishing to lose the opportunity of expounding their doctrines before a general religious council. Faces kindled and voices rose.

"Let a Cæcilian enter one of our churches now" exulted Purpuris, "and we'll place our hands on his head, not to choose him as our shepherd, but to crack his skull!"

Many forgot the purpose of the meeting and engaged in subtle discussions, seeking converts. The Basilidian, Triphon, who hailed from Egypt, surrounded by curious hearers, exhibited a transparent chrysolith amulet, bearing the mysterious word "Abraxa."

"He who shall understand the meaning of the word *Abraxa*," Triphon was saying to the group around him, "shall receive all freedom, shall become an immortal, and, tasting all sins, be sullied by none. *Abraxa* represents by letters the number of the mountains in heaven, three hundred and sixty-five. Above the three hundred and sixty-five celestial spheres, above the hierarchies of angels and archangels, there is a certain Nothingness, nameless, and more beautiful than any light, a motionless and sterile Nothingness. . ."

"The motionless and sterile nothingness is in your own stupid head!" growled an Arian bishop, striding straight up to Triphon.

The Gnostic, according to his custom, became silent, locking his lips in a contemptuous smile, and raising a forefinger—

"Wisdom! Wisdom!" he exclaimed, and vanished in the crowd.

The prophetess of Papusa, among her anxious Copts, stood up, terrible, pale, half-swooning, and groaned, as if her troubled eyes saw nothing, as if her ears heard nothing—

"*Maran Atha*"—"The Lord is coming!"

The disciples of the youth Epiphanes, a Pagan demi-god or Christian martyr, worshipped in the oratories of Cephalonia, were declaiming brotherhood and equality—

"There are no laws but these: Destroy all; let all be in common—women, lands, riches, like earth, air, and sun!"

The Ophites, serpent-worshippers, raised above their heads a cross, round which a tame adder was coiling—

"The wisdom of the Serpent," they said, "gives man a knowledge of good and evil; behold the saviour, Ophiomorphos, the serpentiform! Fear nothing! Hearken to him! Taste the forbidden fruit, and ye shall be even as gods!"

A perfumed and curled Marcosianist, lifting on high a crystal cup full of water with the skilful gestures of a juggler, invited curiosity—

"Look at this miracle! the water's going to boil and be turned into blood!"

Colabasians were there, counting their fingers with inconceivable celerity, and demonstrating that all the numbers of Pythagoras, every mystery of heaven and earth, were comprised in the letters of the Greek alphabet—

"Alpha, Omega—the beginning and the end, and between them the Trinity; Beta, Gamma, Delta—the Father, the Son, and the Holy Spirit! You see how simple it is!"

Fabionites, gluttonous Carpocratians, debauched Barbelonites stood up, preaching such follies that hearers possessing a vestige of morality put their fingers in their ears. Many strove to move their audiences by the attractive force over the imagination possessed by madness and monstrosity. Every man was certain of his own gospel. Yet all were enemies. Even the minute sect, hidden in remote provinces of Africa, the Rogationists, were certain that Christ returning upon earth would find the true comprehension of the Gospel only amongst themselves, in a few Mauritanian villages, and nowhere else.

Evander of Nicomedia, forgetting Juventinus, could scarcely scribble down the new heresies on his tablets fast enough, happy as a collector who has lit upon a new set of trinkets.

And meantime, in the upper gallery, the young Emperor, surrounded by his white-robed philosophic friends, was gazing down upon the maddened tumult with malign satisfaction. The Pythagorean Proclus, Nymphidian, Priscus, Ædesius, old Iamblicus, the pious bishop Hekobolis, were at his side. They neither laughed nor jested. Their faces remained almost impassive and their attitude a becoming one; only from time to time across their closed lips flitted a furtive and pitying smile. From the shadow of the purple hangings they looked down on the spectacle, as gods must regard the hostilities of men, or circus-lovers the beasts of the arena. It was indeed a banquet for Hellenic sages.

In the midst of the general confusion the effeminate young Caïnite leapt on the tribune and shouted, with such conviction in his voice that everybody turned round, overwhelmed at the impiety—

"Blessed be rebels against God! Blessed be Cain, Shem, Judas, the inhabitants of Sodom and Gomorrah! Blessed be their brother, the Angel of Infinite Darkness!"

The bishop Purpuris, who for an hour past had not been able to get a hearing, to relieve his feelings rushed at the Caïnite and raised his sinewy hand to close the lips of the blasphemer.

A crowd dragged him back.

"Father, it is unbecoming!"

"Let me be, let me be! I will not endure such abomination," roared Purpuris; "take this, seed of Cain!"

And the bishop spat in his face.

A general fray followed, which would have enlarged into a battle if Roman soldiers had not intervened. These parted the Galileans, with the words—

"You must not act so in this place! Have you not got enough churches to fight each other in?"

Purpuris was dragged off, and ordered to quit the atrium.

He called out—

"Leona, deacon Leona!"

The deacon thrust the soldiers aside, felled two of them to the earth, freed Purpuris, and set the terrible mace of the Circumcellions whirling above the heads of the heresiarchs.

"Glory to God!" shouted the African, seeking a victim.

Suddenly the club sank out of his loosened hands. All stood petrified. Then a sharp cry, uttered by one of the Coptic servants of the prophetess of Papusa, rent the general hush. Kneeling, his face transfigured by fear, he pointed to the tribune—

"The Devil! The Devil! Look at the Prince of Evil!"

It was Julian the Emperor, on the marble daïs above the crowd, in his white chlamys, his arms crossed on his breast. Terrible glee burned in his eyes; and to many indeed, at that moment, the recreant prince appeared dreadful as Satan, his brother.

"Is this how you fulfil the law of love, Galileans?" he said to the dumbfounded assembly. "How much your mercy and forgiveness are worth! . . . Verily the wild animals have more compassion than brethren like you! In the words of your Master: "Woe upon you, law-makers, because you have taken the key of the house, and, hindering others from entering, have not entered in yourselves! Woe to you, Pharisees! . . ."

And enjoying their silence he added after a pause—

"If you cannot rule yourselves, Galileans, I say to you, in order to prevent greater misfortunes, you shall now obey, and submit yourselves to me!"

VII

Just as Julian, leaving the Atrium of Constantine, was descending the great flight of steps and proceeding to sacrifice in the direction of the little Temple of Tyche, the goddess of happiness, near the palace, the old bishop Maris, blind, white-haired, and bent double, approached him, led by a child. A great crowd had gathered at the foot of the staircase. With a solemn gesture, the bishop stopped the Emperor and said to him—

"Listen, peoples, tribes, young and old, all that be upon the earth, listen to me! And ye powers above, Angels, who will blot out soon this martyr-maker! It is not the Amorite king who shall fall, nor Ogyges, King of Thebes, but the Serpent, the Great Spirit, the revolted Assyrian, the common enemy, who shall cause a multitude of threats and violences upon earth! Hear, O heaven, and inspire the earth! . . . And thou also, Cæsar, listen to my prophecy, for today, by my mouth, God speaks! . . . Thy days are numbered! Soon wilt thou perish! Like dust lifted by the tempest, like the hiss of an arrow, like the noise of thunder, like the swiftness of light! The spring of Castaly shall be dried up forever, and a mockery to us that pass by! Apollo shall become again a worthless idol, Daphne a tree bewept in fable, and the grass shall grow in your temples overturned. O! abominations of Sennacherib! so we have foretold it. We Galileans—despised of the earth—adorers of the Crucified—ignorant disciples of the fishermen of Capernaum—we, weakened by long fasting, half-dead, who struggle in vain, we nevertheless shall overcome you! . . . Unfold to me, Imperial sophist, your speeches, your syllogisms, your antitheses; and we shall see how, on our side, ignorant fishermen can speak!

"David shall chant again—David, who with his strange pebbles from the brook slew Goliath. Thanks be to Thee, O Lord! the Church today is purified by persecution! O pure virgins, kindle your torches, array the bishop with a fair robe, for our ornament is the robe of Christ!"

The old man almost chanted the last words as in a liturgy, and the crowd, with emotion, murmured approval. Someone cried out aloud—

"Amen!"

"Have you finished, old man?" asked Julian, calmly.

The Emperor had listened to the long speech imperturbably, as if it had been addressed to someone else.

"Here are my hands, executioners. . . bind them! . . . Lead me to death! . . . Lord, I accept Thy crown!"

The bishop raised his faded eyes skyward.

"Do you imagine, brave man, that I shall send you to execution?" said Julian. "You are mistaken. I shall bid you go in peace. In my heart there is no anger whatever against you. . ."

"What is he saying?" the crowd asked each other.

"Tempt me not! I will not deny Christ. Hence, enemy of mankind! Headsman, lead me to death! . . . I am ready. . ."

"There are no headsmen here, my friend; they are only simple good folk, like yourself. Set your mind at rest. My existence is more wearisome and ordinary than you imagine. I have heard you with curiosity, for I admire eloquence, even when it is Galilean! . . . And how much there was in it. . . the abomination of Sennacherib, the king of the Amorites, the stones of David and Goliath! The style of your discourse can scarcely be called simple. Read our Demosthenes, Plato, and particularly Homer. These were really simple in their words as children, or gods. Yes, Galileans, learn the greatness of calm from them! . . . God, remember, was not in the tempest but in the silence. That is all my lesson. That is all my vengeance, since vengeance you must have from me. . ."

"May God strike thee blind, renegade!" began Maris.

"God's wrath will not give thee back sight by striking me blind!" answered Julian.

"I thank God for my blindness!" exclaimed the old man; "it does not allow me to see your damned face, Apostate!"

"What spitefulness! in so frail a body! You are always speaking of humility and love, Galileans; and yet what hate is in everyone of your words! I have just quitted an assemblage where the Fathers of the Church were ready to fly at each other like wild beasts. And now comes this unbridled speech of yours! Why this hatred? Am I not your brother? Oh, if you knew at this moment how kindly my heart feels towards you! May the Olympians soften your cruel and suffering soul, poor blind man! Go in peace, and remember that the Galileans are not the only men who can pardon! . . ."

"Believe him not, brethren! . . . It is a trick, a snare of the Serpent. God of Israel, have no mercy!"

Paying no attention to the curses of the old man, Julian, in his white tunic, made his way through the crowd with the haughty bearing of one of the old sages.

VIII

It was a stormy night. At rare intervals a weak moon-ray darted between hurrying black clouds and mingled itself strangely with the throbbings of lightning. A warm salt-laden wind was blowing violently. On the left shore of the Bosphorus a horseman was approaching a lonely ruin. In immemorial Trojan times this fortification had been used as a watch-tower. It was now little more than a heap of stones and half-demolished walls, overgrown by tall grass. But at its foot a small chamber still served as shelter to shepherds and poor travellers.

Tethering his horse under a dismantled doorway, and brushing through the burdock-leaves, the rider knocked at a low door—

"It is I, Meroë! Open! . . ."

An old Egyptian woman opened the door and admitted him to the interior of the tower. The traveller came near a torch which lighted up his face. He was Julian the Emperor.

The two went out, the old woman, who knew the place well, leading Julian by the hand. Parting the briers and thistles she revealed a low entry in one face of a little ravine in the cliff, and went down the steps within. The sea lay near, and the shock of the waves below made the cliff tremble, but arched rockwalls completely sheltered them from the wind. The Egyptian halted—

"Here, my lord, is a lamp, and the key. You must turn it twice. The monastery-door is open. If you meet the guardian brother, fear nothing; I have given him money. Only make no mistake; it is in the upper passage, the third cell to the left."

Julian opened the door and took a long time descending a steep slope of huge stone-hewn steps. The tunnel soon became a passage, so narrow that two men could not pass each other in it. This secret way joined the watch-tower on the opposite bank of the chasm with a new Christian monastery.

Julian emerged high above the sea, but still between steep cliffs washed by the tide. He began to climb a narrow rocky stair by daylight. Arrived at the summit he found a brick wall, which he climbed with some difficulty. He found himself in the little cloistered garden.

He penetrated farther into a small court, in which the walls were hung with wild roses. The air was full of perfume. The shutters of one of the windows on the ground floor were not closed from within.

Julian gently opened them, and entered through the window. A gust of imprisoned air filled his nostrils with odours of moisture, incense, mice, medicinal herbs, and fresh apples, with which the cautious nuns had filled their stores.

The Emperor went along a corridor into which opened two rows of doors. He counted the third to the left and softly opened it. An alabaster lamp faintly lighted the cell. He made his breathing as noiseless as possible.

A woman, dressed in the dark robe of a nun, lay stretched upon a low bed. She must have fallen asleep during prayer, too weary to undress. Long lashes shadowed the pale cheeks, and the brows wore a slight majestic frown, like the frown of the dead.

Julian recognised Arsinoë.

She had greatly changed. Her hair alone had remained unaltered. It was still golden brown at its roots, and at its ends pale yellow, like honey standing in the sun.

The eyelids trembled. She sighed.

Before Julian's remembrance arose that proud body of the young Amazon bathed in light, dazzling as the mellow Parthenon marbles, and, with a gesture of irresistible love, Julian stretched out his arms to the nun sleeping under the shadow of the tall black cross. He murmured—

"Arsinoë!"

The girl opened her eyes, and gazed at him without astonishment or fear, as if she had known he would come. But returning to herself, she shivered, and passed her hand over her forehead.

He came near her—

"Fear nothing; at a word from you I will go away."

"Why have you come?"

"I wished to know if indeed. . ."

"What matters it, Julian? We cannot understand each other."

"Do you really believe in 'Him,' Arsinoë?"

She made no answer and lowered her eyes.

"Do you remember our night at Athens?" continued the Emperor. "Do you remember then how you tempted me, the Galilean monk, as now I am tempting you? The old pride, the old force, are still on your face, Arsinoë, and not humility, O slave of the Galilean! Tell me the truth."

"I wish for power," she said in a low tone.

"Power! Then you still remember our compact—our alliance?" exclaimed Julian joyfully.

She shook her head, with a sad smile—

"Oh no! Power over the people is not worth the labour of obtaining it. *You* have learned that!"

"And this is why you go forth into the desert?"

"Yes. . . and for freedom's sake."

"Arsinoë, as of old, you care only for yourself!"

"I wish to love others as 'He' commands, but I cannot. I detest them, and I detest myself!"

"Then it is better not to live!"

"One must conquer oneself," she said slowly. "One must conquer in oneself not only the distaste for death but also distaste for life, which is very difficult, because a life like mine is much more terrible than death. But if one succeeds in self-conquest to the end, Life and Death become as nothing, and a greater liberty is gained!"

Her fine brows were knit into a frown of indomitable will.

Julian looked at her in despair.

"What have they made of you?" he murmured. "You are all, all, executioners and martyrs! Why do you keep torturing yourselves? Do you not see that within your soul there is nothing but hate and despair?"

She fixed on him eyes full of anger—

"Why did you come here? I never summoned you. Go! . . . What matters it to me what you think! My own thoughts and sufferings are enough for me to bear. There is an abyss between us which none living can cross over. You tell me that I do not believe. . . That is precisely the cause of myself-hatred. I do not believe, but I wish to believe. Do you understand? I wish and I shall believe. I shall force myself. I shall torture my flesh—dry it up by hunger and thirst, make it more unfeeling than stones. I will tame my intelligence, I will slay it, I will kill it, because it is the Devil, and more seducing than any passion. That shall be my last victory, and the best, because it will set me free. Then I shall see if anything will dare revolt in me and say, 'I do not believe!'"

She stretched her joined hands heavenward, with a suppliant gesture—

"Lord, have mercy upon me! Lord, where art Thou? Hear me, and pardon me!"

Julian flung himself on his knees before her, drew her to himself, and his triumphant eyes sparkled—

"O girl, I see now, you are not able to leave us! You willed it, but willed the impossible! Come! Come now with me! Tomorrow you shall be the spouse of the Roman Emperor, mistress of the world! I have entered this place like a thief; I shall go out with my prey like a lion! What a victory over the Galileans! Who can hinder us? We will dare everything, and walk as gods!"

The face of Arsinoë became sad and tranquil. She looked at Julian pityingly, without thrusting him away—

"Unhappy man! . . . You are unhappy as I. You yourself know not whither you wish to lead me. On whom do you reckon? In whom put your trust? Your gods are decaying, dead. . . I will flee into the desert, far from contaminating fables, far from this terrifying smell of rottenness. Leave me. . . I can aid you in nothing. . . Go. . ."

Wrath and passion shone in Julian's eyes; but more calmly still, and so pityingly that his very heart shivered and froze as under the blow of deadly insult, she went on—

"Why do you delude yourself? Are *you* not wavering, perishable, as we all are? Think: what means this charity of yours? These guest-houses— these sermons of the sacrificial priests? All that is new, unknown to the ancient heroes of Hellas. . . Julian! Julian! are *your* gods the ancient Olympians, luminous and pitiless—terrible sons of the azure—rejoicing in the blood of victims and in the pains of mortals? Human blood and suffering were the very nectar of the old gods! Yours, seduced by the faith of the fishermen of Capernaum, are sick and humble weaklings, full of compassion for men. . . But that pity is mortal to your gods!

"Yes," she continued implacably; "you are sick, you are all too weak for your wisdom! That is your penalty, Hellenists of too late a day. You have strength neither for good nor for evil. You are neither day nor night, nor life nor death; your heart wavers, here and there. You have left one bank, and cannot reach the other. You believe, and you do not believe. You betray yourselves, you hesitate; you will, and you do not will, because you do not know on what to set your will. They alone are strong who, seeing one truth, are blind to all other. They will conquer us—us who are wise and weak!"

Julian raised his head with an effort, as if waking from some evil dream, and said—

"You are unjust, Arsinoë. My soul does not know fear, nor my will weakness. The forces of destiny are leading me. If it is written that I shall die too soon—and I know it is so—my death shall not be unworthy of the sight of the gods. Farewell. I bear you no anger, because now to me you are as one dead!"

IX

Above the marble portico of the guest-house of Apollo, built for the poor, for pilgrims and the disabled, ran these letters in Homeric Greek along the pediment:

> *"Strangers and beggars are all sent by Zeus,*
> *And dear to them is the little we give."*[1]

The Emperor went into the inner court. A graceful Ionic colonnade ran round it. The hospice had formerly been a palæstra or wrestling-ground. It was a soft and sunny afternoon, before sunset, but a heavy atmosphere came to the portico from the inner rooms.

There, massed together, children and old men were crawling about, Christians and Pagans, the sound and the sick; folk disabled, deformed, enfeebled, dropsical, consumptive; folk bearing on their faces the stamp of every vice and every form of suffering.

A half-naked old woman, with a tanned skin like the colour of dead leaves, was rubbing her sore, pockmarked back against the pure marble of a pillar.

In the middle of the court stood a statue of the Pythian Apollo, bow in hand, quiver on shoulder. At the foot of the statue was seated a wrinkled monster who seemed neither young nor old. His arms were huddled round his knees, his head rested on one side; and swinging himself from right to left with a stupid air, he kept declaiming in a monotone—

"Jesus Christ, the Son of God, have mercy upon us, the lost, lost, lost!"

At last the principal inspector, Marcus Ausonius, appeared, pale and trembling—

"Most wise and merciful Cæsar, will you not deign to come into my house? The atmosphere is hurtful here. . . there are contagious maladies. . ."

"No, I am not afraid. Are you the inspector?"

Ausonius, keeping in his breath in order not to breathe the vitiated air, bowed low.

---

1. *Odyssey*, xiv. 57, 58.

"Are bread and wine distributed everyday?"

"Yes, as you have ordered, divine Augustus. . ."

"What filth!"

"They are Galileans. To wash, is for them a sin. It's impossible to make them take baths."

"Bring me the account-books!" ordered Julian.

The inspector fell on his knees, and for long could not utter a word. Finally he faltered—

"Sire. . . everything is in due order, . . . but unfortunately. . . the books have been burnt. . ."

The Emperor's brow clouded.

At that moment, cries arose from the crowd of sick persons—

"A miracle! A miracle! . . . Look, the paralytic can walk!"

Julian turned round, and saw a tall man, wild with joy, stretching out his hands towards him with a look full of simple faith.

"I believe! I believe!" cried the paralytic; "I believe thou art no man, but a god descended upon earth. Touch me, heal me, Cæsar!"

All the halt and maimed were shouting—

"A miracle! Glory to Apollo! Glory to the Healer!"

"Come to me," called the sick, "say a word, and I shall be cured!"

Julian turned, and looked at the god in the light of sunset, and for the first time all going on in the hospice seemed to him a sacrilege. The clear eyes of the Olympian should look down no more on these monstrosities. Julian felt a wild desire to purify the ancient palæstra, to rid it of all Pagan and Galilean vermin, to sweep out the whole human dunghill. Oh, had Apollo lived again, how his eyes would have lightened, his arrows flown and purged the place of the paralytic and infirm!

Julian left the hospice of Apollo in haste. The Emperor had understood perfectly that his information was correct and that the principal inspector was a peculator. But such fatigue and disgust rose in his heart that he had no courage to push further his investigation of the rascality.

It was late when he returned to the palace. He gave an order that he would receive no one, and withdrew to the terrace which looked out on the Bosphorus.

Previous to his visit to the guest-house, the whole day had worn away in wearisome details of business, legal decisions, and the audit of accounts. A great number of instances of peculation had been brought to light, and allowed the Emperor to see that even his best friends were deceiving him. All these philosophers, these rhetoricians, poets, panegyrists, were robbing the treasury, and robbing it just as much as had the eunuchs and Christian bishops in the reign of Constantius. Guest-houses, alms-houses for philosophers, inns of Apollo and Aphrodite, were so many pretexts for gain by the cunning, and the more so that not only to Galileans, but also to Pagans themselves, these institutions seemed a fantastic notion, even a sacrilege, on the part of Cæsar.

Julian felt his body aching under ceaseless and profitless fatigue. Extinguishing the lamp, he lay down upon his narrow camp-bed.

"I must reflect in quiet," he said to himself, gazing at the nocturnal sky. But the power of reflection did not come. A great star was shining in the darkened ether and Julian through half-closed eyelids looked at it. Coldly, coldly, the star's image sank into his heart.

X

At Antioch the great, the capital of Syria, not far from Syngon, the principal street, splendid hot baths, *Thermæ*, stood just at the meeting of four roads.

These baths were fashionable and expensive. Crowds of clients used to go there to learn the last gossip of the town. Between the *apodyterium*, the room for undressing, and the *frigidarium*, or room for cooling and rest, lay a fine hall with mosaic floor and marble walls; this was the hot-air bath, the *sudatorium* or *laconicum*.

From adjoining halls came laughs of the bathers and the noise of powerful jets of water falling into huge basins. Naked slaves ran hither and thither, jostling one another and opening jars of perfume.

At Antioch bathing was considered neither as an amusement nor as a necessity, but as the principal charm and most varied art of life. The capital of Syria was moreover renowned, the world over, for the abundance, the exquisite taste, and the purity of its waters. A full bath or a full bucket seemed empty, so transparent were the streams from the aqueducts of Antioch.

Through the warm and milky vapours of the sudatorium could be caught glimpses of the red and naked bodies of notable citizens. Some were half-reclining, others seated. Some were being rubbed over with oil; all, with the utmost solemnity, were talking together, while they perspired. The beauty of a pair of ancient statues, an Antinous and an Adonis, placed in niches overhead, threw into still greater prominence the hideousness of the living.

A fat old man came out with a majestic, albeit misshapen, body. He was the merchant Bouzaris, whose finger and thumb controlled the whole of the corn-markets of Antioch. A sprightly young man was respectfully supporting him under the arm. Although both were naked, it was easy to distinguish at a glance which was patron and which client.

"Let the vapour be turned on me," commanded Bouzaris, in his hoarse voice. From the profundity of his tones could be calculated the prodigious number of millions which he commanded on the market.

Two metal taps were turned, and the warm steam, escaping with a hiss from the vent-hole, enveloped the figure of the merchant in thick mist. He stood in the middle of the white cloud, like some squat and monstrous god in process of apotheosis, tunding his red and fleshy belly like a drum.

Sitting hard by in a prominent place was Marcus Ausonius, the former inspector of the guest-house. Huddled up, crouching on his heels by the massive side of the merchant, the meagre little man resembled a featherless and shivering chicken.

Julius Mauricus, the scoffer, was there, trying to make his dry nervous body perspire. He was lean as a stick.

Garguillus, too, was stretched on the mosaic floor, still well-fed, soft as gelatine, enormous in bulk as the carcass of a slain boar. A Paphlagonian slave, panting under the protracted effort, was scrubbing the blubber of his back with a piece of damp cloth; while the now wealthy poet, Publius Porphyrius, was staring in a melancholy manner at his own gouty legs.

"Do you know, my friends?" he asked, "about the letter from the white bulls to the Roman Emperor?"

"No. Tell it."

"One line only: 'Conquer Persia, and we are doomed!'"

"Is that all?"

"What more was there to say?"

Undulations of laughter heaved the body of Garguillus.

"By Pallas, it's telling and to the point! If the Emperor comes back in triumph from Persia, he'll offer in sacrifice to the Olympians such masses of white bulls that these animals will get rarer than the bull Apis! . . . Slave! Rub the small of my back, the small of my back! . . . harder, harder!"

And, in turning over, his body made the sound, against the mosaic floor, of a great bundle of wet linen flopped on the ground.

"Ha! ha! ha!" laughed Julius, "they say from the Isle of Taprobane, in the Indies, they're sending great numbers of very rare white birds and big wild swans from Scythia. All that for the gods! The Roman Emperor is fattening the Olympians. It's true they have had time to get hungry since the days of Constantine!"

"The gods guzzle while we starve!" cried Garguillus. "It's now three days since one has been able to get a decent Colchis pheasant in the market, or even a tolerably eatable fish."

"He's a greenhorn and an innocent!" remarked the corn-merchant.

Everybody turned round respectfully.

"A greenhorn, I tell you!" resumed Bouzaris. "I say that if you pinched the nose of your Roman Cæsar you'd find nothing but milk in him like a babe of two weeks! . . . He wanted to lower the price of bread; forbade us to sell it at the price we set on it! And so he brought four hundred thousand measures of wheat from Egypt. . ."

"Well, did you lower the price?"

"Listen! I stirred up the wheat-sellers. We closed the shops. Better let our grain rot than give in. So the people ate the Egyptian corn. We won't give him ours. He's made his cake, let him eat it!"

Bouzaris triumphantly clapped his palms on his belly.

"That's enough steam! Now pour!" ordered the merchant.

And the handsome curly-headed slave, who resembled Antinous, unsealed over his head a slender amphora containing the costliest Arabian cassia. The aromatics flowed over the red sweating body. Bouzaris spread the thick scented drops over himself with satisfaction, and then wiped his gross fingers in the golden hair of the slave standing with bowed head before him.

"Your excellency has quite rightly observed that the Emperor was nothing more than a greenhorn," said the parasite friend, with a profound bow. "He has recently published a pamphlet aimed at the inhabitants of Antioch and entitled, *The Beard-hater*, in which, in response to the insults of the populace, he says in effect—'You laugh at my beard and my coarseness of manners. Laugh as much as you please! I, too, laugh at myself. But I don't want trials, informers, prisons, or punishments!' Now is that worthy of a Roman Emperor? Is it dignified?"

"The Cæsar Constantius of pious memory," declared Bouzaris, "can't be spoken of in the same breath with Julian! In his clothes, in his bearing, one could see at once he was a Cæsar. But this one, God forgive me, is only an abortion of the gods, a lame monkey, a bandy-legged bear who hangs about the streets unshaven, uncombed, unwashed, with stains of ink on his fingers. Why it makes me sick to see him! . . . Books, learning, philosophy. . . Ah, we'll make you pay dear for all that! A ruler mustn't laugh with his people! He must keep them in hand. Once let the people slip, and he'll never get a grip on them again. . ."

Then Marcus Ausonius, who up to that time had been mute, murmured thoughtfully—

"Well, one can forgive most things, but why does he take away the last remaining joy in life—the circus, and the fights of gladiators? My friends, the sight of blood causes, and will always cause, an inexplicable pleasure to man. . . 'Tis a sacred and mysterious enjoyment. There's no gaiety without bloodshed, no greatness on the earth. The smell of blood is the smell of Rome!"

The last scion of the Ausonii glanced naïvely round at his hearers. Sometimes he looked like a boy, sometimes like an old man. The swollen torso of Garguillus heaved on the floor. Raising his head, he glanced at Ausonius.

"Neatly put. Smell of blood, smell of Rome! . . . Go on, Marcus, you're inspired today. . ."

"I say what I feel, my dear fellows. Blood is so pleasant to man that even the Christians can't do without it. They want to purify the world through bloodshed. Julian is making a great mistake. In taking away the circus from the people he's robbing them of their chief enjoyment, which is naturally sanguinary. The populace would have pardoned almost anything; but it won't pardon that!"

Marcus pronounced the last words solemnly, and then suddenly slipped a hand behind his back and his face beamed.

"Are you perspiring!" asked Garguillus.

"Yes!" answered Ausonius, with a rapturous smile. "Rub, slave, rub!"

He lay down on the couch. The bath-slave fell to kneading the poor anæmic limbs, which had a deadly bluish tint.

From their porphyry niches the figures of ancient time looked down with scorn through the milky smoke.

Meanwhile at the cross-roads, outside the baths, a crowd was collecting.

At night Antioch glittered with thousands of lights, especially along the Syngon, which ran through the city for a distance of twenty-six stadia, with porticoes and colonnades thronged with shops throughout its length.

In the crowd, pleasantries about the Emperor ran from mouth to mouth. Street boys rushed about from group to group shouting satirical ditties. An old woman caught one of the little vagabonds, and, lifting his shirt, administered sound correction with the sole of her sandal.

"Take that! and that! to teach you to sing such disgraceful things!"

The urchin uttered piercing squeals.

Another, clambering on the back of a comrade, drew on the white wall with a piece of coal a long-bearded goat, crowned with the Imperial diadem, while a third wrote underneath in big letters, "This is the impious Julian!" and trying to make his voice formidable yelled—

"The butcher comes With a big, big knife!"

An old man in the long black ecclesiastical habit passing by, halted, listened to the boy, and cast up his eyes to heaven—

"Out of the mouths of babes and sucklings proceedeth wisdom! Were we not better off under Cappa and Khi?"

"What do you mean by Cappa and Khi?"

"Don't you understand? The Greek letter Cappa (*K*) begins the name of Constantius, and Khi (*X*) is the initial of 'Christ.' I mean by that, that Constantius and Christ did no harm to the inhabitants of Antioch while the philosophers. . ."

"True, true! One was better off under Cappa and Khi!"

A drunken man, overhearing this colloquy, hawked the saying about the streets, and the pleasantry circulated through Antioch, and being manifestly absurd tickled the popular fancy.

A scene of still greater animation might have been witnessed in the tavern situated opposite the baths. This tavern belonged to the Armenian Syrax, who had long ago transferred his commercial undertakings from Cæsarea to Antioch. From bulging wine-skins and enormous jars, wine was pouring freely into tin cups. Here, as everywhere, the conversation turned on the Emperor's doings.

The little Syrian soldier Strombix, the same who had taken part in Julian's campaign against the barbarians in Gaul, was distinguishing himself by special eloquence. By his side lolled the faithful giant, his friend, the Sarmatian, Aragaris. Strombix felt as happy as a fish in water; he loved risings and rebellions better than anything in the world.

He was preparing to make a speech. An old rag-picker had just brought in a sensational piece of news—

"We're all doomed! . . . The Lord's hand is heavy on us. . . Yesterday a neighbour of mine told me something which at first I refused to believe!"

"Tell us, good woman!"

"Well, it was at Gaza. The Pagans seized a convent. They made the nuns come out. They tied them to gallows in the market-place, beat 'em to death, and after rolling their warm bodies, all hacked to pieces, in grains of barley, threw 'em to the swine!"

"I saw myself," added a young weaver, "a Pagan at Hieropolis, who was eating the liver of a deacon!"

"What an abomination!" murmured the auditors crossing themselves.

With the help of Aragaris, Strombix clambered on to a table, which was still sticky with the spilth of wine, and striking an oratorical attitude, addressed the crowd, while Aragaris proudly contemplated his friend.

"Citizens," began Strombix; "how long shall we wait before we rebel? Don't you know that Julian has sworn, if he returns a conqueror from Persia, to gather together the holy defenders of the Church and throw them to beasts in the amphitheatre? To turn the porticoes of basilicas into granaries, and the churches into stables. . ."

A hump-backed old man, livid with fear, tumbled over on the tavern floor. It was the husband of the rag-picker, himself a glass-blower. Rising, he slapped his thigh despairingly, stared at the company, and faltered—

"Ah, what a situation! . . . And there are two hundred corpses in the wells and the aqueducts!"

"Where? What corpses?"

"Hush! . . . Hush!" murmured the glass-blower.

"They say that the renegade has long taken his auguries from the intestines of living men; and all this for his war against the Persians and his victory over the Christians!"

Overcome with satisfaction he muttered under his breath—

"Why, in the cellars of the palace at Antioch they've discovered chests full of human bones. . . and in the city of Karra, near Edessa, the Christians have found, in a subterranean temple, the corpse of a woman hanging by her hair with her body slit open. . . Julian wanted to inspect the liver of an infant for his cursed war."

"Eh? Gluturius! Is it true that human bones are found in the sewers? *You* ought to know!" said a shoemaker, a confirmed sceptic.

Gluturius, the scavenger, who stood near the door, not venturing in because he smelt badly, being thus addressed, began, according to his custom, to smile and to blink his inflamed eyelids:

"No, worthy friends," he answered humbly. "Newborn infants are sometimes found there, or skeletons of asses and camels, but I never yet saw a corpse of man or woman."

When Strombix resumed his speech, the scavenger listened religiously, rubbing his bare leg against the door post.

"Brother men," cried the orator, with fiery indignation, "let us be revenged! Let us die like ancient Romans!"

"No use bursting *your* lungs," grumbled the shoemaker. "When we get to that stage, you'll be the first to turn tail and let the others die!"

"You're a set of cowards," chimed in a painted woman, dressed in a poor and tawdry dress. She was a street-walker, nicknamed by her admirers the She-wolf. "Do you know," she went on wrathfully, "what the holy martyrs Macedonius, Theodulus, and Tertian replied to their executioners?"

"No, She-wolf, tell us."

"Well, I've heard. At Myrrha, in Phrygia, three young men, Macedonius, Theodulus, and Tertian, had burst into a Greek temple by night, and smashed the idols to the glory of God. The proconsul Amachius had them seized, stretched them on dripping-pans, and ordered fires to be lighted under them. The three martyrs said: 'If you want to taste cooked flesh, Amachius, turn us over on the other side, that we may not be served up to you half-cooked!' and all three laughed and spat in the face of the proconsul. And everybody saw an angel come down out of heaven with three crowns! *You* wouldn't have spoken so! You're too fearful for your skins. . . It's heart-breaking, just to look at you!"

The She-wolf turned away in disgust.

Cries rose from the street.

"Perhaps they're breaking up idols?" suggested the shoemaker pleasantly.

"Forward, citizens! Follow me!" shouted Strombix, waving his arms; but he slipped on the table, and would have fallen had not Aragaris caught him.

Everybody rushed to the door. An enormous crowd was advancing down the principal street and, filling the narrow cross-roads, brought up before the baths.

"Old Pamva! Old Pamva!" the idlers were shouting. "He's come from the desert to help the people; to pull down the great, and to save the humble and poor!"

XI

The old man had a coarse face, with high cheek-bones, bearded to the eyes. A patched piece of sacking served him as inner robe, and a hooded sheep's skin as cloak or chlamys. For twenty years, Pamva had never washed himself, considering cleanliness sinful, and believing that a special fiend presided over any acts of care for the body. He dwelt in a fearful desert, the Berean, round Chalybon, to the east of Antioch, where serpents and scorpions swarmed at the bottom of the arid water-courses. His lodging was the deep sandy hollow of a dried-up well, called *coubba* in Syriac, where he used to feed himself on five stalks a day of a sweet and flowery kind of reed. He had nearly died of starvation. His disciples descended to feed him by means of ropes. Then, during seven years, he lived on a half-measure of boiled lentils. His sight grew feeble; his skin became leprous and scurvy; he therefore added a little oil to his lentils, and accused himself of worship of the belly.

Pamva, learning from his disciples that the Emperor Julian, the fierce Anti-Christ, was persecuting the Christians, left his retreat and came to Antioch to strengthen weak-kneed believers—

"Listen! listen! . . . he's going to speak."

Pamva climbed the staircase of the baths and halted on a broad landing. His eyes glittered with condensed ire. He stretched out his arms, pointing out to the people palaces, pagan temples, baths, shops, courts of justice, all the monuments of Antioch.

"Not a stone of these shall remain! All shall crumble and disappear. The holy fire shall burn up the universe. The heavens, like a smouldering palace, shall sink away! That shall be the terrible judgment of Christ, the unimaginable spectacle. Whither shall I turn mine eyes, and what shall I wonder at, if it be not the groaning of kings, cast down into darkness? If it be not the terror of Aphrodite, the goddess of love, shivering in her nakedness before the Crucified? If it be not the flight of Jupiter, and all the Olympians, before the thunders of the Most High? . . . Triumph, ye martyrs, and rejoice, ye persecuted! See your judges, the Roman proconsuls, seized by more terrible flames than yours. Nor shall the syllogisms of Aristotle, nor the demonstrations of Plato save you, philosophers, hurled into hell! And, on that stage, their actors shall roar, as the heroes of Sophocles and Æschylus never roared before! And their rope-dancers, trust, me, shall dance a quicker step in that fire!

And we, the poor and ignorant, shall rejoice and say to the strong, wise, and the haughty: Behold the Crucified, the son of the carpenter and the work-woman, the King of Judæa, crowned in purple and thorns! Behold the Sabbath-breaker, the Samaritan woman possessed of the devil! See Him, whom you led bound with cords into your prætorium, Him whose thirst you quenched with vinegar and hyssop! And we shall hear in answer weepings and gnashings of teeth. We shall laugh, our hearts overflowing with joy! Come, come, come, Lord Jesus!"

Gluturius, the cleanser of sewers, fell on his knees, and blinking his inflamed eyelids as if he saw Christ descending, stretched out his arms. The metal-founder clenched his fists, collected his forces like a bull ready to charge. And the livid-faced weaver, trembling in all his limbs, with an amazed smile was murmuring, "Lord, let me, too, suffer!"

The animal faces of beggars and sharpers expressed the mischievous triumph of the weak over the strong; of slaves over their masters. The She-wolf grinned in silence, and an insatiable thirst for vengeance twinkled in her drunken eyes.

Suddenly, the jingle of weapons and the heavy step of horses. The Roman legionaries of the night-watch wheeled round the corner of the road. At their head strode the prefect, Sallustius Secundus, a man with aquiline nose, open face, and a look of calmness and kindly intelligence. He wore the senatorial laticlave, and gave an impression of self-confidence and patrician nobleness. Above the distant Pantheon, erected by Antiochus Seleucus, slowly arose the great reddish moon, and its rays were glittering on shields and breastplates—

"Disperse, citizens!" said Sallustius, addressing the crowd. "By order of Augustus crowds are forbidden in the streets of Antioch by night."

The populace groaned and murmured. Street-boys whistled, and one audacious voice sang—

> *"Goodbye to the white cocks!*
> *Goodbye to the white ox!*
> *For Julian knocks them on the head*
> *To feed his devils and the dead!"*

There was a threatening clash of arms. The legionaries unsheathed their swords and prepared to charge. Old Pamva struck the marble flags with his staff, and shouted—

"Hail, gallant army of Satan! Hail, wise Roman dignitary! You'll probably remember the time when you burned us, when you taught us philosophy, and we prayed God to save your lost souls! Welcome to you!"

The legionaries gripped their swords, but the prefect with a gesture stopped them. He saw that the crowd was in his power.

"What are you threatening us with, blockhead?" asked Pamva, addressing himself to Sallustius. "What can you do? All we want for vengeance is a black night and two or three torches. You fear the Alemanni and the Persians. We are more terrible than they. We are everywhere in the midst of you, inviolable, innumerable! We have no boundaries, no father-land; we recognise but one republic, the universal republic! Born but yesterday, already we are filling the world, filling your cities, your fortresses, your islands, city councils, camps, palaces, senates, forums! We leave you your temples! . . . And but for our humility, our fraternity, choosing rather to die than to slay, we should have blotted you out. . .

"We want neither sword nor fire! So many are we, that if we withdrew, you would perish. Your cities would become solitudes, you would be frightened at your own loneliness, at the silence of the universe! All life would stop, at that death-touch! Remember the Roman Empire exists only on sufferance, sustained by the mercy of us Christians!"

All eyes being fixed on Pamva no one perceived a man clothed in the old chlamys of a wandering philosopher, with a lean yellow face, curling hair, and long black beard, quickly coming through the lines of legionaries, who respectfully made way for him. He was followed by a few companions, and, leaning towards Sallustius, whispered—

"What are you waiting for?"

"They will perhaps disperse of themselves," responded Sallustius. "The Galileans have already too many martyrs for us to make anymore of them. They fly towards death as bees to honey!"

But the man in the philosopher's robe advanced and cried out with a distinct voice, like a captain accustomed to command—

"Scatter the crowd. Seize the ringleaders!"

Everybody wheeled round, and in alarm shouted—

"Augustus! Augustus Julian!"

The soldiers charged with drawn swords. The old rag-picker was knocked down, struggling and shrieking under the feet of the legionaries. Many fled, and Strombix was the first to take advantage of the general confusion. Stones hurtled through the air. The metal-founder, defending old Pamva, hurled a large jagged flint at a legionary. It struck the She-wolf, who fell with a slight cry, covered with blood, and convinced that she was dying a martyr.

A legionary seized Gluturius; but the sewer-cleaner gave himself up so readily (the prospect of becoming an admired martyr appearing so enviable in comparison with his present occupation), and his rags gave off such a stink, that the disgusted soldier immediately released his prisoner.

In the midst of the crowd there was a market-gardener who had chanced by, leading an ass laden with cabbages. Mouth agape, he had listened to old Pamva from beginning to end. Noticing the danger, he now tried to flee, but his ass starkly refused. In vain was the beast belaboured. Buttressed against his forefeet, with ears lowered and tail lifted, it uttered a deafening series of brays, drowning in its triumphant stupidity the death-rattle of the dying, the oaths of the soldiery, and the prayers of Galileans.

Oribazius, who was among the companions of Julian, came up to the Emperor—

"Julian, what are you doing? Is it worthy of your wisdom? . . ."

The Emperor cast on him a stern look, and Oribazius was silent, not daring to finish his protest.

In the last few months Julian had not only changed but grown old. His worn face had the sad and terrible expression of those gnawed by some long and incurable malady, or absorbed in some fixed idea akin to madness. His powerful hands were unconsciously tearing to pieces a roll of papyrus. At last he said in a deep voice, with eyes kept steadily on Oribazius—

"Away! I know what I am doing. . . With these scoundrels who have no faith in the gods, one cannot deal as with human beings. They must be destroyed like wild beasts. And for the matter of that, what harm would be done if a dozen Galileans were slain by the hand of the Hellenists?"

Oribazius mused—

"How like he is now, in his fury, to his cousin Constantius!"

Julian spoke to the crowd, and his voice appeared to himself even strange and terrible—

"By the grace of the gods I am still Emperor! Galileans, obey! You may mock at my beard and clothes, but not at the Roman law. . . Remember, I am punishing you for rebellion and not for religion. Chain that rascal!"

With a shaking hand he pointed to Pamva, who was promptly seized by two fair-haired Batavians.

"Thou liest, atheist!" shouted Pamva triumphantly. "You are punishing us for our faith. Why do you not pardon me, as you did Maris the blind Chalcedonian? Where is now your philosophy? Have the times changed? Have you overshot your mark? Brothers, fear not the Roman Cæsar, but the Almighty God!"

The crowd gave up all idea of flight. All were infected by the fever of martyrdom. The Batavians and the Celts were startled by the sight of a mob rushing joyfully on death. Even children threw themseves on the swords and lances. Julian wished to stop the massacre. He was too late; the bees were making for the honey. He could only exclaim, in scorn and despair—

"Unhappy people! If life weighs on you, is it so difficult for you to shorten it for yourselves?"

And Pamva in bonds, lifted by sinewy arms, retorted with joy—

"Exterminate us, Roman, we shall multiply the more! The dungeon is our liberty; weakness, our strength: death, our victory!"

XII

At about five miles from Antioch, up the course of the river Orontes, stood the celebrated wood of Daphne, consecrated to Apollo. Therein a temple had been built, where every year the praises of the Sun-god were celebrated.

Julian, without saying anything of his intention quitted Antioch at the break of day. He wished to ascertain for himself whether the inhabitants remembered the ancient sacred feast. All along the road he mused of the solemnity, hoping to see lads and virgins going up the steps of the temple, clad in white as a symbol of purity and youth, the crowd of the faithful, the choirs, and the smoke of incense.

The road was difficult; from the rocky Berean hills a gusty burning wind came down. The atmosphere was laden with the bitter smell of burnt wood, and thick with a bluish fog which spread itself over the deep gorge of Mount Kazia. Harassing dust filled eyes and throat, and crackled between the teeth of the traveller. The very sun through the smoky vapour seemed red and sickly. But hardly had the Emperor penetrated into the wood of Daphne than fragrant coolness surrounded him. It was difficult to believe that such a corner of Paradise could be found at a few paces from the scorching road. The wood was twenty-four stadia in circumference, and perpetual twilight reigned in its almost impenetrable alleys of gigantic laurels, planted centuries before. The Emperor was surprised at the solitariness of the wood—no worshippers, no victims, no incense, nor any preparation for the solemn feast-day. Thinking that the people must be assembled near the temple, he pushed on farther. At every step the wood became more lonely. It was as untroubled by any sound as an abandoned cemetery. Birds were few, the shadow of the laurel-grove being too thick, and no song of theirs was heard. A grasshopper began his shrill cry in the grass, and quickly ceased, as if startled at his own voice. Insects alone were humming faintly in a slender ray of sunlight, but ventured not to quit its beam for the neighbouring gloom. Sometimes Julian pushed his path along wider alleys, bordered with titanic walls of weird cypress, casting shade dark as a moonless night. Here and there subterranean waters made the moss spongy. Streams ran everywhere, chill as melted snow, but silently, with no tinkling ripples, as if muted by the melancholy of that enchanted wood. In one nook, a rift in the rock, clear drops were falling slowly, glittering, one by one. But moss stifled the sound of their fall, and they sank away like the tears of an unspoken love.

There were broad glens of wild narcissus, many lilies, and even butterflies. But these were dark-winged and not gay-coloured, for the sun-rays filtered through the thick laurel became almost lunar-pale, and pensive as if fallen through the smoke of a funeral torch. It was as though Phoebus had grown faint and inconsolable after the final loss of Daphne. And she, remaining, overcast and shadowy under the most burning kisses of the god, here kept impenetrable coolness and bloom under her branches forever.

Everywhere in that wood reigned the abandonment, the tender melancholy of the god who loved in vain.

Already in sight, and dazzling through the cypresses, shone the columns and pediments of the temple raised in the time of Seleucus Nicator. But not a worshipper yet had Julian encountered. At last he saw a child of twelve years old, on a path overgrown with wild hyacinth. His dark eyes shone strangely brilliant in his finely cut pale face. Golden hair fell in curls on his slender neck, and his blue-veined temples were transparent as the petals of a flower grown in the shade.

"Do you know, child, where are the sacrificers and the people?" Julian asked.

The child made no answer, as if he had not understood the question.

"Listen, little one, can you not lead me to the priest of Apollo?"

He shook his head, smiling.

"Why will you not answer me?"

Then the boy put a finger to his lips and then to both his ears, and shook his head gravely this time.

Julian thought—

"This must be a deaf-mute."

The child looked shyly askance at the Emperor, who grew almost fearful in the silent twilight of the deserted wood in the company of the elf, who stared at him fixedly and haughtily as a little god.

Suddenly, he pointed out to Julian an old man, clothed in a patched and tattered tunic; Julian immediately recognised a temple priest. The weak and broken old man stumbled along in drunken fashion, laughing and mumbling to himself as he went. He was red-nosed and completely bald except for a fringe of downy grey hair. His watery and short-sighted eyes had an expression of childlike benevolence. He was carrying a large basket.

"The priest of Apollo?" asked Julian.

"I am he. I am called Gorgius. What do you want, good man?"

"Can you direct me to the high-priest of this temple and the people worshipping here?"

Gorgius made no answer at first, but put his panier on the ground. Then he rubbed his bald pate and, standing with arms akimbo, held his head on one side winking mischievously with his left eye.

"And why am *I* not the high-priest of Apollo?" he asked, "and what worshippers do you mean, my son? . . . May the Olympians protect you."

He smelt strongly of wine. Julian thought his behaviour indecent and prepared to administer a rebuke—

"You seem to be drunk, old man."

Gorgius, in no wise perturbed, continued to rub the back of his neck.

"Drunk? I don't think so. But I may have tossed off five cups or so, for the sake of the celebrations; and as to that, I drink more through sorrow than merriment. Yes, my son, may the Olympians have you in their keeping! . . . Who are you? By your dress perhaps a wandering philosopher, or a professor from the schools of Antioch?"

The Emperor smiled and nodded his head in acquiescence. He wished to make the priest talk freely.

"You have hit it. I am a teacher."

"Christian?"

"No, Hellenist."

"Ah, that's good. There are many others of your way of thinking who hang about this neighbourhood."

"You have not yet answered me as to where the people are: whether many victims have been sent from Antioch; whether the choirs are ready."

"Victims? Small thanks for victims," said the old man, laughing and stumbling so violently that he nearly tumbled down. "Many's the long year, my brother, since we saw that kind of thing! . . . Since the time of Constantine. . ." Gorgius snapped his fingers despairingly and whistled. "It is all over—done for! . . . Phut! . . . Men have forgotten the gods. Not only have we no victims, but we don't even get a handful of wheat to cook a cake; not a grain of incense, not a drop of oil for the lamps. . . There's nothing for it but to go to bed and die! . . . Yes, my son! may the Olympians protect you! . . . The monks have taken everything! . . . and they fight each other; they're rolling in fat. . . Our tale is told. . . Ah!

bad times these. And you say 'Don't drink!' But it's hard not to drink when one suffers. If I didn't drink a bit I should have hanged myself long ago."

"And no one has come from Antioch for this great feast day?" asked Julian.

"None but you, my son. I am the priest, you are the people! We will together offer the victim to the god."

"You have just told me that you received no victims!"

Gorgius rubbed the back of his neck, grinning—

"We received none from others, but there is my own offering. Weve eaten little for three days, Hepherion and I, to save the necessary money. Look!"

He raised the lid of the basket. A tethered goose slid out its head, cackling and trying to escape.

"Ha, ha, ha! is not that a victim?" asked the old man proudly. "Although it isn't a fat young goose it is nevertheless a sacred bird! Apollo ought to be glad of it just now. The gods consider geese a delicacy."

"Have you long dwelt in this temple?" questioned Julian.

"For forty years and perhaps longer. . ."

"Is this your son?" asked Julian, pointing to Hepherion, who was staring at him as if he were trying to follow the conversation.

"No. I have neither relatives nor friends. Hepherion helps me at the hours for sacrifice."

"Who are his father and mother?"

"I do not know the father and I strongly suspect that no one knows who he is. But his mother was the great sibyl Diotima, who long lived in this temple. She would never speak nor raise her veil before men. She was chaste as a vestal. When she brought this child into the world we were all astonished, and at a loss what to think. . . but a learned centenarian, a magian told us. . ."

Gorgius, with a mysterious air, put his hand before his mouth and muttered in Julian's ear as if he feared the child could catch his words—

"The hierophant told us that he was no son of man, but a god come down by night to the sibyl while she was asleep within the temple! See how beautiful he is!"

"A deaf-mute son of a god?" murmured the Emperor, surprised.

"In times like ours if the son of the god and of the sibyl were not a deaf-mute he would die of grief," answered Gorgius. "See how thin and pale he is already!"

"Who knows," said Julian, with a sad smile, "but that you are right, old man. In our days it is well for a prophet to be a deaf-mute."

Suddenly the child approached Julian and looking at him fixedly, seized his hand and kissed it. A thrill ran through Julian.

"My son," said the old man, gravely, "may the Olympians shield you; you must be a good man. That child never kisses the evil nor the impious, and he flees from the monks as from the plague. I think he sees and understands more than either of us but can utter nothing. I've often surprised him sitting before the statue of Apollo for hours, gazing at him with joy as if he were talking with the god."

The face of Hepherion grew dark and he went away.

Gorgius smote his head and said—

"I am wasting time in gossip. The sun is up; the sacrifice must be performed. Come!"

"Wait," said the Emperor. "I wished to ask you something more. Have you ever heard that the Emperor Julian desired to restore to honour the worship of the old gods?"

"Yes, but. . . what can *he* do, poor man? He will not succeed. I tell you—all's over!"

"Have you faith in the gods?" asked Julian. "Can the Olympians quit us so forever?"

The old man sighed, and hanging his head—

"My son, you're young; although there are white hairs shining in your dark locks, and furrows on your brow already. But in the days when my hair was black and young girls used to look at me with favour, I remember sailing in a ship, near Thessalonica, and seeing Mount Olympus. Its base and its girdle melted into blue, and its snowy summit seemed hanging in the air, dominating sky and sea, golden and inaccessible. I mused 'Behold the dwelling of the gods!' and I was full of emotion. But on this same ship there was a scoffing old man who called himself an Epicurean. He pointed out Mount Olympus, and said to me: 'My friend, travellers have long ago climbed Olympus, and they saw that it was an ordinary mountain, like other mountains, on which there was nothing but snow, ice and stones!' And those words sank so deep into my heart that I shall remember them all my life."

The Emperor smiled—

"Old man, your faith is childish. Suppose there were no Olympus—why should not the gods exist above, in the kingdom of the eternal Ideas, in the realm of the soul's light?"

     DMITRY MEREZHKOVSKY

Gorgius hung his head lower yet—

"Yes, yes, yes! . . . but. . . nevertheless all is over. Olympus is deserted."

Julian gazed at him, surprised.

"You see," continued Gorgius, "the earth breeds nowadays only hard men or weak men. The gods can only laugh at them, or grow wrath with them. They are not worth destroying. They will perish of themselves by sickness, debauchery, or decline. The gods are grown weary and they have departed!"

"And do you think, Gorgius, that the human race must disappear?"

The priest shook his bald head—

"Ah, ah, ah! The earth is in pain. The rivers flow more slowly; the flowers in spring have not their old fragrance. An ancient fisherman lately told me that one can see Etna no longer as we used to do. The air has become thicker and darker, the sun is waxing weak; the end of the world is near. . ."

"Tell me, Gorgius, can you remember better times?"

The old man brightened up, and his eyes shone.

"When I first came here in the first years of the reign of Constantine," he said joyfully, "grand festivals were celebrated every year in honour of Apollo. What numbers of lads and virgins used to come to this holy wood! How the moon used to shine! How exquisite the smell of the cypresses! How the nightingales used to sing! And when their chant ceased, the air would tremble with nocturnal kisses and sighings of love, as with the beatings of invisible wings."

Gorgius was silent and plunged in thought.

At that moment the sound of church-singing came from behind the trees.

"What is that?" asked Julian.

"The monks," answered the priest. "Monks praying over a dead Galilean."

"What, a Galilean in the wood sacred to Apollo?"

"Yes; they call him the martyr Babylas. Ten years ago the brother of the Emperor Julian, Cæsar Gallus, transferred the bones of this Babylas from Antioch into this wood, and had a superb sarcophagus made for him. From that day the oracle ceased. The temple was sullied and the god departed."

"What sacrilege!" exclaimed the Emperor indignantly.

"That year the virgin sibyl Diotima gave birth to a deaf-mute child, a bad omen. Only one sacred spring was left us and did not dry up, the spring called Tears of the Sun. . . over there, where the child is now sitting. . ."

Julian turned round. The boy was sitting in front of the mossy rock, motionless, and in his open palm receiving the falling drops. Julian almost imagined he saw two transparent wings trembling behind the divinely beautiful child. So sad, so pale, so enchanting his look, that the Emperor mused—

"He must be Eros, the little god of love, dying in our century of Galilean moroseness, and in his hand receiving the last drops, the last tears of love, tears of the god over Daphne, over the vanished beauty of Daphne!"

The deaf-mute remained motionless, and a great black velvety butterfly alighted on his head. He neither saw it, nor stirred. Like a malign shadow the butterfly opened and shut its wings, while the Tears of the Sun dropped, one by one, into the hand of Hepherion. Louder and louder in the distance rose funereal psalms.

Suddenly from behind the cypresses came the sound of voices disputing—

"Augustus is there."

"Why should he go alone to Daphne?"

"Why not? today is the great festival of Apollo. See, there he is. . . Julian, we have sought you since the morning!"

They were Greek sophists, men of science and rhetoricians, habitual companions of the Emperor, and with them the Neo-Platonist Priscus of Epirus, the bilious sceptic Julius Mauricus, the wise Sallustius Secundus, and the celebrated orator Libanius.

Julian vouchsafed them not the least attention.

"What's the matter?" murmured Julius to Priscus.

"He must be displeased that there has been no preparation for the feast! We have not sent a single offering. . ."

Julian addressed the former Christian rhetorician, now the high-priest of Astarte, Hekobolis—

"Go into the neighbouring chapel, and inform the Galileans praying there of my will. Let them come here."

Hekobolis went.

Gorgius, still holding his basket, stood petrified, with eyes and mouth wide open. He rubbed his bald head. Had he not drunk too much? It must all be a dream! But when he remembered all he had said about Julian and the god to the pretended professor, a cold sweat broke out on his forehead, his legs trembled, and he fell on his knees—

"Pardon, Cæsar! Forget my words!"

One of the philosophers wished to thrust away the old man; but Julian stopped him—

"Do not insult the sacrificial priest. Rise, Gorgius, there is my hand; fear nothing. So long as I live, none shall do harm to you or to your little lad. You and I both came for the festival, both love the old gods. We will be friends and rejoice together at this feast of the Sun!"

The psalms had meantime ceased. Frightened monks appeared coming up the alley of cypresses, deacons and superiors still in the sacerdotal dress and led by Hekobolis. The arch-priest, a fat man with a shining red face, walked swaying from side to side, much out of breath and wiping his brow. He saluted Augustus profoundly, reaching one finger to the ground, and said in a pleasant bass voice—

"May the humane Augustus pardon his unworthy servants!"

He bowed lower yet, and two novices skilfully assisted him to rise again. One of them had forgotten to put away the censer, from which the incense was escaping in thin fillets of smoke.

At the sight of the monks Hepherion fled. Julian said—

"Galileans, I order you to rid the sacred wood of Apollo of the relics of your co-religionist. We do not desire to use force against you, but if our will is not carried out, I must myself see that Helios is delivered from such sacrilege. I shall send here my soldiers, who will disinter the bones, burn them, and scatter the ashes to the winds."

The arch-priest coughed, and finally said in a humble tone—

"Most merciful Cæsar, that is hard on us, for these relics have long rested here, in a place blessed by the will of Cæsar Gallus. But as it is a matter beyond our jurisdiction, we are forced to refer it to the bishop."

A murmur ran through the crowd; an urchin hidden in a laurel bush shouted—

"The butcher comes With a big, big knife!"

But he received such a buffet that he fled, howling.

The arch-priest, feeling that decency obliged him to defend the relics, coughed again and began—

"If it pleases your High Wisdom to give this order on account of the idol. . ." he quickly corrected himself.

"Of the Hellenic god, Helios. . ."

The Emperor's eyes sparkled with rage.

"The 'idol,'" he interrupted, "'idol' is your word. For what imbeciles do you take us, if you think that we worship the matter that represents our gods, metal, stone, or wood. All your preachers preach this, but it is a lie. We worship not these things, but the soul, the living soul of beauty in these models of the purest human beauty. It is not we, the idolaters, but you—you, who devour each other like wild beasts for the sake of an iota; you, who kiss the rotten bones of criminals punished for breaking the Roman laws; you, who call the fratricide Constantius an 'Eternal Holiness!' To deify the splendid sculptures of Phidias, which breathe Olympian beauty and goodness, is that less reasonable than to bow before two crossed beams of wood, a shameful instrument of torture? Must one blush for you, pity you, or hate you? It is the pitch of mad degradation for our country, to see sons of the Hellenes, who read Plato and Homer, rushing to an outcast tribe, a tribe almost blotted out by Vespasian and Titus, in order to deify a dead man! . . . And you still dare to accuse us of idolatry!"

The arch-priest imperturbably stroked his long beard, and looking at Julian askance, wiped the perspiration from his glistening forehead.

Then the Emperor said to Priscus the philosopher—

"My friend, accomplish the Delian mysteries with which you are familiar. We must purify the Temple of Apollo. He will return to his dwelling, and once we have taken away the stone which seals the spring, the oracle will speak again."

The arch-priest terminated the interview with a deep bow and the same obsequious manner, in which an invincible tenacity could be felt—

"Let your will be done, Cæsar. We are the children, you are the father; but there is no power above the power of God."

"Oh, you hypocrites, I know your obedience and your humility! Your humility is the serpent's fang! Why not struggle against me at least like men?"

Julian turned round to depart, when a little old man and woman issued from the crowd and prostrated themselves at his feet. They were poorly but cleanly dressed, and bore a surprising resemblance to each other, reminding him of Philemon and Baucis.

"Protect us, just Cæsar," whispered the old man. "We have a little house near Antioch at the foot of the Stavrinus. We've lived there twenty years, and now the town-senators, the decurions, are come. . ." The old man clasped his hands despairingly, and the old woman, imitating him, did the same.

"The decurions come and say, 'This house does not belong to you!'—'What—the Lord be with you—we've been here twenty years!'—'Yes; but you had no right. The land belongs to the temple of the god Æsculapius, and your house is built with the temple-stones. It must return to Æsculapius.' What does this mean? . . . Have mercy, all-powerful Augustus!"

The two old people, with their clear and childlike faces, were kneeling before him, and weeping, kissed his feet.

Julian perceived an amber cross on the woman's neck.

"Are you Christians?" he asked, his brow growing sombre.

"Yes."

"I should like to grant your prayer. . . but how is it to be done? The land belongs to the god. . . Nevertheless, your property shall be paid for."

"No, no," cried out the old people, "we're rooted there by all our habits. We don't ask for money. But there everything is ours; we know every blade of grass. . ."

"There everything is ours," repeated the old woman like an echo. "The vine, the chickens, the cow, the olives, the pigs—everything is ours. And there's the step too, on which in the evening we have warmed our old bones in the sun, side by side, for these twenty years."

The Emperor, without listening, turned toward the startled crowd—

"Latterly the Galileans have overwhelmed me with demands for the return of lands belonging to the churches, and the Valentinians accuse the Arians of having robbed them of their properties. To cut short dispute I have given half of those lands to the Gallic warriors and the other half to the Imperial Treasury; and I am decided to act similarly in future. By what right, you ask? But is it not more easy for a camel to pass through the eye of a needle than for a rich man to enter the kingdom of heaven? You glorify poverty, Galileans? Why murmur against me? In taking property which you yourselves have taken from your brother-heretics, or from Olympian temples, I am only restoring you to wholesome poverty and the narrow way into the heavenly kingdom."

An evil smile curled his lips.

"We're injured unjustly," groaned the two old people.

"Well, suffer the injustice!" answered Julian. "You should rejoice in persecution. What are these sufferings to eternal bliss?"

The old man, unprepared for this deduction, stammered in dismay, as a forlorn hope—

"We are your faithful slaves, Augustus. My son serves on the military staff, in a distant fortress of the Roman frontier, and his superior officers think well of him. . ."

"Is he also a Christian?" interrupted Julian.

"Yes," sighed the old man, and was immediately dismayed at the avowal.

"You have done well to warn me. As proved enemies of the Roman Augustus, Christians must not henceforth occupy high Imperial office, above all in the army. I am more of your Master's opinion than you are yourselves. How should disciples of Jesus do justice according to the Roman law, when He has said, '*Judge not, and ye shall not be judged*'? How should Christians rightly defend the Empire by the sword, when they were taught by Him '*He who shall take up the sword shall perish by the sword*'; and again, '*Resist not evil*'? Therefore, for the safety of your souls, we shall withdraw Christians from the law and from the army of Rome; that helpless, and disarmed, and free from frivolous earthliness, they may reach the kingdom of heaven!"

Smiling inwardly, and so robbing his hatred of still greater bitterness, the Emperor strode rapidly toward the Temple of Apollo.

The old people stretched their arms after him, sobbing—

"Cæsar, we did it unwittingly! Take our house, our land, all that we have, but have pity on our son!"

The philosophers wished to enter the temple, but the Emperor waved them back—

"I came to the festival alone. I alone will offer the sacrifice!"

"Let us go in," he added, addressing Gorgius.

"Close the doors, and let none of the unconsecrated enter. . ."

And the doors were shut in the faces of his philosopher friends.

"'Unconsecrated?' How do you like that?" asked Garguillus moodily.

Libanius stood sulking in silence.

Mauricus, with a mysterious air, dragged his friends into a corner of the portico, and touching his forehead with a finger murmured—

"Do you understand?"

All were dumbfounded.

"Is it possible?"

Mauricus began to reckon—

"First, pallor, feverish appearance, disordered hair, irregular step, incoherent speeches; second, excessive harshness and nervousness; third, this stupid war against the Persians! . . . By Pallas, it clearly means madness!"

The friends drew closer, and began to tell each other all sorts of anecdotes. Sallustius, who held aloof, contemplated the group with a bitter smile.

Within the temple Julian found Hepherion, who brightened on seeing him, and several times during the rite gazed into the Emperor's face, as if the two had some secret in common. Shining in the sunlight, the colossal statue of Apollo stood in the midst of the temple, its body ivory and its garments golden, like those of the Zeus by Phidias at Olympia. The god, stooping slightly, was pouring the nectar of his cup to the Earth-Mother, praying her to restore him Daphne.

A slight cloud passed above the temple. Shadows ran over the time-yellowed ivory. It seemed to Julian that the god benignly stooped still lower, to receive the offering of the last adorers—the weak priest, the apostate Emperor, and the deaf-mute son of the sibyl.

"This is my reward," thought Julian. "I wish for no other glory, nor guerdon, O Apollo! I thank thee for the curses of the crowd; and for thy grace, in making me live and die alone, like thyself! There, where the populace prays, there is no god! Thou art here, in this sanctuary profaned. O god, scorned by mankind, now art thou far more beautiful than of old when they adored thee! On the day marked for me by the Fates, let me be joined again to thee, O Radiant One! Let me die in thee, Sun, as the fire of the last offering dies in thy rays!"

So prayed the Emperor, tears streaming down his cheeks, and one by one the drops of the victim's blood fell like tears on the half-consumed embers.

XIII

A profound obscurity enveloped the wood of Daphne on all sides. A hot wind was hunting the clouds along. For days not a drop of rain had fallen on the cracked and arid earth. The laurels were shaking their black branches to heaven. The low roar of the cypresses in their titanic alleys was like the murmur of a crowd of angry old men.

Two persons were gliding cautiously through the shadow towards the Temple of Apollo. The smaller, who had green eyes like a cat, saw clearly through the night, and was leading the more stalwart by the hand.

"Oh! oh! you scoundrel! we shall break our necks in some ditch!"

"There is no ditch here! What are you afraid of? Since you adopted the new religion you've become a regular old woman!"

"An old woman! . . . When I used to hunt the bear my heart had never a throb the quicker! But here. . . this isn't a job like that! . . . We shall swing for it, side by side, on the same gallows, my boy."

"Nonsense! Be quiet, you great fool!"

The small man again began dragging along the bigger, who carried an enormous truss of hay and a pickaxe.

They arrived at a postern door of the temple.

"Here, use the pick!" muttered the little man, groping with his hands for cracks in the stone. "And you can cut the cross-timbers with the axe. . ."

Suddenly there came a cry, like the complaint of a sick child. The tall man trembled in all his limbs—

"What is it?"

"The Demon!" exclaimed the little one, his eyes staring with affright, clutching at the clothes of his companion—

"You won't desert me, old fellow?"

"It's an owl! . . . Well, he can plume himself on having scared us!"

The enormous night-bird, startled from his nest, flew away with a sobbing cry.

"Let's give it up," said the tall man. "That will never kindle."

"Why not? The wood's rotten, dry as tinder in the sun, and all worm-eaten. . . A single spark will do. Come, work along!"

And the little man shoved the taller.

"Now, push the straw into the hole! . . . more, more, for the glory of the Father, of the Son, and of the Holy Ghost!"

"Why are you fidgeting about like an eel?" said the tall man, in annoyance. "And what is there to laugh at?"

"Ha, ha, ha! What? The angels of heaven must be rejoicing. . . Only remember, uncle, if we're taken, don't deny what we've done. We'll have a pretty little blaze! . . . Here, take the flint and steel!"

"Go to the devil!" answered the other. "You sha'n't tempt me, cursed little snake! Pah! Kindle yourself!"

"Ah, you're crying off. . ." and trembling with rage the little man seized the big man by the beard.

"I'll be the first to denounce you; I shall be believed. . ."

"Leave me alone, damn you. Give me the flint. . . I've had enough of this."

The sparks sprang out. The smaller man, for greater comfort, or to complete his resemblance to a young snake, laid himself flat on his stomach. Thin tongues of flame ran through the straw, which had been soaked in pitch. Thick smoke arose. A mass of flame shone ruddily on the distressed face of the giant Aragaris, and the monkey-like visage of the little Syrian, Strombix, who began leaping and laughing like one drunk or mad—

"We'll destroy it all, in the name of the Father, Son, and Holy Ghost! Ho! ho! ho! A pretty little blaze, eh!"

There was something ferocious in his destructive glee.

Aragaris, pointing to the darkness, muttered—

"Don't you hear something?"

Not a soul was in the wood, but the incendiaries, in the roaring of the wind and the moaning of the cypresses, imagined that they heard voices.

Aragaris began to run.

"Take me on your shoulders, comrade! You've long legs."

Aragaris halted; Strombix sprang on the shoulders of the Sarmatian like a squirrel, and they fled away. The little Syrian dug his knees into his companion's ribs, and put his arms round his neck to avoid falling. In spite of his fear he laughed and shouted with joy. The pair gained the open field. Between the clouds, the moon in its last quarter was shining, and the wind roared harshly. Strombix on the giant's shoulders seemed an evil spirit riding his victim to hell. The idea in fact suddenly struck Aragaris that the Demon, in the shape of a great cat, was hunting him along with his claws to the abyss. The giant made desperate bounds to shake off his burden. The hair bristled on his head, and he yelled with terror. The black, double figure of the pair running, stooped towards the dry, hard earth, over the withered fields, was silhouetted against the pale horizon.

At the same hour, in his chamber in the palace at Antioch, Julian was having a secret interview with the prefect Sallustius Secundus—

"Where shall we obtain, well-beloved Cæsar, the necessary food for such an army?"

"I'll send to Sicily, to Egypt, to Apulia, in all directions where the harvests are abundant," answered the Emperor. "I can answer for it that there will be food enough. . ."

"And money?" asked Sallustius. "Would it not be better to postpone this campaign till next year? Wait a little?"

Julian strode up and down the room. Suddenly he halted before the other man.

"Wait!" he exclaimed angrily. "One would say the word was a kind of pass-word, it is repeated to me so often! . . . Wait? As if it were possible to wait now, to weigh, vacillate, hesitate! Are the Galileans waiting? Understand, Senator, I must achieve the impossible; I must return from Persia great and terrible. . . or not return at all. No more conciliations, or half measures, are possible! . . . Why speak of reason? Did the Macedonian Alexander conquer the world by reason—the beardless young man who, with a mere handful of soldiers, went to fight the monarchs of Asia? Was he not mad, in the sight of reasonable men like you? What gave him victory?"

"I do not know," responded the prefect evasively. "I suppose the valour of the hero. . ."

"No," exclaimed Julian. "The gods! Understand, Sallustius, the Olympians can grant me the same grace, and a greater still, if it please them. I will cross the world from east to west, like the great Macedonian, like the god Dionysus. When I come back victorious from Asia we shall see what the Christians have to say, whether they will mock at the sword of the Roman Emperor as they mock at the plain robe of the philosopher."

His eyes seemed glittering with madness; and Sallustius, seeing that further objection was useless, said nothing. But when Julian began to walk up and down, the prefect shook his head and deep pity was expressed in the kindly gaze of the old man.

"The army must be ready to march," continued Julian. "I desire it, do you hear? I will have no excuses nor delays. Arsaces, the Armenian king, has promised help. There is bread. What more is lacking? I must know that I can at any moment set out against the Persians. On this depends not only my glory, but the safety of the Roman Empire and the victory of the gods against the Galileans! . . ."

The warm wind, blowing into the chamber, agitated the three flames of the lampadary. A shooting-star scored the dark blue night-sky and vanished. Julian saw it, and was strangely thrilled.

Outside the door voices were heard. Someone knocked.

"Who is there? Come in!" said the Emperor.

They were his philosopher friends. Libanius, at their head, seemed more emphatic and sullen than usual.

"What is your desire?" asked Julian coldly.

Libanius knelt, still retaining his arrogant air—

"Let me depart, Augustus. I can no longer endure life at your Court. My patience is exhausted. Everyday there is some new insult to put up with. . ." and he spoke at length of rewards, the moneys received by him no longer, of ingratitude in view of his services, and the splendid panegyrics with which he had glorified Cæsar.

But Julian, unheeding, gazed at the celebrated orator with disgust. Could this really be the same Libanius whose speeches he had admired so much in youth? What baseness! what vanity!

Then all the philosophers began speaking at once. Their voices rose, they mutually accused each other of impiety, debauchery, peculation, repeating the most fatuous scandals. The scene was a petty civil war, not of the wise, but between parasites waxed fat through prosperity, ready to fly at each other's throats through pride, anger, and idleness.

At last the Emperor uttered a word which brought them back to their senses—

"Masters!"

All were silenced like so many frightened magpies.

"Masters!" repeated Julian, with bitter irony, "I have heard you long enough. Permit me to relate you a fable: 'An Egyptian king had a set of tame apes, trained to perform a war-dance of Epirus. They were costumed in helmets and masks; their tails were hidden under the Imperial purple, and while they were dancing it was difficult to believe they were not human. This spectacle gave general delight for years. But on one occasion one of the spectators happened to throw on the stage a handful of nuts! And what happened? The warriors tore off their purple and masks, readjusted their tails, dropped on all fours, and began to bite each other.' How do you like my fable, masters?"

Everybody was silent. Suddenly Sallustius took the Emperor by the hand and pointed to the open window. Under the sombre masses of clouds a reddish light, tossed by a violent wind, seemed slowly spreading.

"Fire! fire!" all present cried.

"On the other side of the river," some suggested.

"No, at Garandâma," others cried.

"No, it must be at Gezireh, in the Jew quarter!"

"It's neither at Gezireh nor at Garandâma," exclaimed a voice, with the exultant tone of one in a crowd at sight of a conflagration. "It is in the wood of Daphne!"

"Apollo's temple!" murmured the Emperor, whose heart was beating wildly. "The Galileans!" he shouted with a mad voice, rushing to the door, then to the staircase.

"Slaves, . . . quick! My charger and fifty legionaries!"

In a few moments all was ready. A black colt, trembling all over and with a dangerous look in his bloodshot eyes, was led into the courtyard.

Julian rode at a breakneck speed through the streets of Antioch, followed by his legionaries. The crowd scattered in terror before them. One man was knocked down and another trampled to death, but their cries were drowned by the thunder of hoofs and the clatter of arms.

The open country was reached. Julian knew not how long the mad gallop lasted; three legionaries fell with their foundered horses. The glow became brighter and brighter and the smell of smoke perceptible. The fields with their dusty vegetation assumed a yellowish hue. A curious crowd rushed up from every side, like moths to a flame. Julian noticed the joyousness of their faces, as if they were hurrying to a festival.

Tongues of flame glittered, in thick smoke-clouds, above the wood of Daphne. The Emperor penetrated into the sacred enclosure. There the crowd was bellowing, and exchanging pleasantries and laughter.

The calm alleys, abandoned by all for so many years, were swarming. Rioters profaned the wood, broke down branches of ancient laurels, befouled the springs, and trampled on the sleeping flowers. The cool odour of narcissus and lily strove with the stifling heat of the fire and the breath of the people.

"A miracle from God," murmured the crowd gleefully. "I myself saw lightning fall from heaven and kindle the roof!"

"No, thou liest! The earth split in the midst of the temple and vomited flames underneath the idol!"

"'S death! . . . It was after the abominable order to shift the relics. They thought they could do it without let or hindrance. . . Pooh! . . . So much for your Temple of Apollo and prophecy from the sacred spring! It is a blessing!"

Julian saw in the crowd a woman half-dressed, as if newly risen from bed. With a stupid smile she was wondering at the fire, while cradling on her arm an infant at the breast. Tears still trembled on the eyelashes of the little one; but he quieted himself sucking vigorously at the breast, against which he had propped himself with one hand, while stretching the other towards the flames as if for a new plaything.

The Emperor reined up his horse. Further advance was impossible, by reason of the heat. The legionaries stood awaiting orders. But Julian saw that the temple was doomed. From base to roof it was enveloped in flames, like an immense brazier. Walls, joists, and carven cross-beams were falling in, with crash after crash, and whirlwinds of sparks mounted to a sky which came down lower and lower, lurid and menacing. The flames seemed to lick the clouds, struggling against the embraces of the wind and, roaring, flapped like great sails. The laurel leaves writhed in the heat, and doubled themselves as in torture. The peaks of the cypresses, kindled like huge torches, gave up the smoke of sacrifice. Drops of resin fell thickly from the centenarian trees, old as the temple.

Julian gazed haggardly at the fire. He wished to give an order to the legionaries; but drawing his sword from the scabbard and curbing his restive horse, he could only exclaim impotently between clenched teeth—"Oh, wretched, wretched people!"

Shouts of the crowd sounded in the distance. Julian recollected that the entrance to the treasury was at the back; and the idea occurred to him that the Galileans were pillaging the wealth of the god. . . He made a sign, and dashed in that direction, followed by the legionaries. A melancholy procession brought him to a halt. A few Roman guards, who had run up in haste from the village of Daphne, were carrying a rude litter.

"What is it?" asked Julian.

"The Galileans have stoned the priest Gorgius to death."

"And the treasury?"

"It is untouched. Standing on the threshold of the door, the priest defended the entrance. He never left his post until a stone stretched him on the ground. Then they killed the child. The Galilean horde, after trampling them under foot, would have got into the treasury if we hadn't arrived in time."

"Is he still alive?"

"Hardly breathing."

The Emperor leapt from his horse. The litter was laid gently down; and Julian stooping, cautiously lifted a corner of the old chlamys of the priest, which covered both bodies. The old man was stretched with closed eyes and scarcely heaving breast on a bed of fresh laurel-branches. Julian's heart shook with pity when he saw the red-nosed old drinker, whom he had thought so scandalous a few days before. He remembered the poor goose in the wicker basket, the last offering to Apollo. On the snowy hair drops of blood stood like berries, and laurel leaves enlaced lay in a wreath on the priest's head.

By his side lay the little body of Hepherion, his cheek resting on his hand. He seemed asleep. Julian thought—

"Such must Eros be, son of the Love-goddess, killed by the stones of Galileans."

And the Roman Emperor knelt in veneration before the martyrs to Olympus. In spite of the loss of the temple, in spite of the stupid triumph of the mob, Julian felt in this death the presence of the god. His heart softened; even his hate disappeared, and with humble tears he kissed the old man's hand. The dying man opened his eyes.

"Where is the child?" he asked under his breath.

"Here, near you."

Julian gently placed the hand of Gorgius on the locks of Hepherion.

"Is he alive?" asked Gorgius, stroking the child's curls for the last time. He was so weak that he could not turn his head, and Julian had not the courage to reveal the truth.

The priest fixed a suppliant look on the Emperor—

"Cæsar! I entrust him to you. . . Do not abandon him. . ."

"Be assured; I will do all that I can for the little one."

So Julian took under his protection one to whom not even a Roman Cæsar could now do good or harm.

Gorgius let his hand remain on the head of Hepherion. Suddenly his face lighted; he tried to say something, and stammered incoherently—

"Rejoice! Rejoice!"

He gazed before him with eyes wide open, sighed, paused in the midst of the sigh, and his look faded. Julian closed the eyes of the dead.

Suddenly exultant songs were heard. The Emperor wheeled round, and saw a long procession marching down the cypress-alley. A great crowd of priests, in dalmatics of cloth of gold covered with precious gems, deacons swinging censers, black monks bearing lighted tapers, virgins and youths clothed in white, children waving palm-branches, and above the crowd on a lofty car the relics of Babylas, in a glittering silver shrine. They were the relics expelled, by Cæsar's orders, from Daphne to Antioch. The expulsion had become a victorious march. The people were singing the ancient Psalm of David glorifying the God of Israel—

"He is clothed in clouds and darkness!"

Above the moanings of the wind, and the roarings of the fire, soared the triumphant chant of the Galileans to the lurid vault of the sky—

"Clouds and darkness surround Him, fire tramples out His enemies before Him, and the mountains melt like wax before the face of the Lord, the Lord of all the earth!"

Julian grew pale at the audacity of joy resounding in the last line—

"Let all those who serve and boast themselves of their idols tremble, And let all gods bow down before Him!"

The Emperor leapt upon his horse, drew his sword, and shouted—
"Soldiers, follow me!"

He was about to rush in, disperse the triumphant mob, overset the shrine, and scatter the bones of the saint, but a firm hand seized the bridle of his horse—

"Out of the way!" cried Julian furiously, lifting his sword.

Next moment his arm fell. Before him stood the stern, calm face of Sallustius Secundus, who had just arrived from Antioch.

"Cæsar, do not strike the unarmed! Be yourself!"

Julian put back his sword in the scabbard.

His helmet scorched his head; he tore it off and flung it to earth, wiping away great drops of sweat. Alone and bareheaded he advanced towards the crowd, signing them to halt.

"Inhabitants of Antioch," he said almost calmly, restraining himself by a supreme effort, "know that the rioters, and setters on fire of the Temple of Apollo, will be punished without mercy. You scorn my pity? We shall see how you will scorn my anger. The Roman Augustus could blot your town from the earth, so that men should forget that Antioch the great ever existed. But I go forth to war against the Persians. If the gods grant that I return in triumph, woe be to you, rioters! Woe to thee, Nazarene, the carpenter's son!"

And he stretched out his sword above the heads of the crowd.

Suddenly he fancied he heard a voice saying—

"The Nazarene, son of the carpenter, makes ready thy shroud!"

Julian thrilled, turned round, but saw no one. He passed his hand over his eyes. Was it an hallucination? At that moment from the interior of the temple came a deafening noise. Part of the roof had fallen on the statue of Apollo, which reeled from its pedestal. The procession went on its way, taking up again the Psalm—

"Let those tremble who serve and boast themselves of their idols,
And let all gods of the earth bow down before Him!"

XIV

Julian passed the winter in preparations for his Persian campaign. At the beginning of spring, on the fifth of March, he quitted Antioch with an army of sixty-five thousand men. The snow was melting from the mountains. In fruit-gardens the leafless young apricot trees were trimmed with pink blossoms. The soldiery marched gaily to the war as to a festival.

The dockyards of Samos had built a fleet of twelve hundred ships, wrought of enormous cedars, pine, and oak from Taurus gorges, and the fleet had ascended the Euphrates as far as the city of Leontopolis.

By forced marches Julian passed by Hieropolis to Carrhæ, and thence along the Euphrates as far as the southern Persian frontier. In the north, another army of thirty thousand men had been sent out under the generals Procopius and Sebastian. Joined to the forces of the Armenian Arsaces, these were to lay waste Adiabene, Apolloniatis, and traversing Corduene rejoin the principal army on the banks of the Tigris at Ctesiphon.

All had been provided for, combined and planned with ardour by the Emperor himself. Those who understood the plan of campaign were amazed, and not without reason, at its wisdom, simplicity, and greatness of conception.

At the beginning of April, the army reached Circesium, a post remarkably fortified by Diocletian on the frontier of Mesopotamia, at the junction of the Araxes and the Euphrates. There a bridge of boats was constructed, Julian having given the order to cross the frontier on the following morning. Late that evening, when all was ready, he returned to his tent, fatigued but satisfied. He lit his lamp in order to resume his favourite work, for which part of his night was reserved. It was a study in pure philosophy: *Against the Christians*. He used to write it in snatches, within sound of the trumpets and camp-songs and challenging sentries. He rejoiced in the idea that he was fighting the Galilean with every weapon lying to his hand; by battlefield and book, by Roman sword and Hellenic learning. Never did the Emperor part with the works of the Fathers, ecclesiastical canons and creeds of the councils. On the margin of the New Testament, which he studied with no less care than Plato and Homer, he would make caustic annotations with his own hand.

Julian took off his dusty armour, sat down before his table, and dipping his reed-pen in ink, began to write. His leisure was immediately invaded. Two couriers had just arrived in camp, one from Italy, the other from Jerusalem. Their news was by no means agreeable. An earthquake had destroyed the city of Nicomedia in Asia Minor, and subterranean rumblings had raised to the highest pitch the terror of the inhabitants of Constantinople. The books of the sibyls, moreover, forebade the crossing of the frontiers before the year had elapsed. The courier from Jerusalem brought a letter from the dignitary Alipius of Antioch. By a strange contradiction Julian, the worshipper of the manifold Olympus, had decided to rebuild the temple, destroyed by the Romans, of the one God of Israel, in order to refute, in the face of time and the world, the prophecy of the Gospel, "*There shall not be left here one stone upon another that shall not be thrown down*" (Matt. xxiv. 2). The Jews responded with enthusiasm to the Emperor's appeal. Gifts flowed in from all sides. The plan of rebuilding was a superb one. The work was promptly taken in hand, and Julian confided the general supervision to his friend, the learned and noble Alipius of Antioch, formerly proconsul of Britain.

"What has happened?" asked Julian, before unsealing the missive, perturbed at the sombre face of the courier.

"A great misfortune, well-beloved Cæsar!"

"Speak, fear nothing."

"So long as the workmen were working at the ruins and demolishing the old walls, all went well. But hardly had they proceeded to lay the first stone of the new edifice, when flames, in the shape of balls of fire, escaped from the vaults, overturned the blocks, and scorched the workmen. On the following day, on the order of the most noble Alipius, the works were resumed. The miracle was repeated, and so also a third time. The Christians are triumphant; the Hellenes in despair; and not a single workman will consent to go down into the vaults. Nothing remains of the edifice, not one stone!"

"Hush, fool! You must be a Galilean yourself!" exclaimed the Emperor. "These are old wives' tales!"

He broke the seal, unfolded, and read the letter. The courier spoke the truth. Alipius confirmed his words. Julian could not believe his eyes. He re-read the message carefully, bringing it nearer to the lamp. His face flushed with anger and shame. He bit his lips and threw the crumpled papyrus to the physician Oribazius, who stood hard by.

"Read! . . . Either Alipius has gone mad, or indeed. . . No! that's impossible!"

The young Alexandrian doctor picked up and read the letter with the calmness which never deserted him. Lifting his clear and intelligent eyes to Julian's, he answered—

"I see in this no miracle. Scientific men described the phenomenon long ago. In the vaults of old buildings which have been sealed from the air for centuries, there collects a dense inflammable gas. To go with a lighted torch into these vaults is enough to explain the explosion and kill the rash workman. To the ignorant and superstitious this of course appears a miracle, but it is perfectly natural and explicable."

He laid the letter on the table with a slightly pedantic smile on his thin lips.

"Ah, yes! to be sure," said Julian, not without bitterness. "The earthquakes at Nicomedia and Constantinople, the prophecies of the sibylline books, drought at Antioch, conflagrations at Rome, inundations in Egypt, all are perfectly natural! Only it is odd that everything is in league against me, earth and water, fire and sky, and even the gods, I believe!"

Sallustius Secundus came into the tent.

"Sublime Augustus! Tuscan wizards, charged by you to ascertain the will of the gods, beg you to wait; not to cross the frontier tomorrow. The birds of the oracles, despite all prayers, refuse food, and will not even pick at the grains of barley!"

At first Julian frowned angrily, but his face immediately brightened, and he burst into a surprising fit of laughter.

"Really, Sallustius? They won't peck at anything, eh? Then what must we do with these obstinate beasts? Suppose we retrace our steps to Antioch, amid the laughter of the Galileans? . . . My dear friend, go back immediately to these Tuscan wizards and tell them my will. Let the fowls be thrown into the river. Do you understand? These pampered birds are not pleased to eat. Let's see if they will drink. . . Carry my orders."

"Is this some jest, Cæsar? Do I understand you rightly? In spite of everything, we are to cross the frontier tomorrow?"

"Yes! And I swear by my next victory, and the greatness of Rome, that no prophetic bird shall daunt me, neither water, earth, nor fire, not even the gods! It is too late! The die is cast. My friends, is there anything in all nature superior to the will of man? In all the sibylline books is there anything stronger than the words 'I will'? More than ever I feel the mystery of my life. No auguries shall enmesh me. Today I believe in, and yet I laugh at them. Is it sacrilege? So much the worse. I have nothing to lose! If the gods abandon me I will deny them!"

When everybody had gone out, Julian approached the little statue of Mercury, with the intention of praying, as he usually did, and casting some grains of incense on the tripod; but suddenly he turned away with a smile, lay down on the lion-skin which served him as bed, and extinguishing the lamp fell into a deep and careless slumber, as folk often do on the brink of misfortune.

Dawn had hardly risen when he awoke in higher spirits than on the evening before. The trumpet sounded. Julian leapt on horseback and rode to the banks of the Araxes. It was a cool April morning. A gentle wind bore the nocturnal desert warmth from the banks of the great Asiatic river. All along the Euphrates, from Circesium as far as the Roman camp, stretched the fleet, over a space of nearly two miles. Since the reign of Xerxes no such display of forces had ever been seen here. The sun's first rays glittered behind the mausoleum raised to Gordian, the conqueror of the Persians, killed in that place by the Arab Philip. The edge of the purple disk rose from the desert like a burning coal, and all the tops of the masts and sails grew red in the morning fog. The Emperor raised his hand, and the earth-shaking mass of sixty-five thousand men began the march. The Roman army began to cross the bridge that separated it from the Persian frontier. Julian's horse carried him over the bridge and up a high sandy hill on the enemy's soil. The centurion of the Imperial Guard, Anatolius, the admirer of Arsinoë, marched at the head of the palatine cohort.

Anatolius looked at the Emperor. A great change had come over Julian during the month passed in the open air, amidst the healthy toils of campaigning. It was difficult to recognise in this masculine warrior, so hale of visage, whose young glance was brilliant with gaiety, the thin and yellow-faced philosopher, dull-eyed, ragged-bearded, nervous in movement, with ink-stained fingers and toga, Julian the rhetorician, who had served as butt for the street-boys of Antioch.

"Hark! hark! Cæsar is going to speak!"

All was silent. The clink of arms, the noise of waves lapping sides of ships, and the silky rustle of the standards were the only sounds audible.

"Warriors, my bravest of the brave," said Julian in his strong voice, "I read such gaiety, such boldness on your faces, that I cannot help addressing you some words of welcome. Remember, comrades, the destiny of the world is in our hands! We are going to restore the old greatness of Rome! Steel your hearts; be ready for any fate. There is to be no turning back.

"I shall be at your head, on horseback or on foot, taking all dangers and toils with the humblest among you; because, henceforth, you are no longer my servants, but my children and my friends! If fate kills me, happy shall I be to die for our great Rome, like Scævola and the Curiatii and the noblest of the Decii. Courage, then, my comrades! and remember that the strong are always conquerors!"

He stretched his sword, with a smile, toward the distant horizon. The soldiers in unison held up their bucklers, shouting in rapture—

"Glory, glory to conquering Cæsar!"

The galleys glided down the reaches of the river. The Roman eagles hovered above their cohorts, and the Emperor rode on his white horse, to meet the rising sun, across the cold blue shadow, on the desert sand, cast from the pyramid of Gordian. Soon, soon was Julian to quit the light of day for the long shadow of the solitary grave.

XV

The army was marching along the left bank of the Euphrates; on the broad plain, level as the sea, and covered with silvery wormwood, not a tree was in sight. On all sides lay grass and sweet-smelling bushes. From time to time, troops of wild asses appeared on the horizon, raising clouds of dust. Ostriches were seen running; and the soldiers used to roast the delicate flesh of the bustard at their camp-fires. Jests and songs lasted till night-fall. The desert received these soldiers, hungry for glory, booty, and blood, with mute caresses, starry nights, gentle dawns and sunsets, night-coolnesses breathing the bitter smell of wormwood. Deeper and deeper they plunged into the solitudes, without meeting the enemy. Hardly had they passed when calm descended on the plain, as on the sea over a sunken ship; and the grass, trampled by the legionaries, lifted up anew its soft spears.

Suddenly the desert became menacing. Clouds hid the sky; rains began; and a soldier watering his horses was killed by lightning. At the end of April came the heats. Soldiers envied their comrades who marched in the shadow of a dromedary or of a wagon. The men of the north, Gauls and Sicambri, began to die of sunstroke. The plains became sad, bare, tufted here and there with scorched grass, and every step sank into the sand. Fierce gusts of wind assailed the army, tearing the standards from their poles, and blowing away tents. Then again a calm was restored which in its strangeness and profundity, seemed to the frightened soldiers more terrible than tempest. Raillery and marching-songs ceased; but the march went on, day after day; and yet they never caught a glimpse of the enemy.

At the beginning of May the palm-groves of Assyria were reached.

At Mazeprakt, where lay ruins of the enormous wall constructed by ancient Syrian kings, the enemy was seen for the first time. The Persians hastily retreated, and under a rain of poisoned arrows the Romans crossed the wide canal joining the Euphrates to the Tigris. This magnificent piece of engineering, made of Babylonian brick, cutting Mesopotamia in two, was called Nazar Malka, the River of Kings. Suddenly the Persians disappeared. The waters of the Nazar Malka rose, overflowed the banks, and flooded the vast surrounding plains. The Persians had organised the inundation by opening the sluices and dykes which lay on all sides, threatening the friable wastes. The foot-soldiers marched on, up to the knees in water, and their legs sank deep into mud. Entire companies disappeared into invisible ditches. Even horsemen and dromedaries with their burdens vanished suddenly. The track had to be sounded for with poles. The whole desert was transformed into a lake, and the palm-groves appeared like islands.

"Whither are we going?" the cowardly began to murmur. "Why not retire at once to the river, and get on shipboard? We are soldiers; not frogs made for dabbling through mud!"

Julian marched on foot with the infantry, even in the most difficult places. He helped to haul the labouring chariots out of mud-holes by their wheels; and laughed at his own soaked and clay-stained purple. Fascines and floating bridges were formed of palm stems; and at night-fall the army succeeded in reaching a dry place. The soldiers fell asleep, utterly exhausted.

In the morning they saw the fortress of Perizaborh.

From the tops of walls and inaccessible towers, spread with thick carpets and goat-skins, to defend them from the shock of siege-weapons, the Persians poured down scorn upon their enemies.

The whole day passed in the exchange of insults and projectiles. Then, profiting by the darkness of a moonless night, the Romans, in absolute silence, carried the catapults and battering-ram from their ships (which had all this way accompanied the march) and propped these weapons against the walls of Perizaborh. The fosses were filled with earth, and by means of a *malleolus*, or enormous spindle-shaped arrow, full of an inflammable matter, made of pitch, sulphur, oil, and bitumen, the Romans succeeded in setting the goatskin carpets on fire.

The Persians rushed to extinguish the conflagration, and profiting by the momentary confusion the Emperor ordered an attack by the great battering-ram. This was a huge pine-stem, swung by chains from a pyramidal tower of beams, and pointed by a ram's head in metal. A hundred strong legionaries, hauling in rhythm on thick ropes made of ox-sinew, slowly heaved and balanced the enormous shaft. The first blow sounded like the rumbling of thunder. Earth shook and the walls resounded. The furious ram butted his metal head in a swift and tremendous succession of blows against the walls. There was a great crash; an entire corner of the wall had given way. The Persians, with despairing cries, fled in all directions; and Julian, the star of whose helmet glittered through clouds of dust, bright and terrible as the star of Mars, galloped into the conquered town.

For two days the army rested under the fresh and shadowy groves on the other side of the city; the men regaling themselves with a kind of wine made of palm-juice, and amber-clear dates from Babylon.

Then they resumed their march and entered a rocky plain.

The heat was painful. Men and horses died in great numbers. At noon the air danced above the rocks in burning rays, and through the ashen-grey desert wound the silvery waves of Tigris, like a lazy serpent basking his coils in the sun.

The Romans saw at length, beyond the Tigris, a lofty rock rising, rose-coloured, bare and jagged. This was the second fortress defending Ctesiphon, the southern capital of Persia. It was a place far more difficult to take than Perizaborh, and soared to the clouds like an eagle's nest.

The sixteen towers and double enclosing walls of Maogamalki were built with the famous bricks of Babylon, sun-dried and mortared with bitumen, like all the ancient monuments of Assyria, which fear not the centuries.

The attack commenced. Again the ungainly slings groaned, and the pulleys of *scorpions* and *onagers*, or frames for flinging stones. Again huge flaming beams hissed like arrows from their engines. At the hour when even lizards go to sleep in fissures of the rock, the sun-rays fell vertically on the backs and heads of soldiers, stifling them like a crushing weight. The desperate legionaries, in defiance of their officers and of increased danger, snatched off their helmets and bloodied armour, preferring the chance of wounds to enduring that fearful heat. Above the brown towers and loopholes of Maogamalki, vomiting poisoned arrows, lances, stones, leaden bullets, and Persian fire-darts of choking sulphur, stretched the dazzling blue-grey of a dusty sky, blind and implacable as death.

The heavens beat down the hatred of men. Besiegers and besieged, utterly exhausted, ceased fighting. And a silence of noon-day, more sullen than the blackest night, fell on both hosts.

The Romans lost no whit of their courage. After the taking of Perizaborh they believed in the invincibility of the Emperor, compared him to Alexander the Great, and expected miracles from him.

For several days, on the east side of Maogamalki where the rocky steep was less abrupt, soldiers were set to hollow a tunnel. This mine, passing under the walls of the fortress, led up to the centre of the town. The width of the passage—three cubits—allowed two soldiers to proceed abreast. Huge beams at intervals supported the ceiling. The diggers worked gaily. The damp and obscurity seemed delicious to them after the excess of sunlight.

"A day or two ago we were frogs and now we're moles," said the soldiers to each other, laughing.

Three cohorts, the Mattiarians, Lactiniarians, and Victorians, fifteen hundred picked men, keeping the sternest silence, crawled into the subterranean passage, impatiently waiting orders to burst into the town. At daybreak the attack was expressly directed on two opposite sides, in order to divert the attention of the Persians, and Julian himself led up the soldiers by a single narrow path under a hail of stones and arrows.

"We shall see," he said to himself with glee at the danger; "we shall see if the gods preserve me, or if, by a miracle, I shall escape death even now."

Some irresistible curiosity, or thirst for the supernatural, urged him to expose himself, and with a defiant smile to challenge Fate to do her worst. It was not death he feared, but only defeat in his purposeless and intoxicating game against the higher powers.

The soldiers followed him on, fascinated by and catching the contagion of his mad mood.

Meantime the Persians, laughing at the efforts of the besiegers, were singing on the battlements songs in glory of King Sapor, "Son of the Sun." And from the precipitous terraces they shouted to the Romans:

"Julian will scale the heavenly palace of Ormuzd before he gets into our fortress!"

When the fire of action had risen to its hottest, the Emperor, in a low voice, sent word to his officers on the far side of the city.

The legionaries hidden in the tunnel burst out into the interior of the city, and found themselves in the cellar of a house where an old Persian woman was kneading bread. She uttered a piercing cry at the sight of the Roman legionaries, and was promptly killed. Then, gliding unperceived, they threw themselves on the rear of the besieged. The Persians flung down their arms, and scattered into the streets. The Romans then rushed to the city gates, and by the double assault the town was taken. From that moment not a legionary doubted that the Emperor, like Alexander of Macedon, would conquer the whole of the Persian Empire as far as the Indies.

Leaving its larger ships behind on the Euphrates, the army now drew near to Ctesiphon, on the river Tigris. But Julian, whose almost unnaturally feverish imagination gave his enemies no time to recover, made practicable the old Roman canal, hollowed by Trajan and Septimius Severus between the Tigris and the Euphrates; the same channel that had been filled in and flooded by the Persians. By this means the whole fleet left the Euphrates and reached the Tigris a little above Ctesiphon. The conqueror found himself thus at the centre of the Asiatic Empire.

On the following day Julian summoned a council of war and declared that the troops should be transported that night to the other bank, under the walls of the capital. Dagalaïf, Hormizdas, Secundinus, Victor, Sallustius, all seasoned warriors, were terrified at this idea. For hours they strove to persuade the Emperor to relinquish so rash a project, urging the fatigue of the soldiers, the width and rapid currents of the river, the steepness of the banks, the proximity of Ctesiphon, and the innumerable army of Sapor; the Persians being certain to make a sortie at the moment of disembarkation. Julian would listen to nothing.

"Wait as long as we will," he exclaimed impatiently, "the river will not grow narrower nor the banks less steep; and the Persian army will get bigger everyday we delay. If I had listened to your advice, we should still be at Antioch."

The chiefs left his tent in consternation.

"He cannot last long in this mood," murmured the well-tried and wily Dagalaïf, a Goth grown old in the service of Rome. "Remember what I tell you. He seems gay, and even laughs, but there is something ill in his expression. I've seen it in people who are close to despair or death. That gaiety augurs evil."

The warm misty twilight descended rapidly on the immense river-reaches. At a given signal five galleys bearing four hundred warriors, were unlashed from their moorings, and for long nothing was heard but the regular dip of their muffled oars. Then, silence. The obscurity became impenetrable. Julian gazed fixedly in the direction in which the boats had disappeared, concealing his emotion under affected cheerfulness. The generals muttered among themselves. Suddenly a blaze lit up the night. Everyone drew his breath, and all looks were turned on the Emperor. He understood what that blaze meant. The Persians had succeeded in setting light to the Roman ships, by means of fire-balls hurled from engines on the other bank.

Julian grew pale, but immediately collecting himself and giving his soldiers no time to think, he rushed into the first ship lying along shore and shouted to the army—

DMITRY MEREZHKOVSKY

"Victory, victory! Do you see that fire? They have landed and are masters of the bank. I myself ordered the cohorts to light the bonfire as a signal of success. Follow me, comrades!"

"What is this?" muttered the prudent Sallustius in his ear. "All is lost; that fire is on board our galleys. . ."

"Cæsar has gone mad!" groaned the terrified Hormizdas to Dagalaïf. That wily barbarian shrugged his shoulders in perplexity.

With an irresistible impulse the legions dashed down to the river, all ranks elbowing each other and shouting "Victory! victory!" Jostling, falling into the water, dragging each other out, the men swarmed on board.

A few small boats nearly sank; and there was no room on the galleys to take over all. Many cavalry swam across, hanging to the manes and tails of their horses. The Celts and Batavians flung themselves into the water, pushing over, afloat, their great hollowed leather shields. Through fog they swam, many being caught and whirled round in eddies, but regardless of danger they too shouted "Victory, victory!" from the water. So great was the number of ships that the current was slightly broken, thus aiding the swimmers. The conflagration of the first five galleys was extinguished without difficulty. Then only did all ranks understand the Emperor's audacious ruse. But the spirit of the soldiers rose still higher after the avoidance of such a danger. Now everything seemed possible.

A little before dawn they made themselves masters of the heights of the far bank, but hardly had the Romans time for a brief rest on their arms when they saw at daybreak a vast army sally from the walls of Ctesiphon into the plain round the city.

The battle lasted twelve hours. The Persians fought with the fierceness of despair. Julian's army here saw for the first time the great war-elephants which could crush a cohort like a tuft of grass. Never had the Romans won such a victory since the great days of the Emperors Trajan, Vespasian, and Titus.

On the following morning at daybreak Julian brought a grateful offering to Ares, the god of war. It consisted of ten white bulls, beautiful beasts like those on the old Greek bas-reliefs. The whole army was given up to merrymaking. Only the Tuscan wizards, who at every victory of Julian's had become more sombre, mute, and enigmatic, remained obstinately sullen.

The first bull, arrayed with laurels, was led to the smoking altar. He walked slowly and passively. Suddenly he stumbled to his knees, lowing pitifully, almost humanly, so that a thrill ran through the spectators; and then, burying his muzzle in the dust, shuddered. Before the axe of the slayer had touched his forehead he had reeled over and died. A second bull similarly fell dead, then a third and a fourth. All paced weakly to the altar, seeming hardly able to stand upright, as if attacked by some mortal malady.

The army was in dismay at the presage. Some said that the Etruscan wizards had poisoned the bulls, to revenge themselves for the Emperor's contempt for their art. Nine bulls thus fell, and the tenth, snapping his bonds, escaped, and rushed bellowing through the camp beyond hope of recapture.

The ceremonial became disorganised, and the augurs smiled among themselves a satisfied smile. When the entrails of the dead bulls were opened Julian, being skilled in magic, saw at a glance terrifying omens in the organs. He turned aside, his brow dark with wrath, attempting but failing to assume carelessness.

Turning again he approached the altar and spurned it violently with his foot. The altar reeled, but did not fall. The crowd uttered deep sighs and the prefect Sallustius rushed towards the Emperor, whispering—

"The men are looking! It would be better to cut short the sacrifice. . ."

Julian waved him away, and overturned the altar with his foot. The embers were scattered and the fire extinguished, but the fragrant smoke still thickly ascended.

"Woe, woe upon us! The altar is profaned!" groaned a voice.

"I tell you he is mad," growled Hormizdas, grasping Dagalaïf's arm. "Look at him. . . How is it that the rest don't see it?"

The Etruscan augurs watched the proceedings, motionless, with imperturbable faces.

Julian's eyes kindled and he raised his arms to the sky. He cried—

"I swear by the eternal joy, locked here, in my heart, I renounce You, as you have renounced me! I abandon you as you have abandoned me, impotent Deities! Single-handed against you, phantom Olympians, I am like unto you, but not your equal, because I am a man and you are only gods! . . . Long, long has my heart aspired to this deliverance; and now I break our alliance, laugh at my superstitious terrors, at your childish oracles. I was living like a slave, and I might have died a slave! I understand that I am stronger than the gods, because, vowed to death, I have conquered death! No melancholy, no fear, no victims, no prayer! All that is past. Henceforth in my life there shall

DMITRY MEREZHKOVSKY

not be a single shade, nor trembling. Nothing! except that everlasting Olympian smile which I have learnt from you, the Dead! Nothing, but the sacred fire of which I rob you, O Immortals! Mine be the cloudless sky in which you have dwelt till now, and from which you have died, to give place to man-gods! Maximus! Maximus! you were right; over my soul your mind hovers still. . ."

An augur of ninety years old put his hand on the shoulder of the Emperor.

"Speak lower, my son, speak lower. If thou hast understood the mystery, rejoice in silence! Tempt not the crowd. Those who hear thee cannot understand."

The general murmurs of indignation became louder.

"He's raving," said Hormizdas to Dagalaïf. "Take him to his tent, or all will go ill!"

Oribazius, like the devoted physician that he was, took Julian's hand and began to persuade him soothingly.

"Well-beloved Augustus, you must take rest. There are dangerous fevers in this country. Come into the tent. The sun is hurtful. . . Your illness may get worse!"

The Emperor looked at him with a pre-occupied air.

"Stay, Oribazius, I have forgotten something. . . Ah, yes, yes! . . . It is the chiefest thing of all! Listen. Say not, 'The gods are no more,' but rather 'The gods as yet are not.' They are not, but they shall exist; not in fables, but on earth. We shall all be gods, all; only to become so we must create in ourselves such daring as no man has yet felt, not even Alexander!"

The agitation of the army became more pronounced. Murmurs and exclamations joined into a general hum of indignation. No one clearly understood; but everyone had a suspicion that something abnormal was going on.

Some cried:

"Sacrilege! Set up the altar again!"

Others answered:

"The sacrificial priests have poisoned Cæsar because he would not listen to them! Let us kill them! They are bringing ruin on us!"

The Galileans took advantage of the occasion, and slipped about from group to group, whispering and inventing pieces of scandal.

"Were you watching the Emperor? It is the chastisement of God on him. Devils have seized him and troubled his mind. That's why he revolts against his own gods. He has renounced the One God!"

As if awaking from a deep sleep, the Emperor looked slowly over the crowd, and at last asked Oribazius, indifferently:

"What is the matter—these shouts? What has happened? Ah, yes! . . . the altar upset!"

And contemplating the extinct embers with a sad smile he said:

"Do you know, my learned friends, one cannot offend people more than by telling them the truth! . . . Poor simple children! . . . Well, let them cry, let them weep, they will get over it! Come, Oribazius, we will go into the shade. You are right, the sun is dangerous. I am tired, and my eyes hurt me. . ."

Julian went slowly away leaning on the arm of the doctor. At the door of his tent he made a languid sign that all should leave him. The door-curtain was lowered, and the tent plunged in darkness.

The Emperor went up to the camp-bed, a lion's skin, and sank on it exhausted. He remained stretched thus a long time, holding his head tightly in his hands, as in childhood, after some fit of anger or disappointment.

"Quiet! quiet! Cæsar is ill!" the generals said, to calm the soldiers.

And the men were immediately dumb.

Throughout the Roman camp, as in the chamber of the dying, reigned the silence of painful expectation. The Galileans alone took time by the forelock, gliding furtively hither and thither, penetrating everywhere, hawking about sinister rumours, and, like reptiles waked by the sun's warmth after their winter's sleep, ceaselessly whispered:

"Do you not understand? This is the punishment of God on him!"

XVI

More than once did Oribazius prudently lift the door-curtain, bringing refreshing drink to the sick man. Julian refused it, and kept asking to be left alone. He feared human faces, noise, and light. Keeping his hands pressed against his head, and closing his eyes, he endeavoured to keep his mind a blank; to forget where he was, to forget every emotion. The protracted effort of will sustained during the last three months had changed him, and left him weak and broken, as after a long illness. He knew not whether he was asleep or awake. Visionary scenes, trains of pictures glided before his eyes one after another with amazing swiftness and intolerable precision. Sometimes he fancied he was in bed, in the great hall at Macellum. Old Labda had given him her blessing for the night. The snortings of the horses picketed near the tent became the dull snoring of Mardonius, which the boys used to laugh at.

He felt happy and again a young boy, unknown by anyone, far from the world, hidden amongst the Cappadocian mountains.

He smelt the fresh and subtle smell of hyacinths, in the first warmth of the March sun, within the little courtyard of the priest Olympiodorus. He heard the silver laughter of Amaryllis and the murmur of the fountain, the metallic clink of the cottabos, and the voice of Diaphane: "Children, the gingerbread cakes are ready!"

Then all vanished.

Then the only sound he heard was of the first flies, humming in a nook out of the wind, on the white warm-sunned wall, by the seashore. And he was blissfully watching sails bathed in the infinite softness of the blue Propontic Sea, and he believed himself alone in a delicious solitude, undisturbed by a single face, and, like the little dancing gnats of the white wall, luxuriated in sheer happiness of living, in the sunlight, in the calm.

Suddenly, half-waking, Julian remembers that he is in the heart of Persia; that he is the Roman Emperor; that he alone is responsible for the lives of sixty thousand legionaries; that the gods are no more, that he has thrown down the altar of sacrifice. He shivers, and an icy chillness invades his body. He is falling, falling through the void, with nothing, nothing in the universe to arrest his fall.

Perhaps an hour, perhaps twenty-four hours, may have elapsed in this kind of half-slumber.

Then no longer dreaming, but in reality, he hears his faithful slave saying, as he thrusts his head under the door-curtain:

"Cæsar, I am afraid of disturbing you, but I dare not disobey. It was your order that you should be immediately informed. . . The chief Ariphas has just arrived in the camp. . ."

"Ariphas!" exclaimed Julian, rising, "Ariphas! . . . Bring him, bring him here quickly!"

This was one of his bravest commanders, sent with a detachment to ascertain whether the auxiliary army of thirty thousand men, under the command of Procopius and Sebastian, was not coming, with the troops of his ally Arsaces, to join the Emperor under the walls of Ctesiphon. Julian had long been awaiting this help, on which the fate of the principal army depended.

"Bring him!" exclaimed the Emperor. . . "or no, I myself will. . ."

But his weakness was not yet dissipated, despite this momentary over-excitement. His head swam, he closed his eyes and had to support himself against the canvas wall of the tent.

"Give me wine. . . strong wine. . . mixed with cold water."

The old slave rapidly executed the order, and gave the cup to the Emperor, who drank slowly and issued from the tent. It was late in the evening. A storm had passed far into the distance across the Euphrates, and the wind was still fresh with the smell of rain. Rare stars, trembling like watchlights in the breeze, shone in the gapped cloud. From the desert came up the barkings of jackals. Julian laid bare his breast, held his forehead in the wind, surrendering himself to the soft breath of the sinking gale.

He smiled at the thought of his own cowardice. His weakness had disappeared, strength returned to him. He was sensible of the tension of his own nerves, and felt eager to command, to act, to pass the night without sleep, to battle and play with life and death, and again to conquer peril. Only from time to time was he conscious of shivering.

Ariphas came.

The news was lamentable. All hope in the help of Procopius and Sebastian was lost. The Emperor was abandoned by his allies in the middle of Asia. There was even reason to suspect treason on the part of the wily Arsaces.

At this moment it was announced that a deserter from the camp of Sapor desired to speak with the Emperor.

This Persian prostrated himself before Julian and kissed the earth.

His body was monstrous. His hideous head had been disfigured by Asiatic torture. The ears cut off, and the nostrils torn from the face, made his visage like that of a human skull. But the eyes were bright, intelligent, and resolute.

He was robed in rich fire-coloured silk, spoke Greek villainously, and was accompanied by two slaves.

The Persian called himself Artaban, a satrap calumniated to Sapor, who had therefore tortured him. He had come to the Romans, he said, for revenge on his own king.

"O Lord of the Universe!" said Artaban, with fallacious emphasis, "I will deliver Sapor up to thee, bound hand and foot, like a sacrificial lamb. I will lead thee by night to the camp and softly shalt thy hand take the king, as children take young birds in their snares. Only hearken to Artaban: Artaban has plenitude of power, and knows the king's secrets."

"What reward do you expect from me?" asked Julian.

"Vengeance! Come with me!"

"Whither?"

"To the north; through the desert—three hundred and twenty-five parasangs—then through the mountains eastward, straight on Susa and Ecbatana. . ."

The Persian pointed to the horizon.

"Over there, over there," he repeated, fixing his eyes on Julian.

"Cæsar," said Hormizdas to the Emperor, "take care! . . . I don't like this man's face! He's a sorcerer—a brigand, or perhaps much worse? . . . Sometimes queer things happen in these latitudes. Get rid of him! . . . Don't listen to him. . ."

Julian paid no heed to the words of Hormizdas.

He felt the strange fascination of the Persian's supplicating eyes.

"Do you know every step of the road which leads to Ecbatana?"

"Oh yes! yes!" exclaimed the Persian with a contented laugh. "How should I not know it? Every grain of sand in that desert. . . every roadside well. . . Artaban knows the meaning of the birds' song, hears the grass growing, and the waters flowing under the earth. He will run before thine army, nosing the scent, tracing the road. Believe me, in twenty days all Persia, as far as the Indies and the ocean, shall be thine!"

The heart of the Emperor began beating violently.

"Can this be the miracle I was waiting for?" he mused. "In twenty days, Persia shall be mine!"

He could scarcely breathe at the thought.

The monster, kneeling before him, murmured.

"Hound me not away from thee! Like a hound shall I remain lying crouched at thy feet! From the moment I saw thee, I loved thee, Lord of the Universe, because thou art the proudest of men! Oh, that thou wouldst walk over my body, that thou wouldst trample on me, and I would lick the dust from thy feet, chanting: 'Glory, glory to the son of the Sun, to the king of the East and of the West, Julian!"

He kissed the Emperor's feet; and the two slaves prostrating themselves also, repeated after him, "Glory, glory, glory!"

"But what to do with the ships?" thought Julian aloud to himself. "Leave them unarmed in the hands of the enemy or keep them?"

"Burn them," breathed Artaban.

The words thrilled Julian, who looked strangely at the Persian.

"Burn them? What sayest thou?"

Artaban raised his head and looked steadfastly into the Emperor's eyes.

"Hast thou *fear*? Thou! . . . No, no. Men alone are fearful, but not the gods! Burn the ships, and thou shalt be free as the wind. Thy ships shall not fall into the power of the enemy and thine army be swelled by the soldiers that work the fleet. Be great and bold to the very end! Burn them, and in ten days thou shalt be under the walls of Ecbatana. In twenty days all Persia shall be thine! Thou shall be greater than the son of Philip, who conquered Darius. Only. . . burn thy ships and follow me! . . ."

"And if these are but lies—if I can read in your heart that you are lying!" exclaimed the Emperor seizing the Persian with one hand by the throat and with the other menacing him with a dagger.

Hormizdas uttered a sigh of relief.

For some instants Artaban sustained the gaze of the Roman without speaking, and Julian again felt the fascination of those eyes, so intelligent, audacious, and servile.

"If thou dost not believe me, let me die by thy hand," repeated the Persian.

Julian relaxed his hold, and returned the poignard to its sheath.

"It is terrible and pleasant to look thee in the eyes," continued Artaban. "Thy visage is that of a god! That, as yet no one knows; I alone know that thou art. . . Do not repulse thy slave, sire."

"We shall see," murmured Julian thoughtfully. "Long have I desired to fight your king, in the desert. . . But the ships. . ."

"Oh, yes, the ships!" murmured Artaban. "Thou must set out at once. . . this night. . . so that the inhabitants of Ctesiphon cannot see us. . . Thou must burn them. . ."

Julian did not answer.

"Take them away," he said, pointing out the deserters to his legionaries. "Keep them under close watch!"

And returning to his tent, he halted and raised his eyes—

"Is this true? So quickly and so simply! I feel that my will is the will of the gods. I have but to think, and it is accomplished."

The joyfulness in his heart became intenser. Smiling, he pressed his hand on his breast to suppress its tumultuous beating. He still was conscious of shiverings, and his head felt leaden, as if he had passed the day in too fierce a sun.

Ordering Victor, an old general blindly devoted to him, to come to his tent, he confided to him the golden ring bearing the Imperial seal.

"To the commanders of the fleet, Constantius and Lucilian," Julian ordered laconically. "Before daybreak they must burn the ships, except the five largest freighted with bread, and the twelve smaller ones which serve as pontoon bridges. Burn all the rest. Anybody opposing this order will answer for it with his head. Keep the most absolute secrecy. . . Go!"

He gave him a piece of papyrus on which was written a curt order to the commander of the fleet. Victor, as usual, astonished at nothing, kissed the hem of the Imperial purple, and went out. Julian then, in spite of the late hour, convoked a council of war. The generals met in his tent, moody, suspicious, and secretly irritated. In a few words Julian explained his plan of going northwards to the centre of Persia, and then eastwards towards Ecbatana, to seize the king unawares. All revolted against the idea, raising their voices simultaneously, and not hiding the fact that Julian's plan seemed to them sheer madness. Fatigue, lack of confidence, and spite were expressed on the faces of the oldest and wisest soldiers. Several spoke curtly—all in opposition.

Sallustius Secundus said, "Whither are we going? What more do we want? Think, Cæsar: we have conquered half Persia. Sapor offers better conditions of peace than ever Asian monarch before has offered to any Roman conqueror, even to the great Pompeius, Septimius Severus, or Trajan. Let us, then, conclude peace before it is too late, and win back to our own country!"

"The soldiers are grumbling," observed Dagalaïf. "Don't push them to despair; they're worn out; the number of wounded and sick is great. If you lead them farther into an unknown desert, we can answer for nothing. Have mercy on them! . . . And are not you yourself in need of rest? You must be more tired than any of us."

"Let us turn back!" cried all the generals. "To go on would be madness."

At that moment a dull, menacing sound broke out behind the tent, a sound like the rumbling of a furious sea. Julian leant ear, and immediately understood. It meant mutiny.

"You know my will," he said coldly to the chiefs, motioning them to the door. "It is unshakable. In two hours we must be upon the march. See that all is ready."

"Well-beloved Augustus," answered Sallustius, with respectful self-possession, "I will not leave this tent without telling you what I ought to tell you. You have spoken with us, your equals not in power but in valour, in a manner unworthy of a Roman pupil of Socrates and Plato. We can only pardon your words by setting them down to a momentary weakness of the nerves, which clouds your Imperial understanding."

"Is that so?" exclaimed Julian, sarcastically, growing pale with stifled anger. "Then, my friends, it is the worse for you, for you are now in the hands of a madman! I have just given the order to burn the ships, and my orders are at this moment being carried out! I foresaw your sage counsel, and have cut off your means of retreat. Now your lives are in my hands, and I shall oblige you to believe in miracles!"

All stood overwhelmed; Sallustius alone pushed towards Cæsar, and taking his hands cried—

"It is impossible, Cæsar. . . surely. . . you have not. . . actually. . ."

He broke off the sentence, and dropped the hands of the Emperor.

All the company stood up, listening.

The cries of the legionaries became louder and louder—the noise of mutiny came nearer, like the sound of tempest over immense forests.

"Let them shout," said Julian calmly. "Poor children! Whither will they go without me? You understand? That is why I burn the ships, the last hope of the cowardly and the idle. There is now no possible return, except by miracle. Now are you bound to me for life and death. In twenty days Asia will be ours. I have girt you with terror, that you may conquer all and become like me. Rejoice! Like Dionysus, I will lead you through the world, and you shall be the masters of men and gods! . . ."

Hardly had he pronounced these words when a cry of infinite despair resounded through the host—

"They are on fire! . . . they are burning!"

The generals rushed out of the tent, followed by Julian.

They saw the glow of conflagration. Victor had transmitted the Emperor's orders literally, and Julian himself watched the flaming spectacle with a smile.

"Cæsar! . . . May the gods protect us! . . . He has escaped!"

With these words, a centurion fell at Julian's feet, pale and trembling.

"Who has escaped? What mean you?"

"Artaban! . . . Artaban! . . . Woe be on us! Cæsar, he has deceived thee!"

"Impossible! . . . And the slaves?" stammered the Emperor, overwhelmed.

"Have just confessed under torture that Artaban was not a satrap, but a tax-collector of Ctesiphon. He invented this device to save the city, and lead you into the desert to deliver you to the Persians. He knew that you would burn the ships. They also said that Sapor was advancing at the head of a great army."

The Emperor rushed to the river-bank to find Victor—

"Put out the fires!—quench them quickly as possible!"

But his voice failed. Staring at the huge blaze Julian perceived that no human force could conquer the flames, which were augmented by a violent wind.

He held his head in his hands, and although with no faith nor prayer in his heart, raised his eyes to heaven, as if there seeking succour. The stars were shining above, faint, almost invisible.

The mutiny rolled on, becoming more and more menacing.

"The Persians have burned the ships!" groaned some, stretching their arms toward the river.

"No, no, it was the generals, to drag us still farther into the desert and leave us there," others cried incoherently.

"Kill the priests!" yelled some. "The Etruscans have poisoned Cæsar, and sent him mad!"

"Glory to Augustus Julian, the conqueror!" shouted the faithful Gauls and Celts. "Silence, traitors! so long as Cæsar breathes we have nothing to fear!"

The cowardly were weeping—

"Our country! Our country! We won't go a step farther. We would sooner die. Ah, we shall sooner see our own ears, than see our own land again! We are lost, comrades! The Persians have us in a trap!"

"Do you see clearly now?" said the exultant Galileans. "He is possessed of demons. Julian has sold his soul, and they're dragging him to the abyss. Are we going to let a demoniac lead us?"

And nevertheless Julian, seeing nothing, hearing nothing, murmured as in a dream—

"What matters it? The miracle will be accomplished!"

XVII

It was the sixteenth of June, and the first bivouac on the night of the retreat. The army had refused to go farther. Neither prayers, commands, nor threats of the Emperor had brought them to reason. Celts, Romans, Pagans, Christians, brave men and cowards, all had answered in the same words—

"Let us go back to our own country!"

The chiefs rejoiced in secret; the Tuscan augurs openly triumphed. After the burning of the ships there had been a general insurrection. And now not only the Galileans but the Olympians and Hellenists were persuaded that a curse was on the Emperor's head, and that the Furies were pursuing him. When he walked through the camp talk would cease and people edge away from him in fear. Sibylline books and the Book of Revelation, Tuscan wizards, Christian prophecies, gods, and angels, joined forces to crush the common foe. The Emperor then announced that he would lead his men homewards northward through the fertile provinces of Apolloniatis and Adiabene. According to this plan of retreat, while retaining a hope of forming a junction with the troops of Procopius and Sebastian, Julian consoled himself with the thought that he was keeping within the borders of Persia, and that he might still encounter Sapor's army, deliver battle, and win a decisive victory.

The Persians were no longer visible. Desiring to weaken the Romans before a crushing attack, they set on fire their own rich champaigns of barley and wheat, and destroyed every store and granary in the country.

Julian's soldiers marched through a black desert, still smoking with traces of fire.

Famine soon set in.

In order to augment the invaders' distress the Persians had broken the canal-dykes and flooded the fields, being aided in this endeavour by brooks and torrents which had overflowed their courses owing to the melting of the snow on the Armenian mountains. The flood dried up quickly under the burning rays of the June sun, but left the warm soil coated with slimy mud. Asphyxiating vapours and the bitter odour of ashes and of rotting vegetation loaded the air every night, and befouled the drinking water, the food, and even the rags of the soldiers. Myriads of insects rose from corrupted marshes. Mosquitoes, venomous horse-flies, rose in clouds round the beasts of burden and fastened themselves on the men. Their subtle hum went on night and day. Maddened by stings, the horses died or stampeded, the oxen broke their traces and overturned the wagons. After exhausting marches through defiles and fords the soldiers obtained no rest; tents were no refuge against the insects, and to get any sleep the men had to wrap their heads in stifling cloaks, while the bites of a certain small transparent dung-coloured fly produced swellings and boils which gradually became a horrible purulent plague. During the last days of the march the sun was invisible. The low, dense, stifling sky was a white cloth of cloud; and its motionless glare still more painful to the eyes than the naked sun.

And so they kept marching, wasted, weak, with hung head and feeble step, day after day, between the implacable sky and the black, burnt earth.

"Surely," they thought, "Anti-Christ, the man apostate from God, must have intentionally led them into this accursed place, to leave them to their doom." Some murmured, "Curse the generals!" but incoherently, as in a dream. Others kept praying and whining like sick children, begging a crust of bread or a mouthful of wine from their companions. Many from weakness dropped and died on the road.

The Emperor ordered the last rations kept for himself and for his staff to be distributed among the famished rank and file. He contented himself with a thin soup of flour and suet, a fare from which the meanest soldier would have revolted. Thanks to extreme temperance, he felt continually full of nervous excitement, and at the same time a lightness of body, as if he had wings. This lightness sustained him and increased his strength tenfold. He attempted not to think of the future. But to return to Antioch or Tarsus, defeated, and to submit to Galilean ridicule, that he certainly would never endure.

One night the soldiers were resting, the north wind having driven off the flies. Oil, flour, and wine, from the last Imperial supply, had assuaged their hunger. The hope of return gradually revived. The camp became silent. Julian withdrew to his tent. Now he was wont almost to dispense with sleep, or if he slept at all, it was towards daybreak. If by chance profound slumber overtook him, he would wake terrified, with drops of cold sweat on his forehead. He had need of full possession of consciousness to stifle the dull pain gnawing at his soul.

Entering his tent, he trimmed the lamp with a pair of snuffers. Rolls of parchment and the Gospels lay around him on the ground in disorder. He began to write his favourite work, *Against the Christians*, begun two months previously at the opening of the campaign. Reclining, with his back turned to the tent door, Julian was re-reading the manuscript, when suddenly he heard a slight noise.

He turned round, uttered a cry, and sprang to his feet. He thought he saw a ghost. On the threshold stood a youth, clothed in a ragged brown garment of camel's hair; a dusty sheepskin, the "melotes" of the Egyptian anchorites, flung over his shoulders. His bare feet were shod in sandals of palmwood.

The Emperor scanned him, waiting, unable to pronounce a word.

"Do you remember," said a well-known voice. "Do you remember, Julian, how you came to me in the convent? Then I repulsed you. But I have not been able to forget you, because we are singularly like each other, singularly near each other. . ."

The lad threw back his black hood, Julian saw the bright brown hair, and recognised Arsinoë.

"Whence—why have you come? Why are you clad thus?"

He still feared lest this might be some spirit, which would vanish as unexpectedly as it had appeared.

In a few words Arsinoë narrated to him her fortunes since their last parting.

After leaving her guardian Hortensius and giving the greater part of her wealth to the poor, she had long lodged with the anchorites to the south of Lake Mareotis, west of the Nile, among the sterile mountains of Libya, in the terrible Nitrian and Sciathian deserts. She had been accompanied by the young Juventinus, the disciple of old Didimus. They had been taught daily by the ascetics.

"And then," asked Julian, not without a certain apprehension, "and then, girl, did you find among them what you were seeking for?"

She shook her head, and said sadly—

"No. Flashes of light, allusions, hints, as always, elsewhere."

"Speak on! Tell me all," implored the Emperor, his eyes brilliant with hope and gratitude.

"How can I?" she answered slowly. "For, my friend, I was seeking the freedom of the soul; but it has no existence here!"

"Yes, yes! is not that true?" cried Julian, exultant. "That was what I told you, Arsinoë."

She seated herself on a stool covered with a leopardskin, and continued her tale calmly, with the same sad smile, Julian listening in an avidity of joy. . .

"Tell me, how did you leave those unhappy desert-folk?" demanded Julian.

"I was tempted once," replied Arsinoë; "once in the desert among the rocks I found a fragment of white marble. I picked it up and long wondered at it, sparkling in the sun, and suddenly I remembered Athens, my youth, my art, and you! I awoke, and I decided to return to the world, to live and die as God had created me; as an artist. At that moment the old Didimus had a vision in which I was the means of reconciling you with the Galilean. . ."

"With the Galilean!" exclaimed the Emperor.

His face darkened, his eyes lost their fire, the triumphant laugh died on his lips.

"Curiosity, too, drew me again towards you," continued Arsinoë. "I wished to know if you had attained truth in the way you pursued, and what summit you had reached. I resumed the habit of a monk. Brother Juventinus and I descended the Nile as far as Alexandria; then a ship took us to Antioch; and we have journeyed with a great Syrian caravan through Apamea, Epiphania, and Edessa to the frontier. After a thousand dangers, we crossed the Mesopotamian desert, abandoned by the Persians, and not far from the village of Abuzat, after the victory at Ctesiphon, we saw your camp. And so I am here! . . . And you, Julian?"

He sighed, and hung his head without answering. Then scanning her, he demanded—

"And now you too detest Him, Arsinoë?"

"No; why?" she answered simply. "Why detest Him? Did not the sages of Hellas come near, in their teaching, to the message of the Galilean? Those who in the desert martyrise soul and body are far from the humble Son of Mary. He used to love children, freedom, cheerfulness, and the fair white lilies of the field. He loved beauty, Julian! . . . We have wandered from Him and become entangled and embittered. All call you the Apostate, . . . but it is they who are the apostates. . ."

The Emperor knelt down before Arsinoë and raised upon her eyes full of prayer; tears coursed slowly down his lean cheeks.

"It must not be," he murmured. "Do not speak. Why? Why? Let be what has been! . . . Do not again become mine enemy!"

"No, no! I must say it all to you," exclaimed Arsinoë. "Listen! I know that you love Him! It is so, and that is the fatality upon you. Against whom have you revolted? What kind of enemy are you for Him? When your lips are cursing the Crucified, your heart is aspiring after

Him. When you are struggling against His name, you are closer to Him, closer to His spirit, than those who repeat with dead lips, 'Lord, Lord'! . . . And it is they who are your enemies, and not He. Ah! why do you torture yourself more than the Galilean monks?"

The Emperor tore himself from the clasp of Arsinoë, and stood up, pale as one dead. His face again grew restless, and in his eyes shone the old hatred. He muttered with sorrowful irony—

"Away with you! Go from me! I know the devices of the Galileans!"

Arsinoë gazed at him in fear and despair, as at one insane—

"Julian! . . . Julian, what is the matter? Is it possible that a mere name. . ."

But he had regained cold self-possession. His eyes were lustreless, his air indifferent, almost contemptuous; the Roman Emperor was speaking to a Galilean.

"Depart, Arsinoë. Forget all that I have said. It was a moment of weakness which is over. I am tranquil. You see, we must remain strangers. The shadow of the Crucified is always between us. You have not renounced Him, and he who is not His enemy cannot be my friend. . ."

She fell on her knees before him—

"Why? why? What are you doing? Have pity on me; have pity on yourself, before it is too late! For this is madness. Return, or you must. . ."

She paused, and he completed the sentence for her with a haughty smile—

"Or I must perish, you mean, Arsinoë? Be it so. I shall follow my road to the end, lead where it may! If, as you say, I have been unjust toward the wisdom of the Galileans, remember what I have borne at their hands. How numberless, how despicable were my enemies! . . . The other day some Roman soldiers found before my eyes, in a Mesopotamian marsh, a lion tortured by flies. They had buried themselves in his throat, in his ears, in his nostrils, choking his breath, sealing his eyes, and in their stinging myriads had mastered even his powers at last! Such shall my death be, and such the victory of the Galileans over Cæsar!"

The girl still held out towards him her pale hands; but without a word, without a hope, like a friend towards a friend who is dead. Between the two lay still that abyss which is not to be crossed by the living.

Towards the twentieth of July the Roman army, after a long journey across burnt plains, found a little grass which had escaped from the devastators in the deep valley of the river Durous.

A field of ripe wheat was found hard by. The soldiers reaped it and rested in the valley three days. Unspeakably happy, the legionaries threw themselves down on the verdure, breathing the delightful moisture of the earth, and brushing the cool blades of grass against their dusty faces.

On the morning of the fourth day the Roman sentinels perceived a cloud of smoke or dust. Some supposed it to be the wild asses, which usually roamed in herds for safety against the attack of lions. Others affirmed that it was Saracens, attracted by the news of the siege of Ctesiphon. A few expressed their fears lest it should prove to be the principal army of King Sapor.

The Emperor ordered the call to arms to be sounded on the bugles. The cohorts in strict defensive order, sheltered by their locked shields, as by walls of metal, formed a camp half-circlewise on the river bank. The cloud of smoke or dust remained on the horizon until evening, nor could any divine with certainty what lurked behind it. The night was dark and still, with not a star in the sky.

The Romans did not sleep. They stood round huge bivouac-fires in mute restlessness, awaiting the dawn.

XVIII

At sunrise they saw the Persians. The enemy was advancing slowly. Experienced soldiers estimated their number at nearly two hundred thousand. Hill after hill unmasked new bodies of men, and the glittering of the arms on these detachments, in spite of distance and dust, was almost dazzlingly bright. The Romans, with hardly a word in the ranks, left the valley of the previous night and ranged themselves in battle-order. Their faces were stern, but not sad. Danger now stifled their hatred, and all looks were fixed upon the Emperor, Christians as well as Pagans seeking to surmise from his expression whether they might still hope for success.

At that hour Julian was beaming with joy. Long, long, had he awaited this encounter with the Persians, awaited the miracle in which victory would give him such renown and power that the Galileans could no longer resist. He was haughty as one of the old heroes of Hellas. Danger seemed to spiritualise him; and a gay and terrible light was in his eyes.

The heavy and dusty morning of the twenty-second of July seemed the prelude to a day of burning heat, and the Emperor objected to wear a breastplate, and remained clad in a light silken tunic. Victor, the general, came up holding a coat-of-mail, and said—

"Cæsar, I have had a bad dream; tempt not fate; wear armour!"

Julian silently waved his hand in negation. The old man fell on his knees—

"Put it on! Have pity on your slave! . . . This battle will be perilous. . ."

Julian took a shield, flung the light purple of his chlamys over his shoulder, and vaulting on horseback said—

"Let me be, old friend! I need nothing."

He vanished, his golden-crested helm glittering for a while in the sun, while Victor anxiously followed him with his eyes.

Julian disposed his army in a peculiar form, like a crescent. The enormous half-circle was to bury its two points in the Persian mass and squeeze it inwards from two sides. The right wing was commanded by Dagalaïf, the left by Hormizdas, Julian and Victor leading the centre. The trumpets sounded. The earth trembled under the soft and heavy tread of the Persian elephants, wearing huge plumes of ostrich-feathers on their foreheads. Turrets of hide were lashed on the back of the beasts by thick thongs; and each turret held four archers, who shot flaming arrows of tow and pitch.

The Roman horse did not stand the first shock. With deafening roars and raised trunks the elephants opened their huge moist gullets. The legionaries felt in their faces the hot wind of the monsters, maddened before battle by a special drink made of wine, pepper, and spices. With foot spikes painted in vermilion and tipped with steel, the elephants disembowelled horses, and their trunks whirled horsemen from the saddle and dashed them against the ground. The torrid heat of the afternoon raised from the trumpeting beasts a rank odour of sweat which made the horses wince, rear, and tremble violently.

One cohort had already taken flight. It happened to be a body of Christians. Julian pursued them, and striking the chief decurion full in the face, cried furiously—

"Cowards! I suppose praying is the only thing you are good for?"

The light Thracian archery and Paphlagonian skirmishers now advanced against the elephants. Behind them marched Illyrians, skilful throwers of the leaded javelins, the "Martiobarbuli." Julian gave the order to aim arrows, stones, and javelins at the legs of the elephants. An arrow struck an enormous Indian beast in the eye. He trumpeted and reared, the girths snapped, saddle and leather turret slid and upset, shedding the Persian archers like birds from a nest. Confusion followed among the huge pachyderms. Wounded in the legs they staggered and fell, and their squadron became little more than a mountain of grey masses. Their feet in air, their trunks bleeding, their armour smashed, they lay amid ruins of the turrets, half crushed horses, and piles of Roman and Persian dead.

At last the elephants took flight, and rushed headlong against the Persians, trampling them underfoot. This particular danger had been foreseen by the barbarian tacticians. The previous instance of the battle under Nizibis had shown that an army may be defeated by its own allies. Now the mahouts began to slash the monsters with curved cutlasses between the two joints of the spine lying nearest the skull; a single blow in this exact spot sufficing to kill outright the largest and strongest of the great beasts. The cohorts of Martiobarbuli charged, clambering over the wounded and pursuing those in flight.

At this instant Julian galloped to support the left wing. On that side rode the Persian *Clibanarii*, a famous body of cavalry, bound man to man by a strong chain, and clad in invulnerable scale-armour. They received the waves of battle like a row of bronze equestrian statues. They could only be wounded through narrow slits left for mouth and eyes.

Against the Clibaniars Julian sent his old faithful friends, the Batavians and the Celts. They would die for a smile from Cæsar, gazing at him with eyes of childlike adoration. The right wing of the Romans was assailed by Persian chariots, drawn by galloping zebras. Scythes were affixed to their axles, which, sweeping along with incredible swiftness, mowed legs from horses and heads from soldiers, and lopped bodies in half, easily as the reaper's sickle takes the corn.

Towards the end of the day, weighed down in their overheated armour, the Clibaniars wavered. Julian massed all his forces against them. They broke, and re-formed, but their ranks at last became confused and fled. A cry of triumph broke from the Emperor's lips. He galloped ahead, pursuing the fugitives, not perceiving that he was far in advance of his main body. A few body-guards surrounded the Cæsar, amongst them old General Victor. This old man, though wounded in the hand, was unconscious of his hurt, not quitting the Emperor's side for a moment, and shielding him time after time from mortal blows. He knew that it was as dangerous to approach a fleeing army as to enter a falling building.

"Take heed, Cæsar!" he shouted. "Put on this mail of mine!" but Julian heard him not, and still rode on, on—his breast lying bared to drink in the wind—as if he, unsupported, unarmed, and terrible, was hunting his countless enemies by glance and gesture only from the field. Laughter was on his lips; through the cloud of dust, raised by the furious gallop of the horse, shone the Boeotian helmet, and the outspread folds of his chlamys streamed into two great wings of purple, that seemed to bear him farther and yet farther.

In front, a small detachment of Saracens was in flight. One of these horsemen, turning in his saddle, recognised Julian by his raiment, and pointing him out to his comrades, uttered a guttural cry like that of an eagle—

"*Malek, malek!* . . . The king, the king!"

All wheeled round, and at full gallop sprang upright, standing on their saddles, their long white vestments streaming, and lances poised above their heads. The Emperor saw the bronzed face of a young robber, one little more than a lad. Riding rapidly towards him on a Bactrian dromedary, from whose shaggy hair lumps of dry mud swung and dangled, Victor parried two lances aimed at the Emperor by Bedouins.

Then the lad on the camel aimed, his fierce look glittering and white teeth showing while he cried gleefully—

"*Malek, malek!*"

"That boy is happy," was the thought that flashed through Julian's mind, "and I too. . ."

He had no time to finish; the lance hissed, and grazing the skin of his right hand, glanced over the ribs and buried itself below the liver. Julian thought the wound a slight one, and seizing the double-edged barb to withdraw it, cut his fingers. Blood gushed out. Julian uttered a cry, flung his head back, fixed his staring eyes on the pale sky, and slid from his horse into the arms of the guard.

Victor supported him with tender veneration, gazing with trembling lips at the closed eyes of his sovereign. The tardy cohorts in the rear came up.

XIX

T he Emperor was carried into his tent, and laid on his camp-bed. Still in a swoon, he groaned from time to time. Oribazius, the physician, drew out the iron lance-head, and washed and bound up the deep wound. By a look Victor asked if any hope remained, and Oribazius sadly shook his head. After the dressing of the wound Julian sighed and opened his eyes.

"Where am I?" he asked in surprise with a glance round. Then hearing the distant noise of battle he remembered all, and with an effort rose upon his bed.

"Why have they brought me here? Where is my horse? Quick, Victor!"

Suddenly his face writhed with pain, friends hastened to support him, but he thrust back Victor and Oribazius.

"Permit me! I must be with them to the end."

His soul was struggling against death. Slowly, with infinite difficulty, he tottered to his feet, a faint smile playing on his lips, and the old fire in his eyes.

"You see, I am able-bodied still. . . quick! give me my sword, buckler, horse!"

Victor gave him the shield and sword. Julian took them and made a few unsteady steps, like a child learning to walk. The wound re-opened; he let fall his arms, sank into the arms of Oribazius and Victor and looking up cried contemptuously—

"All is over! Thou hast conquered, Galilean!"

And making no further resistance, he gave himself up to his friends, and was laid on the bed.

"Yes, yes," he repeated softly, "I am dying."

Oribazius leaned towards him, consoling him, assuring him that the wound would heal.

"Why deceive me?" answered Julian; "I am not afraid. . ." Then he added gravely, "I hope I shall die the death of the righteous."

In the evening he lost consciousness. Hour after hour went by. The sun went down. Fighting ceased. A lamp was lighted in the tent, and night slowly descended.

Julian did not recover consciousness. His breathing grew weaker; he was thought to be breathing his last. But later his eyes opened, little by little; his look was fixed steadily on a corner of the tent. A rapid whisper broke from his lips: he was in delirium.

"Thou, here, why? . . . what matters it? All is over. Canst Thou not see that? . . . Go. Thou hatedst laughter. . . And so we can never forgive Thee. . ."

Then, regaining his faculties, he asked of Oribazius—

"What hour is it? Shall I see the sun?"

And he added dreamily—

"Oribazius, can it be possible that reason should be really so powerless? I believe it is a weakness of the body. . . blood fills the brain, creating phantoms. . . One must conquer. . . reason must. . ."

His ideas anew became confused, and his gaze resumed its fixity—

"I will not! Do you hear? . . . Go, Tempter! I do not believe! Socrates died like a god. Reason. . . Victor, ah, Victor! . . . what do you want from me? Thou, the unappeasable, the implacable? Thy love is more terrible than death. . . Thy burden is the heaviest of all. . . Why dost thou look at me so? How much I have loved thee, Good Shepherd! . . . Only Thou? No, no! The pierced feet, blood? . . . The death of Hellas. . . darkness? . . . I want sunlight, the golden sun. . . on the Parthenon marble! . . . Wouldst thou veil the sun? . . ."

It was one o'clock in the morning. The legions had returned to camp, with no exultation over their victory. In spite of fatigue, scarcely any slept, all waiting for news from the Imperial tent. Many stood sleeping, leaning on their lances round the half-extinguished camp-fires; and the breathing of picketed horses could be heard, munching captured forage of corn.

Between the dark rows of tents, faint white lines showed on the horizon. Stars became yet more chilly and pale. The mists kept spreading, and the steel of lances and shields was clouded with dew. Here and there crew a cock, belonging to the Tuscan soothsayers. A calm sadness hovered over heaven and earth. The scene was illusive as a mirror; the near seemed far off and the distant came near.

At the entrance to Julian's tent stood a throng of generals, friends, and familiar companions, all looking like phantoms in the misty twilight. Still deeper silence reigned within the tent. Oribazius, the physician, was pounding simples in a mortar to make a refreshing drink. The sick man lay calm, and the delirium had left him. At dawn, collecting himself, he asked impatiently—

"When will the sun rise?"

"In an hour," answered Oribazius glancing at the clepsydra.

"Call the generals," ordered Julian. "I must speak. . ."

"Well-beloved Cæsar, it may be hurtful. . ."

"What matter! I shall not die before the sun rises. Victor, raise my head."

He was told about the victory over the Persians, the flight of the enemy's cavalry, and of the two sons of Sapor the king; of the death of fifty satraps. Julian showed neither astonishment nor gladness. He remained indifferent.

Dagalaïf, Hormizdas, Ariphas, Lucilian, and Sallustius came in, headed by the general Jovian. Many, with an eye to the future, had wished to see on the throne this weak and timid man, who could be dangerous to none. It was their hope under his rule to recover from the anxieties of the tumultuous reign of Julian. Jovian possessed the art of pleasing all. Tall and handsome in person, he in no way differed from the crowd, aiming at all-round benevolence. Among the intimate friends stood also a young centurion of the Imperial horse, the future famous historian, Ammianus Marcellinus. Everyone was aware that he was writing an account of the campaign, and amassing documents for a great historical work. Stooping under the tent-door Ammianus drew out tablets and stylus. A keen and impartial curiosity animated his stern face; and with the coolness of an artist or a man of science he prepared to take notes of the speech of the dying Emperor.

"Lift the curtain!" Julian ordered.

It was raised, and everyone stood aside so that the fresh air of the morning might blow on the face of the dying. The door faced east, and the view to the horizon was unbroken.

"Now put the lamp out."

The order was executed, and the tent filled with twilight. Everybody stood waiting in silence.

"Listen, friends," Julian began; his voice was low but clear, his whole presence breathed a triumph of mind over body, and invincible will still gleamed from those eyes. The hand of Ammianus trembled, but he wrote down the words uttered. He knew that he was writing on the tables of history, and transmitting to men unborn the last words of a great man.

"Listen, friends; my hour is come, perhaps too soon. But you see, like an honest debtor, I am not sorry to give back my life to Nature, and in my soul is neither pain nor fear; nothing but cheerfulness, and a fore-feeling of the long repose. I have simply done my duty, and have nothing to repent of. From the days when I daily expected death, like a hunted beast, in the palace of Macellum, in Cappadocia, up to the day of greatness when I took on the purple of the Roman Cæsar, I have tried to keep my soul stainless, I have aspired to ends not ignoble. If I have failed—and I have failed—to do all that I desired, you will not forget that most of our earthly affairs are in the hands of Destiny. And now I thank the Eternal for having allowed me to die neither after long sickness nor at the hands of the executioner, but on the battlefield—in mid-youth—in mid-endeavour, half-way to achievement. . . And dear, dear friends. . ."

His voice ceased; everyone present knelt down; many were weeping.

"No, no, my dear friends," said Julian smiling; "why weep for those who are going back to their own country? Take heart, Victor!"

The old man tried to answer, but in vain; then hiding his face in his hands, he sobbed aloud.

"Soft! Soft!" cried Julian; and then turning toward the sky: "Ah, there He is!"

The morning clouds were growing rosy, and the twilight in the tent had become warm and mellow; the first beam of the sun washed over the rim of the horizon. The dying man held his face towards the light, with closed eyes.

Then Sallustius Secundus went up to Julian and kissing his hand said—

"Well-beloved Augustus! whom do you name as your successor?"

"What matters it? Let Destiny decide! We must not resist her. Let the Galileans triumph. We shall conquer later on. And then shall begin on earth the reign of the equals of the gods, souls laughing forever like the sun. . . Look, behold him!"

A faint shiver ran through his body, and with a last effort Julian stretched out his arms, as if he would have rushed to meet the rising orb. Blood gushed from his wound, and the veins swelled on neck and temples.

"Water! water!" he whispered, choking.

Victor lifted a golden cup of spring-water to his mouth. Julian, looking forth from the tent drank thirstily of the ice-cold draught. Then his head fell back, and the last murmur came from his half-open lips—

"Helios! receive me into thyself. . ."

The eyes went out. Victor closed their lids. The face of the Emperor, lying in the sun-rays, took on a look of one of the Olympians sleeping.

XX

Three months had elapsed since the shameful treaty of peace signed by Jovian with the Persians. At the beginning of October the Roman army, exhausted by famine and forced marches through the deserts of Mesopotamia, had at last reached Antioch. During this melancholy retreat Anatolius, the centurion of Imperial cavalry, had formed a close friendship with the historian, Ammianus Marcellinus. The two friends had decided to betake themselves to Italy, to a secluded villa at Baiæ, whither Arsinoë had invited them, to rest from the fatigues of the campaign, and to heal their wounds at the sulphur-baths.

On this journey, they had made a halt of some days at Antioch, where great festivals were in preparation, in honour of Jovian's accession to the throne and of the return of the army.

The peace concluded with King Sapor was dishonourable for the Empire. Five rich Roman provinces lying along the farther banks of the Tigris, together with fifteen frontier fortresses, including Singara, Castra Maurorum, and the invincible Nizibis, all these passed into the hands of Sapor. Little did the Galileans care for the defeat of Rome. When the news of Julian's death arrived at Antioch, the timorous citizens believed at first that it was some new device of Satan, fresh toils in which to capture the righteous. But when the news was confirmed their joy became delirious.

In the early morning the noise of festival and the cries of the people reached the sleeping-chamber of Anatolius. He had decided to pass all day indoors, the rejoicing of the populace being repugnant to him. He attempted to sleep again, and failed. A strange curiosity woke in him. Without a word to Ammianus, he dressed quickly, and went out into the street. It was a fresh and pleasant autumn morning.

Great round clouds, in sharp contrast with the deep blue of the sky, sailed over the innumerable colonnades and marble porticoes of Antioch. In the forum and the markets everywhere ran the murmur of fountains and streams; and down the long dusty vistas of the bright streets flowed wide currents, artificially-channelled waters, crossing each other in a perfect network of rills. Here and there pigeons were cooing and picking grains of barley. The scent of flowers and incense issued from the open doors of churches. Near the fountain-basins young girls were sprinkling their baskets of pale October roses with water, or singing joyful psalms, and garlanding the columns of the Christian basilicas. A noisy crowd was pouring through the streets. Chariots and litters were forging slowly down the middle of the pavements. At every moment rose cries of—

"Hail to Jovian Augustus, the great and happy!"

Some added: "The conqueror," but with a certain diffidence, as if the word smacked of irony.

The same urchin who had once caricatured Julian on the walls of the town was there now clapping his hands, beating his drum, whistling, tumbling in the dust, and shouting (although he had no notion of the meaning of the words)—

"The Wild Boar has perished, the Devastator of the Garden of Eden!"

An old woman, bent double in her rags, came out like a black-beetle into the sun, rejoicing with the rest. She was brandishing a stick and vociferating in a cracked voice—

"Julian has perished! The evil-doer has perished!"

An infinite sadness filled the heart of Anatolius; but urged by curiosity he wandered on, and in following the Syngon, approached the cathedral. There he saw an official connected with the quæstorship, Marcus Avinius, coming out of the basilica, accompanied by two slaves, who elbowed a passage for him through the crowd.

"What is this?" wondered Anatolius. "Why should this enemy of the Galileans be here?"

Crosses embroidered in gold adorned the violet chlamys of Avinius, and were even sewn on his crimson leather shoes.

Julius Mauricus, another friend of Anatolius, accosted Avinius—

"How do you do, my reverend friend?" he asked, after a surprised and mocking scrutiny of the dignitary's new costume.

Julius was a free man, having an independent fortune; and for him the change of religion was a matter of indifference. He was by no means surprised at the transformation of his official friends, but took pleasure in putting teasing questions whenever he met them, assuming the air of a moralist who concealed indignation under the mask of irony.

The people were hurrying to the entrance of the church, and upon the deserted steps outside the friends were soon able to talk freely. Anatolius, ensconced behind a column, listened to the dialogue—

"Why didn't you stay to the end of the service?" asked Mauricus.

"Palpitations. I was half-stifled. I'm not accustomed. . ." and Avinius added thoughtfully—

"The new preacher has an extraordinary style. His exaggerations act too violently on my nerves. A style. . . like the scratching of iron on glass!"

"Really, how touching!" laughed Mauricus. "Here's a man who has abjured conscience! . . . But *style* . . ."

"No, no; perhaps I didn't understand him well!" interrupted Avinius. "Don't disbelieve it! Mauricus, I am sincere."

From a downy litter the head of the chancery himself, Garguillus, got out, groaning—

"I think I'm late. . . But that's of no great importance; I'll remain on the space outside. . . God and the Holy Ghost. . ."

"Here's another miracle!" laughed Mauricus. "Texts from the Bible, in the mouth of Garguillus!"

"May Christ forgive you, my son!" quoth that imperturbable quæstor; "what are you always racking your soul about?"

"Oh, but up to now I haven't been able quite to get over it! There are so many conversions, so many transformations! I had always imagined that your opinions. . ."

"Pure stupidity, my dear son! I have only one opinion, which is, that the Galilean cooks are no worse than the Hellenist cooks. The Hellenists put me on a lenten diet. . . which would make anybody ill. . . Come and dine, O philosopher, and I'll bring you over to my belief. You will lick your fingers after it! And, after all, isn't it the same thing to eat a good dinner in honour of the god Hermes, and to eat it in honour of St. Mercurius? All these things are prejudices. I don't see anything irritating in trifles like this." And he pointed to the little amber cross, which dangled amidst the perfumed folds of an amethystine-purple robe, upon his enormous belly.

"Look, there's Hekobolis, the arch-priest of the goddess Astarte-Dindymene! The hierophant has repented, and is now in black Galilean vestments again! . . . Oh, Ovid, singer of *Metamorphoses*, why art thou not here?" chanted Mauricus, pointing to an old man with a red face seated in a covered litter—

"What's he reading?"

"It surely can't be the laws of the goddess of Pessinus!"

"What divine humility! . . . Fasting has thinned him! . . . Look how he's sighing and throwing up his eyes!"

"Do you know the story of his conversion?" asked Garguillus with a cheerful laugh.

"He went to find Jovian, the Emperor, and I suppose, as formerly with Julian, fell at his feet. . ."

"Oh, no! he invented something entirely new. There was a sudden public repentance. He prostrated himself at the door of a church, just as Jovian was coming out, and in the middle of the crowd, Hekobolis shouted 'Trample on me! trample on me! I am Dead-Sea fruit!' and, with tears, kissed the feet of the passers-by."

"Ah. . . that's new! And was it successful?"

"By Jove! he had a private interview with the Emperor. Oh, people like him have got nine lives! Everything turns to gold in their fingers. When they slough the old skin, they get young again. Learn, my children. . ."

"And what did he manage to say to the Emperor?"

"How can I tell?" sighed Garguillus, not without a certain secret jealousy. "He may have said perhaps, 'Cling to Christianity till not a Pagan be left upon earth! The religion of the just is the basis of your throne!' Now his fortune is made; and far more securely than in the time of Julian. What exquisite sagacity!"

"Oh, my benefactors, protect me! Snatch Cicumbrix, the humblest of your slaves, from the claws of the lions!"

"What's happened?" asked Garguillus of the consumptive shoemaker, who was being dragged off by two of the town police.

"They're going to throw me into prison!"

"Why?"

"For pillaging a church. . ."

"What? You have. . ."

"No, no! I was in the crowd, and I just cried out once or twice 'Beat them!' That was under Augustus Julian. Then they said, 'Cæsar desires that the Christian churches shall be destroyed.' But I didn't go into the church; I stayed outside. My shop is a wretched little place; but it's on a crowded square, and if anything happens I'm always lugged up as a witness. O defend me! Have pity on me!"

"Are you a Christian or a Pagan?" asked Julius.

"I don't know myself. Before Constantine's time I sacrificed to the gods. Then I was baptised. Then, under Constantius, I became an Arian. Afterwards I had to become a Hellenist. Now I want to be an Arian again; but it's all mixed up in my head! I obey orders, and I never can happen to profess the true religion at the right time. I have fought for Christ, and also for the gods. . . But it's always either too soon or too late! One gets no rest. . . I have children. . . Protect me, benefactors!"

"Fear nothing, my friend; we will get you off. I remember you once made me a handsome pair of shoes."

Anatolius, unperceived by his friends, now went into the church, desiring to hear Theodorite, the young and celebrated preacher. The sun was shining through clouds of incense, and one of the slanting rays fell on the red beard of the speaker in the pulpit. His frail hands were transparent as wax; his exultant eyes feverishly bright, and his thrilling voice thundered in an avenging cry.

"I desire to write, as on a sign-post of infamy for future generations, the history of Julian, the foul renegade. May all ages and peoples read my inscription, and tremble before the justice of the Lord! . . . Come hither, torturer, serpent of wisdom, today we will scoff at thee! Together, my brothers, let us rejoice; let us sound our timbrels, and chant the chant of Miriam over the destruction of the Egyptians in the Red Sea. O Emperor! where are thy ceremonies, thy mysteries? Where now are thy invocations and thy divinations? Where are thy Persian and Babylonish glories? Where are the gods that accompanied thee—thy defenders, Julian? All have deceived thee, all have vanished!"

"Ah, my dear! What a beard he has!" said an ancient rouged patrician lady, standing near Anatolius, to her neighbour. "It's a sort of gold, of brown-gold colour!"

"Yes, but how about his teeth?" answered the other.

"What—teeth? With a beard like that, teeth are nothing!"

"No! ah no, Veronica, don't say that! Can one compare him with brother Tiphanius. . ."

Theodorite continued—

"Julian bred evil in his soul as wild beasts secrete venom. God waited till all his cruelty was manifest, to strike him. . ."

"Don't miss the circus today," murmured another neighbour of Anatolius into the ear of his companion. "There are going to be she-bears from Britain."

"You don't say so! Real ones?"

"Yes. One's called Mica Aurea (grain of gold), and the other Innocentia! They're fed on human flesh. And then, there'll be the gladiators!"

"Lord Jesus! . . . we mustn't miss that! Let's not wait for the end! Let's run, in order to get a seat in time!"

Meantime Theodorite was praising Julian's predecessor for his Christian benevolence, pure life, and love for all his family.

Anatolius felt choked by the crowd. He went out of the church, and once quit of the smell of incense and oil, drew a deep breath of fresh air under the blue sky.

Outside the church portico a loud conversation was going on undisturbed. A grave rumour was circulating in the crowd; the two she-bears were being led through the streets to the amphitheatre. Those who heard the news precipitately left the church before the end of the sermon, asking each other anxiously—

"Are we still in time? Is Mica Aurea ill?"

"No, it's Innocentia who had a fit of indigestion today. But now she's going on quite well."

"Thank God. . . thank God!"

The church quickly emptied. Anatolius saw panting multitudes running in the direction of the circus from every street, from every alley, from every basilica. They crushed each other, trampled on women and children, hurled abuse, lost their sandals, but halted for nothing in the race. Every face wore a careworn expression denoting that life depended on getting a seat in the amphitheatre. Two names full of sanguinary promise passed from lip to lip—

"Mica Aurea! Innocentia!"

Anatolius followed the crowd into the amphitheatre.

According to the Roman custom a vast awning, the velarium, sprinkled with perfume, protected the people against the rays of the sun, and spread a pleasant coolness. Thousands of heads already swarmed round the circus.

Before the opening of the games, the highest dignitaries in Antioch carried the bronze statue of Jovian into the Imperial box, so that the people could enjoy a sight of the new sovereign. In his right hand Augustus was holding a globe surmounted by a cross. The sun lighted up the placid bronze countenance of the Emperor. The officials kissed the feet of the statue, and the populace yelled with joy—

"Hail to the saviour of the country, Augustus Jovian!"

Multitudes of hands waved coloured girdles and linen kerchiefs. The crowd acclaimed in Jovian its symbol, its soul, its image regnant over the world. In its scorn of the dead Emperor the mob next addressed itself to Julian, as if he were there, still alive in the amphitheatre, and could hear them—

"Well, philosopher, the wisdom of Plato and Crisipus wasn't much good to you! Jupiter and Phoebus didn't protect you! Now you are in the claws of the devils! Ah, you godless idolater, Christ has conquered! We, the humble of the world, have conquered!"

All were convinced that Julian had been slain by a Christian, and returned thanks to God for the blow. But the furious enthusiasm of the crowd reached its highest pitch when they saw the gladiator prostrate in the claws of Mica Aurea. Their eyes started out of their heads to glut themselves with the sight of blood; and to the roaring of the wild beast the people responded by a roar wilder still—

"Glory to the most pious Emperor Jovian! Christ has conquered!"

Anatolius felt overcome with disgust at the sweltering breath and odour of the human horde. Closing his eyes, attempting not to draw breath, he ran out into the street, returned to his lodging, closed door and shutters, and flung himself on his bed until night-fall. But it was impossible to escape the populace.

Hardly had twilight descended, when the whole of Antioch was illumined by thousands of lights. At the angles of basilicas and Imperial edifices huge torches were aflare, and cressets flaming in every street. Through the cracks in the shutters of the sleeping-room of Anatolius came in the glow of bonfires and the stink of pitch and tallow. Songs of drunken legionaries were bellowed from neighbouring taverns, amidst the shrill laughter of prostitutes. Dominating all, rose the praises of Jovian, and curses on Julian the renegade.

Anatolius, with a bitter smile, raised his arms skyward, crying—

"In truth, thou hast conquered, Galilean!"

I t was on board a great merchant galley with three banks of oars, laden with soft Asian carpets and amphoræ of olive-oil, on the voyage between Seleucia, the port of Antioch, and Italy.

Sailing and rowing amongst the islands of the Archipelago, the vessel was now making for Crete, where she was to take on board a cargo of wool, and disembark some ecclesiastics, bound for a Cretan monastery. Old men, seated on the fore-deck, were passing the days in pious gossip, prayer, or in their monkish avocation of weaving baskets from slips of palm-leaf. In the stern, under a light violet awning, other passengers were installed, with whom the monks, considering them Pagans, were anxious to have nothing to do. These were Anatolius, Ammianus Marcellinus, and Arsinoë.

The evening was calm. The rowers—slaves from Alexandria—heaved and lowered their long oars to the beat of an ancient chant. The sun was sinking amid ruddy clouds. Anatolius was gazing at the waves, thinking over the poet's phrase, *the many-laughtered sea*.

After the hustling, the heat and dust of the streets of Antioch, after the smoke of torches, and the fiery breath of the rabble, he was lulling his mind with the thought: "Thou of the many laughters, take me and cleanse my soul!"

Isles of Calypso, Amorgos, Astypalæa, Thera, arose like visions, now lifting themselves from the sea, now melting away, as if, all round the vessel, the Oceanides were still leading their eternal dance. In those waters Anatolius felt himself far back in the days of the Odyssey.

His companions did not disturb his meditations, for each was absorbed in work. Ammianus Marcellinus was putting in order his memoirs of the Persian campaign and the life of the Emperor Julian; and in the evenings he used to read the remarkable work of the Christian master, Clement of Alexandria, entitled, *Stromata: The Patchwork Quilt*.

Arsinoë was making models in wax for a large marble statue. It was the figure of some Olympian deity, the face of which wore an expression of super human sadness. Anatolius wished, but hesitated, to ask her whether it represented Dionysus or Christ.

The artist had long ago abandoned the robes of a nun. Pious folk had turned from her with horror, and called her the recreant; but her name, and the recollection of generous gifts formerly made to Christian monasteries, safeguarded her from persecution. Of her great fortune but a small portion remained, just enough to secure independence; and on the shores of the Gulf of Naples, not far from Baiæ, she still owned a small estate, and the same villa in which Myrrha had passed her last days. Thither Arsinoë, Anatolius, and Marcellinus had agreed to retire after the stormy troubles of recent years, to pass their lives in peace as servants of the Muses.

The former nun now wore the same robes as before her consecration. The noble and simple lines of the peplum restored her resemblance to some ancient Athenian vestal. But the stuff was sober in colour, and her splendid hair thickly veiled. A wisdom almost austere lay in those deep unsmiling eyes. Only the white arms of the artist, bare to the shoulder, relieved the sombre hues of her robe. She toiled impatiently, almost feverishly, moulding the soft wax; and her pale hands impressed Anatolius with a sense of extraordinary power.

That evening the galley was coasting an islet of which none knew the name. Far off, it looked like an arid rock. In order to avoid dangerous reefs the trireme had to pass close in to shore. Under the steep cliff the sea-water lay so clear that sand and weed at the bottom could be clearly distinguished. Beyond the grim rocks could be seen green pastures, and sheep feeding round a plane-tree.

Anatolius saw, seated at the foot of the tree, a lad and a young girl, probably children of poor shepherds. Behind them, among cypresses, was a small rough figure of Pan playing the flute. Anatolius turned towards Arsinoë to point out this remote and peaceful nook of a lost Hellas; but the words died on his lips. Wholly rapt, and with a look of strange gaiety, the artist was intent on her creation, the waxen statuette, with its face of haunting sadness, and proud Olympian attitude.

Anatolius felt her mood like a rebuff. He asked Arsinoë in a harsh unsteady voice, pointing at the model—

"Why are you making that? What does the thing stand for?"

Slowly and with effort, she raised her eyes to his; and he mused—

"The sibyls must have eyes like those!" and then aloud: "Arsinoë, do you think that this work of yours will be understood?"

"What matters it, friend?" she answered, smiling gravely. Then she added in a lower tone, as if communing with herself: "He will stretch out His hands toward the world. He must be inexorable and terrible as Mithra-Dionysus in all his strength and beauty; yet merciful and humble. . ."

"What do you mean? is not that an impossible contradiction?"

"Who knows? For us, yes; but for the future. . ."

The sun was descending lower. Above him, on the horizon westward, a storm-cloud was impending, and the last rays illuminated the island with a soft, almost melancholy, glow.

The shepherd lad and his companion approached Pan's altar to make their evening sacrifice.

"Is it your belief, Arsinoë," continued Anatolius, "is it your faith that unknown brothers of ours shall pick up the threads of our existence, and, following the clue, go immeasurably farther than we? Do you believe that all shall not perish in the barbaric gloom which is sinking on Rome and Hellas? Ah, if that were so? If one could trust the future. . ."

"Yes!" exclaimed Arsinoë, a prophetic gleam in her sombre eyes, "the future is in us, in our madness and our anguish! Julian was right. Content without glory, in silence, strangers to all, and solitary among men, we must work out our work to the end. We must hide and cherish the last, the utmost spark amongst the ashes of the altar, that tribes and nations of the future may kindle from it new torches! Where we finish they shall begin. Let Hellas die! Men shall dig up her relics— unearth her divine fragments of marble, yea, over them shall weep and pray! From our tombs shall the yellowed leaves of the books we love be unsealed, and the ancient stories of Homer, the wisdom of Plato, shall be spelt out slowly anew, as by little children. And with Hellas, you and I shall live again!"

"And with us, revives the curse on us!" exclaimed Anatolius, "The struggle between Olympus and Golgotha will begin over again!—Why? And when shall that struggle end? Answer, sibyl, if thou canst!"

Arsinoë was silent, and her eyes fell. Then she glanced at Ammianus and pointed to him—

"There is one who will answer you better than I. Like ours, his heart is shared between Christ and Olympus, and yet he keeps the lucidity of his soul."

Ammianus Marcellinus, putting aside the manuscript by Clement, had been quietly listening to the discussion.

"In truth," said the Epicurean, addressing him, "we have now been friends for more than four months, and yet I do not know whether you are a Christian or a Hellenist?"

"Nor I myself," answered the young Ammianus frankly, with a blush.

"What? No torture of doubts? No suffering from the antagonism between the Greek and the Christian doctrine?"

"No, my friend; I think that the two teachings in many points agree. . ."

"But how—from what point of view—do you intend to write your account of the Roman Empire? One of the two scales of the balance must sink and the other rise?"

"Not consciously, I hope," answered the historian; "My aim is to be just to both. Julian the Emperor I love, but even for him I shall be impartial. No one shall know which side I join, any better than I know myself. . ."

Anatolius had already proved the bravery, the chivalrous friendship of Ammianus, and now he was daily discovering in him other qualities no less rare.

"You are born to be a historian, Ammianus, to be the judge of our passionate age, and to bring its warring philosophies, in some sort, to a reconciliation!"

"I shall not be the first to do that," answered Ammianus. He rose to his feet and pointing with enthusiasm to the parchment-rolls of the great Christian master—

"All you suggest is already written here; and with far ampler powers than mine. This is the *Patchwork* of Clement of Alexandria, in which he proves that the greatness of Rome and the philosophy of Hellas paved the way for the teaching of Christ, and, by maxims and numberless forecasts, made the first decided steps toward the earthly kingdom of God. Plato is the forerunner of Jesus the Nazarene."

The last words, spoken with perfect simplicity, profoundly impressed Anatolius. He seemed to remember the whole scene as from some previous existence: the island flushed by that setting sun; the smell of tar on board the galley; and the words of Ammianus. The vista of a new world was momentarily opened to his mind.

Meanwhile the trireme was heading round the cape; the little wood of cypress had almost disappeared behind the cliffs. Anatolius threw a last look at the lad and girl before the altar of Pan. The girl was pouring out the evening offering of goat's milk and honey; the boy beginning to play on his reed-pipe. The thin blue smoke of sacrifice could be seen rising above the wood after the human figures had vanished and while the trireme made for open sea.

From the fore-part of the ship there came upon the silence a solemn music; the old monks were chanting in unison their evening prayer. . .

But over the still water came faint and clear notes of another melody. It was the little shepherd, piping his nocturnal hymn to Pan, the old god of gaiety, of freedom and love.

Anatolius felt a thrill of wonder and surmise.

"*Thy will be done on earth, as it is in heaven*," the monks chanted.

The silvery notes of the shepherd's flute, floating high in the sky, mingled with the words of the Christians.

The last beams faded from that happy islet, leaving it dull and hueless in the midst of the sea. Both hymns ceased.

The wind blew sharply in the rigging and whipped up grey and white waves. The straining galley-timbers creaked and groaned. Shadows approached from the southward and the sea grew swiftly dark. Huge clouds massed overhead, and from beyond the horizon came the first long intermittent roll of thunder.

Night and Tempest, hand in hand, were striding on apace.

THE END

A Note About the Author

Dmitry Merezhkovsky (1866–1941) was a Russian novelist and poet. Born in Saint Petersburg, Merezhkovsky was raised in a prominent political family. At thirteen, while a student at the St. Petersburg Third Classic Gymnasium, Dmitry began writing poetry. Soon, he earned a reputation as a promising young writer and enrolled at the University of Saint Petersburg, where he completed his PhD with a study on Montaigne. In 1892, he published *Symbols. Poems and Songs*, a work inspired by Poe and Baudelaire in which Merezhkovsky explores his increasingly personal religious ideas. In 1895, he published *The Death of the Gods*, the first novel in his groundbreaking *Christ and Antichrist Trilogy*. With these novels, Merezhkovsky was recognized as a cofounder of the Russian Symbolist movement. In 1905, his apocalyptic Christian worldview seemed to come to fruition in the First Russian Revolution, which he supported through poetry and organizing groups of students and artists. Formerly a supporter of the Tsar, Merezhkovsky was involved in leftist politics by 1910, but soon became disillusioned with the rise of the radical Bolsheviks. In the aftermath of the October Revolution, Merezhkovsky and his wife, the poet Zinaida Gippius, were forced to flee Russia. Over the years, they would find safe harbor in Warsaw and Paris, where Merezhkovsky continued to write works of nonfiction while advocating for the Russian people. Toward the end of his life, he came to see through such leaders as Benito Mussolini, Francisco Franco, and Adolf Hitler a means of defeating Communism in Russia. Though scholars debate his level of commitment to fascist and nationalist ideologies, this nevertheless marked a sinister turn in an otherwise brilliant literary career. Nominated for the Nobel Prize in literature nine times without winning, Merezhkovsky is recognized as an important figure of the Silver Age of Russian art.

A Note from the Publisher

Spanning many genres, from non-fiction essays to literature classics to children's books and lyric poetry, Mint Edition books showcase the master works of our time in a modern new package. The text is freshly typeset, is clean and easy to read, and features a new note about the author in each volume. Many books also include exclusive new introductory material. Every book boasts a striking new cover, which makes it as appropriate for collecting as it is for gift giving. Mint Edition books are only printed when a reader orders them, so natural resources are not wasted. We're proud that our books are never manufactured in excess and exist only in the exact quantity they need to be read and enjoyed.

bookfinity™

Discover more of your favorite classics with Bookfinity™.

- Track your reading with custom book lists.
- Get great book recommendations for your personalized Reader Type.
- Add reviews for your favorite books.
- AND MUCH MORE!

Visit **bookfinity.com** and take the fun Reader Type quiz to get started.

Enjoy our classic and modern companion pairings!

Classic & Modern